HELL'S
HERESIES

HELL'S HERESIES

KAT D. COFFIN

CITY OWL
PRESS

HELL'S HERESIES

CITY OWL PRESS
www.cityowlpress.com

Cover Design by Darling Santamaria.

Edited by Danielle DeVor.

For information on subsidiary rights, please contact the publisher at info@cityowlpress.com.

Print Edition ISBN: 978-1-64898-482-2

Digital Edition ISBN: 978-1-64898-483-9

Printed in the United States of America

 CITY OWL PRESS
Escape Your World ♦ Get Lost in Ours

To Tina, who never allows me to have writer's block.

ONE

SOMETHING SNATCHED Emerie's ankle and yanked her off the bed.

At first, she assumed she'd rolled the wrong way and sat up, trying to figure out why her bed was so hard and cold. She blinked owlishly at the leaning tower of laundry across from her. She registered that one of her windows was open, which accounted for how cold her bedroom was. But before she could center herself and fully realize she was no longer on her ebony sleigh bed, an invisible force grabbed her leg and pulled her out the open bedroom door. She snatched desperately at the door jamb, but it slipped through her fingers. She heard it vibrate ominously as she was towed along.

"Hey!"

Her head hit several boxes as she careened down the hallway. Emerie attempted to seize the wall, but only succeeded in slamming her body back and forth against the plaster like a pinball. She kicked her free leg fiercely at the imperceptible aggressor. She felt something icy-cold, as though she plunged a bare foot in slush—but she was released.

Emerie scrambled to her feet and punched the air wildly. She was at the tail end of their long hallway, almost in the upstairs parlor. Monsters crouched in the darkness until her eyes adjusted and they became unpacked boxes strewn across the room. She squinted and steadied her breathing. There was nothing there. As usual.

Dylan poked his head out of their bedroom. His eyes narrowed.

"Emerie?" His clicked his teeth. "Did it happen again?"

"No," Emerie said. "I just—went to get a glass of water. Tripped on a box."

Dylan snorted audibly. But Emerie knew three a.m. was too late for this particular fight for her early bird boyfriend. He retreated into their bedroom and she sighed with relief. This wasn't the first time she had been forcibly jerked out of bed and dragged down the hallway. She considered herself lucky it always pulled her into the parlor, rather than making a sharp right turn at the end of the hall to push her down the stairs. These unfortunate instances were just one of the many examples Dylan had of why they *should not have moved into this house.* But Emerie refused to accept that kind of negative thinking about their home renovation plans.

She started to follow him back to bed and bit back an angry squawk —she stepped in a paint roller tray. Creamy-cold goop covered her foot.

Her lip curled and she carefully removed her bare foot, resisting the urge to kick the roller tray against the wall. This was getting ridiculous.

She took care to walk on the plastic sheeting which covered the floor and detoured into the bathroom to wash off the paint in the clawfoot tub. She loved that tub, with its strange taloned feet and a showerhead faucet combination styled like an old-fashioned telephone. It was one of the reasons she moved in—along with the huge kitchen overflowing with cabinet space, three extra bedrooms, and wraparound porch. She exhaled as she flicked the light—they'd been having electricity problems since the move. Thankfully, it buzzed on.

"Are you kidding me?!"

The doors of the medicine cabinet were flung open. Their collective toiletries littered the floor. Her Spider-Man toothbrush floated sadly in the toilet over Dylan's electric toothbrush head. She stared at the mess, balancing on one foot. Dylan would be furious. His assortment of hair products far outnumbered her own and he had organized them *so care-*

fully. She scooped them up and haphazardly stuffed them back into the medicine cabinet. Gingerly, she reached inside the toilet and threw both toothbrushes away. She eyed the shower curtain, which had been torn down for good measure.

Scowling, Emerie hopped on one foot to the tub. She twisted the knob and hissed as the icy water blasted the paint off her foot. She had not been getting much sleep since they moved in. Their first night here, booming explosions of thunder woke them up repeatedly through the night—but the skies were completely clear. After making sure there was no hidden bowling alley in the attic, she blamed the neighbor's pickup truck.

The following night a high-pitched scream interrupted them while they tried to unpack the dining room boxes, shattering a crystal tea set. Emerie didn't much care for the gaudy collection, so she made an offhand comment about the squeaky pipes in the basement and pretended she had dropped the tea set. At this point, Dylan began to grow suspicious.

After a week, Emerie started feeling cold pokes and prods, like someone slipped ice cubes down her shirt. Of course, this eventually evolved into chilly hands that wrenched her out of bed and towed her down the hallway. Terrifying the first time, scary the second, and then painfully annoying the rest—not that the experience wasn't frightening. But an awful case of carpet burn converted fear into deep irritation.

Not to mention, different rooms kept getting trashed—like their bathroom. The longer they stayed, the more the activity seemed to increase.

Emerie stepped away from the tub, shaking her foot dry. An ice-cold draft enveloped her body and she shivered. She noticed with alarm the water in the toilet bowl had frozen. She wrapped her arms around herself as the mirror fogged over. Words started to appear on the condensation.

Emerie squinted. "LLIK...Lick? Wait, are you trying to write 'kill'?"

The words halted.

"It's a mirror." Emerie placed her hands on her hips. "Are you on the other side of the mirror? Then you'll have to write words backwards."

The mirror fogged over again and new words appeared. **KCUF**

"Yeah, well, kcuf you too!" Emerie yelled at the mirror. She stalked out of the bathroom and climbed into bed. Dylan mumbled something at her presence but she ignored him. After hijacking the majority of the pillows, she nested comfortably. Just as she started to drift off, a loud blast of organ music shook the entire house.

Bach's Fantasia in G minor.

"Where is that coming from?!" Dylan demanded into his single pillow. "We don't have an organ!"

"You're dreaming!" Emerie yelled over the organ music as she buried herself in the rest of the pillows. "I don't hear anything!"

———

Of course, Emerie had heard the organ music. She was also quite aware their new house was, in all likelihood, haunted. Emerie Fox and her boyfriend moved to Milton, Massachusetts about three weeks ago. She'd fallen in love with the fixer upper with a bright red door, an outdoor upstairs balcony, and a large varnished back porch that overlooked a small patch of forest. It was within walking distance of the library and fifteen minutes away from I-95. Aside from the supernatural pest problem—the house was perfect.

Unfortunately, the real estate agent had not been forthcoming about the paranormal infestation.

Her boyfriend had been less than enthusiastic about the purchase of the house with or without hauntings. He claimed they were the only people their age in the world who were buying houses and what's more, he wanted to live in Boston, not Milton.

Dylan didn't like Milton. He had an aversion to small towns and did not share Emerie's love of the obscurely historical. His family hailed from Chicago; he was used to having his home be a touring spot for his favorite bands and twenty-four-hour conveniences. There was not much to do in Milton, unless you enjoyed early American history or taverns that Washington Irving drank in. No concert venues, no clubs, no Broadway shows or any sort of night life. Instead there were churches, houses that dated back to the 1700s, a quaint Main Street, a pleasant forest preserve...and even more churches.

Worse still, Dylan's hour-long commute to his job in Boston was aggravating—Emerie understood this, but as she'd pointed out several times, it was too expensive to live there.

He didn't understand, of course. Probably because the high cost of living was a motivator, not a detractor. Dylan had never had to worry about things like if a paycheck would cover rent and groceries. If he fell in love with an apartment out of their budget, he would simply go to his parents for assistance. (His father was a high-profile politician and his mother ran a lifestyle web series where she explained which thousand-dollar table setting was the most striking.)

Emerie could not conceive of asking her parents for help. Once she had moved out, that meant she was *done*. It was now up to her to take care of her family, not the other way around! Her mother was getting older and her father had just retired. That needed to factor into Emerie and Dylan's budget.

Of course, his usual rejoinder was the restorations on their new house were far more costly than a high rent. Emerie would finish the conversation (he claimed it was an argument, she insisted it was a conversation) by declaring their house was *an investment* in their life together. Dylan would generally give up at that point.

The poltergeist was his latest gripe, a technically understandable irritation, but frankly, Emerie wasn't about to let a little thing like a haunting stop her home makeover plans. Which was why she tried her best to ignore the entity.

This was easier said than done. Particularly since the poltergeist was becoming bolder with its antics with each passing day.

After managing to get a few scrapes of sleep, Emerie awoke and trudged downstairs for her morning fix, the found that her coffeemaker was missing.

Emerie had unpacked the coffeemaker the first day and they had been enjoying steamed lattes every morning since. Their love for all things caffeinated bonded them as a couple and neither one of them were particularly pleasant until their second cup. It simply wasn't possible for the machine to have been lost in the move. After she checked every single cupboard twice, Emerie was forced to deliver the bad news to Dylan.

"This is the last straw, Emerie!" Dylan stormed into the kitchen. He was already dressed, in camel-colored slacks and a salmon dress shirt. He had forgotten to iron his dress shirt, which gave him a somewhat rumpled appearance. Emerie toyed with letting him know but ultimately chose to allow him to continue his rant.

"What are we supposed to do? Drink *tea*?!" Dylan's tone suggested that forcing him to drink tea could lead to unemployment, disenfranchisement, and homelessness in one fell swoop.

"I like tea," Emerie said mildly. She was seated cross legged on the counter, still in her dinosaur-patterned pajamas. To prove this point, she took an exaggerated sip of herbal tea out of a mug shaped like Edgar Allan Poe's head.

"The thumps and thuds are one thing." He snatched the box of Froot Loops and poured them into a Star Trek mug. (The bowls were not yet unpacked). "It's an old house. We could chalk it up to faulty construction or boxes falling over or—whatever."

Emerie nodded earnestly.

"The organ music at three a.m.—we could live with that, it makes us more cultured," Dylan continued, setting down his mug. His fingers tangled in his white and blue striped tie. He was trying and failing to tie it round his neck, but only succeeded in making a noose.

"But stealing our *coffeemaker*?!" He then took a large gulp from his mug of Froot Loops. Ordinarily, Dylan was fairly finicky in his breakfast tastes, preferring egg white omelets with skim milk, perhaps some Greek yogurt and fruit. But desperate times—being late for work, not having proper groceries yet, their kitchen not fully unpacked, a haunt terrorizing them—led him to fall back into college habits and subsist purely on cereal.

"Nothing has stolen our coffeemaker," Emerie assured him as she grabbed a small pot and filled it with cereal herself. Unlike Dylan, Emerie had no stress-related qualms about eating breakfast cereal.

"We have just misplaced Norman. We will find him."

"Stop naming our appliances!" Dylan nearly garroted himself with his necktie. Emerie hopped off the counter.

"You used to think it was cute." She tied a Windsor knot easily and took a step back.

"This is all your fault." Dylan accidentally tripped over the garbage can. "*You*

encouraged it."

"What are you talking about?!" Emerie said, stung.

"The offering! When the lights started flickering, you set out a tray of mochi and salt water like the damn thing was a visiting neighbor!"

Well, that was unfair. That was how you dealt with spirits in Japan. You appeased them with a food offering, everyone knew that. And in her defense, the spirit *had* taken the food—the tray was empty the following day—although its activity increased.

Dylan would not let up. "How do you misplace a two-hundred dollar coffeemaker? It's a Keurig! It's priceless!"

"Well, it's not priceless." Emerie pointed out reasonably. "You just said the price. Two hundreds."

Dylan's face went purple. He was generally a handsome man, with a somewhat roguish look—high cheekbones, prominent brows, classically handsome. Emerie thought he looked a bit like Errol Flynn on a good day. But the purple somewhat ruined his countenance.

"I cannot live in this town, much less this house, without coffee!"

Emerie sighed. Dylan's repulsion to the house had some valid points —she could admit it was a trifle unfair they lived so close to her work and so far from his. The ever-present fear of purchasing a money pit was legitimate. The house needed a *lot* of repairs and the moving/renovating process was constantly hampered by ghostly pranks and burglaries.

Emerie took a deep breath. "It's garage sale season. I'm sure I could find a Mr. Coffee for a reasonable—"

"*I want my Keurig.*"

"All right, all right." Emerie munched her Froot Loops. "I'll find it. Norman's around here somewhere."

Dylan rolled his eyes at her refusal to stop calling their MIA coffeemaker Norman and exited the kitchen for a moment. He returned with his phone and handed it to her. He'd Googled the address—and apparently came upon some poorly designed websites. Emerie's brow furrowed.

"I'm pretty sure *this* is why we got the house so cheap," Dylan said as she scrolled with her thumb.

"Hm." Emerie handed the phone back to him. "I did tell you the house had a colorful history."

Dylan coughed. "*Colorful?* Apparently all manner of occult practice and ritual went on here. Spiritualist clubs came from all over the world to conjure and perform the darkest spells…did you know about this?!"

"The entire town of Milton is built on ghost stories." Emerie explained patiently. "It's part of the tourist trade."

That was the other side of Milton. Unfortunately, neither Nathanial Hawthorne nor Washington Irving ever wrote any short stories about the town, but Milton was still resolutely proud of its haunted woods, local goblins that apparently terrorized farmers in the 1970s, and their documented persecution of witches in the 1600s. A few B-movie horror films had been shot in town—nothing of true notoriety, but enough to warrant the occasional cult status. Emerie thought of Milton as a sort of less renowned Salem.

But it seemed Dylan's opinion of the town's supernatural folklore had shifted. "This house has a historical marker for the Lucifer Club. A crazy bunch of old biddies that summoned demons for laughs!"

"Did you know that in New Orleans they have little signs outside their properties that say if it's haunted or not haunted?" Emerie asked conversationally. "It's part of the allure. But none of it's real."

"How can you say that?" Dylan raked his fingers through his hair. "You have been dragged off your bed and down the hall three times this week!"

"I'm going to the doctor next week." Emerie slurped the milk out of her pot. "I bet it's a sleep disorder."

"And the organ music?!"

"You know, we live near several churches. Maybe we're in, like, a sound wave Bermuda triangle kind of area and we just *absorb* all of the churches' sound waves—"

"Emerie!" Dylan held up his hands. "Stop. Listen to yourself. You sound like a lunatic."

The lunatic line was an old favorite of Dylan's. He used it when she first found the house and excitedly pointed out the magenta living room and the possibly broken beyond repair antique oven in the attic. But while Emerie would concede her home décor taste was less than usual, being called a lunatic in this context annoyed her.

"You're the one talking about ghosts and haunted houses." Emerie placed her drained pot in the sink. "Just because I don't believe in the boogeyman doesn't make me a lunatic. Stop being condescending."

"I'm not being condescending." He poured the rest of his breakfast into the sink in disgust. "I'm being realistic—I'm being an adult. We can't live in this house!"

Emerie placed her hands on her hips. "*You're* being an adult?! You're the one who wants to abandon our house without even giving it a fair shot! Who's being the immature one?"

It was perhaps not the best idea to get into a "who's more of an adult" argument while she was clad in dinosaur-patterned pajamas—Dylan's suit shook the foundation of her point. But she stared at him resolutely, not giving an inch.

"Maybe we have different ideas of what constitutes adulthood," Dylan said finally.

"Maybe," Emerie agreed, "but I'm not *quitting*, Dylan. I'm sticking it out—I have to! I bought the house, I made the commitment, and I am *not* wasting the money Ji-Ji left me. This house is mine. I hope you'll make it yours too."

She had brought up the big guns. Dylan *knew* how devastated she'd been upon her grandfather's death. It had been his idea to use the money from her inheritance to purchase a small home, but hers to refurbish an old home—just like her Ji-Ji had done back in Hokkaido. The idea had shortly turned into an obsession, whether Dylan liked it or not.

There was an awkward pause as Dylan avoided her gaze and absorbed his surroundings—the piles of unpacked boxes, the stacked paint cans, the ratty curtains. The kitchen certainly wasn't looking its best. The window overlooking the sink revealed a daunting jungle of wild hedges and giant trees that littered leaves all over their front lawn. Those trees did an excellent job of blocking light into the kitchen, which gave the room a very gloomy atmosphere. Some of the black-and-white floor tiles were missing, the wallpaper was peeling, and the light fixtures were dingy. Like everything else in the house, it could do with a complete overhaul.

"I have to go," Dylan said finally. "My flight's in an hour. Emerie, if this haunting shit doesn't let up, *we are leaving.* We are not sticking around to become the next Amityville!"

Still stung by the "lunatic" comment, she folded her arms. "I will say this one more time. There is nothing wrong with this house. We are not going anywhere. Is that clear?"

Before he could respond, there was a mighty CRASH—all the pots and pans hanging over the kitchen island fell to the floor. The mini-egg skillet ricocheted off Dylan's forehead.

Emerie glanced upwards. "I will get that fixed by the time you return."

————

Dylan was attending a "Pioneers in Digital Marketing" conference in New York. The conference only lasted a week, but he had sworn he would spend an additional two weeks taking a detour in Boston to look for reasonably priced apartments, no matter what Emerie said.

They hadn't even been living together for that long yet it seemed they were fighting constantly. She kept hoping he would see her side of things and join in on the project with gusto…but everything he did to help seemed to be done only to appease her, not because he understood or even cared about her feelings for the house.

It was unfortunate Dylan left right after a fight. But by late afternoon, Emerie felt energized and motivated. She ripped the rest of the magenta wallpaper from the living room, she sanded down the floors, she swept, she scrubbed the kitchen, she replaced tile, and she contemplated paint colors. Projects were healing. Sweat provided a sense of Zen towards her situation. Tasks distracted her from thinking too hard about her boyfriend's dampening attitude. She wondered if he really *would* find an apartment in Boston. He'd agreed to move in with her—after all, the house was in her name, not his. Dylan came to Milton for her…he didn't have as much riding on the house as she did.

It would be easy for him to call it quits. The entity was especially hard on Dylan, who seemed to carry the brunt of the haunts—not counting it occasionally dragging Emerie down the hallway. All of his left socks disappeared in one night, along with his boater shoes, and his Netflix queue was abruptly deleted. He complained of the drafts more than Emerie and constantly whined something was *watching* him.

Emerie sighed. She opened the fridge (named Midge) and helped herself to some cold pizza—they had pretty much been subsisting on Chinese food and pizza. She retrieved another Guinness and walked into the living room, ready to settle in on the couch for an early dinner.

She froze and nearly dropped her pizza. There was large, graffiti-like writing on the wall where she'd intended to hang her flat screen.

HE'S A JERK, EMERIE. DUMP HIM.

She continued to stare. The words were a blood color and faintly glistened in the light. It was recent.

It was one thing to receive condensation mirror messages at three-a.m. on her bathroom mirror—she could chalk up to being half-asleep if she were feeling particularly rational. But this…?

Emerie set her dinner down, turned on her heel, ran out of the living room into the foyer and raced up to her bedroom to retrieve her large wooden bokuto—a Japanese wooden training sword—from the closet.

Emerie's mother's side of the family came from Hokkaido, Japan. Emerie spent most of her summer holidays there, staying with her Ji-Ji and Ba-chan. When Emerie was ten, she became enchanted by a Japanese swordsmanship demonstration at a Tanabata festival. Upon her return, her father had signed her up for kendo, much to the delight of her mother.

This phase hadn't lasted long, as the bokuto was her approximate height, which made wielding it a difficult affair. Her instructor insisted over and over that her diminutive size would have no bearing on her skill, as long as she practiced regularly. Unfortunately, Emerie wasn't exactly diligent and the wooden sword constantly fell from her fingers when she raised it over her head. Her kendo obsession lasted about as long as her ice-skating interest.

Still, Emerie had kept the weapon. Now she patrolled the house and looked for signs of…anything.

Nothing. All the doors were locked. All the windows were snapped shut. No signs of forced entry.

Emerie exhaled deeply.

"This is getting ridiculous," she muttered, retreating to the living room. "I will not live with a ghost! Especially a ghost that dispenses relationship advice! I have girlfriends for that job!"

Nothing responded.

Furiously, she stormed upstairs to her bedroom. She was going to figure out a way to de-haunt her house before Dylan returned.

TWO

THE REFRIGERATOR WAS UPSIDE DOWN.

For the first time in a while, Emerie was not dragged from her bed in the middle of the night. She awoke in the morning refreshed, rejuvenated, and delighted she was not covered in rug burns. She'd padded downstairs for another Keurig hunt and had found her refrigerator, still plugged in—but upside down.

She tentatively cracked the refrigerator door and saw in outrage that everything was neatly and tidily organized, as though the poltergeist had taken everything out, flipped the interior shelves and the refrigerator, and carefully placed everything back inside.

This was an outrage. How dare the spirit reorganize her fridge and flip it upside down!

Emerie would probably need Dylan's help to turn it right side up. She pulled out a quart of half-and-half and shut the lopsided fridge with a sigh. Tea first. Upside down fridge later.

The Keurig was still MIA, but her rice cooker somehow had ended up in a box marked "Living Room". All the "Living Room" boxes were in the kitchen and all the "Kitchen" boxes were in the living room and all the "Bathroom" boxes were in her bedroom. Was it the ghost? Or was it her poor organizational skills? Both possibilities offended Emerie.

She placed her rice cooker on her kitchen counter. Her rice cooker, as innocuous as it was a hand-me-down from her grandfather—her wonderful and cantankerous Ji-Ji. The plastic was peeling on it, but it still worked fine. She scooted it where the Keurig used to stand.

The granite countertops had been another selling point of the house. She loved the kitchen, despite the trees that loomed over the window. Sky-blue cabinets surrounded the room and extended into a small hall-way. Peacock-blue glass fixtures on the ceiling fans provided the majority of the light and created constellations of shapes on the smooth tile floors. The kitchen was nearly always cold, but the gas stove more than made up for that—Emerie had already celebrated this triumph by toasting marshmallows over its open flame on her first day here.

She also especially admired the vintage corbels lining the doorway into the dining room. They intricately webbed across the corners, looking sort of like demonic lyres. The hallway ended in a roomy dining room with a sparkling chandelier that flung specks of light every which way. She was undecided on the startling turquoise and gold wallpaper rimming the dining room walls and she didn't have a dining room table yet. She wanted something special for such a magnificent room; her college dining table was far too plain.

Emerie began to stack a colorful assortment of bowls on the counter, and then transferred them into the cabinet next to the sink. She'd had a short conversation with her mother last night, after she'd discovered the writing on the wall. It had not gone well. Her mother flexed between repeated pleas to move back home and to start having grandbabies.

Emerie hadn't mentioned the ghost problem. It was too embarrassing and she had no idea what her mother would even make of it.

Besides, Emerie couldn't back out now. She couldn't let the terrorists (or poltergeists) win.

Still...a part of her did want to ask her mother for advice. There were old family stories about how she grew up in an old hot springs resort in Hokkaido. Her mother had hated the house; she described it as having 'terrible energy', whatever that meant.

Emerie's grandfather, the owner of the aforementioned Hokkaido house, passed away last January. He had been a man of unusual quirks and interests, much like Emerie herself—and perhaps a man of simmering grudges. He had not left Emerie's mother anything in his will. Ji-Ji's small estate went solely to Emerie, his eldest grandchild.

This bizarre stipulation had shocked Emerie's family. His Hokkaido house, haunted or not, would be sold and the money would go to Emerie. Everything else, save a few knickknacks apparently reserved for her younger brother Falcon, would be donated.

Her mother had barely reacted to the fact Ji-Ji left her out of his will. She simply shrugged and said something in Japanese about respecting his wishes, requested that some of the personal letters be saved, and left Emerie to it. Her mother suspected, perhaps correctly, that Ji-Ji had never forgiven his daughter for marrying an American.

Still, it put Emerie in a rather awkward position with her family, who had very little trust in her to handle the money responsibly...

She finished with the bowls and strolled into the living room. Arms akimbo, she surveyed her defaced walls.

She needed more information. That was how she tackled articles at work—gather all the information she possibly could, review it carefully, and draw a conclusion. She could no longer ignore the metaphorical and literal writing on the wall—it was time to act.

Emerie's initial projects since moving in had involved a great deal of painting. The living room's ceiling and walls, for whatever reason, were previously a violent pink topped off with magenta wallpaper. Not only that, the former owners thought green and violet velvet blanket-style curtains pulled the room together. Everything was topped off with a crimson glass chandelier, which amplified the room's red glow. It had been unnerving to walk into the room and be thrust into blush-colored light. Three days ago, Emerie had transformed the shocking pink into a serene pearl. The cream color relaxed the room, made it more welcoming. Which made it particularly aggravating the ghost had chosen to leave its judgmental message *right after she painted...*

Neither here nor there. At least she still had paint left. It had taken several coats to cover that shade and ripping wallpaper was always a trial. Emerie smiled grimly at the memory.

She methodically painted over the words, ignoring the shiver that went down her spine once she reached her name. **HE'S A JERK, EMERIE. DUMP HIM.** She paused and scratched at one of the letters with her fingernail. She frowned at the rust-colored flecks on her thumb. It sure looked like blood...

After an hour or so of work, the living room no longer looked like the inside of a bordello. Emerie did keep the crimson light fixtures, as she thought they added "atmosphere" to the room. She shoved her favorite easy chair next to the east-facing bay windows and positioned her lumpy couch so it was angled near her small bookshelf and flat screen. While moving her easy chair, she discovered the window lock was broken—she would need to get that fixed sooner rather than later. She completed her work by setting a coffee table that used to be an old railroad trunk before her sofa and adding an end table that used to be a tea tray.

Emerie took a seat on her couch and smiled at her newly hung flat screen. It did occur to her that the haunt might still write on the wall, even with the television blocking it—but for now, she was satisfied with her small victory.

She flicked on the television and idly flipped channels. In a moment of terrifying coincidence, a horror film was on one of the movie channels. Emerie watched with interest as a priest splashed water on a young girl writhing on her bed.

Holy water...now there was an idea.

———

For $17.80, Emerie could purchase holy water from the Dead Sea online.

Holy water, according to the internet, was water blessed by a priest and used for protection against evil. She wasn't sure if this would be effective. Salt was also recommended, but this resulted only in Emerie accidentally getting salt in her eyes—and a new incredibly disconcerting message, this time painted on her kitchen cabinets:

ARE YOU SEASONING YOURSELF FOR DINNER?

It occurred to Emerie that the message was likely a joke in bad taste, as spirits and ghosts (as far as she was aware) did not eat new homeowners. Did they? Surely a big budget horror film would've been made about ghosts eating people if it were true. The internet provided varying opinions on the matter. She wished she could ask her grandfather. Ji-Ji knew everything.

He didn't visit very often; Emerie's mother would bring them to Japan over the summer holidays. He no longer ran the hot springs his daughter grew up in and had retired to a smaller cottage a mile away. (He told his grandchildren to steer clear of the hot springs and Emerie and Falcon were far more interested in his backyard pool)

Ji-Ji knew the best remedy for a cold was *tamago-zake*, a sweet and strong mixture of what Emerie originally thought was just raw egg and honey. Turned out Ji-Ji often added a couple of shots of sake to it too, much to her mother's displeasure. (For all her mollycoddling, it *did* work.) He knew her little brother's big earlobes meant he was extraordinarily lucky.

When Emerie and her brother hid from thunderstorms, her grandfather's kind and craggy face would appear at their hiding spot and gravely tell them to protect their belly buttons or the god of thunder would strike them down.

Ji-Ji had no idea why his daughter requested he leave, after that. "Smart, sensible children hide from thunder gods," he'd said approvingly.

Emerie had nightmares about Thor-like giants chasing her with lightning bolts.

She shook herself for a moment and returned to her research. She couldn't tell if bottled holy water was incredibly overpriced or an excellent deal—what was the going rate? But according to the description, it came with a certificate and house blessing card, in order to prove its authenticity.

Still…$17.80?! It was *water. Salty* water. Bottled water was a scam in any respect, but at least it was usually no more than a dollar or two. Even with the tempting certificate of authenticity, Emerie could not bring herself to spend that much money on a bottle of water. It felt like buying overpriced snacks at the movies instead of sneaking them in your purse like a proper American.

So Emerie decided to get some a different way.

It was a relief to leave her house. She had spent the morning painting over the ambiguous message on her cupboards and attempting to fix the lock on her living room window. The paint fumes and fury that she had the wrong kind of screw caused her to fling her screwdriver across the room, narrowly missing the beloved antique light fixtures. She needed the break—and she needed to see if holy water would be a solution to her supernatural pest problem.

As she put on her jacket and entered the foyer, she was startled to find a parting message painted on her door.

WEAR A SCARF, IT'S CHILLY.

Emerie scowled. She defiantly ignored the advice, added "buy red paint for front door" to her shopping list, and strode outside.

Autumn had been kind to Milton, decorating the sugar maples and oak trees in varying shades of flame. The weather was just chilly and sunny enough for a brisk walk and Emerie stepped forth onto her sidewalk, snuggled into a charcoal-colored blanket cape. Given a choice in the matter, she would wear nothing but blankets and pajamas forever.

Emerie's house stood on the corner of Crenshaw and Cambridge streets. A left took her down Cambridge into the heart of Milton. Pavement became cobblestones, houses bled into folksy shops, selling everything from antiques to taxidermy. A barbeque restaurant caused her to stop short and inhale deeply—she had been living on fast food for too long. Across from the barbeque restaurant was a coffee shop called "Witch's Brew", which made Emerie smile. She noticed quite a few new age shops too…Milton apparently wanted to capitalize on its history of witch persecution as much as Salem.

Farther down was the courthouse (built in 1790), and across the street from the courthouse was St. Julian's Parish.

St. Julian's looked almost gothic in appearance, as though a hunchback might swing from its expansive bell tower at any moment. It was certainly bigger than the Baptist church down the street from Emerie's house, and it loomed over Cambridge Street with grave authority. The stained glass windows were gruesome, with graphic pictures of angels slaying monsters with spears and clubs. It was impressive—the little plaque before the main entrance boasted that it was one of the oldest Catholic churches in Massachusetts. Emerie especially liked the gargoyles that decorated the front.

She hesitated at first, then boldly strode up the front steps as though she knew exactly where she was going. It was mid-afternoon, so there was no fear of her interrupting the service. She would just nip into the back, dunk her Wonder Woman water bottle in the nearest holy water fountain, and be on her way.

Unfortunately, as Emerie was not a practicing Catholic, she was unaware of the afternoon mass.

For a moment, she thought she'd interrupted the service. But she got lucky—the mass had just concluded. The sparse congregation were focused on gathering their purses and coats, greeting each other with small smiles, and chatting with the priests. Emerie flushed at the few people who blinked at her, and surreptitiously approached a large baptismal font near the doors. Acting quickly, she plunged Wonder Woman into the water.

No one seemed to notice this—the collective congregation seemed more intent on exiting the church. Emerie sighed with relief and pulled the water bottle out, screwing the cap on tightly.

"Can I help you?"

Emerie jumped and almost dropped her water bottle. She shoved it into her bag and whipped around. A man with a white clergy collar looked down at her suspiciously. He was a striking black man who looked to be in his early forties. Something about his stern gaze and crew cut made her wonder if he was ex-military.

"Nope, I'm good." Emerie started to back away from the baptismal font. "It was a great sermon, Pastor. Great job."

"Father." He gently corrected her and folded his arms against his chest. "We're priests, not pastors. I will be sure to relay the message to Father Simon."

She smiled brightly at him. He did not smile back. She continued to smile pleasantly and walked backwards out of the church, her hand gripping Wonder Woman tightly. He continued to stare her down as she tripped out of the doors.

Emerie half-expected to be struck by lightning once she entered the bright sunshine. But it seemed God didn't mind her stealing holy water.

As she made her way home, she was feeling pretty good about herself. She stopped at the barbecue restaurant and ordered some dinner to go, picked up a bottle of wine at the liquor store, and was feeling pleased her venture outside the house had been rather productive. She paused outside a new age store, but pressed onward. If the holy water didn't work, she'd try there next.

Emerie was just about to turn the corner on Crenshaw Street to her house when she noticed a yard sale across the street. An older woman was starting to close it down, folding up tables and boxing up the unsold items. This did not seem to deter her neighbors however, who continued to mill about, deciding between vases and old clothes.

Unable to resist a good yard sale, Emerie crossed the street to check out the bookshelves. She always seemed to be in need of more book-shelves. There was a lovely window seat under the stairs she wished to turn into a book nook.

Emerie crossed into the yard and stopped in front of a small black bookcase, about three feet high. She felt the woman's eyes upon her, so she cast a tentative smile at her neighbor who nodded happily.

"I'm just about done." Her neighbor's voice was pleasantly husky, like an old forties film star. "I'm practically giving away this stuff!"

She was a little strange looking, if Emerie were to be honest. She was wearing something that appeared to be a turquoise muumuu and had more necklaces around her neck than Emerie even owned. Her hair was an ashy blonde, streaked with gray, and her round pale gray eyes gave her an almost owlish appearance.

Emerie gave her a thumbs-up. "Good! I'm still looking for some new furniture. I just moved here. My name's Emerie."

"Oh, you're the new one to the neighborhood!" The woman exclaimed. "My name's Sunflower. I've been wondering who my new neighbors are."

Emerie resisted the urge to comment on the name "Sunflower." Her house was a little smaller than Emerie's, but it still had a classic Victorian turret and a wraparound porch. Her porch looked almost jungle-ish; it was overflowing with vibrant greenery. Approximately a thousand wind chimes lined the lacy overhang over her porch. They seemed to be made of everything from seashells to coke bottles. A sudden burst of October wind nearly knocked a flimsy chair over and the cacophony of wind chimes clanged and tinkled a discordant harmony. A few of the lingering shoppers grimaced at the racket.

"It's just me and my boyfriend." Emerie raised her voice over the wind chimes. "He's out of town right now."

"That's too bad!" Sunflower cleared off another card table. Her hands were slender and a large crystal ring encircled every finger. One finger got caught on an old scarf and Sunflower impatiently shook it off.

"You look around my daughter's age, as a matter of fact." Sunflower heaved another box onto the porch. "She's up in Boston; her work keeps her *so* busy, she doesn't often come down here. Life in the big city, I guess. I'm glad at least some young people still have an appreciation for small towns."

"Well, home ownership is no picnic," Emerie examined an old leather jacket with a patch that read CC LOVES EM. "I've been up to my ears in paint and boxes and old wallpaper. But I really like projects."

"I completely understand," Sunflower rooted through the depths of her box like a caver. "It's more fun to fix those kind of places up with someone who shares your vision. I'm so happy my daughter helped me refurbish my home!"

No kidding, Emerie thought with a grumpy huff. *Some people actually LIKE working on projects with their loved ones!*

"Wait a second."

An elderly woman interrupted her and stood between Emerie and Sunflower. She had the face of a gremlin—wrinkled, with large ears and wiry gray hair. She wasn't that much bigger than one, either. She carried a paper bag filled to the brim with buttons.

"You moved into Hell Haven?" The old woman's tone was frankly accusatory.

Emerie's lips twisted. "Excuse me?"

"That's what we used to call it." The old woman maneuvered around one of the folding tables, plodded up the steps, and began to count out pennies on the porch railing. "Hell Haven. Or Hell House. Most haunted house in Milton."

"Well, I don't know about *most* haunted!" Sunflower sputtered out. "My house is full of spirit activity. I am a medium, you know. I own an elemental store in town."

This did not strike Emerie as surprising. But the gremlin-faced woman paid her no heed, simply continued to pick out pennies, occasionally murmuring in approval if she found a nickel in the bunch.

"You're a damned fool," she said, as she slowly held up a silver dollar in Emerie's direction, "if you think you can renovate *that* house."

A woman at the next table heard this and inclined her head. She was blonde with a distinctly "mom" haircut in expensive athleisure wear. Emerie felt a little embarrassed at the woman's cool expression—apparently restoring rumored haunted houses was not in her Martha Stewart Bible.

A balding middle-aged man looked up from a collection of golf clubs. "Don't mind my mother. She has a story for every house on this street. Hurry up, Ma, they're closing down!"

The old woman finally finished her budgeting and shoved two handfuls of pennies and assorted nickels toward Sunflower, who responded with a rather fixed smile. Emerie coughed, glad to recuse herself from the conversation.

The first table revealed quite a few fake plastic roses, marked for a nickel each. There were also several chipped teacups, a swan necklace, and several Hot Wheels cars, most missing tires.

The second table looked more promising. Underneath the card table, she saw an old record player from the 1940s. It was about the size of a coffee table, made of cherry wood, standing proudly on four nubby feet. A little wood polish would really make it shine, though she wasn't sure she could get rid of the scuff marks around the legs. It didn't appear to be in working condition and there were no nearby records to go with it, but she fell in love with it anyway. Maybe she could fix it. She loved fixing things! Dylan used to love it too, haunting garage sales, finding old beat-up stereo systems or computers they would monkey around with over the weekend. Surely she could find some instructions online. For twenty-five dollars, it was worth a shot.

She was just about to stop Sunflower and pay for the record player when something caught her eye. The last table was covered in board games and puzzles—Risk, Monopoly, Mouse Trap...but there was something else buried under a mountain of castle-themed ten-thousand-piece jigsaw puzzles. Her heart leapt to her throat as she dug out a long, flat rectangular box. She was staring at a classic Ouija board.

Carefully, Emerie tucked the box under her arm and trotted up the front steps. Sunflower looked up from counting the old woman's pennies and smiled brightly.

"How much for the old record player and this?"

"Well—" Sunflower started to say.

"You ought to give it to her for free!" The old woman shouted from across the yard. "If she's dumb enough to play with it in the Hell Haven!"

Sunflower blanched. The balding man said exasperatedly, *"Mom."*

"You can take the spirit board for free," Sunflower cleared her throat, "and if you're interested in that sort of thing, we have some much nicer ones at my shop. I'll take twenty dollars for the record player."

Emerie dug a twenty from her bag and handed it over to Sunflower. She then carefully balanced the Ouija board on top of her new old record player and crossed the street to her house.

When she opened the front door, she came upon another blood message—this time marking up the beautiful teal ceiling of the foyer.

YOU HAVE AWOKEN ANCIENT EVIL

"Then go back to sleep!" Emerie yelled upwards. She set the record player down with the Ouija board and her dinner balanced on top and stormed down the hallway. She furiously sprinkled her purloined holy water in the kitchen and dining room and repeated her work in the living room. She spritzed the mud room facing the backyard. She splashed water on every step leading upstairs, the upstairs parlor, the spare bedrooms, and her own bedroom. She even ventured into the expansive attic and flicked water in every corner. Nothing screamed or burned, but at least it felt like she was doing something.

She exhaled and retreated downstairs once more. She paused for a minute, considering the record player and Ouija board. Not tonight. She would figure out where to put *both* in the morning.

She grabbed her dinner and wine and marched into the kitchen. She seated herself on a barstool and sullenly ate her barbecue burger. She really needed a dining room table.

There was a sudden banging on the front door. Emerie choked on her burger. She slid off the barstool and stormed into the dining room. The lovely chandelier was swinging ever so slightly. Emerie glared at it accusingly and strode into the entryway.

"What?!"

She took a few steps forward and saw the message on the front door again.

DID YOU BRING ME ANY BRISKET?

Emerie screamed in frustration.

Holy water was a joke. At least she hadn't wasted seventeen-dollars on it.

THREE

IT WAS AMAZING how much work Emerie got done in the wee small hours of the morning.

Sleep was officially out of the question. She didn't relish getting dragged out of bed again and it seemed more likely to happen with Dylan gone. So instead, she finished unpacking the dining room and hallway, dragged the record player into the living room from its temporary spot, and piled the now empty boxes in the mudroom to be taken to the curb at a saner hour. She then moved upstairs searching for more things to do. Unfortunately, she was nearly finished with the upstairs, aside from retiling the bathroom.

It occurred to her that the attic probably needed a good sweeping. At the end of the upstairs hallway, across from the master bedroom, was a heavy chestnut door. Emerie hadn't had a chance to spend much time in the attic, aside from shoving all her Christmas boxes haphazardly up there—but now seemed as good a time as any. So she pulled open the attic door and climbed the narrow steps, broom in hand. Once she reached the third floor, a cobweb attacked her face and she grimaced, fending it off with the dustpan.

The attic was one of the best rooms in the house. It was neither dark nor dreary—windows lined every wall, providing a gorgeous view of her neighborhood. The ceiling was vaulted, and wood paneling arced against the slanted corners of the room. Emerie even contemplated turning it into a library of sorts, it was such a lovely space for quiet—but hauling bookshelves up the rickety attic stairs did not strike her as a pleasant task.

She swept furiously, awakening ancient dust-bunnies from their slumber. She reached the old cast-iron stove at the far end of the attic. She wiped it down with an old T-shirt, letting the rhythm match her breathing. She still wasn't sure what to do with the thing—it didn't work and even if it did, what would they cook in an attic? Dylan had suggested selling it online, but she hated the idea of something so obscurely historical leaving her house. She had named it Eunice.

Dylan...Emerie winced. She should have called him by now...but then again, he hadn't called her either. Perhaps he really *was* looking for a shiny Boston apartment—and perhaps a new girlfriend.

She sat on her heels in thought. It hadn't always been like this with Dylan. They used to laugh themselves silly at each other and Emerie's antics amused rather than annoyed. She had thought of him as her straight man, the Abbott to her Costello, the Hanshin to her Kyojin, the Greg to her Dharma. She swallowed a little hard. Perhaps he had outgrown her.

She decided that she ought to clean the inside of the old stove, so she cracked it open. She blew inside, to try and scare off spiders, and wiped the interior.

Her fingers brushed against something. Emerie started and pulled out a packet of papers. They were bound in twine—letters and photographs.

She rolled the twine off and flipped through them. The spidery script was hard to read; she needed better light. They were photographs of different women in old-fashioned Victorian clothing. In one photograph, they were sitting in an ornately decorated room with a sparkling chandelier.

Emerie leaned in closer. That was *her* chandelier...that was *her* dining room.

There was something on the table—a board of some sort. Their hands were all touching it. Emerie squinted. Was that a Ouija board? Did they have Ouija boards back then? But she recognized those symbols; they looked exactly like the one she owned. But the planchette wasn't plastic. The planchette was much fancier—perhaps made of mother-of-pearl or ivory.

She turned the photograph over. It was hard to make out, but she was pretty sure the inscription read: Order of the Rosy Eden, 1898.

"Weird," Emerie muttered to herself. She stood and brushed herself off. She crossed the room and opened the attic door, descending the constricted stairs. She made her way down the bedroom hallway, continuing to flip through the photographs, until she reached the upstairs parlor. She found another photo, this one of a middle-aged woman, seated in the same parlor. The inscription read, "Fairy Lemp, 1881."

It seemed as though Dylan had been right—Fairy Lemp really did have a club in this house. Some women played bridge; maybe these women played with spirits. Were they responsible for her poltergeist? Or had they used their spirit board to try to rid themselves of the mischievous spook?

There could be a way for Emerie to find out. She trotted downstairs to her living room glancing gout the window. It was still fairly dark out, but dawn would be here soon enough. She placed her Ouija board on the ottoman in front of her couch, made herself a cup of instant coffee (her coffeemaker was still MIA, but they had a spare electric tea kettle), and examined the board carefully.

By all accounts, the game looked a little silly.

Despite the box, which promised surefire scares, it just looked like a board game with a piece of plastic. She couldn't recall ever playing with one before—she and her brother were more Scrabble and Boggle players than anything else. But at least she had a possible way of communication.

"All right then," she announced to the house. "I'm sick and tired of repainting my walls. Can you communicate with me this way?"

She rested her fingertips gently on the pointer. Nothing happened.

Emerie shook her head angrily. Why had she even tried? This was a board game! What kind of lunatic bought into this nonsense?

Still…wasn't she a little past the point of skepticism?

She cleared her throat again. "Look—my name is Emerie Fox. I want to make this house my home. I found some fairly suspect photographs in the attic. Are you trying to hurt me?"

This time, the pointer quivered. Emerie sucked in her breath as the planchette suddenly flew out from under her fingertips and landed firmly on the word NO.

A shiver went down her spine. Her breathing grew shallower and she tentatively drew the pointer back to her.

"Are you—are you trying to make me leave?" She swallowed, suddenly afraid of the answer.

The pointer hesitated before it moved again.

NO

Emerie let out the breath she'd been holding. "Okay. Are you...a ghost of someone who died here?"

NO

"A ghost from somewhere else? I heard this house was buried over part of the cemetery..."

NO

Emerie's brow furrowed.

"Are you a ghost at all?"

NO

Her heart began to hammer. If not a ghost...

"Then you're something else, right?" She wrapped her hands around her coffee mug, absorbing its warmth. "Some kind of entity..."

YES

"So then..." Her fingernails tapped a rapid rhythm on her mug. "What—what are you?"

A book fell off the bookshelf next to the bay windows. Emerie jumped, accidentally spilling coffee on herself. She swore and stood, moving to the window. She wiped her wet sleeve absently on the curtain and bent down to pick the book up. One of Dylan's.

The Screwtape Letters by C.S. Lewis. She turned it over and skimmed the back cover.

Ice prickled through her veins. Like a child afraid of monsters, she jumped up and turned on all the lights. The room started to drink in the morning sunlight, but she couldn't seem to quell her nerves. She set the book down and placed her trembling fingertips on the pointer.

"Are you a demon?"

The pointer leapt out from under her fingertips.

YES

A little cry came from her mouth. She wanted to scream, but couldn't muster the full noise. Ghosts were one thing—her mother and grandfather treated them as more of a nuisance than anything else. But demons?

A thousand horror films flew through her mind...Linda Blair vomiting pea soup, Barbara Hershey screaming, Katie Featherston smiling wickedly at her boyfriend's camera ...

I should move. I should get the hell out of here. I should leave this town in my dust...

Suddenly, the image of Dylan's smirking face entered her mind. *"I told you so! I told you this would happen! You know, if you just listened to me more, Emerie ..."*

Emerie shuddered. Somehow, facing down a demon was preferable to her smug boyfriend.

"Okay," Emerie took another deep breath. "A demon...hey, wait a minute. If you're a demon, how come the holy water didn't work?!"

The pointer moved between the letters rapidly.

STOLEN

She tucked a lock of her hair behind her ear as heat filled her cheeks. Whoops. Somehow it hadn't occurred to her that stealing holy water might make the water less holy. She exhaled slowly.

"Fair point...so you're a demon. But...you're not going to hurt me?"

NO

"You're not going to possess me, are you?"

This time, the pointer spelled out something. Emerie carefully scribbled out the message on an old receipt.

NOT WITHOUT YOUR PERMISSION

Emerie blinked. "You're asking my consent?"

The pointer flew to YES.

Unexpected.

Emerie's eyes narrowed. "Do you want to drag me to Hell?"

NO HELL IS LAME

"Do you want me to sell my soul to Satan?"

NO SATAN'S A DICK

At that, Emerie had to laugh. Then inspiration struck.

"Maybe I'm not the target." She said grimly. "If you're not after me, are you after Dylan?"

The pointer hesitated.

NOT IF YOU DONT WANT ME TO BE

The message was so stilted, so reluctant, it made Emerie laugh again at the absurdity of it all. She pinched the skin between her brows.

"All right," she sighed, "if you're not after me or my boyfriend... what is it you want?"

There was no response from the Ouija board. Emerie's lips twisted. Perhaps the demon was tired of talking.

"Let's try something different." She hummed a little. "How about a name? I'm guessing Mephistopheles? Beelzebub? Stormagedden?"

MY NAME IS SAMAEL

"Samael..." When she said his name, the lights flickered. Shadows filled the room like scattering goblins. Emerie craned her neck towards the window—the rising sun was hidden behind clouds.

"This is crazy." Emerie said, half to herself. "This is crazy. But...I mean, it's not like I'm making this all up. Samael...Samael, have you been in the house this whole time?"

YES INCORPOREAL

"I don't know anything about western demons." Emerie stood, pen and receipt in hand, and started to pace in a circle around her coffee table. Western demons were connected to Christianity, right?

Demons were different in Japan. They were called *yokai* or *mononoke*. They weren't evil, exactly, more mischievous. Something to be wary of. *Yokai* was often translated into the word *demon*, but a better word might be fairy or trickster spirit...not that Emerie believed in any of that nonsense. Ghosts were one thing—humans were real, after all. But demons?

"Anyway, I'm agnostic. So...what type of demon are you, exactly?"

LAZY

This demon had a weird sense of humor.

"Come on." Emerie prompted. "What kind?"

PART INCUBUS

PART BELIEL

"I have no idea what the hell a beliel is. But an incubus…so what's that mean? You trying to seduce me?"

The pointer hesitated again, circling awkwardly.

IF I WERE TRYING TO SEDUCE YOU

There was a pregnant pause, as though for dramatic emphasis.

YOU WOULD KNOW

"Oh yeah?" Emerie placed a hand on her hip.

At that precise moment, Emerie's record player turned on. She slowly turned towards it—she hadn't found the time to fix it yet. But Bruce Springsteen was crooning "You've Got It."

She decided to sit down. "Seriously? That's the song you're going with?"

AWESOME SONG

"Whatever." Emerie stretched. "So it was you, right? The weird messages? Dragging me along the ground every which way? Scaring the hell out of Dylan?"

YES

"Okay…I just…I still don't understand why." Emerie watched the pointer rattle against the board before doing a backflip. "You haven't answered me. You haven't told me what you want."

The pointer vibrated. Finally, it scooted across the letters and spelled out one word:

THIS

"This?" Emerie threw up her hands. "What's 'this'? To talk to me?"

YES

"But—why?!"

LIKED THE FOOD

"The offering! So it did appease you," Emerie sat back in her seat. "But then again, no it didn't. You're still here. What is it you want?"

The music stopped abruptly. The pointer halted. Emerie stared at the board and flicked the pointer with her finger. Nothing moved. Samael had exited the conversation.

———

According to ninety-eight percent of the demonology and paranormal websites Emerie perused the next day, contacting a demon through a Ouija board was an absolutely terrible idea. Several ghost hunters cited credible-ish statistics which stated the number one reason a house becomes haunted is through a user playing with a Ouija board. Under no circumstances should you converse with a demon—demons were liars, deceivers, and cheats. They would do anything to enact their malicious ends. Furthermore, acknowledging a demon's presence, allowing its influence into your life, was sure to lead to absolute calamity.

But it was too late now, so Emerie decided to keep going with it.

Apparently, the demon—Samael—described himself accurately. He was somewhat lazy and didn't often feel like talking to Emerie, even through the use of a Ouija board. Or he would become bored and refuse to talk to her, but he would flick the living room lights and radio as if distracting her from her work deadlines was just as good as conversation. When she watched TV, he enjoyed mimicking the scores on the piano, which was simultaneously eerie and amusing.

He stopped vandalizing her walls, accepting the Ouija board as a replacement. But whenever she tried to ask him about where he came from or how he got here, he would abruptly leave the conversation. This seemed out of character. Most of her internet research indicated a demon would try and trick her—in fact, they weren't generally supposed to admit they were demons. She read about cases where they would pretend to be ghosts to gain the trust of the residents.

So why was Samael so upfront about what he was?

She turned to the letters and photographs she'd found in her attic, but much of it remained a mystery. There was one jarring thing she'd found on a few scraps of paper. At the top of one page, in clear black letters, the name **SAMAEL** was written out. Underneath was a bullet point list of odds and ends, almost like a grocery list. Key of Solomon, lamb's blood, virgin's kiss, snakeskin…and on the margins of the notebook:

SAMAEL THE DESTROYER
SAMAEL THE ACCUSER
SAMAEL THE SEDUCER

VENOM OF GOD
BLINDNESS OF GOD

None of these titles sounded positive. Furthermore, Fairy Lemp had drawn little hearts around each title, which was confusing.

In an effort to collect more information, Emerie brought the Ouija board into the kitchen and placed it on the island. She cracked open a Guinness and kept her eye on the pointer.

HI EMERIE

"Hi Samael." Emerie tapped her fingers on the board. "So tell me. Have you interacted with other people in this house?"

NOT REALLY

"Why not?" Emerie leaned in a bit.

UNINTERESTING

"So, you find me interesting." She crossed her arms over her chest. "Why?"

No response.

"You know, in horror movies, the demon is always after the baby," Emerie pointed out. "Are you after my hypothetical unborn child that you want to turn into the antichrist?"

TOO MUCH WORK

CHILDCARE IS A PAIN IN THE ASS

She snorted into her beer. "Okay, fair enough…but you're still being weirdly evasive. You said you weren't trying to make me leave. Shouldn't you be scaring me?"

I AM SCARING YOU

"Dragging me out of bed and knocking things over isn't scary, it's just annoying," Emerie retorted. "My brother and I liked to terrorize each other when we were younger. You'll have to try a lot harder than that."

SO YOU ARE A LITTLE HARDER TO SCARE

BUT THAT IS JUST BECAUSE

YOU ARE WEIRD

Emerie snorted and took another sip of beer.

JUST YOU WAIT

"Yeah, good luck with that." She rolled her eyes. "Look, this is getting a little ridiculous. I just don't have the personality or energy to be haunted. You'd best clear off now, you're just setting yourself up for disappointment."

The pointer sat up, as though it were offended. It suddenly flipped through the air and bonked her on the nose.

"Fine!" Emerie stood from her barstool and snapped the board shut. "I warned you."

She flipped the lights off and made her way upstairs to call it a night.

———

Samael's determination to haunt her properly began in earnest the following morning. When Emerie awoke, she found that none of the lights in her house worked. After an angry call to the electric company (who denied all culpability), she lit candles, which elicited an eerie, Dracula-esque atmosphere.

"Joke's on you!" She shouted at the ceiling. "I *like* gothic novels, so there!"

The books on her bookshelf promptly fell off in unison. This did not annoy Emerie, however, as she felt there was nothing more relaxing than figuring out a new way to reorganize her books. Last time, she had organized them by genre and alphabetically (with a subsection by publication date). This time, she would try organizing them by color.

Presumably, Samael realized she enjoyed any excuse to reorder her books, so instead he set about cracking her picture frames. Emerie promptly removed the broken glass from the frames and let her pictures hang bare. Samael retaliated by scribbling over Dylan's face in every picture. Emerie ignored the vandalism and remarked loudly the macabre touch to their photographs added whimsy to the house.

Samael continued his irritating habit of stealing Emerie's things. To top it off, he would also return them several days later—but place them in the most incongruous of places. Emerie's hairbrush would disappear from her bedroom and turn up in the oven only to find a new home several hours later in the crockpot.

When Samael stole her flash drive which contained most of her unfinished drafts for work, Emerie knew it was time to declare a truce. She taped a white napkin to a pencil and sat before the Ouija board once more. She waved the napkin in emphasis.

"What's it gonna take to get my flash drive back, asshole?"

The pointer paused before pirouetting over her hand. It spelled out:

I SCARED YOU

"Yes, you scared me with the threat of unemployment, which any self-respecting twenty-something fears," Emerie said impatiently, tearing the white flag in impatience. "I'm serious, Samael, give me back my flash drive. I have two articles due next week."

VICTORY

"The flash drive, please!"

FINE ITS NEXT TO YOUR COFFEE

She whipped around to find her Keurig was *still missing*—but a freshly brewed latte was sitting on the countertop, as though it had been there the whole time. She slid off her stool and sure enough, the flash drive was seated right next to it.

"You have a sick sense of humor," Emerie informed the Ouija board, taking a sip of latte.

HAHAHAHAHAHA

"Yeah, laugh it up, jerk!" Emerie yelled at the game. "I'm calling a priest!"

HAVE FUN WITH THAT

FOUR

DYLAN HAD A FEW RELIGIOUS BOOKS, remnants of his private school confirmation classes. He went to Lutheran schools most of his life and Emerie would occasionally run across a stray Concordia study Bible or little blue Luther's catechism as she unpacked box after box of books. His copy of *The Screwtape Letters* was one of these leftovers, though C.S. Lewis apparently did not have any solid advice about what to do about a semi-friendly demon living in your house, just amusing pieces of their correspondence.

She couldn't come up with any other options on what to do about her situation—aside from returning to St. Julian's.

Her family had attended Christmas and Easter services, more for the sake of her father's parents than anything else. Emerie's lingering memories of western churches involved itchy dresses, falling asleep against her mother's shoulder, and counting the crosses in the sanctuary until the endless sermon was over. Once she'd reached high school, she expressed her desire to spend the holidays sleeping in, and her parents did not put up much objection.

Every once in a while, they would take a trip to visit Ji-Ji and her mother's extended family in Hokkaido. Shrine visits there were short and perfunctory—much more appealing than the endless Protestant services she'd been subjected to.

She had intentions of creating a shrine for her grandfather in her house… somewhere isolated, where Dylan couldn't complain about the smell of incense. But every time she started to gather the materials, a lump would form in her throat and she couldn't complete the task. It was too final.

She couldn't think about Ji-Ji now. It would only distract her from her mission.

But if her house did have a demon—if she wasn't slowly going insane —then she needed more in-depth research than the internet could offer. Who would know more about demons than a priest?

Still, she hesitated at the steps of St. Julian's Parish. After all, she had sort of stolen holy water from this church and that had been something of a fiasco. Wouldn't she have better luck at the Baptist church on Crenshaw? And besides, weren't the priests who got killed in *The Exorcist* Catholic? That didn't bode well for her…

She turned away from the front church steps and started to walk, her back to the church. But before she reached the sidewalk, she noticed a little side path that wound its way around the church, then disappeared into hedges and trees. There wasn't a gate or anything blockading the path, so she assumed it was open to the public.

It was still early in the day and Emerie didn't particularly want to go home. She stepped onto the dirt path and started on her way.

She assumed correctly. The path went straight into the trees and led to a small, shaded churchyard. That was something remarkable about these old Massachusetts towns—they never seemed to disrupt the New England woods. The streets and buildings just sort of grew around them, with patches of trees sprouting in unexpected places. The churchyard was clearly old, with weathered stones scattered helter-skelter. Some of the headstones were modern and neatly ordered, gleaming in the sunlight. Others looked older. She couldn't read the inscriptions, but she thought she could see some faint dates from the 1700s. The further she went into the churchyard, the more she realized the older headstones seemed to form a spiraling pattern. She stopped at one suddenly, squatting down. The inscription had struck her…Lemp…Florence Lemp?

"Welcome back."

Emerie squawked and lost her footing. The same priest who had cornered her during her thievery within the church watched her carefully. He was leaning against a spade and held coral gardening gloves in one fist—Emerie noticed daisies were stitched on the cuff.

She stared at him for a moment before blurting out, "Your gloves are pink."

"My mother got them for me," the priest replied coolly.

He continued to stare her down and Emerie wondered if he'd been burying a body. Then she realized he was holding a flowerpot filled with bright orange blossoms.

"Nice to see you again!" She put on a winning smile. "I like your…carnations?"

"Mums." He corrected. "Have you returned for more holy water?"

Emerie winced. "Oh…you saw me?"

The priest's stony expression plainly told her the indiscretion had been anything but covert. He put the gargoyles to shame in both silence and disapproval.

"I'm surprised you didn't bust me and report me to the Pope." Emerie scratched her neck.

"If holy water relieves people's worries, they are welcome to it." The priest folded his gloves into his jeans pocket neatly. "I've no objection to you bringing some home. Next time, please ask."

"Okay…" She cleared her throat. "Er—well, I don't need anything, thanks."

"Are you paying your respects here?" He gestured towards the headstone.

Emerie considered lying but she had a funny feeling the priest would be able to tell. "No…I was just doing some research. Or trying to."

"Research on what?" The priest looked pointedly towards a flowerbed. Catching on, she knelt gently in the dirt, smiling a little as her knees sank into the warm soil. It reminded her of gardening with Ji-Ji. (Though Ji-Ji would be complaining about Emerie's refusal to pull what she called "the pretty weeds.")

They were near a large headstone with a fat winged stone baby peeking overtop. She watched the priest carefully remove the plastic green tub which encased the chrysanthemums. The soil was still packed into the shape of the tub.

"I guess you could say…theology?" Emerie pulled a stray dandelion away from the flowerbed and tied the stem in a knot.

"Theology?" The priest stopped for a moment and looked at her piercingly. "So you came to a cemetery?"

She squirmed. "Okay, you win. I chickened out from coming inside again. I saw the garden path and decided to take a walk. It's pretty back here."

To her surprise, he gave her a rare smile. It completely changed the attitude of his face, like the sun emerging from the clouds. She suddenly felt less like she was in the principal's office and more like she was having a friendly chat with a neighbor.

"It's an extremely old garden," the priest told her as he removed a small pair of clippers from his basket. "It was here before the church, actually. I've had…disagreements with some of my colleagues about it. There are some who wish to turn some of the older sections into a parking lot."

"Paving paradise, huh?" Emerie traced a finger into the dirt. It felt cool and moist on her finger. "That's a shame."

He rumbled in assent, reminding her vaguely of a rottweiler. "What sort of theology questions do you have?"

Emerie looked at him furtively, but he didn't meet her gaze. He took out a small trowel and started to dig into the soft earth.

"So…" She twisted the knotted dandelion stem between her fingers. "What's—what's the church's stance on demons?"

To her relief, the priest did not laugh at her. His digging slowed for a moment, but aside from that, his only reaction was a raised eyebrow. "Demons?"

She nodded. He reached into the hole he created and tested its depth. She watched in surprise as he picked up his mums and snipped the flowers clean off. Only the green sprouts remained.

"It is best to pinch your chrysanthemums." The priest continued to trim some of the green. "It keeps them hardy during the winter." He ignored the decapitated flowers, his attention wholly on the sprouts.

"So. Demons. I'm guessing you're a horror buff." The priest's tone was light and casual.

"Um, no." Emerie watched as he planted the green sprouts into the ground, firmly packing it all around. "I just moved here. I don't really have a frame of reference for all the witchcraft, witch burning, cults, and demon stuff the town seems to thrive on. I've been trying to research, but it's not exactly an academic area of interest."

"That is true," The priest said. "Most seminaries don't cover demonology." He took out another green plastic tub of chrysanthemums from his basket and repeated the procedure.

"Did yours?"

The corners of his mouth lifted. "Somewhat. Though not in the way you'd expect. You see, the church's stance on demons and demonic possession has…evolved, I guess you could say. We have a lot more scientific resources and medical knowledge than we did a thousand years ago. That changes our context."

"Okay—so what are demons, anyway? Christian demons, I mean. I'm not really clear on where they came from."

"There are a multitude of views." The priest stood from his work and brushed the dirt off his jeans. "Some religious scholars and theologians don't even believe in demons or find them necessary to the faith. Others believe they are simply forces of evil, bent on wreaking havoc on God's creation and tempting humanity away from Christ."

"I thought they were fallen angels." Emerie glanced suspiciously at the fat baby angel statue leering at them from its headstone.

"That's another view." The priest lifted his head and inhaled the fall air deeply. "*If he oppos'd; and with ambitious aim/Against the Throne and Monarchy of God/Rais'd impious War in Heav'n and Battel proud/With vain attempt. Him the Almighty Power Hurld headlong flaming from th' Ethereal Skie/With hideous ruine and combustion down/To bottomless perdition, there to dwell.*"

Emerie stared at him blankly.

"Paradise Lost." The priest clarified, and offered his palm to help her stand. "Milton—our town's namesake, actually. As the story goes, there was a great war in Heaven over humanity. Some angels chose to fall with

Lucifer and rebel against God. Others chose to stand with God and protect creation."

"Why did Lucifer rebel against God?"

"Well, according to the story," the priest paused by a cherry tree and examined the bark critically, "because of us. Because he hated God's love for humanity. That's why—traditionally speaking, that is—demons are seen as forces of torment to humans. Evil beings that would like nothing more than to destroy someone."

A breeze shook the cherry tree branches and Emerie shivered. Is that what Samael wanted? Was that his endgame? To destroy her?

Then why was he so *bad* at it?

"So there's no way...no way a demon could be nice to a human?" she asked. She still held the dandelion. She picked at it anxiously, her fingers becoming sticky from the stem.

"Well, these are all hypotheticals." The priest moved towards what appeared to be an empty flower bed and touched the dirt, as though measuring the moisture with his fingers. "I'm explaining Christian *mythology* more than anything else. When we talk about demons now, we might talk about struggling with depression, with alcoholism, PTSD...or we might talk about demons as a metaphor for general evil. Something against God cannot be for humanity."

"R-right." Emerie tripped on a small stone obscured by leaves. "And...if a demon were to...I don't know, talk to a human...it would probably be a trick. A trick to tempt them into Hell or whatever..."

The priest didn't answer her, but moved towards the stone she stumbled over. He circled it and Emerie realized it was a small headstone, perhaps for a stillbirth. Once he was satisfied she hadn't disturbed it, he continued on his way through the garden.

"Wait a second." She said suddenly and jogged to keep up with him. "What if I don't even believe in Hell—or anything, really. How could a demon tempt me away from God when I don't have anything to do with God in the first place?"

The priest stopped short and looked at her severely. "My dear, you are human. That in itself means you have something to do with God."

Emerie frowned. It was one thing to have her house haunted by a demon, it was quite another to be haunted by God.

"Well, thanks for the talk." Emerie backed away from him slowly. "And the uh, gardening tips. Sorry about the holy water."

"You'd be surprised at how many of these sorts of conversations I have with visitors." The priest's tone was rather dry. "Milton's a funny place that way. But if you're still concerned about demons, we'd be happy to come to your house and administer a blessing."

"What does that entail?" Emerie asked warily. "Because no offense, the holy water I used didn't really work."

"It wasn't administered by a priest." He looked as though he were resisting the urge to lecture her. "We send someone over, recite a little prayer, etc. Nothing as exciting as the movies might lead you to believe." The priest pulled out his wallet from a back pocket and withdrew something. "If you're interested, here's my card. Give us a call and we'll set a date."

Emerie took his business card—who knew priests had business cards? It read: Boaz Zebulun of St. Julian's Parish.

She thanked him again and exited the churchyard.

————

The priest who came to her house was not Boaz Zebulun, but a shorter balding man who said his name was Simon. He smiled pleasantly at her, in an almost patronizing way, and set to work.

Emerie admitted to him, a little awkwardly, that she wasn't Catholic. This did not seem to surprise Father Simon, who alluded to the fact it was fairly commonplace for Milton newcomers to have priests and clergy bless their homes. He did encourage her to attend St. Julian's, and she politely feigned interest.

She'd expected dramatics, but all Father Simon did was recite a rambling sort of prayer that mentioned casting out evil spirits, sprinkle her with holy water, and sprinkle her living room with holy water. Then he waved at her vaguely, told her he hoped to see her at Mass, and walked out the door.

Emerie didn't hear anything for a while and wondered if his little ritual had worked. No messages on her walls, no flickering lights...her stomach flipped a bit when she considered the idea that perhaps Samael was gone forever. Back to Hell, wherever that may be. Then it would be just her in the house, until Dylan came home.

Nevertheless, when she entered the kitchen to prepare her dinner, her faucet turned on of its own accord.

She narrowed her eyes and looked down the kitchen hallway into the dining room. The pointer was rattling on her Ouija board.

Sighing, Emerie trudged towards the table and crossed her arms. She looked down at the board expectantly.

RUDE

"You're calling me rude?" She placed her hands on her hips. "You're the one who won't scram!"

THOUGHT YOU ENJOYED MY COMPANY

"Oh, come on, Samael, no one wants a demon stuck in their house." Emerie retorted. "The only thing hellish about this house should be the mortgage."

There was no answer. She noticed a photograph of her grandfather was crooked so she crossed the dining room to adjust it. Her fingers lingered on the photo before she trudged back to the table.

"Well, apparently the priest blessing didn't work anyway." Emerie collapsed into a chair, "So it's not like you should even be offended."

OF COURSE IT DIDNT WORK

"What's that supposed to mean?"

IT DOES NOT WORK IF YOU DONT MEAN IT

THAT GUY DID NOT MEAN IT

Emerie narrowed her eyes. "What do you mean he didn't mean it? He said the prayers, he sprinkled the holy water, (which he did NOT steal) he asked me to join his church."

HE DOES NOT BELIEVE IN DEMONS

She blinked at this pronouncement. The pointer continued to move.

HE BLESSES HOMES FOR LITTLE OLD LADIES WHO DO

There was another pause before the pointer went on.

HE LIKES GIVING PEACE OF MIND NOT EXORCISMS

Father Zebulun had told her not all Catholics believed in demons, but it hadn't occurred to her clergy were counted among that fold. She wondered again if Father Zebulun himself believed.

NOT A BAD PERSON

NOT A BAD PRIEST

BUT YOU CANT GET RID OF SOMETHING YOU DONT BELIEVE IN

"Fair enough." Emerie twisted her lips. "I don't know what else to do. Do *any* pastors or priests believe in demons anymore?"

I WOULD NOT INVITE THEM OVER

MOST HAVE NO IDEA WHAT THEY ARE DOING

"Well, we're in the same boat then," she said grimly, "but come on, Samael. You can't stay here forever. Don't you want to leave?"

CANT LEAVE

"Why not?

The pointer rattled along the board restlessly, refusing to settle on any of the letters. Finally, it started to spell a sentence out.

DO YOU REALLY WANT ME TO LEAVE

Emerie hesitated. Her first instinct was to yell, "OBVIOUSLY!" But she held back—why was she holding back? It was a demon, for Christ's sake. But then again…was he really so bad? Despite what Father Zebulun had said, he didn't seem all that dangerous. Thus far, all Samael had done was talk to her, turn lights off and on, steal her possessions (and give them back) and mildly deface her house. He was more like an irksome roommate than a malevolent poltergeist.

"I'm going to bed." Emerie muttered. "Good night, Samael."

GOOD NIGHT

FIVE

THE SHOP WAS CALLED "The Enchanted Attic". It wasn't a large store—cramped, really, squashed between "The Witch's Brew" coffee shop and an athletic shoe store. Like Emerie's neighbor's home, the awning was bedecked in a thousand multicolored wind chimes and the glass window had strange symbols cheerfully painted at each corner. Emerie accidentally knocked over a sandwich sign, which advertised herbal teas and palm readings Thursdays through Saturdays at four p.m.

It took Emerie a minute to enter. Outside the church, she'd been afraid the people within would judge her. Outside the new age shop, she was afraid the people outside would judge her for going in.

The door jangled as she entered and she was immediately hit by a wave of patchouli incense. She started forward, grimacing at the scent, and briefly became distracted by a naked fairy statue holding an enormous box of mood rings.

"Welcome to—oh!" Sunflower, Emerie's neighbor, scurried towards her and smiled in pleasure. She was wearing a marvelously magenta muumuu and her waist-length hair was tied in a rope-like braid. "Hello, again!"

"Hi there." Emerie sidestepped the naked fairy statue and blinked at an impressive wall tapestry with rainbow-colored astrological symbols.

"Just wanted to, um…check out your store. It's super unique. Love the dragons."

She pointed to a large bookshelf across from the tapestry that was covered in ceramic dragons.

"Well, thank you!" Sunflower rubbed her hands eagerly. Emerie admired a prominent skull ring made of jade.

"Were you looking for anything in particular?" Sunflower asked hopefully, dancing on her feet a little. "If you'd like a nicer spirit board, I have a wonderful collection on the back wall."

She pointed towards the far end of her store. There was a little corner of the store rimmed with bookshelves filled with an assortment of odds and ends.

"Mine actually works pretty well." Emerie cleared her throat. "I guess I was just…doing some research. Or I've been trying to. Just about some rumors I've heard about my…my house."

Sunflower smiled and placed a hand on Emerie's upper arm. "You mustn't mind Mrs. Wellen. She's been in the neighborhood forever— when I was a little girl, she was a teenager, and she enjoyed scaring the pants off of us with her spooky stories. Her son Jason is a transplant surgeon, you know."

"Well…in this case, she might've been right about my house." Emerie admitted with a cough. "I have the feeling that it's…sort of haunted. I know that sounds crazy."

Sunflower tsked. "Oh, I don't like that word. Crazy, my dear, is relative. Besides, I'm in the business of believing in the impossible. Have you tried burning sage?"

"I've tried a couple of things." Emerie reached out and selected a stick of incense. Pumpkin spice latte. She inhaled the scent and replaced it.

"The thing is," Emerie turned to face Sunflower fully, "the thing is, it doesn't feel…it doesn't feel like it wants to *hurt* me. If that makes sense. Doesn't feel…demonic."

"You think it's a demon?" Sunflower's eyes widened in interest. She fiddled with the full moon ring on her forefinger.

Emerie shrugged. "Do you believe in those?"

"Well…" Sunflower beckoned her over to the far corner of the store.

Emerie followed and was surprised to see it was exceedingly well-orga-nized. Three bookshelves: the first containing modern witchcraft for the busy practitioner, the second about dream interpretation, the third about supernatural creatures—ghosts, demons, angels, fairies, and so on. There was a little round table in the middle of everything with stacked, hand-carved spirit boards and what appeared to be wands.

"You see, it depends on what you mean by the word *demon*." Sunflower fumbled with the scooped neckline of her muumuu until she triumphantly withdrew a pair of bright red glasses on a silver chain. She slipped them on her nose and started perusing the bookshelves.

"I guess I mean…the Christian ones. The things that try and hurt humans…?" Emerie offered, leaning against an end table idly. She glanced down and resisted the urge to fiddle with an ivory and ebony wand. Her fingers itched a little and she swung them casually. "They live in Hell? They possess and terrorize people?"

"And the entity inhabiting your house…it has done these things?"

Emerie shifted uncomfortably. "Not exactly. I mean, it's been *super annoying*, don't get me wrong. And I think it did try to terrorize me, at least in the beginning. But now it's sort of mellowed out. Especially since my boyfriend left for Boston."

"Perhaps the entity has grown attached to you." Sunflower suggested. Her voice was a little too enthusiastic about the idea.

"You see, what the common layperson regards as a *demon*, others might see as a mischievous spirit, wishing to bestow favors and wisdom upon those open enough to receive them."

That sounded like *youkai* <u>again</u>. *Youkai* could be good and generous, but they could also be real pains in the ass.

"Let me ask you this." Sunflower twirled a loose strand of silver-streaked hair around her finger. "Have you communicated with this spirit? Through your spirit board?"

"Yeah." Emerie burred like a horse.. "He said he wasn't a ghost. He said he was a demon."

"He used the word 'demon'?"

Emerie paused. What *was* the word he used? No, he hadn't used any words. He'd knocked a book off the shelf. A book about demons. But he hadn't argued with her when she'd called him a demon. Hadn't he said he was part incubus or something? But what did that even mean anyway? Perhaps he was more of a mischievous spirit than an actual demon?

"I was told…" Emerie could not meet Sunflower's kind, albeit loopy gaze, so she focused on the multicolored ribbons in her hair. "I was told spiritualists congregated in my house. In fact, I've been doing a little research on someone by the name of Fairy Lemp."

Sunflower nodded, though her expression did not hold any recognition of the name. "I am aware of many wise and connected people who lived in our neighborhood. They held a great deal of power and had exceptional knowledge of the spirit world."

This didn't sound like Fairy Lemp. Everything in Emerie's research indicated that Fairy was…well…a bit of a loon and flake. Her doodles were nonsensical. Still…Sunflower had more experience in this realm than she did…then again, she was also getting loon and flake vibes from Sunflower.

Still, it didn't hurt to ask. "Have you heard of something called the Key of Solomon? It was referenced in one of her journals."

Sunflower tilted her head at the question. "Hmm. That's very old school, my dear, very old school indeed. Outdated, I hesitate to say… still, it's excellent to know for foundational purposes. It's essentially a book, a book that has pentacles and chants for summoning spirits. Renaissance magic. Influential on modern practice."

"I don't suppose…" Emerie hesitated. "I don't suppose you have a copy?"

"I'd have to order it." Sunflower went to the computer behind the counter. "You know, those old texts are so—well, I won't bias you. But we practitioners have come a long way. But not to worry, I'll order it and it should be here in two or three days."

Emerie approached the counter and idly fidgeted with a display of moonstone necklaces. She noticed framed pictures on the wall, of Sunflower with a little girl. The little girl had dark hair like Emerie and quite a dour expression, as though she were annoyed at the constant photography.

Sunflower typed a few things into her computer and smiled in satisfaction. She lifted her head towards Emerie and locked gazes.

"You know, you don't need all this to communicate with your spirit." Sunflower leaned into the counter and tapped her fingers together. "You simply have to…open yourself up. It's not about trappings and ancient rituals and tools—as fun as they are. It's about your soul. And your will-ingness to be guided."

Emerie shrugged uncomfortably. "I'm just trying to get rid of him, honestly. Before Dylan comes home."

"That's a shame." Sunflower sighed and handed her a complimentary stick of incense—Purple Rain. "Spirits have a lot to teach us, you know."

Emerie did not know. But she gave Sunflower a tight smile and thanked her for ordering the book.

———

When Emerie returned home, she set out the Ouija board on the coffee table and poured herself a glass of wine. She thought about what Sunflower had said about 'opening herself up to communication' and thought grimly of the priest's failure to get rid of Samael. She also wondered if she even truly *wanted* to get rid of him…not to mention, Dylan hadn't texted her in a while. He used to text her pictures of weird things he encountered on his trip to New York—an anime themed coffee shop in the Chinatown, the Museum of Sex in Midtown, that sort of thing. Nowadays he seemed less inclined to indulge her eccentricities. It was nice to have a little company.

"Samael?" she asked. "Are you around?"

The Ouija board pointer flicked. **YES**

"Good," She took a sip. "We need to talk."

NEVER A GOOD IDEA WHEN A WOMAN SAYS THAT

"Har, har," Emerie said dryly. "I'm serious, Samael."

GO AHEAD

"First up—who is Fairy Lemp?"

UGH

"Aha! You do know her!" Emerie said triumphantly. "I'm not the only woman you've talked to after all!"

NOT LIKE WITH YOU

FAIRY TRIED TO SUMMON ME

Emerie blinked. "Tried? What do you mean 'tried'?"

GOT SCARED HALFWAY THROUGH

RAN OUT

LEFT ME STUCK BETWEEN PLANES

She stared at the Ouija board. She dug through her photographs and examined the strange symbols and designs she'd seen in Fairy's notes. They weren't idle doodles! They were markers, little preview sketches before she and her club tried summoning a demon. But apparently they'd chickened out midway through the ceremony.

"You can't go anywhere?" Emerie asked slowly. "You're just trapped in this house?"

BETWEEN HEAVEN AND HELL

"Can't your—I don't know, your demon buddies help you get unstuck?"

WHY SHOULD THEY CARE

There was apparently no loyalty in Hell. Emerie's brow furrowed.

"So how long have you been stuck here?"

NOT LONG

ABOUT

150 YEARS

"One-hundred and fifty *years*?!" Emerie squawked. "You've just been stuck here? Haunting this house?"

YES

She sat back against her couch, dizzy. She glanced out the window. The afternoon had melted into a golden amber and she tucked her knees under her. She looked towards the Ouija board again.

"Why exactly did she want to summon you? Just for laughs?"

The pointer scooted from one end of the coffee table to the other. After a few moments of this ritual, it finally spelled out letters properly.

I AM VERY GOOD COMPANY

Emerie considered this. She remembered how Fairy Lemp had doodled little hearts around Samael's name…and his other titles. Samael the Destroyer. Samael the Accuser. Samael the *Seducer*.

She snorted. "Wow. She went to all that trouble and then backed out at the last second."

Samael did not respond, instead continued to rhythmically spin the pointer around the coffee table, from each corner to the next. She watched this repetitive motion and wondered if this was supposed to be eerie or it was Samael's way of playing with a fidget spinner.

"Well now, I'm curious…what do demons look like?"

The pointer halted. Finally, it spelled out:

ALL TYPES

"Okay," Emerie poured herself another glass of wine, "what do you look like?"

The pointer spun in agitation. And then:

GIANT CENTIPEDE

Emerie shuddered. "Ew! Seriously?"

NO

JUST WANTED TO SEE YOUR REACTION

She drummed her fingers on the board. "Well, that's a relief. Can't stand centipedes. I'm guessing cloven hoofs? Maybe a pitchfork?"

INCORPOREAL

"You have to have some kind of form, right?"

NOT ON THIS PLANE

"What plane are you on, then?"

PURGATORY NETHERWORLD IN BETWEEN UPSIDE DOWN

Emerie wasn't sure if he was distinguishing different places or saying variant names of the same thing.

"There's no way I could see you?" She sipped her wine. "Short of summoning you?"

NO

Emerie sighed in frustration. "Fair enough."

The wine was making her feel contentedly fuzzy. The pointer quivered again and she warily watched it scoot across the board.

YOU COULD HEAR ME

"Hear you? How?"

ENTER YOUR BODY

Emerie's eyes widened. "You want to possess me?!"

NO

YES

SHORTLY

ENTER YOUR MIND

HEAR MY VOICE

She scrunched her face. "This sounds like a really bad start to a horror film."

IT IS

She sighed. "This also sounds like a dangerous and terrible idea."

YES

"Then why are you suggesting it?!"

LESS DANGEROUS THAN YOU SUMMONING ME

Her lips twisted. "I never said I would summon you."

YOURE THINKING ABOUT IT

DONT

"But how do I know you won't make me do anything? Or go full Pazuzu?"

The pointer twirled in consideration. **SCOUTS HONOR**

Emerie snickered. "Funny."

WELL I CANT EXACTLY SWEAR ON THE BIBLE

She laughed again as she considered. The wine was pleasantly fuzzing her impulse control and frankly, she'd done dumber things after a few beers. "Okay...I mean...five minutes. Just for five minutes."

ARE YOU SURE

Emerie drained her wine and nodded.

POSSESSION IS INTIMATE

She quirked a brow. "Intimate?"

INTIMATE

The whole thing struck her as an intensely reckless and stupid idea. Many a time she had yelled at the TV screen, when some stupid character started down the steps of a basement in pursuit of a strange noise. But the wine had given Emerie a sort of brazen courage only cheap vintages could provide.

"Five minutes, Samael. What do I do?"

STAY STILL

EMPTY YOUR THOUGHTS

CLOSE YOUR EYES

Emerie complied. She shut her eyes and she took a deep breath, clearing her mind. She recalled an ancient yoga class where her instructor told her over and over again to breathe. "Stop trying to do advanced poses, Emerie!" She wasn't much for breathing. She preferred action.

She suddenly felt drowsy, her limbs falling heavier. She wasn't quite asleep; she could still hear the sounds of her newly installed dishwasher and the AC running. But she couldn't feel the vibration or the coolness from the vents. Her senses were muffled.

Something tingled her toes. A ticklish feeling spread through her legs and rose up her torso. Her heart pounded in hesitation. She felt something prodding her, requesting her to open the door. She slowly nodded.

"Samael?" Emerie whispered. "Are you there?"

"I'm here."

She gasped. She heard him! She heard his voice! It wasn't at all what she expected. For understandable reasons, she couldn't quite escape the feeling her demon would sound scary and monstrous. But in fact, Samael had a smoky earthy voice. It reminded her of Bruce Springsteen or Bob Dylan's voice. Relaxed and mellow, with a gravelly intonation.

"Wow. I can really hear you." She experimentally stretched out her legs onto the couch—she was relieved to find she was still in control of her body.

"It's nice to talk to you without using that stupid board game."

She shrugged. "Hey, don't knock the Ouija board. It's been pretty useful. I've named it Harriet."

"Your Ouija board is named Harriet, your fridge is named Midge, and your toaster is named Stanley. Why do you name inanimate objects?"

"To be fair, with you around, they're hardly inanimate," Emerie pointed out, "and I do wish you'd stop trashing everything."

"I can't always help it."

"If you say so. Just don't make me throw up pea soup."

She waited for a response but didn't hear anything. Odd memories started to flit through her head randomly—old birthday parties, horse camp, Hokkaido in the summer. She inhaled sharply.

"Are you poking around in my head?"

"Yup. You miss your grandfather a lot."

"I do. He was important to me." She exhaled deeply—she could see her grandfather's stern expression as he told her not to swing on the outside gate. Then he laughed without warning and started to swing on the gate himself. She was seven at the time.

"He trusted you."

"I don't want to talk about him." Emerie blinked away tears. "I just want to know why you're so interested in communicating with me. What do you want from me?"

There was no response. The sun had set completely and Emerie half-registered she ought to turn on the living room lights. Things felt dim right now. She took another deep breath and shivered at the warm electricity tingling from her toes to her ears.

"Samael?" Emerie called. "I can still feel you inside me…it feels really good. Talk to me." She flushed. She hadn't realized how *filthy* that sounded. She then heard a smoky chuckle, and it dawned on her that Samael felt her embarrassment.

"Okay, five minutes are up," she ordered. "Out you go!"

"You're the boss. It felt good to be inside you too."

"Out!"

The warmth dissipated and Emerie was left alone on her couch in the darkness of her living room. She registered an odd heaviness to her limbs. She exhaled slowly and stood.

"Going to make dinner," she said softly to her Ouija board. "See you later, Samael."

SEE YOU LATER

HARRIET SAYS LATER TOO

Emerie laughed and left the room. She flicked on the hallway light and strode into her kitchen, flicking on that light as well. She pulled out a box of pasta shells from the cupboard and searched for tomatoes. She had just bought some tomatoes. They were around here somewhere…

"That was stupid." She muttered to herself as she filled a pot with water. "This whole thing is stupid. What kind of demon respects my boundaries like that?" It was not becoming *vital* to get him out of her house. She was getting attached to his presence.

SIX

"BEFORE COMMENCING OPERATIONS," Emerie read aloud, "the Master and his Disciples must abstain with great and thorough continence during the space of nine days from sensual pleasures and from vain and foolish conversation…"

She quirked a brow. She was sitting at the Witch's Brew café with a black coffee and a cranberry orange scone, reading *The Key of Solomon*. The book had arrived at Sunflower's shop a full day earlier than expected, to the utter delight of Sunflower and the slight trepidation of Emerie. The book meant business. The book meant she was actually going to do this.

And according to the book, during her nine days of abstinence, she needed to recite the Prayer and Confession frequently. On the seventh day, she was supposed to bathe herself in consecrated water, and recite "The Lord Adonai" while she did so.

She was beginning to realize why Dylan hated his catechism classes.

"How am I supposed to get a bathtub full of consecrated water?" Emerie leaned back in her chair. It was just a little too brisk for coffee outside, but she traded the somewhat punishing autumn breezes for the possibility of someone looking over her shoulder.

"What am I supposed to do? Call Father Zebulun and ask him to bless my tub?" she muttered as she took out a mechanical pencil from her purse. She sketched a rough doodle similar to the ones she'd found in Fairy Lemp's journals—a pentacle. Currently, hers looked more like a wonky star than a pentacle.

Emerie traced her handiwork in her notebook critically. If she couldn't get it right on paper, she would hardly be able to get it right in her attic.

That was her plan. She was going to summon Samael.

She had not come to the decision lightly. She had given the idea a good hour or so of thought—about the same amount of time she had given to buying a house.

So sue her. She didn't think coming to decisions quickly was necessarily a *bad* trait.

The fact of the matter was there didn't seem to be any other way to get Samael out of her house. If she asked for a priest to perform an exorcism, she would either get the impotent Father Simon or the terrifying Father Zebulun—and something deep inside her, something she couldn't quite explain, told her to leave the priest out of it.

And goodness, what a production it all was! The movies made summoning a demon seem so easy. But the truth was far more complicated. She was to fast three days beforehand, bathe in consecrated water, pick up incense, a knife, a 'sickle of the magical art', lantern, candles…

Some artifacts weren't too hard to find. Emerie owned a beautiful old knife her father had given her years and years ago, after a trip to Bosnia. She hoped a Hori Hori knife from the local gardening store counted as a sickle. Candles were simple enough to find. The real trouble was marking the floor with a pentacle. Emerie was not good at sketching stick figures, let alone complex intertwined circles decorated with sigils.

Once she finished her coffee, she shut her notebook and decided to ask Sunflower for advice about the pentacle. Maybe she had some large pentacle stencils hidden away.

The Enchanted Attic was right next door. As Emerie entered the shop, a woman about her age exited. She paid no heed to Emerie but strode straight towards her car with a slight scowl. Emerie would not have noticed her had she not recognized her—she had seen this woman before, in the pictures hanging up behind Sunflower's counter.

"Hiya neighbor." Emerie waved at Sunflower. "I'm just here to pick up some supplies."

"More candles?" Sunflower chuckled. "You about cleared us out last time! I'm so *thrilled* you're interested in the craft!"

Emerie raised and lowered one shoulder. "Actually—I'm trying to draw a pentacle on the floor of my attic, but I'm not much of an artist. Any advice? I don't suppose you have any stencils I could use…?"

"I'm afraid not. That would be helpful, wouldn't it?" Sunflower hummed to herself and twisted her waist-length plait in thought. "But you know what? We have some lovely posters you could probably trace over. Would that work?"

"That would work perfectly!" Emerie exclaimed. Sunflower rushed behind a curtain and Emerie heard the shuffling of papers and boxes being shoved aside.

She returned triumphantly with a large purple poster with a silver pentacle, about the same size as Emerie's poster of David Bowie she had in her room growing up, which covered two-thirds of her bedroom wall. The pentacle did not look exactly like the sketch in the Key of Solomon, but the shape was close enough that if Emerie sketched it out, she could complete the rest herself.

When she paid for the poster, she found herself staring at the photographs. Sunflower caught her gaze.

"Did you see my daughter?" Sunflower smiled. "She visits me every few weeks or so. A marvelous practitioner."

"Like you, huh?" Emerie humored her and rolled up the poster, sticking it in her bag.

"My craft came from careful practice and study," Sunflower said regally, "but my beautiful Zephyr—she is a natural witch."

"Huh." Emerie shrugged.

"In fact, I'll give you her name and number. In case you run into trouble." She grabbed one of her business cards, scribbled something on the back, and handed it to Emerie.

She accepted the business card and turned it over. Sunflower's loopy handwriting read: ZEPHYR MOON, ESQ. She tucked it into her wallet, next to Father Zebulun's card.

———

When Emerie returned home, her phone rang. Dylan remembered he had a girlfriend.

"How was the conference?" Emerie asked as she pulled out the pentacle poster. She spread it across her dining room table and nodded in satisfaction.

"Emerie, it was amazing!" Dylan gushed. "You have no idea how explosive the market is becoming with all these new innovations. I have so much to show you—they have all the PowerPoints on the website! We'll go through them when I get back."

"Sounds fun." Emerie lied.

"And even better—I found us an apartment."

Emerie stopped rummaging through her canvas tote. "Excuse me?"

"I found an apartment. In Boston. It's *perfect*."

Emerie pulled out a large purple candle and dug her thumbnail into the wax. She exhaled slowly.

"We don't need an apartment, Dylan." Emerie's voice strained with friendliness. "We have a house. A gorgeous house. A house I sunk all my money into."

"Our money. And you still have some left," Dylan pointed out.

Emerie ground her teeth. "That's weird, because I can read Japanese, and strangely enough, all of the legal documents read Emerie Fox." (Technically they read her Japanese name, but Dylan got the gist.)

"You said we were in this together."

"We are!"

"It's a *haunted* house. Get real, Emerie. At least come up here and look at the apartment. It has two rooms we could turn into offices. You'd have a place to work on your articles."

"I have a place to work on my articles right here." Emerie noticed her volume had increased and tried to modulate the key. "I don't need to see any other places. Because I have a place. Here. In Milton."

"Milton is not that far from Boston. Be reasonable, Emerie."

"I am being reasonable!" Emerie exploded and dropped her bag. Multicolored candles scattered across the floor of the dining room. "You wanted to explore other options if the haunting shit didn't let up. Well, guess what! I am taking care of the haunting shit!"

"Oh yeah? How?"

Emerie stared at the pentacle poster. What exactly happened here? When she and Dylan agreed to live together, it was supposed to be this exciting thing. He knew she was obsessed with HGTV and daydreamed about restoring historical homes. He knew she was attracted to the obscure and loved things with character. Sure, he didn't share most of her hobbies, but he'd always been supportive, she thought. Or did she mistake support for just listening to her ramble? She knelt down and gathered her candles rapidly, shoving them back in her tote.

"Give me a week, Dylan. Look at other apartments if it makes you feel better. But I'm telling you, I just need a week. I'm taking care of it."

She could feel her irritation with her words as she wandered into the kitchen. Why on earth was she compromising with him? It was *her* house…maybe that was the whole problem. Maybe Dylan felt left out or emasculated or…

WHY ARE YOU MAKING EXCUSES FOR HIM was spelled out in refrigerator magnets. Emerie blinked and she heard Dylan sigh on the phone.

"Fine. But in a week, you're coming up to Boston and looking at this apartment."

She shut her phone off. It was easier than fighting with him. She'd pay for it later, certainly, but right now she had work to do. And when Emerie was in project-mode, it was far easier to shift her anxieties about her changing relationship aside.

Almost as if the cosmos were chastising her for hanging up on him, she heard a crash coming from the living room. She exited the dining room and saw that several books had fallen from her living room shelf and the TV had switched on. A medical procedural was on. Emerie glanced towards her coffee table and noticed the pointer on her Ouija board was rattling.

"What?" She demanded, walking over.

WHAT DO YOU THINK YOU ARE DOING

"Redecorating." Emerie dug into a plastic bag and pulled out two cans of spray paint.

ARE YOU SERIOUSLY
CASTING A CIRCLE
IN YOUR BASEMENT
DO YOU KNOW HOW STUPID THAT IS

"I'm not casting a circle in my basement," Emerie declared, hoisting up a paint roller in victory. "I'm casting a circle in my attic. More space up there. I can't have a demon haunting my house forever! Dylan will be back soon!"

YOU HAVE NO IDEA WHAT YOU ARE DOING

"I can't believe there's a dress code required. The Key of Solomon requires white ceremonial garb. What does that constitute? I don't think I own anything white…"

EMERIE STOP
YOU COULD UNLEASH SOMETHING A LOT WORSE THAN ME

Samael had a point. But if there was one thing that made her dig her heels in, it was someone telling her what to do.

"I'll risk it." Emerie shook one of the cans of spray paint. "I'm a quick learner, Sam. It'll be all right. If Fairy Lemp can do it, so can I."

FAIRY LEMP DIDNT
THATS THE POINT
DO NOT DO THIS

She ignored him, grabbed her keys, and added one more item to her grocery list.

DID YOU JUST CALL ME SAM

———

No matter how many electric lamps Emerie dragged up to her attic, nothing could quite remove the eerie effect of her marked-up floor. There was something wholly disconcerting about the intricate designs, littered with foreign symbols, each point marked with a long tapering candle. The design was a tilted square, each point with an equally sized circle around it. Within the square were two more circles, the four cardinal directions clearly marked. The poster, which Emerie had used as a giant stencil, ensured everything was even and in proportion.

Tomorrow night, she would begin.

She grabbed a broom and began sweeping clockwise around her seal. The book recommended that her area be as clean as possible, and the attic seemed to be a veritable conference room of spiders and dust. She took special care to wipe down the old oven in the attic—it had no place in the ritual, but she felt it was owed some respect. After all, she discovered Fairy Lemp in the old woodstove.

She was just about to head downstairs when she noticed writing on the wall.

STOP

Samael had gone back to his old trick of defacing her wall in garish red paint. At least she hoped it was paint. Emerie frowned.

"Knock it off, Samael."

There was a rustling in the corner of the attic. She watched as a bright red ornament darted towards her and bonked her on the head.

"Hey!" Emerie snatched the little red ball. It was slightly chipped.

"I'm *trying* to help you!"

She heard a scratching noise and turned her head towards it. There was a message on the left wall, near the attic door.

YOU ARE NOT HELPING

"Well, how do you know if I don't try?"

This time, her Christmas star came whirling out of the darkness. She ducked and it hit the back wall. It was made of plastic, so it didn't break, but Emerie started to become concerned about her older family ornaments.

"Sam, you're not going to bully me out of this!"

She watched in fascinated horror and annoyance as a long strand of Christmas lights snaked across the floor towards her. They looked like spiky pythons and she watched as they tried to scratch out her etchings —but she had thought ahead. She had not chalked her pentagram; she physically painted the symbols on the floor.

"Are you going to give it up, now?"

The strand of Christmas lights then darted towards her and wrapped around her ankle. "Hey!"

Just then, her phone rang.

She tried to kick the Christmas lights off her ankle, but they only wound up her leg more tightly. Swearing profusely, she dug her phone out of her pocket and answered in a slightly breathless tone

"Hello?"

"Miss Fox? It's Father Zebulun."

"Oh, hey!" Emerie tried to keep her voice as sunny as possible, while simultaneously trying to rip the Christmas lights off her leg. A box of ornament hooks levitated and were promptly dumped on her head.

"Er—how did you get my number?"

"Father Simon and I had a brief conversation about the cleansing and…I know this is abrupt, but we really ought to meet. Would it be possible to get a coffee with me tomorrow?"

"Oh, uh…" Emerie attempted to shake the ornament hooks out of her hair and successfully freed herself from the Christmas lights—only to be captured by the sparkly red garland.

"I'm actually busy tomorrow!" Emerie stumbled towards a box of recycled wrapping paper and desperately searched for scissors. "But I could meet with you on Sunday!"

"Sunday would be fine. Father Simon will cover for me; it's important we speak. Shall we say eleven a.m.? At the Witch's Brew?"

"You got it!"

She dropped her phone and snatched a pair of old fabric scissors from the box. She hacked the garland off her leg and scrambled to her feet, her arms raised in warning.

"Now, look, Sam." Emerie backed up to the door. "At this point, you've seen how stubborn I am. You can try and wreck the attic all you like—I'll just move everything to the basement. I am going to do this. You can either help or stay out of the way!"

The lights flickered. But no other Christmas ornaments attacked her. She sighed in relief. It was a little nerve-wracking how deeply Samael did *not* want her to summon him. Why was he so against it, anyway? Even if it was a bad idea to summon a demon in your attic—which it probably was—Emerie was under the impression demons *liked* leading you to do stupid, reckless things. Or so the movies had told her.

Speaking of…what would she do once he was there? Well, for a few moments at least, he'd be trapped in her circle. If anything went wrong, she had her knife. Oddly enough, the Key of Solomon had several contingency plans if the first few summonings didn't work, and a firm sort of prayer if the demon or spirit got a little mouthy.

She was out of her depth either way. With a sigh, she flicked the attic light off and headed downstairs. She would need a good night's sleep— she suspected she wouldn't get much of it tomorrow.

SEVEN

A MIDDLE-AGED BLONDE woman ran errands.

She was indistinguishable from about a hundred other middle-aged blonde women who lived in Milton. She wore athletic buttery-soft leggings and a crisp, pink shirt. Her streaked blonde hair was cut in a razed bob, complete with chin-length tendrils that were blown and flat-ironed into submission. She wore oversized black sunglasses and her phone seemed permanently glued to her cheekbone.

Her errands began near Emerie's house. The woman noted Emerie's lawn needed cutting and she sprinkled something with her free hand (she still held her cell phone to her cheek) that looked like pesticide on the crabgrass bleeding onto the sidewalk. The woman began a long rant to an unknown person about homeowners who couldn't properly care for their lawns and promptly started her journey.

Her first stop was the Milton Public Library, where she entered, pushed her way to the front of the line, and announced a book she wanted was in.

The librarian pulled up her account and stated the book was not, in fact, in. The woman told her friend on the phone to "hang on a sec," and proceeded to scream at the librarian viciously for daring to tell her such a thing. She had received a *confirmation email* just this morning *assuring her* that her book was in. And no, she could not pull it up right now, couldn't this woman see that she was on the phone? When the librarian checked again and could not find the book, the middle-aged woman devolved into a completely separate rant about some of the books the Milton Public Library stocked and how they were inappropriate for children and she intended to lodge a complaint with the City Council.

Once the librarian dissolved into tears, the woman smiled in satisfaction and exited the library. She stopped just outside of the building as she continued to gab on the phone and sprinkled something in the dirt. She scuffed the soil a bit with her Coach tennis shoe and continued on her way.

Her next stop was a popular tourist attraction in Milton, the Corbin Courthouse, on Ladue Street, which ran parallel to Cambridge Street. According to local legend, Judge Corbin had been the unforgiving man who sentenced over a hundred women to death by hanging for witchcraft. The courthouse was rumored to be haunted (as most Milton buildings were considered to be) and was a local hot spot for curious tourists —but there was a lovely café most of the court employees frequented as it was an excellent place for lunch. The outdoor patio was nicely shaded and they had toasty outdoor heaters for cooler nights.

The woman sat down at a table and ordered a Cobb salad with light vinaigrette and a venti non-fat latte with two shots of espresso. She made sure the waitress was aware she ordered "non-fat", because last time they had given her 2%.

The woman complained on the phone how long her food was taking and about fifteen minutes later, the waitress arrived with her order. At which point, the woman raised holy hell because there was *bacon* in her Cobb salad and she specifically had said *no bacon*, because she knew for a fact the Corbin Mansion did NOT serve turkey bacon and she was not about to give herself or her family swine flu due to their carelessness. It took two managers, a nasty Yelp review, and a free lunch before the woman calmed down. When she had finished her meal (while the two managers soothed the waitress, who was in the midst of an anxiety attack), the woman continued her conversation on her cell phone. She pulled out something from her purse and sprinkled it at the base of the tree next to her table. She stuck a sparkly pink manicured finger into the dirt and flicked it, before wiping her index finger off with a napkin. She didn't even pause to take a breath in her conversation.

After lunch, the woman continued down Ladue Street until she reached the Memorial Park. It was a small plot of land where the town of Milton, (determinedly copying Salem as much as possible) had created a memorial site to honor the women who had been persecuted as witches. The signs begged silence and reverence, but at the moment, the lot was anything but quiet.

There was a protest going on over abortion. Two large crowds of people screamed at each other, waving colorful signs and each accused the other of denying rights. The woman disappeared into the mob (it was impossible to tell which side). She reappeared on the other side, brushed a bit of dirt off her shoulder, and stuck her bottle back into her purse. She looked approvingly at the crowd and said something into her phone— the crowds' yells made it impossible to hear.

She left the park and headed up Crenshaw Street and reached Father Zebulun's church. She entered the narthex and headed downstairs into the church basement where the Ladies' Group was meeting. She was greeted with hugs and pleasantries and they went right to business. Over pink lemonade and gluten-free cookies, they discussed seriously a pair of married men and their three kids who wished to join the church and attend Sunday School. Father Zebulun had agreed readily, but the Ladies' Group was Concerned about Those Children attending Sunday School with Their Precious Babies. They intended to speak with Father Zebulun about it AND alert the Cardinal.

(There had been a flurry of angry emails to Father Zebulun about the matter, which he had ignored and consigned to his spam folder and the Cardinal had long given up on trying to order Father Zebulun to do anything.)

After the Ladies' Group meeting, the woman volunteered to clean everything up. She put away the pink lemonade and wiped down the tables. Then she pulled out something from her purse once more—and carefully sprinkled each corner of the basement with it.

Once she finished, she headed back upstairs and exited the church.

She stepped into her black Cadillac parked a block from the church, and drove out of the downtown area. She cruised past the suburbs, almost to the edge of Milton—right into a small park, marked by the tree line of the large forest that patched in and out through Milton and Framingham. Once she parked on the side of the road, she got out of her car.

She was still on the phone. She strode forward, past scattered picnic tables and a rusted playground that needed more money and care than Milton could afford. She pushed into the forest and walked into the shaded darkness.

After a mile or so of hiking uphill chatting away the entire time, she reached her destination. The northernmost point of the town—the Witch Caves. She entered a clearing, criss-crossed by boulders and large, partially collapsed stone hutches and tunnels. Local legend held that women, on the run from the vicious Judge Corbin, hid out in the caves and hutches—hence the name. No one knew where they came from. They pre-dated the early colonists and native tribes. Archaeologists couldn't seem to agree on whether they were manmade or naturally formed. Nowadays, they made for an enjoyable hike for tourists and families. But the place held a somber presence, as if the ancient stone walls remembered the shivering women, hiding in the shadows, terrified for their lives.

The woman regarded the caves; her phone conversation paused. She thought of the women of the past, trembling in fear as they hid from their pursuers—and smiled. She carefully tucked one more item into the dirt.

A child's skull glinted in the dying light. She pushed it into the tunnel farther, ensuring the stark whiteness of bone was undetectable.

"All set," the woman said into her phone. "I'll see you tomorrow."

She hung up.

EIGHT

EMERIE WAITED until Saturday night before she started the summoning.

The book was crystal clear that any practitioner who wished to speak to a demon *must* wait until nightfall. They simply would not show up if you tried it during the day. It also had precise directions on the type of weather and phase of moon for demon summoning. Her phone reported the weather was *supposed* to be clear, with a nice half-moon visible, but the sky remained a sickly gray for most of the day.

She'd tried fasting as the book directed, but eventually got too hungry and demolished a family size bag of Doritos. Maybe the forces of Hell wouldn't notice her full stomach. What were they going to do, check her fingernails for cheese dust?

Samael had not spoken to her the entire day, nor had he made any sign of his presence. She tried not to let this bother her; tried to put out of her head how vehemently he did not want her to summon him.

After a light dinner of a chicken salad sandwich and tomato soup, Emerie made her way upstairs into the attic. She flicked on the light and stared at her work. The design on the floor of her attic seemed...okay. At least it looked even. It was a fairly simple star, like the ones she used to doodle on her homework, with a ring around each point. Every point of the star was marked with a different colored candle—red, white, black, green, and blue. The gap between the points of the star contained little doodles—she didn't know what they meant. But drawing the sigils had brought back painful memories of calligraphy drawing in the Japanese classes her mother insisted she take on Saturday mornings. She never could get her brush strokes even…

She had spent the day completely clearing out her attic. She had moved the Christmas decoration boxes into the basement, in case Samael got any more funny ideas. Aside from the attic stove and her various candles, everything was bare. She pulled a lighter out of the right pocket of her dress and flicked it on. She then circled her designs, careful not to accidentally knock over any of the tapers. She slowly lit every candle.

Thunder rumbled outside and she glanced nervously at one of the attic windows. Rain started to patter against the glass. The book had warned her not to proceed with the ritual if the weather wasn't calm. She rubbed her arms, smoothing away the goosebumps. Well, it was too late to stop now. She had everything ready.

Emerie turned on her lantern. She wasn't fool enough to turn off her attic lights and perform the ritual by candlelight—that seemed a little too cloak and dagger for her. She scanned her notes quickly and proceeded to walk clockwise and counterclockwise past the designs. At each design, she bent down and wrote—what the book claimed—were the four names of God, on the southern, northern, western, and eastern points of her circle. She tried to recite one of the Psalms but couldn't remember it all the way through, so instead finished with Robert Frost's "Stopping By Woods on a Snowy Evening" and a few of her favorite Leonard Cohen songs.

She'd never been much good at recitations. In the eighth grade, she was supposed to memorize a poem for class, but she could only really memorize Kate Voegele songs. Her teacher had not been impressed.

Emerie pulled out *The Key of Solomon* from the left pocket of her dress. She flipped ahead to chapter eight—"An Extremely Powerful Conjuration." Fairy Lemp's notes had mentioned that the previous conjurations were subpar.

"Behold," Emerie said aloud. "We command ye and potently ordain ye by the most strong and powerful names of God, who is worthy of all praise, admiration, honor, glory, veneration, and fear...that ye delay not longer but that ye appear before us without any tumult or disturbance, but, on the contrary, with great respect and courtesy, in a beautiful and human form."

She looked up expectantly. Nothing happened. She glanced at the lights above her head, but they remained steady, with no flickering or sputtering. Thunder growled outside and rain began to pound the roof. She sighed and looked at the next passage.

Let not the Master on that account lose his courage, for there is nothing in the world stronger and of greater force to overawe the Spirits than constancy, the book told her cheerfully. Emerie cleared her throat and leaned over the edge of her circle to pick up a bowl of table salt. She tossed salt towards each of the four corners and knelt down. She carefully pointed her father's knife north. She lifted up her other arm in an open embrace.

"By the holy names of God, by the other holy and ineffable names which are written in the Book of Life, we conjure ye, Samael, to come unto us prompt and without any delay—um, tarry not, appear in a beautiful and agreeable form—I mean, you don't *have* to come out looking like Trevor Noah, but if you want to—er, by these holy names: Adonai, Tzabaoth, El, Elohi, Elohim, Shaddai, and Eheieh, Yod He Vau He which is apparently the Great Name of God...who uh, dwelleth in the heavens, who rideth upon the Caribou, I mean, Kerubim, who moveth upon the wings of the wind...I reiterate the conjuration, I conjure ye afresh ye evil and rebellious spirits, abiding in the abysses of darkness."

The wind picked up. It took Emerie a few seconds to realize all her windows were tightly shut—there shouldn't *be* any wind. Her skirt swirled around her and she noticed the flames on her candles sparked and popped. Lightning crashed outside and her heart began to hammer in her chest. Emerie returned to her book, continuing on:

"Ah—approach unto and come before the throne of God, before the holy angels of God to hear the sentence of your condemnation...Come ye then, Samael, I force ye to appear before me, without delay, without rage, without any deformity or hideousness, to execute my will...come ye all from places where you are, from all mountains, valleys, streams, rivers, brooks, ponds, places, baths, temples...come ye angels of darkness, come hither before this Circle without fear, terror, or deformity to execute my commands..."

Emerie yelped. The flames of all five of her candles blazed upwards without warning into thin towers of fire that would leave a nasty burn mark on her attic ceiling. Her circle began to glow, like a streetlight's glare on rainy pavement, and she nervously looked around her. Wind rushed past, filling her ears, and she shrieked when it lifted her off the ground.

At that moment, the lightning cut the power. The thin towers of flames suddenly bent, shot past her, interconnecting into a cage of fire which trapped her in the circle. Tongues of flame singed her dark hair and she kicked desperately against the hot wind. She fell to her knees and her knife clattered to the floor, out of reach. The flames danced all around her. She heard something scream. She heard something laugh.

And then she saw the glow of a thousand pairs of eyes in the darkness. They watched her, ensnared in the circle. She heard the scream-laugh again and the thousand eyes blinked in unison, a silent audience of red eyes, green eyes, brown eyes, blue eyes. Something like an arm, something like an animal, advanced towards her. It entered her flaming circle, like a deformed crab. She watched helplessly, too terrified to cry.

An unseen force pummeled into her and knocked her to her side. She heard an outraged roar and something—something terribly near her cheek—snarled back. She was pressed against the floor while a large and bulky presence blocked her view from those terrible eyes. The flames ignited even more; she could feel their heat all around her and she heard something inhuman howl in a terrifying rage. She tried to scream, but the—whatever-it-was pressed her cheek more firmly into the floor. She shut her eyes, clenching her fists.

All at once, the howling stopped. The candles blew out, her electricity came back on, and the room was suddenly silent. Emerie felt the pressure remove itself from her, but she trembled on the floor, trying to regain her senses. Slowly and surely, she raised herself up, blinking in the familiar yet somehow alien light.

Her attic. The little stove under the window. Her candles knocked askew. A ceiling fan. The rain had stopped. There was only one difference.

There was a demon in the corner, glaring at her angrily.

"YOU IDIOT!"

————

Emerie stared. She tried to form words, but language wouldn't come.

She wasn't entirely sure what she was staring at. A demon, certainly —what else could come up after her summoning ritual—but somehow, her mind refused to process.

Her eyes focused on the wings first. She thought they were a little like bat wings, though there might have been fur or feathers or something lining the edges. They were the color of pitch, at any rate, but she realized if she looked too long at the wings, she began to see other colors too. It was looking at a piece of obsidian catching the light.

Slate gray skin, but it seemed to wear some kind of clothing. Black clothing, of course, but Emerie could still see the slightly clawed hands. It had dark, curly hair that was tousled in an almost boyish sort of way. When the curls caught the light, they were red. But the eyes…the eyes were such a rich brown. At least, she thought they were brown. Every time she thought she could name a color, a thousand more shades of gold and amber took its place.

She couldn't tell if the creature was female or male. The voice had a distinctly husky register, which brought to mind her favorite raspy-throated rock singers. But there was still a sense of androgyny. When she began to think it was male, she noticed the long legs, the smooth lines and expressive eyes. When she thought it might be female, she took in the broad shoulders, the sharp cheekbones, the Bob Dylan-esque gravitas.

Whatever it was…it was *beautiful.*

"Samael?" Emerie whispered.

The creature took a deep breath. *"IDIOT!"* It thundered again. "I told you once, I told you a *thousand* times—"

"It's really you?" Emerie interrupted, completely awestruck. "You're —you're Samael? The Samael I've been communicating with?"

"Of course I'm Samael!" the creature snapped. "You stupid, stubborn, impossible human!"

She continued to stare at him. For all its bluster, the creature wasn't attacking her. It seemed thoroughly annoyed, but it was far from the murderous presence she'd felt previously.

"I can't believe it," Emerie said in wonder. "You're really him."

Samael snorted. "*Him*? I'm not a him."

"Sorry...her?"

"I'm not a him or a her. I'm just Samael."

Emerie swallowed. "That might be a little confusing for me..."

Samael sighed. "You can use 'he'."

She slowly stood and brushed the dirt and debris off her dress. She couldn't stop staring at the creature. Ouija conversations were one thing, but a living and breathing demon, right here in her attic? That was...unreal.

Samael stood as well, his dark brows heavy. She watched him inspect her circle carefully. He snorted at some of her crude designs, before flashing an irked glance.

"Did you close out the Circle?" he demanded.

Emerie blinked. "Did I what now?"

"Close out the Circle!" Samael threw his hands in the air. "I heard your summoning—you skipped a ton of lines and basically invited all of Hell to cross over!"

"I did not," Emerie retorted. "I specifically asked for you by name."

"*And did you close out the Circle?!*"

Emerie glanced downwards, where her copy of *The Key of Solomon* lay upside down. It was smoking slightly; several pages had caught on fire. She scooped it up and patted away the embers. She gingerly flipped a few pages. Her eyes widened towards the final end notes.

"Oops."

"Oops?!" Samael thundered. "Did you just say 'oops'?! You've opened a portal to Hell and all you can say is 'oops'?!"

Emerie raised and lowered one shoulder. "Honestly, I didn't really think I'd get this far."

Samael closed his eyes. His wings were twitching—perhaps a sign of agitation? It reminded her of how a cat would flick its tail in annoyance.

"Can I close it out now?" She gestured towards her book.

"It's too late." Samael kicked a candle—it clattered towards the corner of the attic. He had feet like a gargoyle, with razor-sharp talons. "The Circle is broken—if you can call *that* a Circle. You cracked a hole through dimensions, now *anything* can come out—and something did."

Emerie felt slightly sick. "Something? You mean...that thing with all the eyes...?"

"And more so."

She gave him a long look before checking her handiwork. There was a long crack in her attic floor that hadn't been there before which cut directly through her sigils. She knelt down and peeked through the crack to see if her hallway was visible. She saw nothing but black, which unnerved her enough to scoot away from the crack. She glanced around her...come to think of it, the shadows on the walls were starting to give her the creeps. (The irony that shadows were creepier than the demon she was talking to did not escape her.)

"Well," Emerie said in a tone one might use when they discovered their pipes had broken, "I guess I better figure out how to send it back to Hell and close this portal."

Samael's wings flapped open. She took a step backwards, mesmerized by how much light they caught—and then realized he was incredibly irritated.

"Good luck with that." He kicked another candle for good measure and hissed in pain when his left wing bumped the ceiling fan. "I *told* you, you have no idea what you're doing. Your little ritual was botched from start to finish—you ignored half the instructions in the Key, you skimped every step you could, you didn't recite any of the Psalms a week before and *no*, Leonard Cohen songs don't count!"

Emerie didn't mean to be argumentative, but she did feel he wasn't giving her much credit. (And in her opinion, Leonard Cohen songs were *better* than Psalms.)

"But I *did* get you unstuck." She gestured towards him aimlessly. He towered over her, but everyone towered over her, so it didn't intimidate her.

For a brief moment, she wondered if he might attack her, he looked so furious. But instead he exhaled loudly through his nose.

"You did *not*. You made a mess of things, is what you did. I was barely able to squeeze out before the rest of the hordes of Hell descended —which speaking of, we need to get out of this attic."

As though in emphasis, a loud, horrible groan vibrated the entire house. Emerie jumped when she realized the crack in the design had widened about half a centimeter.

"Well, that's not good," Emerie sighed, placing her hands on her hips. "I wonder how long it will take to fix my attic floor…look, I was only trying to help you."

Samael glared at her and his wings expanded again. *"Help* me?! What kind of human are you?! You don't *help* demons, you fear them and say prayers to keep them away!"

"Well, Jesus Christ, excuse me for—" Emerie started to say. But without warning, the demon was suddenly slammed to the side wall, his head smacking nastily against the antique stove.

"Ow," Samael grumbled, rubbing his cheek. "Please don't do that."

"I did that?! How?!"

"By saying…by saying that name."

Emerie racked her thoughts. "You mean when I said Jesus Christ?"

This time, Samael collided with the ground in a rather undignified manner. He looked like a bird after a crash landing, all tangled up limbs and wings. Emerie gazed at him in amazement. This little trick—saying the Lord's name in vain—might come in handy. She wondered if it would work on anything else that might come out of the crack.

"Sorry…can I…help you up?" She made a move towards him.

"No," Samael snapped, staggering upwards. "I'm *fine.*"

"All right," Emerie was perplexed. But there was nothing to do about it now.

"Let's go downstairs and figure this out. And let's lock the door behind us."

———

Samael's first corporeal experience on the physical plane was a splitting headache.

He hadn't had a migraine in over two thousand centuries—not since his estranged brother Gabriel had put one over on him during that affair with the far-too-clever-for-her-own-good Israelite girl. Gabriel had a special way of aggravating him to the point of physical pain and Samael was beginning to realize this human girl—Emerie—might have the same talent.

Of course, it was absolutely Emerie's fault for causing this catastrophe. But then again, if this hadn't been what he wanted all along, he shouldn't have interacted with her to begin with. He never should have accepted the rice cakes and wine. But it had been *so long* since he'd tasted human food and drink...

Not to mention, it wasn't much fun being cooped up in that stupid house for two hundred years—but corporeal form had such a high price. A price Emerie would certainly pay.

That wasn't his problem, at least. In the meantime, she was making tea.

Samael recognized this as a purely human habit. When in doubt, make tea, make food, keep your hands busy to trick yourself into thinking you're doing something worthwhile. Humans were the only creatures in the world who had *idleness* as a vice—and yet they still found time to blame Hell for it! "Idle hands were the devil's playthings." Not altogether accurate, in his opinion.

He inhaled deeply. Smell. He smelled bergamot flowers. Fresh paint. A little dust. What a marvelous sense scent was...but it was so strange being on the mortal plane again. He couldn't remember the last time he'd been here...the Roman invasion of Britain? Or was it the Jewish exile out of Babylon? There had been that brief bout in southern England, with that silly minister who seemed so intent on burning women while dabbling in black magic himself...but that had been brief, just a quick appearance in the fire.

Things had clearly changed around here. He had been stuck between planes, so at least the house was familiar. But to *touch* things... He extended a claw towards the dark green curtains of the living room. They were velvety soft, like a cat's fur. He stretched out his wings, letting his wing tips brush the ceiling. He would be able to *eat*. He licked his lips. He thought of Emerie in her thin white dress. Warmth curled in his gut.

"Four minutes to steep," she called to him from the kitchen. "It's a precise science."

Samael sighed and continued to peruse the living room. He noticed the piano immediately and held his breath. He reverently extended his claw and clinked a key.

"The piano came with the house," Emerie answered the note from the kitchen. He harrumphed at her, still incredibly irate she had opened a portal to Hell in her attic. Nevertheless, he cautiously plinked out a few notes, transfixed by the sounds.

"Do you play?"

He turned. His powerful wing bumped the piano and slammed it shut. Emerie winced at the noise as she set a steaming teapot, a paper carton, and two mugs on the coffee table. One mug read MALE TEARS and the other had a young woman holding a sword painted on it.

"No." Music was strictly forbidden.

Emerie cocked her head as she poured hot tea into the first mug. "Didn't you once wake us up with organ music?"

Samael cleared his throat as he popped the piano open again curiously. "Look, you need to figure out what you're going to do. Right now, you have a half-open portal to Hell in your attic. It's not going to take long for things to start figuring that out and then we'll have a host of trouble."

Emerie licked her lips and popped open the paper carton. She splashed a little milk into her tea. "Did I let something else out? Something other than you?"

She offered him the mug. Samael ignored her, keeping his attentions on the piano. He stretched out a claw and plinked an F natural. "Yeah. You did."

She poured tea into the second mug. He noticed her hands slightly shook as she set the teapot down. "Where—where is it now?"

"Not in this house. It wouldn't have hung around. It will want... people." He pressed a G# key.

Emerie shuddered. She took a long sip of tea, her small hands wrapped around the mug. She swallowed and exhaled with a hum. She made the tea look delicious. He scowled, grabbed the second mug, and took a gulp. He hated how wonderful it tasted.

After a moment, Emerie opened her eyes. "What can I do to fix this? How can I close the circle?"

Samael gazed at her critically and took another slurp of tea. "*You* can't do anything. You're the one that made this mess!"

"Well, shouldn't I be the one to clean it up, then?" Emerie gestured towards the kitchen. "If you want sugar, it's in the bowl labeled SALT—I can't find our sugar bowl."

He stared at her. What was *wrong* with this human?! Why wasn't she afraid of him?! Why didn't she have the slightest particle of fear or horror at the forces of Hell? She was treating the rift between dimensions like a home repair project.

"I don't want sugar."

"Okay. Why are you staring at me?" She looked at herself and her forehead crinkled. She picked some of the dried wax off the flimsy material and rubbed hard at the ash stains that marred her white dress. "See, this is why I don't wear white."

This innocuous comment sent him over the edge.

"What is wrong with you?!" Samael slammed the mug on the piano. "You have a fully-fledged demon in your house, Emerie Fox! I come from an ancient deep, I was here before the earth was formed and will remain unto eternity...doesn't that—concern you in the slightest?"

She frowned at him and for a brief, shining moment, he thought she understood the gravity of her situation and how much danger she was in. But instead, she stood up from the couch, marched towards him, and snatched the mug off the piano.

"That will leave a ring. Put it on the coffee table on a coaster. Were you raised in a barn?"

It took him a few seconds to remember what a barn was. "I was not."

Emerie exhaled as she took a seat. "Now, look. When that...*thing* came after me, during the summoning—you protected me, didn't you? It backed off after you knocked me down. I think you growled at it."

He bristled. "I did not *growl*, I spoke a language."

"Sure sounded like growling."

"I told it that you were *my* prey and it couldn't have you." He bared his teeth while taking an invigorating slurp. The tea was good. But thirst and hunger were two separately delightful senses.

However, this did not seem to faze Emerie, who took another contemplative sip of tea. He watched her glance at the darkened window, her expression musing. He'd seen this look before. It was the same look she gave her walls when deciding on a paint color.

"I wonder if we'll be able to close the portal and get that demon out of Milton before Dylan gets home," she said finally. "The gate to Hell in the attic will just be one more excuse for him to want to move out. He'll undoubtedly try to push that stupid Boston apartment on me again."

Dylan. Emerie's lover. While Emerie at least had a certain attractiveness and charm to warrant more positive attentions, Dylan's constant whining grated on Samael's nerves. It was *much* better here without him. But as irritating as the little boy was, he had a point.

"A gate to Hell in your attic is enough of an excuse for *most* sensible people to want to leave." Samael mashed two piano notes together. "You weren't even using the right ritual—I already told you, I wasn't *in* Hell, I was caught between planes. You're just lucky I was able to wiggle through."

Emerie directed her gaze to the ceiling, presumably thinking of her attic. There were no cracks in the ceiling—but then again, the crack in the attic would not lead to any place in the house.

"As soon as other demons catch wind of the portal, they'll cross over," he told her. "I won't be able to protect you forever, you know."

She looked at him curiously and he just *knew* she wanted to ask one of her annoying questions about why he *had* protected her.

The truth was...he didn't know the answer. By all accounts he should've eaten her. Or seduced her and *then* eaten her. Or at least possessed her bodily and wreaked a little havoc. But after he'd accepted her food offering, he had left her alone. Mostly.

There was nothing special about Emerie Fox. She was as mortal as they came. It might not even be Emerie Fox he was interested in, it could be humanity in general—it had been a long time since he'd had experience with humans. Samael had spent one-hundred and fifty years watching humans wander to and fro in this house. He had seen their laughter, their curiosity, their fears, their anxieties, their faith, and ulti-mately—their hope. Emerie was certainly not an exception. But her infu-riating pragmatism and bewildering levelheadedness in the face of the paranormal was something new.

He noticed her pull out her phone. "What are you doing?"

Emerie snapped her head up to look at him with disdain.

"I think it's time to call a witch."

NINE

THUNDERSTORMS DID NOT BOTHER Sunflower Moon.

Her daughter had always hated them. Zephyr would raise holy hell if she even heard the slightest grumble of thunder—and lightning would send her hiding in the hall closet. Sunflower would attempt to coax her out with promises of cookies and picture books, but it never made any difference. Even when Zephyr was a teenager, she would blast loud music in her room to drown out the sounds of the storm. Sunflower tried to convey what an important time a thunderstorm was for a young witch —perfect for casting—but her daughter never listened to her.

Sunflower stayed late at her shop that night. Her store was her happy place, cozy and quiet. The backroom was a lovely place to have a cup of tea and a bit of dinner. Since Zephyr had moved out of the house, Sunflower hadn't much liked going home in the evenings. The house was too empty.

She busied herself with balancing her books, organizing the tarot card decks, and restacking the books on her bookshelves. She played an old movie on her laptop, one she loved as a child—*Bell Book and Candle.* Jimmy Stewart's voice soothed as she tidied up her shop and made herself busy. Once the store was spotless, she retreated into the backroom to finish her movie and wait out the storm.

The rain ebbed and roared intermittently. Sunflower made a cup of chamomile tea in the microwave. She sat herself down in a squashy armchair and reviewed her accounts. Zephyr was forever bothering her to get a social media account—an Instabook or a Facegram, to help promote the shop. She could almost hear her daughter's pained exclamation: "You wouldn't constantly be going over your budget if you would just market yourself properly!"

She chuckled to herself. She raised her cup to her lips and just as the hot steam touched her lips, she heard a loud *THUMP* coming from the main store.

Startled, she set her cup down on an old coffee table that showed the moon phases of 1986. She struggled to stand and whisked through the tie-dyed curtain that separated the backroom from the main shop.

It took a moment for her old eyes to adjust to the darkness. The only light came from the star-and-moon shaped twinkle lights that illuminated her front door. The corner bookshelves were untouched. Her jewelry stands were perfectly straight. Her lovely shop seemed at peace.

Sunflower was about to turn around and return to her chamomile tea when she heard another strange noise. Something like a flapping—like a bird's wings or someone flipping through a paperback book. Confused, she went to the counter and flicked on the overhead light.

As soon as the light clicked on, the glass doors of her counter flung open unexpectedly. Before she could register what had happened, something came flying out.

Dozens and dozens of tarot cards flapped around her, whirling like falling leaves. And then all at once...the noise died.

Her hands shook as she bent down and picked up one of the cards. The Devil. Not a bad card to draw during a reading, despite what horror films and Christians would tell you...

It must've been a breeze. A draft, perhaps. Maybe one of the ceiling vents was torn. Her back began to ache as she bent to pick each card up. They seemed to be scattered everywhere. The Hanged Man, the Tower, the Maiden, the Empress, the Hermit...Sunflower tried to keep her mind off the cards she drew. This wasn't a reading. This was a freak incident.

The bells above her door jangled. She looked up in confusion—her front doors were locked. But she could hear something scratching at the door.

There were a few stray cats that roamed around the neighborhood. She would occasionally feed them if business was slow. She blinked suddenly. The small upper light which illuminated her "Enchanted Attic" sign had flicked on of its own accord, partially brightening the entryway.

Sunflower wished she had thought to turn on all of the lights before crossing the room. There was something about the way the shadows fell across her various statues of gargoyles, fairies, and dragons that unnerved her. She stopped in front of her display of crescent moon neck-laces (each with a corresponding horoscope charm!) and shook herself. Her store had *never* spooked her like this. What was going on?

The scratching continued. She swallowed hard and approached the door, squinting at the glass panes. She could see something waiting outside. Something large and black. Too large to be a cat—a figure? Someone who didn't realize her shop was closed? She couldn't see it properly. She needed her glasses.

She was about a foot away from the door when she realized she was not looking outside her shop. She was looking at a reflection. A reflection of something looming right behind her.

Sunflower screamed. She didn't even try to turn around—she launched herself at her front door and desperately tried to escape, but the doors were locked tight. Her keys were in the back. Multicolored crystal wind chimes shattered around her as she banged against the locked doors desperately. Terrified, she turned.

She couldn't see what it was. All she could see was blackness, thick as tar, oppressing the air around her. But the longer she looked, the more she could see the *eyes,* all staring every which way, hungrily gazing at everything in her little shop. The eyes were not human. Animal eyes... dark, heavy-lidded pupils, with no intelligence or sentience behind them.

When they focused on her, she panicked.

In a blur of motion, Sunflower snatched the object closest to her door —in this case, a large cherry wood statue of Buddha—and flung it forward. The Buddha split the creature down the middle, as though it were made more of shadows than mass. To her terror and shock, the creature howled in rage, as though she had done some real damage.

She scrambled forward and tore through her shop, knocking down displays and bookshelves as she went. She could hear it lumbering after her with heavy, clumping steps. She thought she could hear a cacophony of intersecting voices—they were whisper-screaming; they sounded like nails on a chalkboard.

She reached the back. She had to get to her car, she had to reach the stock room door! But in her hurry, she tripped over a large dented singing bowl she'd been trying to repair. Sunflower cried out and grasped her ankle—it had somehow twisted on the woven rug when she fell. She backed up against the far wall, under a poster that displayed all the sabbats.

The light was still on. The curtain separating the backroom and the store was a simple sheer scarf. Her hands shook as she tugged her phone out of her pocket and scrabbled at the screen.

"Please, please," she begged the phone. She could hear it ring, slow and methodical.

A shadow darkened the curtain.

"Please, baby, please!" Sunflower's voice broke. The fifth ring. Her daughter's voicemail.

"Hi, this is Zephyr Moon. I'm not able to take this call, right now, but if you leave a message, my assistant or I will get back with you—"

The curtain tore and Sunflower's screams shattered every window of the store.

———

"Hm. Straight to voicemail. I guess Sunflower's on the phone."

"That woman is an idiot."

Emerie frowned at Samael again. He was leaning against her piano and she wanted to warn him to keep his wings furled. The wing-tips appeared to have claws of some kind and she didn't want them scratching the wood.

"I wouldn't have been able to get as far as I did without her help." She sat down on her couch.

"Having extensive knowledge of witchcraft is one thing." Samael moved away from the piano and examined her bookshelf. "But skimming—dabbling—is dangerous. She encouraged that."

Emerie ignored him and pulled out a business card from her back pocket. "You know what? I'll call her daughter. Sunflower gave me her number."

Samael growled but continued to peruse her books. Emerie dialed the number and turned towards the window. The night was only getting darker and the rain couldn't make up its mind—she could hear it pounding against the roof.

"Hello?" A female voice answered and Emerie cleared her throat.

"Hi," she said a little awkwardly. "Is this Zephyr Moon?"

"Yeah."

"Okay, great. My name is Emerie Fox. So, your mom gave me your number." Emerie scratched her head. "She said if I ran into trouble... you might be able to help me."

"She did?" The voice sounded surprised. "Huh. Well, generally people make appointments with my secretary during normal office hours—and I don't do traffic tickets or anything like that."

Emerie blinked. "You guys handle traffic tickets? That's—interesting. Um, look, I really need some help. I live in Milton, my boyfriend's out of town, and I just—"

"How long have you and your boyfriend been together?" The woman's voice asked matter-of-factly. "Is he a danger to you? Have you contacted the police?"

"Oh, it's not my boyfriend," Emerie tried to clarify. "See, I had this demon stuck in my house, and I tried to summon him to get him unstuck, and I accidentally released something else in Milton, and now we need to track that down and get rid of it."

There was a long silence and then the voice replied with immense irritation, "You're not asking me a legal question, are you?"

"You're a lawyer?" Emerie asked in surprise.

The phone disconnected. Emerie stared at her phone and then rapidly texted:

NEED HELP!!! Please—demons loose in Milton, portal to Hell in my attic, world in mortal danger. Please call. Here's my address.

"That sounded productive," Samael intoned. He was holding a fantasy novel Emerie loved as a child.

Emerie tapped her foot anxiously. "The shop's closed by now...but it is an emergency. Sunflower's probably home. I'm sure she wouldn't mind if we paid her a quick visit."

"What do you mean 'we'?" Samael folded his arms in front of his chest. "Do I look like something that can walk around a human town and not be noticed?"

"It's dark outside. We're just going across the street. No one's going to be out in this weather."

As though the storm wanted to prove her point, a flash of lightning illuminated the living room and thunder cracked the sky. Emerie was surprised to see Samael jump at the storm's commotion—he must not be used to storms. He wrapped his wings around him protectively, like a cloak, and she noticed a serpentine tail near his feet. It twitched like a cat's tail.

Lightning blazed into the room again and this time, across the street, Emerie saw Sunflower. She was getting out of her car and walking towards her house. It occurred to Emerie she wasn't wearing a coat...she must be getting soaked.

"I'll get my jacket." Emerie rushed out of the room into her hallway and pulled a black Star Trek hoodie out of the hall closet. She shoved it on quickly and poked her head into the living room. Samael had not budged from the bookcase.

"Are you coming?" She pulled up her hood.

Samael's dark eyes narrowed. "Why would I do that?" He returned to the book.

"Well—aren't you going to help?" Emerie stuck her hands into her pockets and glanced towards the front door.

"*It was a dark and stormy night.*" Samael read aloud and took a seat on the easy chair. "Hm. Appropriate."

Emerie recognized that technically, this mess was her fault, and

Samael did not owe her any help. But she had spent a fair amount of time bonding with him over the Ouija board and it struck her as grossly unfair he was disregarding that.

"You're being a dick," she shouted at him. "You're no longer stuck in this house—doesn't that count for something?"

Samael did not look up from the book as he spoke. "When the storm is over, I'll be on my way."

Emerie resisted the urge to throw something at him. She instead took another approach and stared at him in icy disapproval.

He ignored her. But to Emerie's satisfaction, his tail continued to jerk and twitch the longer she stared at him.

After her point was made, she left the room, went to the front door, and walked out into the rain-lashed night.

TEN

ZEPHYR MOON DECIDED to prove a point.

Sunflower called *constantly*. In the morning, while she was brushing her teeth, on her way to work, during her meetings, while she was in court—in fact, Zephyr's phone was perpetually on silent because of how many times her mother's incessant phone calls had interrupted her.

On the rare occasions Zephyr *did* answer, it was never anything important. Just Sunflower rambling on about new crystals she recently tried, the upcoming Pagan Picnic, memories that occurred to her, and of course, asking when she was going to visit next. This conversation would eventually end with Zephyr making up an excuse so she could get off the phone.

It wasn't as though Zephyr wanted to be cruel to her mother. She tried explaining how important her career was, how she wanted to set up a life for herself, how she badly needed to build her firm. She could not constantly be interrupted by phone calls from her mother.

Sunflower's usual response was that Zephyr needed to stop focusing so much on *worldly* concerns and start accepting her natural gifts.

Zephyr Moon did not *like* her natural gifts.

She supposed this was abnormal. Millions of children across the world, fed on a diet of superheroes and farm boy fantasy protagonists probably *ached* to have something supernatural about them. How many little girls daydreamed of discovering they had mutant powers? How many children anxiously waited for their Hogwarts letters, checked their closets and wardrobes for secret worlds, eyed their parents' wedding rings skeptically?

But to Zephyr, her gifts always felt like *cheating*.

She knew she was talented. She knew she was a hard worker, intelligent, and driven. From the age of nine, she had desperately wanted to prove herself to the world using *those* abilities, not accidentally charming her teacher into giving her book report an A. She wanted to make friends the *normal* way, not by inadvertently creating a coven of enchanted followers. Winning friends and influencing people happened to her *a lot*, without intent, and was as frustrating as it was heartbreaking. She never could trust that anyone who wished to date her was attracted to her— they may unconsciously be attracted to the magic that clung to her.

Zephyr wasn't exactly *suppressing* her magic—that was dangerous and often led to insanity. She preferred to think of it as *disciplining* her magic.

Her magic was closely managed for outside consumption. She monitored it under the strictest surveillance, allowing it out in controlled bursts—a bit of flight in her steps as she raced down the stairs or dipping a finger in her coffee to warm it again. She ruled her magic in a draconian manner; she never allowed it to influence her workday or the people around her.

Her mother called it *masking*.

Zephyr hated that perspective. Her mother had the luxury to be woo-woo and weird. But there were far more eyes on Zephyr as a trial lawyer and she couldn't afford an overstimulation of magic to affect her work. She was proud of the boundaries she set for herself and her determination to live as a *normal* thirty-something woman. Which included *privacy*. She had a right to have a glass of wine alone in her apartment without her mom interrupting.

Of course, her glass of wine got interrupted anyway when Emily What's-her-face called for a magic consultant.

Zephyr shook her head at the text that lit up her phone. No, no. She would *not* be going to Milton. She was there just a week ago, that should satisfy her mother for a while. She hated the small town, how it copy-catted Salem in style and theme, the claustrophobic community, the Republicans…she poured herself another glass of wine instead. Not to mention, how it was far harder to control her abilities there. The smallest thing would set her off, even if it was as simple as someone sticking a flier underneath her windshield wipers. It was easier to control herself in Boston, where no personal or emotional triggers lay dormant.

It was a perfect autumn evening. It was finally cool enough that if she wanted to, she could enjoy a fire in her fireplace—one of the perks of living in her luxury apartment. But Zephyr never lit it; she kept the flue tightly shut at all times.

Her phone chimed—she had a voicemail. She deleted it without listening. She sipped her blueberry merlot and closed her eyes, letting herself savor her evening. She got the wine from the Nashoba winery, one of her favorite places to go for a weekend.

The flavors danced on her tongue and seeped into her mind. Zephyr smiled. There were a few perks to being a witch. She called it *witchsense*. It wasn't anything terribly impressive. Part of her abilities meant all six senses—yes, *six*—were heightened. When she tasted her wine, she could see the green hills of the Nashoba winery. She could walk the fields of northern Maine where they gathered blueberries, feel the sun on her skin as she tasted hints of raspberry, inhale the warm, flowery breeze.

She opened her eyes to take another sip of wine when something lurched in her stomach.

Zephyr inhaled sharply. Something was wrong. Something had happened. The curdling in her stomach evolved into a powerful throbbing in her gut. Her apartment came in and out of focus and she tried to take deep breaths. She knocked her half-full glass of wine off her kitchen island as she grasped for her phone.

Something was wrong.

She tried calling her mother. But Sunflower did not answer. Zephyr thought of her mother and concentrated hard. She could see her in her mind's eye, scattered and ridiculous, flitting every which way like a hummingbird. But as she pictured her mother, she felt something else too. Some terrible shadowy thing…it was reaching for Sunflower…

Zephyr practically leapt off her stool. In her rush, she kicked on two different colored heels, snatched her purse off the coatrack. Without a second glance, she rushed out the door. She needed to get to Milton NOW.

ELEVEN

EMERIE BANGED ON THE DOOR.

She huddled as close as she could to the screen, keeping well under the porch awning. Massachusetts had apparently decided on cold, relentless rain after the storm and Emerie began to regret trying to get Sunflower's help—surely the portal to Hell in her attic could wait until the morning?

But she still needed to figure out what to do about Samael. Should she just let him go free? Trap him in a cage, maybe? See if she could lock him in the bathroom?

She banged on the door again. "Sunflower, it's Emerie! I need your help! Please let me in!"

She was about to give up when to her surprise, the door slowly opened. She expected to see Sunflower's happy and vague expression, but there was no one at the door. She could see the entryway, with a small niche to the left which held a multitude of candles in various shapes and colors. She smelled incense and essential oils, and a little further in, she saw a narrow, varnished, wood staircase.

"Sunflower?" Emerie stepped inside. "Are you here? It's Emerie! Your neighbor! I screwed up the summoning! I need your help!"

The front door slammed shut behind her and she heard the lock click.

Up to this point, Emerie felt she had dealt with her house's hauntings with patience and good humor. There were certainly disconcerting moments and she had had her fair share of surprising and frightening happenings. But she didn't scare easy and however ludicrous it might seem to the outside observer, she felt that because it was *her* house, she could handle it.

But someone else's haunted house? That was an entirely different matter.

There was something horrible about turning her back to the shadowy staircase, so Emerie backed up, reached behind her, and tried the door-knob. The front door held fast—which of course, made absolutely no sense. A door should lock someone from coming in, not keep them from coming out!

"Well, shit."

Emerie squinted and looked towards the walls. She was trying to spot the light switch—if she could just see in front of her, maybe she could break a window or something to get out of there.

She noticed a likely looking switch towards her right and groped towards it. She flicked it on and for a brief shining moment, the foyer and entryway revealed themselves in brilliant, safe clarity—

And then thunder shook the house and the power went out.

"Are you serious?!"

Emerie pulled out her phone and turned its flashlight on. She exhaled in relief as her phone brightened the entryway. She tried the front door-knob again, but it remained steadfastly locked.

She moved away from the door and gave the dark stairwell a wide berth. Instead, she turned right into the living room, and kept her phone aloft. It seemed like a fairly ordinary living room, with a maroon couch, entertainment center, and a coffee table. Nevertheless, she could see touches of Sunflower here and there. There were dreamcatchers hanging in the windows and the whole room smelled like patchouli. Still, there was nothing particularly scary in the living room, aside from a VCR and collection of old VHS tapes next to it.

Emerie went to the far windows and tried them. They were locked —naturally.

"Sunflower?" Emerie noted a large, heavy candle on the coffee table.

"Hey, I'm really sorry, but I'm about to break your window! I swear I'll pay for it."

She was about to launch the candle at the glass when she heard it.

CLIP. CLOP. CLIP. CLOP.

Her arm dropped. Were those...hooves?

She slowly made her way out of the living room, following the sound. She returned to the entryway and looked up the stairs. At first, she couldn't see anything—even as she held her phone up the steps, the light could not seem to penetrate the thick darkness.

Emerie was about to drop her phone and return to her plan of breaking a window when she saw it. There, at the top of the stairs...two pinpricks of light. An eerie white, the gleam of two animal eyes which stared directly at her.

The darkness melted around the eyes and Emerie found herself staring up at a black goat.

It took Emerie a few moments to register what she saw. The goat remained perfectly stationary—it looked down at her from the top of the steps with an almost bored expression. It was large too, about the size of a mule or pony, with wicked-looking horns.

Emerie continued to gape at the goat. Since when could goats climb stairs? Wait, that was cows... Goats climbed mountains, after all...did Sunflower own a goat? Was she trying to make her own cheese? From what she knew of Sunflower, this was entirely possible, but would she really keep a goat inside the house?

"Hey, there, buddy..." Emerie said to the goat pleasantly. "Uh...your mom around?"

The goat opened its mouth. It let out a horrible sound, like a woman screaming for help and Emerie backed up against the front door in terror, before she remembered that goats bleated like people. She was pretty sure someone told her that a while back. Or maybe they sent her a funny video of a goat screaming like a person.

"Sunflower?" Emerie called. "Are you up there?"

In response, the goat turned from the top of the stairs and she watched it trot down the hallway. The hoofbeats vibrated against the hardwood and Emerie wondered if Sunflower was up there.

She tried the doorknob one more time. It was still locked. With a heavy sigh, she pointed her phone forward and tramped up the steps in pursuit of the goat.

When she reached the top, she cast one more longing glance towards the front door. The upstairs hallway partially overlooked the entryway, and she could hear the rain patter against the narrow side window next to the door. She looked down the hallway and saw the goat disappear into the last bedroom.

Emerie held her phone up. The light fought against the darkness, but she could still see what was in front of her. It occurred to her the upstairs was freezing—did Sunflower have her AC on? As Emerie walked down the hallway, she passed framed pictures of Sunflower and her daughter. Peaceful, ordinary markers of the house.

She reached the end of the hall. The door was ajar. She reached out to push it open when a distinct feeling of dread overcame her. Her heart started to pound and even though she shivered in the drafty hallway, her palms started to sweat.

She shouldn't be here. She could feel it in her bones. She needed to *get out now.*

Emerie whipped around to race down the hallway—but was abruptly jerked backwards, like a rope was tied to her gut. She toppled into the bedroom and slammed against the dresser.

Adrenaline blocked out the pain briefly; Emerie staggered to her feet. She froze when she saw what was lying there.

Sunflower lay on her bed, propped up against the pillows. The bedroom was completely dark, but somehow, the lamp on her night-stand dimly popped on and off. At first, Emerie thought she might be ill...her face was the color of spoiled milk and her eyes flickered, like she was falling asleep. The smell of vomit and rot tinged the air and Emerie looked towards the door. At her glance, the bedroom door shut.

"Sunflower?"

Her eyes did not open at Emerie's plea. But she spoke...

"Who let the fox in the henhouse?"

Her voice did not sound like Sunflower's voice. Sunflower's natu-rally husky and warm vibrato was replaced with a smooth, velvety tenor. Every time the light popped on, Emerie saw the shadow of huge horns around Sunflower. It occurred to her that the goat wasn't in the room.

"Hello, my conjuror."

Sunflower's expression remained impassive and distant. Emerie noticed spit bubbles forming at the corner of her slack mouth. But the voice conveyed a thousand emotions…gratitude, hatred, envy…

Emerie's stomach churned. Samael was right. Something else escaped from the portal in her attic and launched itself into Sunflower.

"You get out of her!" Emerie squeaked. Her head started to throb and she felt dizzy.

The spit bubbles became a small stream of drool. The voice inside Sunflower chuckled.

"Incorporeal form is inconvenient. Skin is better."

"Get out!" Emerie shouted. "I'm warning you!"

"What do you intend to do about it, little conjuror?"

"I'm not afraid of you!"

"You will be."

"I didn't summon you, I summoned *Samael*!"

Her voice vibrated across the room. Emerie suddenly wished at her call he would burst into the room. But Samael was across the street, presumably still engrossed in her book.

"Samael won't mind sharing his snacks. We go way back, Samael and I."

At this, Emerie decided to do something drastic.

There was a glass vanity set to Emerie's right, next to the chest of drawers she was currently pressed up against. In the hope she might startle the thing, she snatched the face mirror off the table and flung it to the ground.

The mirror shattered into a thousand little pieces. The noise was loud enough to cause Sunflower to jerk abruptly, like a robot that malfunctioned. The shards of mirror covered the floor and Emerie heard an angry scream—in each shard, a triangular pupil blazed at her.

On sheer adrenaline, Emerie threw herself at the bedroom door. It did not break, as she was too petite to do any real damage, but she apparently had distracted the thing enough that its attention was no longer on the door. She pounded down the hallway, headed straight for the stairs.

But before she could reach the stairwell, she saw the black goat at the other end of the hallway. It was pawing the ground, head bowed in order to display its powerful horns. She recalled where she had seen this behavior before—something on television, where a bull prepared to charge a matador.

"Oh, you gotta be kidding me."

The black goat charged her. Emerie shrieked like a banshee and flung herself over the balcony.

She expected to land on the hardwood of the entryway, perhaps knocking over an end table or breaking her arm on one of Sunflower's goddess statues. But instead, she didn't fall. She sort of...hung in the air.

"What..."

It was not a comfortable feeling. She felt like a rock climber who'd lost his grip and was now hanging from his safety harness, exposed and stupid. She realized she was staring at a young woman; whose arm reached out towards her, as though she were trying to reach a book on the top shelf.

"Are...are you doing this?"

The woman flicked her wrist. Emerie tumbled to the ground, though perhaps a little more gently than she would have originally.

Emerie scrambled to her feet. The woman's eyes were wide with fury. She was dressed in a well-tailored pantsuit and heels (though mismatched) that cost more than Emerie's car. She was incredibly beautiful and about two feet taller than Emerie. Her eyes were dark brown and her long dark hair was caught up in an elegant bun. She had slender, graceful features, whereas Emerie was more compact.

"Where's my mom?" The beautiful woman demanded without preamble. Her voice was rich and authoritative. It struck Emerie—this must be Sunflower's daughter. The infamous Zephyr Moon, the attorney who'd hung up on her. Emerie had even seen her once, coming out of the shop, though she'd hurried away too quickly for her to recognize her.

"Uh..." Emerie looked upstairs. "Wait, how did you get here so fast?"

"My mom and I have an empathy link," the woman replied, as if that explained sudden teleportation powers. "I'm assuming you're the idiot that summoned whatever's infecting her house?"

"Well..."

"The one that called me?" Zephyr's nose wrinkled. "I smell goat shit."

Emerie tried to think of something to say, but was saved this mercy by an inhuman bellow above them.

The woman made a noise of disgust. She stomped up the stairwell and Emerie followed, keeping close behind. Zephyr stalked towards her mother's bedroom and flung open the door.

The bedroom was still as frightening as ever, but this time Sunflower was crouched on her bed like some sort of goblin. She eyed Zephyr warily, but did not move or attempt to psychically shove her against the wall, as she had with Emerie. Zephyr paid her no heed, instead seemed to collect and critique her surroundings.

"Ugh, Mom," she complained as she gingerly stepped over the broken shards of mirror. "Look at the state of this place. What have you been up to?"

"It wasn't her fault," Emerie volunteered.

"Oh, trust me, I will *get to you*." Zephyr flung open the curtains. The storm had ended, the night now blazed moonlight. Sunflower howled as the silvery light bathed the room. She twisted unnaturally in her bedsheets.

"Okay, you." Zephyr moved to the foot of the bed. "Get the hell out of my mom."

Sunflower hissed at her like a snake. *"Little upstart. How **dare** you presume to command me! Do you know who I am?!"*

"I don't have time to name whatever little angry spirit my mom comes down with. This is your last warning—"

"LITTLE ANGRY SPIRIT?!"

This seemed to truly infuriate it. Emerie watched in horror (while Zephyr watched nonplussed) as Sunflower levitated from her bed, her arms spread out, mimicking the crucifixion. Her eyes rolled to the back of her head, her swollen tongue protruded from her mouth, and thick, tar-like darkness swarmed the room.

"IT WAS I WHO COMMANDED THE ARMIES OF HELL TO CONQUER THE EARTH. IT WAS I WHO REMINDED MANKIND TO FEAR THE WILD HORNED GODS. AND IT WAS I WHO BEDDED A MORTAL WOMAN AND FROM MY LINE SPRANG YOUR KIND—I AM THE FATHER OF ALL WITCHES, IT WAS I WHO TAUGHT THEM MAGIC. FOR I AM AZAZEL!"

Emerie glanced nervously at Zephyr. Zephyr's expression remained neutral. She actually crossed her arms in front of her chest, a silent and judgmental gesture that seemed to indicate she hoped the demon would wrap it up already.

"Taught the first woman magic, huh?" Zephyr snorted. "That was your dumbass mistake."

Before Emerie could marvel at her for calling the demon Azazel a dumbass, Zephyr shouted something unintelligible. She flung something hard and white on the ground, which splintered into a spray of white. Sunflower roared and her floating body charged Zephyr, who clapped her hands sharply. Her mother froze in midair, just as Emerie had, and Zephyr moved towards her. She dragged a chair over and hopped up. She popped her mother's mouth open and looked inside, as if she were checking for strep throat.

"Mm," Zephyr murmured critically. She dug something out of her pocket and popped it into Sunflower's mouth. Emerie wondered if it was a breath mint.

Within moments, Sunflower's body fell onto her bed. She doubled over, breathing hard, and to Emerie's horror, she realized that Sunflower was now puking all over herself.

"Jesus!" Emerie cried out and tried to go to her. Sunflower threw up *harder* at this and Zephyr blocked the way.

"Better out than in." She nodded in approval. "That's it, mom. Get all that nasty out of you."

"It's a demon, not the stomach flu!"

Zephyr snorted. "Like you're an expert on either? Look, you're obviously an idiot for ripping a hole between the spirit world, and you are in *huge* trouble for that, by the way—but unfortunately, this is not the first time my mom has come down with a case of possession. Azazel knew that and that's why he targeted her."

Sunflower retched loudly. Her fists curled into the vomit-soaked sheets and she attempted to aim off her bed onto the floor. Zephyr's expression softened and she went to her mother, patting her back in comfort.

"It's all right, Mommy. I'm sorry I missed your call. I'm here now."

Sunflower's eyes streamed. There was no more liquid in her stomach, so she simply dry heaved. Zephyr made soothing noises and kissed her mother's damp forehead. Emerie gasped—an inky colored puddle started to edge itself off the bed and slide out of the room.

"Let it go," Zephyr told her, although Emerie had absolutely no intention of trying to go after it.

"There's a goat…" Emerie didn't know what else to do, so she started trying to sweep up glass shards with her shoe. "There's a goat haunting the joint too."

Zephyr shook her head. "It's just a shadow. Azazel was possessing my mom. The goat's just something to lure idiots upstairs and to terrorize them."

"So he's…gone now, right? You got rid of him?"

"I got him out of my *mom*." Zephyr's steely gaze found Emerie. "He needs to be exorcised back into the spirit world. Along with whatever else you've unleashed into this town."

"It was an accident!" Emerie bent down and picked up a stray T-shirt, which she used to try and gather the glass shards. "I was trying to get a demon to stop haunting my house. I didn't mean to release the minions of Hell along with him."

"And let me guess." Zephyr swiftly stripped the bed of sheets and blankets. Sunflower watched the proceedings dazedly.

"My mom just had to help you, right? Provided your ingredients, your tools? She never had much sense."

Zephyr helped Sunflower back onto the bare mattress. She gathered up the soiled sheets and tromped out of the room. Emerie kept pace with her, down the steps, across the family room with an impressive collection of Tibetan singing bowls, until they reached the laundry room. The laundry room was next to the kitchen, an unassuming little area that smelled like cat urine and incense.

As they walked, Emerie expected to see the oily puddle oozing about, but it had vanished. She wondered where Azazel was off to next…was he really so powerful? It hadn't taken much for Zephyr to banish him.

She also wondered what he meant by having "history with Samael."

"I need help," Emerie admitted.

Zephyr ignored her as she shoved sheets into the washing machine. "Not my problem, girlie."

"Oh, c'mon! You're a witch! You could probably get rid of these demons like that!" Emerie snapped her fingers in emphasis.

Zephyr flinched at the word "witch." But she resolutely continued to load the washing machine.

"I don't deal with…what you call 'demons'." She hunted around the room for detergent and groaned when she saw a little plastic tub. "Damn it, Mom, do you have to make all of your soaps?"

She grimaced as she poured something white and sticky into the wash. "Mom's as good at making soap as she is at casting spells."

"You don't call them demons?" In an attempt to be helpful, Emerie opened the dryer and pulled out several muumuus, each in a different shade of blue. Muumuus were ridiculous garments to fold, but she did her best.

"Negative energy, trickster spirits, entities of hatred, whatever." Zephyr shut the lid with a slam. "I don't deal with them. Ghosts, maybe. At least that's something *human*. Something you can reason with. But those things? Forget about it."

At least this felt more familiar to Emerie, who's only reference for demons were *yokai* and ghosts.

Zephyr faced Emerie bodily and snatched the muumuus. "This is not my problem."

"It's going to be everyone's problem soon!" Emerie raked her fingers through her hair. "I get that I screwed up—really, I do. But I can't do this on my own!"

Zephyr watched her for a long while. She tapped her fingers along the edge of the washing machine before she leaned towards it and switched it on. The rumble of the wash seemed to make up her mind.

"I have to take care of my mom. What else is new, I *always* have to—never mind. You should leave. This is work for a shaman, not a witch."

And with that, Zephyr stepped around her and exited the laundry room.

Emerie stood there for a few minutes as she tried to figure out what to do. She pulled out her phone and scrolled through her contacts. She didn't know any shamans…but she did know a priest.

TWELVE

THERE WERE many physical pleasures a demon enjoyed, once in corporeal form. Some were obvious—alcohol was popular, sex was a given, and of course devouring your enemies and hearing their screams for mercy. However...there were other surprising pleasures that many demons shared, but did not talk about.

Reading was one of them.

One could never be too careful about what was approved demonic behavior, so most demons kept these milder sort of indulgences to themselves. And as it turned out, Samael badly missed reading.

Emerie's house contained an impressive collection of books in every room. In the living room, the upstairs den, the master bedroom, even both of the bathrooms—there was always something to read. Samael finished the fantasy novel by the time the storm died (he and Emerie both read uncommonly fast—he noticed this the first day, when Emerie chose to power through *The Parable of the Sower* series in two days while utterly ignoring unpacking) and was onto his second, another fantasy book by an English writer who had a simultaneously laughable yet unnerving grasp of the politics of Hell.

Samael heard the intruder approach immediately but did not look up from his book. "What do you want, Azazel?"

A long shadow stretched against the far wall melted and warped—his old partner was having some trouble gaining corporeal form.

Samael pursed his lips in disapproval. "It's your own fault for trying to possess someone right off the bat. It'll take you at least forty-eight hours to get your energy back up to take physical form."

The shadow shifted into that of a large goat, its horns extending across the room. A voice spoke and the entire room vibrated.

"It won't take that long, Samael. Don't you feel it?"

Samael frowned and stuck a claw inside his book to mark his place. He looked at the shadow in annoyance. "Feel what?"

"The town. Someone's prepared it for us."

"Prepared?"

"The gateway in this house is only the beginning. This whole town is going to be ripped to shreds...and we'll take our place once more."

Samael rolled his eyes. "You and your idealistic fantasies. You've been saying that we're going to take over the earth since we got kicked out of the Garden."

"Don't be a fool, Samael. You feel it in your bones, just as I do. You best prepare for the reckoning."

"Reckoning, right. I reckon that hole is going to be plugged up in no time and our sorry hides will end up right back in Hell."

"You haven't been in Hell. You've been here. With that girl."

"With an *assortment* of girls, I'll have you know!" Samael stood up from his easy chair, he was so offended. How dare Azazel accuse him of monogamy!

"I was *stuck*, Azazel. That idiot Lemp woman bungled summoning me and you lot left me stranded!"

"He knew you would be stuck. But he knew another idiot girl would release you. And the rest of us."

"None of that," Samael said wearily. "I don't want to talk to *him*. I don't want to have anything to do with his wild schemes."

"He is already here. I can sense him."

"Well, he can leave me the hell alone. And so can you, if you're in it with him. Now clear off. This house is *mine* for the time being, and so is the girl!"

His wings exploded outward, meeting the shadows in length and width. Azazel's shadow dissolved away from him and Samael heard his brother curse, jeer, and threaten to uproot the foundations of the world for his insolence. Typical younger brother annoyances. But sure enough, he exited the house.

Samael sat back in his easy chair with a sigh. There would be other demons who would claw their way out of the attic. Demons who would be hellbent on wreaking havoc and mayhem on Milton. He was too old for such nonsense. The mere idea of them scrabbling and screeching about gave him a headache.

He heard a key scrape at the front door and Emerie walked in. It occurred to him she *had* been gone a while.

She glared at him in irritation. "*You* look comfortable."

"I've been trapped between dimensions for the past two hundred years," Samael retorted. "I deserve a little downtime."

"Well, you were absolutely no help" Emerie grimaced as she pulled off her sweatshirt and hung it on the coatrack. "I guess we have to go the religious route next. If a witch won't help, we'll have to try a priest."

"*We?*"

THIRTEEN

"I DON'T UNDERSTAND why you're so worried. The house seemed perfectly normal."

Father Zebulun resisted the urge to roll his eyes at the younger priest's naivete. Instead, he counted to ten and kept his voice pleasant and reassuring. Father Simon blinked at his clear agitation.

"I may have nothing to worry about," Father Zebulun reiterated as he slipped off his vestments. "But what you said about the house—particularly *that* house—is of concern."

"I just don't understand how." Father Simon slipped on his raiment and glanced at the clock. Forty minutes till Mass. "It seemed a perfectly ordinary house—give or take her odd decorating style."

"What did you say you saw on the coffee table?" Father Zebulun prompted.

Father Simon sighed. "A Ouija board. But—goodness, it's near Halloween! Sometimes a game is just a game."

"Ouija boards are never games," Father Zebulun said sternly. "And after her conversation with me, and her taking holy water home—I want to be sure she's not doing anything foolish."

Father Simon shook his head mildly and Father Zebulun exhaled slowly. His friend didn't believe in the same things Father Zebulun did—

and who could blame him? Father Simon was born and raised in Milton; he was used to the supernatural being a tourist trap. He was a local priest who had never left Massachusetts, nor felt any desire to.

But Father Zebulun had a different calling.

He waved goodbye to his colleague, thanking him again for covering the Mass. He frowned as he stepped into the sunlight and headed towards the center square. He didn't like the weather today. It was far too sunny. Milton's best weather was overcast or rain. It performed autumn beautifully, but there was something eerily *wrong* about bright, overly warm days in Milton. It felt like a false promise. Or a bad omen.

He had tried to arrive at his office early in order to get some overdue paperwork done before the Mass, but he realized he had forgotten his favorite coffee mug, the nice big red one that read in white letters, "Y'all Need Jesus". He would have to make do with the alternate mug he kept in his desk drawer, the one that declared, "This Might Be Wine"—funny, but it would have been funnier if it had been on a water bottle rather than a coffee mug. Father Zebulun felt sure that if he had flunked out of divinity school, he would've been an excellent Catholic slogan creator.

The storm last night had given him a bad feeling. An autumn storm, so close to All Hallow's Eve...that never meant good things. Particularly if Miss Emerie Fox was up to something.

He hoped, after a strong conversation with her, she would throw her Ouija board away. It was his own fault for not taking her conversation seriously. Most parishioners who complained about demons or ghosts in their homes had other things going on—whether it be leaky pipes or mental illness. That was why he had sent Father Simon to assist her.

That, and of course, strictly speaking, he wasn't supposed to deal with anything demonic or supernatural.

But after his colleague's report...after the intense feeling of *dread* during his contemplative prayer...and after that storm...

Father Zebulun knew when to trust his gut.

The Witch's Brew coffee shop was not far from the sanctuary, so as soon as the early Mass ended, he walked on over. The warm breeze *should* have dissipated his unease, but it only seemed to increase it. He noticed a small gathering of people in the center square, by the fountain. They were mainly young white men, a few he recognized from his congregation. He nodded at them politely and they looked blankly towards him. They wore polo shirts and khakis; most of them had crew cuts. Father Zebulun's pace slowed—he caught the stench of something rank as he passed. Like rotting eggs or decaying meat. It made his stomach churn.

His pace a little more determined, he crossed the street, entered the coffee shop, and purchased a simple Americano. He took a seat on the outdoor patio, so when Emerie arrived, she would see him first thing. As he took a fortifying sip of coffee, he noticed the group of young men had moved from the town square fountain. They now gathered in front of an indie bookstore called Irving Books. They held signs and what appeared to be tiki torches.

A protest? Father Zebulun adjusted his glasses. He couldn't see what the signs read. Maybe a controversial author had arrived for a book signing. He took another sip of coffee as he carefully observed the proceedings. The group stood outside the bookshop. One man waved his sign and shouted something.

The priest wondered if he ought to go over. He knew the proprietors of the bookstore—the Golds. A wonderful old couple who moved to Milton after they sold their successful publishing company. They opened Irving Books as a leisurely retirement activity, as they loved collecting books. Marvin Gold knew Father Zebulun collected rare editions of G.K. Chesterton books and *always* called him first when he found something obscure.

A cloud passed over the sun and Father Zebulun choked on his coffee. One of the young men backed away from the store, picked up a brick, and flung it at the front window.

It was not a good throw. The brick clunked against the door, which made a nasty mark on the wood. Father Zebulun placed a twenty-dollar bill on his table and strode across the street.

The young man had ashy blonde hair and pale blue eyes. He wore a red baseball cap with an incredibly offensive message emblazoned upon it. His friends hooted at him for his poor throw. Determined to regain their approval, he picked up a glass beer bottle, and cocked his arm to fling the bottle once more. But before he could release it, something snagged the bottle out of his hand.

He nearly toppled over. Furiously, he whipped around to see Father Zebulun calmly throw the bottle himself—into a nearby recycling bin.

"Just what do you think you are doing, young man?"

Father Zebulun's voice was quiet. A few of the other youths craned their necks to try to hear. The young man quailed for a minute and then stiffened.

"What's it to you, *priest*?!" He spat at Father Zebulun's feet and called him something that insulted his race and his religion in one fell slur.

Another young man, who also had blonde hair and blue eyes but a squarer jaw, stepped forward. "We have the right to free assembly. Mind your business, *Father*. We have the right to free speech!"

Father Zebulun regarded them. He could see their signs more clearly. The messages ranged from vague to blatant—their country was under siege, immigrants were pouring in, their way of life was under attack… nonsensical hatred under political slogans. Father Zebulun had heard this sort of inane rhetoric before.

"The Golds are friends of mine," he maneuvered in front of the window, to block the shop fully, "and I suggest all of you clear out immediately."

"Get out of the way, priest!" the square-jawed one bellowed. "Or you'll regret it!"

As if to demonstrate this point, the young man in the red cap went to the recycling bin and pulled out the glass bottle. He smashed it against a lamppost and held it up threateningly.

Father Zebulun's expression betrayed nothing. "Put that down, young man."

"Get out of our way."

Father Zebulun started. There was someone in the back of the crowd, who stood next to the red capped man, now brandishing the broken bottle. He was not particularly noticeable, but his features were handsome and entitled. He wore a white polo and khakis, and he was indistinguishable from the rest of the boys—except his arrogant expression was vacant and glazed. His head lolled around his shoulders. The priest's eyes widened.

"Get out of our way. You cannot stop us."

He'd spoken again, but the voice—Father Zebulun was sure of it—did not come from him.

"You did this? You're inside them?!"

For the first time, Father Zebulun actually sounded angry. The young man's head flopped forward until it stared at the ground. But the shoulders jerked up and down, like a puppet on strings. He was laughing.

"We do nothing, priest. You should know that. We do nothing. We simply amplify what is already there."

It was the "we" that was the giveaway. In a horrible instant, Father Zebulun was terribly aware of what was wrong with this man and why these hateful boys were here.

There were demons loose in Milton. And this one—the one controlling the young man in the white polo, the clear ringleader—had sensed the entitlement, the dissatisfaction, the selfish hatred in these boys...and took clear advantage of it. Demons could do nothing on their own. They could only build on the foundation of hatred already there.

"Get out of our way!" The young man in the red cap jabbed the broken bottle in his face. "We won't ask a second time!"

"I would strongly suggest," Father Zebulun said, "that you step away from this shop. Young man, there is clearly a demon among all of you, exacerbating your sins; therefore I will offer sympathy and will guide you towards atonement. But do not test me further."

The young man lunged at him, jagged glass aimed for the priest's throat.

————

Samael was being impossible. For whatever reason, he flat out *refused* to meet with Father Zebulun. So Emerie went to the Witch's Brew by herself.

She had not particularly wanted to go to the priest. She fully intended to blow him off for their coffee date. But due to Zephyr's refusal to help, Sunflower's incapacitation, and the knowledge there were at least three demons running loose in Milton—she was in dire straits.

She bought a black coffee to try to wake herself up (she didn't get much sleep last night—who could when there was a demon reading through her *Lord of the Rings* books in the middle of her living room?) and for a brief shining moment she thought perhaps Father Zebulun had reneged on their date. But that didn't seem likely. She walked onto the patio and leaned against the glass window. She pulled a small notebook from her bag and started a list:

DEMON JAILBIRDS
Samael
Azazel

Emerie tapped her pen against the notebook thoughtfully. *When in doubt, make a list.*

So far, there were two demons loose in Milton. One was sort of contained at her house—though she couldn't be entirely sure of Samael's motives, but she felt confident he wouldn't hurt her.

Azazel was a different story. She needed to figure out a way to contain him and send him back to Hell. Perhaps Father Zebulun would have some ideas...

She paused her pen's journey. It occurred to her that the one person who might have good advice...was her grandfather. Ji-Ji. He knew an uncommon amount about spirits and gods—or at least, stories about them. She felt sure he would have some solid advice.

Several raucous shouts raised Emerie's attention. She saw Father Zebulun across the street. He stood in front of Irving Books, a small gathering of white men surrounding him. They held tiki torches and signs with messages that made her stomach churn and her fists curl. Suddenly nervous for him (nothing frightened her more than a crowd of angry white men), she ran over.

"Are you okay?" She shouted at the priest. He looked at her with real fear on his face—but not for himself, she realized. For her.

The crowd slowly turned from Father Zebulun to pin her with their glassy stares. The leader seemed to be in front—he held a broken bottle. A string of drool hung from the corner of his lip. His eyes rolled back and she stepped away from him as his body *rippled*, as though there was something *crawling* under his skin.

His head swiveled robotically towards her. The young man bared his teeth. *"My conjuror."*

"Oh, shit." Emerie took a step back.

"Miss Fox?!" Father Zebulun demanded. *"What did you do?!"*

Emerie stared at the crowd of young men. She looked nervously over her shoulder and scuffed her foot on the pavement before she finally spoke.

"Hey, Father Z? I'm pretty sure these guys are possessed."

"OF COURSE THEY ARE POSSESSED!" Father Zebulun thundered. "HE JUST CALLED YOU HIS CONJUROR!"

"Silly little conjuror...she did not shut the gate up tight."

Father Zebulun still blocked the door. One of the boys tried to get past him and Father Zebulun shoved him away. The rest of the group stared at each other blankly.

"I absolutely did not conjure him!" Three young men (who all had blonde crewcuts, and were utterly indistinguishable) approached her menacingly. She wished for her bokuto.

"I don't even know—I don't even know what's *in* him."

"Legion." Father Zebulun shoved another young man away from the door. "A demon. He goes after...mobs. Groups of idiots that want to stir trouble."

"Well, I conjured *Samael,* not this freeloader!"

"You shouldn't have conjured anyone!"

Without warning, a bald man with a neatly trimmed beard thrust his fist forward into Father Zebulun's jaw. Emerie cried out in horror—but Father Zebulun barely blinked. He didn't even seem to register the strike. Instead, he looked down at the assaulter with thinly veiled impatience.

"Good Lord," He snorted. "Who taught you to punch?"

The crowd converged on him. Emerie elbowed and kicked her way towards the priest. She swung her bag towards a stocky young man with an inane politician on his shirt. It landed squarely in his face. He recoiled and screamed in pain.

"Get inside the bookshop," Father Zebulun ordered her. "Tell the Golds to lock the doors and drag one of the tables against the doorway."

"Whoa, Father, I'm not just going to leave you—"

"*Now.*"

Without waiting for a response, he seized the door, grabbed her by the scruff of the neck, and flung her inside the bookstore like she was a naughty cat.

The wind was knocked out of her. She took a few seconds to find her breath again. Someone rushed past her and locked the door tightly.

"Hey," Emerie said weakly. "Father Z is out there…"

"We heard him." An older woman turned towards her. She had thick gray hair tied in a practical braid, and deep green eyes. She wore a chunky knit sweater with apples embroidered around the collar. Emerie noticed a small Star of David necklace hung around her neck.

"We're good friends with the priest." A portly man with thick glasses struggled past her and shoved a table against the door. "If he were in danger, he would have come in with you. That's why we left the doors unlocked."

Emerie glanced nervously towards the door. "But—"

"He's a good man." He wiped his brow. "Marvin Gold. This is my wife, Ellen."

Ellen waved at her a little mournfully. Emerie rose to her feet and went to the front doors. She could see a mass of bodies but she could not see Father Zebulun.

"What if they—"

"We've called the police," Marvin said. "They should be here any minute."

"Those boys," Ellen muttered. "We've had threats before, you know. They don't usually stray so far from their mothers' basements or their little chatrooms. No one takes them seriously. But we—"

She was interrupted by a knock on the door. The three of them glanced at each other. It seemed unlikely that a mob would knock.

Marvin went to the door and opened it. There stood Father Zebulun. He looked completely unruffled. The mob had disappeared.

"I'm sorry for the ruckus, Marvin," he said in a pleasant tone. "Please feel free to give the police a detailed report of those hooligans. Now if you wouldn't mind, I'd like to speak to Miss Fox. Privately."

Emerie rushed outside. "What the—how did you—"

"Let's take a walk, Miss Fox."

FOURTEEN

"YOU BETTER EXPLAIN YOURSELF, YOUNG LADY."

"Explain myself?!" Emerie spluttered. "You explain *yourself*! How the hell did you take down a mob?!"

Father Zebulun looked towards the sky, as though he were praying for patience. They walked down Cambridge, away from the bookshop. Town volunteers scurried about, winding autumn leaf garlands around lampposts and rolling out carts and kiosks. Milton was preparing for the Harvest Festival—its busiest time of year.

"I trusted in the Lord," he said finally.

"Oh, *fuck off.*"

He glared at her. "This is not something to be glib about, Miss Fox. How many demons did you summon?"

Emerie felt this was an entirely unfair question. "I already told you, I only summoned *one*! The others are stowaways!"

"Miss Fox." Father Zebulun's expression contorted—Emerie could tell he was struggling to remain calm. "*How many are loose?*"

"Well—three that I know of," Emerie said reluctantly. She pulled out her notepad. "Samael, Azazel...and I guess whatever possessed those boys..."

"Legion." Father Zebulun paused at the curb to allow three men rolling a kiosk **FRESH CANDIED APPLES!** to go by. "I told you. It is called Legion. Legion is attracted to mobs. Crowds of stupid people with entitled resentment."

Emerie took a step back. "Hang on. How do *you* know so much about this? You told me demons were—outdated! Like nowadays, they were alcoholism or depression or whatever…"

"I did not deny the existence of demons, I simply said our context had changed in modern times." Father Zebulun started to cross the street then stopped again with a sigh—another group of people were rolling a kiosk that advertised face painting. "That is the church's current stance!"

"Well, maybe the church could have warned me a little better!"

"It should be common sense not to summon a demon!" Father Zebulun closed his eyes and took a deep breath. "Never mind. You need to take me to your house right now."

"Um…" Emerie watched a woman across the street argue with someone who had a large pickup truck full of hay. "What are you going to do, exactly?"

"I'm going to ask the demon currently occupying your house if he'd like to have tea," Father Zebulun snapped. "What do you *think* I'm going to do?!"

She blinked at him. "So—exorcism? Seriously? That's a thing you can do?!"

"*Yes.* And if you'd come to me sooner, I—"

"I did come to you!"

"Enough!" Father Zebulun stopped short and raised his hands. "We cannot argue about this now. You are right. I should have stepped in sooner and *you* should not have dabbled in something about which you have no knowledge. But that is neither here nor there. There are demons loose in Milton. We have to exterminate them."

"No argument." Emerie sighed. "I'll take you to my house. Follow me."

She felt a vague pang in her chest when she thought of the priest exterminating Samael. He hadn't possessed anyone or tried to cause a riot. He was just sitting in her house reading books, minding his own business…not dissimilar from his actions before she summoned him.

But he was a *demon*. She couldn't just let him be.

Could she?

———

The stench of sulfur interrupted Samael from the third book in his fantasy series.

He frowned and marked his place in the book with Emerie's grocery list. He tried to get up from the easy chair and immediately became paralyzed—his folded wings were awkwardly stuck between the cushions. With a grunt, he jerked himself away. His clawed wingtips tore a rip in the chair and he muffled a curse. That was one of Emerie's favorite easy chairs. He wrinkled at the brimstone scent.

"All right, who is it this time?"

A faint buzzing met Samael's ears. He tensed, and the buzzing grew louder and louder. He tried to follow the noise, following his ears into the foyer and looked up the stairs. All of a sudden, the noise stopped.

Suddenly, Samael was surrounded by a heavy black swarm of flies. He coughed, choked, and roared, swiping angrily at the pestilence. He stumbled blindly back into the living room and screamed several Enochian curses.

A throaty chuckle answered him. *What fun!*

The black swarm folded away from Samael and molded itself into a dark figure. He was a great deal taller than Samael; the crown of his horned head scraped against Emerie's living room ceiling and left a nasty oil spot. He was pale as death, with large, bulbous eyes and a horrifying mouth stalk where his nose should have been. His torso and legs appeared human, but his wings were the delicate transparent gauze of an insect. Despite his proboscis, he had something of a human mouth —lipless, but with thousands of tiny tongues and several needle-like fangs. He grinned at Samael and maggots squirmed between his teeth.

"Beelzebub." Samael's wings extended threateningly. "I guess I can't count on Azazel to deliver messages properly."

"On the contrary!" Beelzebub's voice was liquid; high pitched and slippery. "As soon as I received it, I got here as quickly as I could. Seems there is some confusion on your rank, Samael. It *has* been a while." His wings slid together; they sounded like rubber boots in manure.

Beelzebub. Lord of the Flies, Lucifer's right hand and key advisor, harbinger of pestilence and rot. He was older than Samael—not by much, but still older. Samael and Beelzebub each had a distinct revulsion for the other. Beelzebub found Samael's human-ish appearance, (along with his tendency to seduce and then possess humans) grotesque. Samael thought insects, particularly carrion flies, were equally disgusting.

But the truth was...Beelzebub *did* outrank him. (For reasons Samael would *never* understand or accept...) Still, Samael did not like to be pushed around.

"There's nothing for you in this house." Samael flicked his wrist and the curtains drew themselves, immersing both demons in darkness. "Try the local dump. Or a septic tank."

Beelzebub's eyes glittered. His gigantic compound eyes were by far the most jarring thing about him, even worse than the hairy mouth stalk —there was not a thing human about those eyes. They weren't animal, either...just a kaleidoscope of malice.

"The house is now mine. Orders from the top."

"Oh, come on!" Samael exploded. "*I was here first!*"

Beelzebub paid him no mind. He raised a limb (it was perhaps an arm, Samael could never quite tell with Beelzebub) and touched the wall. Bilious pus squirted from the limb and splattered across the wall, coating the beautiful cream walls in sickening ooze.

"We *just* painted that!"

It didn't occur to Samael he had said "we", but before he realized what he said, he realized the ceiling was moving. Or rather, the thousand iridescent shells of cockroaches that immersed the ceiling began to hiss.

"Oh, hell."

———

"So are you going to explain how you know about demons or what?"

Father Zebulun was certainly not going to explain. He was under strict orders from the Vatican that he was *retired*. He was not to have anything to do with exorcism. After his mistakes in Ukraine, after his dear friend Anton's death...

"Demons are not something to trifle with," he decided was a safe answer.

"Well, I get that *now*. You said—you said you were going to exorcise them, right?"

He sighed as they turned the corner onto Crenshaw. "I have to evaluate the extent of the damage."

Another safe answer. He was the only one at St. Julian's with the proper experience and know-how to observe the marks of demonic possession and summoning. As for exorcisms...he swallowed hard and quickened his pace.

"And then you'll go all Father Merrin on those bitches, right?" Emerie half-tripped over a crack in the sidewalk and he slowed his pace to accommodate her. "The POWER OF CHRIST COMPELS YOU!"

"It's more complex than that." Father Zebulun hated films about demons; they always made exorcisms seem so simple. Eighteen hours was considered a short exorcism.

"Furthermore, I may not be able to do it alone. I may have to call for assistance. And that gets...tricky."

"You seem like this is a pretty standard day for you,"

"It is not." His voice was close to a snap. "Not anymore. And we best pray the infestation is something I can handle, because if it isn't... The Catholic Church requires extensive proof of possession before they will authorize assistance."

"I haven't been possessed." Emerie pointed at her house—it was three doors down. "I mean, I guess those Neo-Nazis have, but—"

"Legion is a relatively minor demon. It was not hard to banish it, though it will in all likelihood find another mob to inhabit. It's actually far more concerning there even *is* a Neo-Nazi group in Milton..." They stopped in front of Emerie's house.

"What was the demon you originally summoned?" Father Zebulun knelt and dug his fingers into the lawn. He withdrew some of the soil and inhaled deeply. Graveyard dirt. This house was built on death.

"Samael. He was the one who was haunting my house." Emerie plucked a few blades of grass and tied them in a knot.

"There are symptoms with demonic possession." Father Zebulun took a few steps forward into her yard. He was hit by a wave of nausea

—he could *feel* the demonic presence wrapping around him like a strait-jacket. It was a wonder it didn't seem to bother Emerie! People could usually feel when places were contaminated by demonic sources.

"I would have to provide tangible evidence," he said wearily, and muttered a Hail Mary for good measure. "Photographs, video record-ings, or—"

The front door flung itself open and something came hurtling outside. A demon landed in a crumpled heap a few feet away from them, like a pigeon that crashed into a window.

Father Zebulun staggered. Humanoid demons were by *far* the most dangerous—and this one was no exception. He was a good seven feet tall, the color of slate, with tar-black wings. Horns crowned his head and a horrifying tail snaked along the ground by his feet. He was straight out of a John Milton play with hypnotic, seductive eyes.

Incubus. Father Zebulun had seen them before.

"Would he work?" Emerie asked Father Zebulun.

"BASTARD SON OF A WHORE TO LUCIFER I WILL FUCKING KILL YOU—"

"Yo Sam! There's a man of the cloth here, tone down the language!" Emerie shouted at him.

The demon whirled around in a fury. Priest and demon stared each other up and down. Father Zebulun took a tiny step in front of Emerie. His hand shifted towards the interior pocket of his jacket.

"You better not throw a crucifix at me!" The demon folded his ebony wings around his shoulders like a cape. "We're locked out."

"What do you mean *locked out*?!" Emerie started towards the door. Father Zebulun snatched her wrist.

"Stay back, Miss Fox. I will deal with the demon inside after I take care of this one." Incubus. Incubi preyed on young women and men, seducing victims with pleasure and lust…sometimes worse.

"Oh, for Lucifer's sake." The demon glared at him. "Trust me, altar boy, you got bigger problems than me."

"What do you mean?" Emerie stepped around Father Zebulun.

"I mean *Beelzebub* is currently inside and is intent on destroying your house."

As if on cue, something punched out the stained-glass foyer window.

The air around the house vibrated and there was a pungent stench of rotting eggs and urine. Before their eyes, piles of garbage appeared on Emerie's front porch, and Father Zebulun heard the distinct sound of something *chewing*.

Emerie screamed in horror and wrenched herself away from Father Zebulun. Ignoring both the demon and priest's bellows of warning, she sprinted to the front door. Despite what Samael had said, she easily yanked it open and disappeared into the dark entryway.

———

Emerie could not have been gone from her house more than a few hours. And yet, her home had become a hoard—piles and piles of garbage carpeted her hardwood floors, unfamiliar ammonia-scented clothing littered every table, and black flies buzzed around every antique light fixture. She choked back a sob when she entered her living room— curtains were ripped down and a thick layer of goo ruined her careful wall painting.

The smell of sulfur grew stronger.

Stacks and stacks of newspapers she'd never seen before littered her couch. She whimpered at the sight of the mess. She had absolutely no idea how to clean it all up and the thought that some nasty demon would ruin all of her hard work made her hyperventilate.

"*IDIOT!*"

Samael's voice was a harsh whisper-yell, like a mom chastising her kids in public. He wasn't exactly tiptoeing—the massive amounts of garbage and clutter all over the floor made that impossible—but his footsteps were careful. He snatched her arm and pulled her in the direction of the foyer.

"We have to get out *now*."

"I'm not giving up my house!"

"Miss Fox," Father Zebulun followed directly behind Samael, crucifix held aloft. "I'm afraid I must agree—"

"You know how much the down payment was?!" Emerie tried to cross the living room to get to the hallway. There were garbage bags in the kitchen—maybe if she started tidying now, she could get it manageable before Dylan came home…

"Did you hear me?!" Samael hissed at her. "*Beelzebub will devour you if you linger!*"

"Fuck Beelzebub!" Emerie shouted at the top of her lungs. "What kinda bills does that asshole pay? Get outta my house!"

There was an audible THUMP coming from the ceiling. Taking advantage of this distraction, Emerie waded away from Samael and Father Zebulun, through ankle-deep garbage, until she reached the hallway and stairwell.

It felt like she was climbing a slippery hill. She reached for the banister and recoiled when she felt how sticky it was. She forced herself up the stairs, ignoring the unpleasant squishes and smells she clambered through.

There was another loud THUMP-THUMP from upstairs. The attic. The demon wrecking her house must be in the attic. It occurred to her that rushing haphazardly into her attic (which was now an apparent hole into the netherworld) to lecture the demon turning her house into a landfill was perhaps not a wise idea. However, as with most of the reckless decisions she had made within the last couple weeks, she decided it was too late to stop now.

"*Miss Fox!*"

Father Zebulun was at the bottom of the stairs. He looked stricken and Emerie was almost touched at how worried the priest seemed. (Samael was right next to him but his expression was one of annoyance, not concern.)

"Get down here!" The priest attempted to stagger up the stairs after her and immediately fell.

"When you get eaten, don't come crying to me!" Samael shouted at her.

Emerie stepped away from them. The upstairs seemed less affected— she could see the floor and the stench wasn't as strong. She was a little nervous that she hadn't run into the demon who booted Samael from the premises. She walked towards the attic door and cautiously opened it.

Nothing sprang out at her. In fact, all was dark, save for a strange sort of gray billowing fog that crept down the attic stairs.

"The tear's grown bigger. The entire attic will be a gateway by sundown."

Emerie jumped. Somehow, both priest and demon had managed to make it up the Everest of garbage. She half-wondered if Samael had magicked them up here, but doubted it—the priest was giving the demon as wide a berth as he could.

"Something's coming down the stairs."

Father Zebulun was right—a dark figure crawled down the attic staircase in slow, stilted movements, apparently having trouble with the steps. It sounded like...hoof beats? Or coconut shells? Emerie was suddenly struck by a mental image of Monty Python and giggled in spite of herself. Father Zebulun looked at her.

Emerie cleared her throat. "Sorry."

"Don't bother with her." Samael snorted. "I've been trying to get her to take this situation seriously from the get-go with absolutely no luck."

Father Zebulun did not answer, only stared at him quite coldly. The three of them watched the creature clop down the stairs—its breaths were hoarse and raspy.

Father Zebulun opened his mouth, perhaps to bellow a damning condemnation of the beast.

"Wait!" Samael said suddenly. "Wait—I know him!"

Emerie stared at him in disbelief. Samael stepped in front of them, peering intently into the silver-gray smoke, which curled around the creature.

"Orobas?" Samael called.

The demon paused in its descent. Its head rose to face the four of them, at the bottom of the stairs, and Emerie was shocked to see the creature had the head of a horse. In all respects, it seemed to be the size of a Maine coon with hoofed back legs...but it stood upright. The torso was human too, but covered in velvety thick fur. Its eyes were somewhat alarming—bright green human eyes on a horse, which gave Emerie a terribly unsettling feeling.

The creature looked like it was about to speak, when suddenly it recoiled, as though being burnt.

"I command you, unclean spirit, whoever you are, along with all your

minions now attacking this servant of God, by the mysteries of the incarnation, passion, resurrection, and ascension of our Lord Jesus Christ—"

Samael howled in pain. Emerie watched, almost paralyzed, as Father Zebulun raised his crucifix and continued in a relentless, unforgiving tone.

"By the descent of the Holy Spirit—see the cross of the Lord, begone you hostile powers!"

"Stop!" Emerie cried. "You're hurting Sam!"

The words were startling. She had known it was his intent to exorcise the demons—all of them. But somehow seeing Samael crumple before her, to experience the ringing in her ears, the persistent, harsh, and cruel words of the exorcism...

"Not yet!" Emerie bellowed. "Just wait!"

Father Zebulun ignored her, his voice dark and terrible. *"Almighty Lord, Word of God the Father, Jesus Christ, God and Lord of all creation—I cast you out, unclean spirit, along with every Satanic power of the enemy, every spectre of hell, and all your fell companions, in the name of our Lord Jesus Christ!"*

The creature on the stairs wailed. Samael fell to his knees as he clutched his head. Emerie shouted again, her words incomprehensible. She tried to grab the crucifix away from the priest, but to no avail; Father Zebulun only held it higher. The entire house shook at Father Zebulun's words and she heard something deep within the bowels of the foundation.

Laughter.

"Something's wrong!" Emerie tried to say. "You have to stop! Father Z!"

The laughter rumbled through the house. Father Zebulun's exorcism marched on. The creature on the stairs began to smoke and Samael cried like a child.

Someone shoved past Emerie and snatched the priest's face. Zephyr Moon stared deeply into his eyes.

"SLEEP!"

At once, Father Zebulun fell against her, nearly knocking her over. She groaned in disgust and shoved Father Zebulun aside none too gently. Emerie stared at her in shock.

Zephyr glared at her. "Are you trying to destroy the entire neighborhood?!"

FIFTEEN

THE CREATURE HAD STOPPED HOWLING. It stumbled away from the attic staircase and looked up at them with an expression of utter betrayal. Samael grunted and Emerie helped him stand.

"I'm going to have *such* a migraine," he grumbled. Once he was relatively stable, Emerie knelt next to the priest and checked his pulse.

"You all are idiots," Zephyr hissed. "Can't you feel what's inside this house?! A simple little priest chant isn't going to do anything!"

"I thought you weren't going to help!" Emerie lowered her voice to match Zephyr's whispers. "I needed *someone*, okay?" She examined the priest carefully. Father Zebulun's breathing was deep and even. He really *looked* asleep.

"You all right, Orobas?" Samael looked towards the stairs. The demon glared at him in displeasure.

"I am feeling aftershocks of residual pain after a partially performed exorcism," the demon called Orobas retorted as it completed its descent down the stairs. "And I am extremely annoyed."

"Join the club!" Zephyr pointed at Father Zebulun. "Grab the stiff. We need to get out of this house."

She pointed at Samael who groaned loudly, but picked up the priest with ridiculous ease. He slung him over his shoulder like a sack of flour. Emerie, however, backed up against the wall.

"I can't leave this house. I can't let Beelzebub destroy it."

"There's nothing *you* can do." Zephyr didn't even bother looking at her; her attention was on Orobas, as though deciding what to do with him.

"I'm not going to abandon my home." Emerie's hands clenched into fists.

Samael's head tilted towards her. "It's my home too. I know it sucks. But Beelzebub is playing with us. We need to regroup. Figure out a plan to get it back."

His voice was surprisingly soft. She blinked at him, a little jarred the declared her house his home too.

"I just…I worked so hard on it." The words broke a little in her mouth.

"I'll help you fix it." Samael promised. He shifted Father Zebulun a little in order to extend his clawed hand towards hers. Slowly, she took it.

The moment was broken by Zephyr snarling at Orobas "Don't make me regret knocking him out. If you try anything, I'll happily finish the exorcism myself."

Orobas glared at her disdainfully. "I *never* betray my conjurer."

He shoved past Zephyr's knees to perform an elaborate bow before Emerie. She nodded awkwardly.

Zephyr pulled out a small plastic bag from her tote. It was filled with rock salt, the sort the residents of Milton put on their driveways and walkways after the first frost. She grabbed a fistful and approached the stairs.

"Hm." She considered the staircase. Somehow, in the last five minutes, the mess had grown *even worse*. It wasn't even a staircase precisely anymore. It just looked like a towering hill of garbage and refuse. Probably exactly what Beelzebub was going for. She looked towards Emerie.

"Any other way downstairs?"

"Uh…" Emerie considered. "I guess jumping out one of the bedroom windows—hey, Sam can fly us out!"

Samael glared at her. "I haven't flown in over two thousand years and I can't carry you all!"

Zephyr frowned. "Sam?"

"She has odd little naming habits." Samael shook his head.

"What if we tried the master bedroom?" Emerie looked down the hallway. "The window's next to a tree…"

Zephyr assented by striding down the hallway and kicking the bedroom door open. Emerie winced visibly at the mark on her door but did not respond—it seemed a minor issue compared to the rest of the chaos within the house. They piled inside and Emerie noticed something strange.

Her bedroom was untouched. The master bedroom had been the only room in the house that was completely unpacked, painted, and decorated. She had replaced the ugly floral drapes with delicate wispy curtains that floated in the breeze. She had torn down the tacky yellow wallpaper (odd wallpaper colors seemed to haunt the house as much as her poltergeist) and painted it a beautiful Tiffany box blue. (Dylan had protested that the color was "girly" and had been subjected to an hour-long rant on assigning gender to paint colors until he submitted out of pure exhaustion.) She had a few framed photographs on her walls (her father was an amateur photographer) and her bookshelves were alphabetized. The largest bookshelf had come with the house, a gargantuan chestnut behemoth, with a garish carving of a monster with seven heads, each lined with ten horns. Dylan had wanted to get rid of it as it "creeped him out", but Emerie refused.

There was no clutter, no garbage, and nothing carpeting her floor with chaos and refuse. Just an eerily cold stillness.

"Um…" Something unpleasant crept into her gut. Emerie edged towards the corner of her bed, where her bokuto lay. She slowly lifted it. "Guys…?"

Zephyr struggled with the window while Samael dumped Father Zebulun unceremoniously onto Emerie's bed.

"Help me open this!" Zephyr snapped.

"It's just—" Emerie took a further step inside. As soon as she did, the door slammed behind her and the room went dark.

It didn't make any sense. It was still daylight outside—sunlight should be streaming through her wafting curtains. And yet, it felt like the power had just been cut in the middle of the night. Emerie swallowed hard and raised her bokuto threateningly. She tried to push away one thought.

Trapped.

"Well, that's not good." Emerie squinted and tried to force her eyes to adjust. "Can anyone see anything?"

"We can."

Samael's eyes glowed amber in the dark while Orobas' green orbs had shifted to a burnt orange. The eeriness of their stares reminded Emerie they were demons…and though Samael clearly did not like Beelzebub, if the tides changed, Emerie and Zephyr were outnumbered.

It seemed Zephyr thought the same. "Emerie. Can you hear my voice? Come over here and take my hand."

The oddly calm voice unnerved Emerie—Zephyr sounded like a mom requesting her child come away from the bobcat in the alley. Emerie took a shaky step forward, keeping a wary eye on Samael and Orobas' unnerving stare, her bokuto not precisely aimed at them, but still between them. She reached out in the direction of Zephyr's voice, fingers groping for her hand.

Something cold and greasy closed over her fingers.

Emerie screamed. But before the shriek was halfway out of her mouth, she was suddenly slammed to the floor. She gasped for breath; tried to tilt her jaw away from the floorboard, but something relentlessly crushed her. She was somehow on top of her bokuto and it was jammed against her windpipe and abdomen.

Zephyr shouted something in a foreign language. All at once, the noontime sunlight burst through the window. The pressure lessened and Emerie twisted to see her attacker.

She would've screamed if she could breathe. Her brain wouldn't even process what she saw in the blazing sunlight—at first it seemed like a horrifying beast with gruesome insect-like features. But as the sunlight raked across its body, it suddenly shimmered and melted—it looked like a thousand centipedes, smothered across her body, skittering and sliming over her torso, pincers stinging any bit of exposed skin. The centipedes frightened her more than the fly monster; Emerie shrieked bloody murder, managed to strain her palms against the floorboard, and shoved herself away with all her might, bokuto swinging wildly at the menace.

As soon as she was on her feet, Zephyr snatched her wrist and pulled her towards the window. The witch bellowed something at Samael, but Emerie could not hear over the rushing in her ears. Before she could understand what they were doing, Zephyr yanked her next to her and they smashed through her upstairs window.

Emerie felt leaves and branches scrape her cheeks. Her eyes were squeezed shut, she still gripped her bokuto, and she braced for a painful landing. But all at once, their flight stopped and Emerie tumbled onto the grass. She blinked in confusion; it felt more like she'd tripped on a step instead of jumping out a second-story window.

"Come here."

Samael did not wait for Emerie to obey the command. He pulled her to him in an oddly possessive way and carefully checked her joints and muscles. He also traced his index claw gently down Emerie's spine, across her chest, and finished by poking her forehead. He even *sniffed* Emerie's bokuto. Satisfied, he nodded grimly.

"He's not in you. Good."

Emerie struggled to catch her breath. "Where's—"

The unconscious body of Father Zebulun landed next to her with a soft flump—much more softly than she would have expected. Zephyr winced a little; apparently levitating people was exhausting.

Samael was still uncomfortably close to her; Emerie stepped away from him, flushing a little. He noticed and smirked in a most annoyingly knowing way.

"Why does Beelzebub even *want* this house?!" Emerie burst out, turning away from Samael's smirk. "It's nowhere near the largest or grandest house in this town. There's nothing special about it."

"There is a fair amount of dark energy about the house," Orobas replied. "Many deaths occurred in the area. It could be a focal point of power."

Whatever *that* meant.

"How long will Father Z be asleep?"

As if on cue, they both heard the priest emit a loud and pained groan.

Zephyr nudged him with the toe of her Louboutin and sighed in exasperation.

"Okay." Emerie swiveled towards Orobas and Samael. "You two know each other. And that *thing* that just infested and kicked me out of my house!"

Orobas and Samael glanced at each other. Emerie tried not to stare at the little demon's gigantic equine head, though it was incredibly hard.

"We know each other," Orobas proclaimed. "Since time began and we were created within the heavens."

Zephyr nudged Father Zebulun with her shoe again, this time poking his shoulder with her spiky red-backed heel. "Orobas is a truth-teller, an oracle. Practitioners summon him because he's the most reliable—unlike most spirits, he never lies, never deceives, and has a weird sense of loyalty to his mortal conjurer."

Emerie cocked her head. "That doesn't exactly sound demonic."

"I already told you, I don't believe in what you deem 'demons'." Zephyr kicked Father Zebulun's back. "They're all just spirits to me. Cranky, lying, mischievous, *irritating* spirits from the netherworld no one has any business messing with. Angels and demons? Black and white morality? That's priest crap."

"Stop that."

Zephyr's efforts had been rewarded. Father Zebulun struggled to stand and massaged this shoulder where Zephyr's shoe had prodded. He breathed heavily and took in the scene: All five of them stood in the front yard of the house, which by all accounts, seemed relatively peaceful. He looked at the demons in alarm but seemed far angrier at Zephyr.

"Who are you?! What happened? Did you *cast on me*?!"

"What did you think *you* were doing?" Zephyr retorted, her hands akimbo. "Trying to exorcise three demons on your own? One of them *Beelzebub*? How stupid are you? You nearly destroyed the entire neighborhood!"

"I had things well in hand…" Father Zebulun's voice became a mumble as he looked toward the house again. He swallowed hard and backed away, pulling out his cell phone. He turned away from them and started talking to someone on the phone—in Italian.

"I need to know *precisely* the ritual you used to summon the demons. But we must leave here immediately."

Father Zebulun glanced over his shoulder at Emerie. "As soon as possible—and stay away from those two!"

He stepped in front of both Zephyr and Emerie, perhaps in an attempt to protect them from any proximity with Orobas and Samael. Orobas meandered over to Emerie's flowerbed and started digging through the soil, looking for earthworms. Samael stepped around Father Zebulun towards Emerie, purposefully disobeying him.

Zephyr rolled her eyes as she interjected. "*Obviously*, she used the Key of Solomon. The Key always summoned preachy spirits."

"Who are you calling *preachy*?" Samael's voice was the epitome of shock and offense.

"In that case, I can fix this." Father Zebulun gestured Emerie to follow him. "We need to leave this place. Right now."

Zephyr barked out a laugh. "*You* can fix this? Like you nearly fixed Beelzebub? I think this is out of your hands, Father."

"Indeed, which is why we need to regroup—" He paused for a moment. Emerie noticed his words became clipped and his brow became stormy.

"*Eccellenza, capisco che non sono più autorizzato a lavorare come esorcista ma questa è un'emergenza. Non penso possiamo aspettare che una squadra arrive da Roma...*"

Emerie watched agape. "I swear. I attract weirdness."

"I am not attracted to you." Orobas felt it necessary to clarify, which was something of a relief from the little horse-headed demon. "But Samael is. Samael has liked humans for a long time and admires your beauty and odd nature."

Emerie turned to Samael for confirmation of this fun fact, who in turn elbowed Orobas and hissed something in a language she didn't understand.

"She asked, I answer." Orobas stretched his horsey mouth into a smug grin. It was frankly terrifying; horses were not meant to grin.

"I didn't really ask—I mean—okay, oracle demon, does this mean more demons are going to come pouring out of my house?"

"Miss Fox!" Father Zebulun shouted at her. "*Do not interact with them. Stay away from them.*"

He returned to his phone conversation."*C'è un'infestazione a Milton. Una delle peggiori che abbia mai visto, si espande a vista d'occhio.*"

Orobas cocked his head towards Father Zebulun. "Hundreds. By the end of the week, thousands. By the end of the month, millions. They sense an opening to the mortal world."

Emerie cast a leery glance towards her house, which still looked quiet and unassuming. Zephyr clenched her fists.

"Well, what do *you* want?" Zephyr gestured towards Samael and Orobas. "Why are you with us? Why don't you go back to where you came from?"

Orobas regarded her coolly. "I wished to leave Hell."

Samael exhaled, but continued to watch Father Zebulun out of the corner of his eye. "Honestly, what makes you think that Hell is any more pleasant for demons than it is for humans?"

Fair point. Emerie thought.

Father Zebulun's voice boomed. "*Non c'è tempo. Dobbiamo occuparcene ora. Non posso aspettare le forze della santa coalizione.*" They all looked at him curiously as he abruptly ended his phone call. He ignored both demons and turned towards both Zephyr and Emerie.

"Who were you talking to?" Zephyr took a tiny step back, as though uncomfortable by his proximity. "The pope?"

Father Zebulun eyed both Orobas and Samael. His hand twitched towards his jacket. Emerie didn't like the look on his face. His expression was stony, as though he were deciding the best way to exterminate them.

Samael stared right back at him and to Emerie's surprise, he suddenly looked nervous—as if he could hear the priest's thoughts and knew it was well within his capabilities. He cleared his throat to speak.

"Look priest—don't do anything rash. Orobas and I won't harm anyone. I don't want the forces of Hell in Milton any more than you do."

"Don't you?" Father Zebulun's voice was almost a whisper.

"Of course not!" Samael's wings flapped out impatiently. "The princes of Hell have been a pain in my ass forever and I really don't want to get dragged into one of their little projects. They have no love for me either—why do you think I got booted from the house?"

Father Zebulun did not look convinced. His right hand edged further into the folds of his jacket, as though reaching for something. Emerie frowned—what was he trying to grab? A crucifix? Holy water? Whatever it was, it almost seemed to *scare* Samael.

"Look." Samael raised his hands in surrender. "Can't we—can't we make a truce? I won't eat anyone—neither will Orobas—and you don't—you don't do what you're thinking about doing. I can help you."

"Why on earth should I believe a demon's truce?" The eerie calm in Father Zebulun's voice was unnerving. Emerie looked towards Zephyr for explanation, but the witch seemed lost as well.

"Because I know the ritual to seal the rip between dimensions—and trust me. You need *me* to enact it. I was the first one summoned so I must be the last one to return to Hell."

Emerie looked at Samael in alarm—he hadn't mentioned *that* before. The demon stared resolutely at the priest and sure enough, Father Zebulun's hand faltered. He exhaled loudly through his nose and ground his teeth together. Finally, he spoke.

"All right. All of you—*all of you*—come with me."

SIXTEEN

"WHY DO YOU DRIVE A MINIVAN?"

Father Zebulun glared at his mirror. "It is *not* a minivan. It's the church's shuttle. We use it to transport our elderly congregants."

It sure looked like a minivan. It was the color of cat litter with a crusty orange carpeted interior and, for some reason, checkered curtains. There were stickers littered across the bumpers—Emerie's favorite read, "We Are Catholics, Sin is Futile, Prepare to Be Baptized." It was certainly roomy enough for two demons and Emerie (Zephyr called shotgun). Orobas immediately discovered the built-in icemaker and happily crunched ice cubes.

"Where *exactly* are we going?" Zephyr wanted to know.

"My house," Father Zebulun answered without looking at her. His hands were clenched tightly on the steering wheel.

"And what will we do there?" Zephyr stretched her legs against the dashboard and examined the minor scuffing on her heels. Perhaps it was an attempt to annoy the priest, but he did not comment.

"Take care of the infestation."

Emerie turned towards Samael, who was in the process of tearing the seatbelt buckle out of the seat. "What did you mean 'you had to be the one to enact the ritual to send all the demons to hell'?"

"Just what I said." Samael attempted to stretch the seatbelt over the bulk of his body but couldn't even get it past his right wing.

"You didn't tell me that." She folded her arms crossly.

"As I recall, I *told* you not to summon me!"

"It's easy to summon a demon." Orobas crunched an ice cube. "It is not so easy to send them back to Hell. As Samael said, it requires the first demon summoned to read aloud the banishing ritual. Not easily done."

Zephyr peered behind them. "That reminds me of an old folktale. Hershel of Ostropol—didn't he trick the king of the goblins that way? By lighting the Hanukkah candles himself?"

"Hershel was always a little shit," Samael muttered.

"Same principle." Orobas lifted the icemaker and shook it over his head. Emerie watched in fascinated horror as an eely tongue emerged from his horse-like mouth and snatched ice cubes out of the air. "Minor demons are simple enough to deceive. Not so with greater demons...and there are *several* greater demons loose in this town."

"Do you know how many?" Emerie fished her phone out of her purse. It was becoming clear she needed to forewarn Dylan.

Orobas lifted his magnificent equine head. "Myself. Samael. Azazel, Beelzebub...and perhaps—"

Something slammed into the roof of the car.

Emerie was flung backwards, practically into Samael's lap as Father Zebulun jerked the wheel and said something colorful that might have earned him a speedy ejection out of the seminary. Brakes squealing, the car veered towards the side of the road and lurched to a halt. Emerie realized they were now sideways.

"What the—"

A thunderous roar interrupted her. The inside of the minivan became oppressively hot and Emerie watched as Father Zebulun kicked his front door open.

"Everyone get out!" He snatched Zephyr's arm and attempted to drag her with him out the door. Zephyr half-heartedly tried to pull away, but suddenly gave in and followed his lead in climbing out.

"What's happening?" Emerie crawled off of Samael to try to kick open her own door. Samael stared at the roof of the car in something like realization. "What—"

There was a sudden ringing in Emerie's ears. It felt as though every-thing around her slowed down as an intense sweltering heat completely enveloped her. But before she could register what was happening, she was surrounded in darkness. It blocked her eyesight while something distinctly leathery grazed against her cheek. She was lifted, choking in the heat.

There was a powerful *BANG* and Emerie found herself tumbling into a drainage ditch. They were on the side of the road, past the suburbs of Milton in some of the neighboring farmlands. There were cornfields across the road. When she regained her bearings, she realized she was staring at the minivan—which was completely engulfed in flames. Samael folded his wings abruptly and dropped Orobas—he'd been holding him by the scruff of his neck. In an instant, Emerie realized Samael was the one who got her out of the minivan.

"*Whoa.*"

Father Zebulun seemed no more worse for wear, save for a large cut on his forehead. Zephyr, however, looked petrified. The color had drained from her expression and her dark eyes were wide as saucers, staring at the burning minivan.

Something was standing on top of the minivan. At first, it was hard to tell through the towering flames, but before long, Emerie saw something solid. It looked almost humanoid, with shiny black coal for eyes. Sparks and embers ran up and down its lightning-like limbs, and when it cack-led, smoke curled and she heard the pop and crackle of pure fire.

"HAIL, MY CONJUROR!"

A flash of blindingly white streaks of flame leapt forth, nearly singeing them all. Father Zebulun stepped towards the minivan, his expression filled with fury. Zephyr was completely frozen at the sight of the fire; she didn't seem able to move. Emerie had never seen her like this—all her self-assuredness had completely vanished. The witch collapsed to her knees and Emerie ran to her. She tried to help her stand and was immediately struck by how violently Zephyr was shaking.

The flame demon screeched with its pop-and-crackle laughter. "MORTALS, MORTALS, HOW I LOVE MORTALS—I WILL TURN YOUR BONES TO ASH, I WILL BLAZE THROUGH YOUR INSIDES, I

WILL CREATE A SACRIFICE UNTO ME—FOR I AM...**AMY, PRESI-DENT OF HELL!**"

Flaming coals rained down around them. Father Zebulun did not even acknowledge them. Zephyr buried her face in Emerie's shoulder like a child while Samael lifted a wing over their heads like an umbrella.

The fire...Zephyr's afraid of the fire!

Emerie blinked.

"I'm sorry...did you say your name is *Amy*?!"

The flame-demon faltered and directed its burning coal eyes at Emerie. The insanity of Emerie's question halted Zephyr's hyperventilating and Father Zebulun stared at her like she was crazy.

The demon recovered quickly. "IT IS I, THE PRESIDENT OF HELL, COMMANDER OF SIXTEEN LEGIONS—**AMY**!"

Emerie couldn't help it. She laughed.

This time *both* Zephyr and Father Zebulun stared at Emerie like she'd lost her mind.

"I'm sorry—Amy? Really? Is your best friend named Helen? Do you go to hot yoga and eat macrobiotic?"

This seemed to throw the flame-demon off once again, but Emerie didn't even give it time to respond. She was on a roll.

"Did you say you were the *president* of Hell? Did you win just this last election season? Who won the popular vote?"

In terrifying situations, there are a multitude of ways to react. Some people freeze, completely paralyzed, others launch into screaming hysterics. Emerie was no different—though her hysterical laughter could probably make an excellent standup comedy routine.

"Is there an electoral college in Hell? That makes total sense, actually, that's probably where we got the idea. Who did you run against? Do we need to call a special counsel to investigate your dealings with the Russians?"

Now Father Zebulun, Zephyr, and Samael were all staring at Emerie like she was completely mad. Orobas was chewing on the remains of a tailpipe.

The demon called Amy, however, was not as amused as Emerie.

"HOW DARE YOU MOCK MY POWER!"

"Is being president of Hell like being vice president of the country?

More a symbolic role where you don't really do anything but pose for photos and write children's books?"

There was a mighty *ROAR* and Samael's wing blocked Emerie fully from President Amy—the flame demon had apparently tired of Emerie's ridicule and had subsequently tried to flambé her.

In that moment, Emerie might have wondered why Samael had now twice stopped this demon from roasting her. But she was distracted by Zephyr running forward and jumping in the drainage ditch.

The witch plunged her palms into the trickle of a stream. *"Demons that have come into my home,"* her voice was low and dark, *"I do not stand alone. I banish you back to whence you came, for I am of Nature, of Light, therefore your bane! EXTINGUISH FLAME!"*

There was a strange gurgling noise and apparently out of nowhere, a huge, twisting, typhoon of water reared its head out of the drainage ditch. Zephyr rose with it, and flung her hands up towards President Amy. A wave of water crashed against the fiery demon and it howled in rage and pain. It whirled around towards her, blazing green and white.

But before it could set the witch ablaze, Father Zebulun charged forward. He drew something from his jacket—a large silver .31 revolver.

Emerie stared at him uncomprehending. What did he think a *gun* was going to do?! But to her surprise, Samael took a nervous step backwards. The flame demon also halted its attack on Zephyr.

Father Zebulun cocked the pistol and fired.

Emerie grew up in Texas. She expected the loud pop to crack through the air and hurt her ears. But she did not expect the air to compress, she did not expect the sky to turn ultraviolet, and she did not expect President Amy to be struck firmly and clearly by a simple .31 bullet. The air *vibrated* at the force of the gun and the entire company, excepting Father Zebulun, fell to the ground. There was a deep and powerful wail of agony from the fiery demon—but then, it vanished.

Emerie slowly turned her head to look at Father Zebulun. The priest's pistol clicked and he slowly returned it to his jacket. She heard him say one word.

"Two."

Zephyr staggered upright. "What the *hell* was that?!"

Father Zebulun ignored her and went to Emerie. He helped her stand

and frowned at something on her cheek—Emerie realized she had a small burn mark, along with a few bruises acquired during her escape from the car.

"Excuse me! Friar Tuck! What the hell did you do? What is that *pistol*? How did it take down a *demon—who the hell are you?*"

Emerie was curious about this herself, so she looked towards Orobas for information. Unfortunately, the horse-headed demon was fast asleep on a stray tire.

"Truth-telling wears him out." Samael shrugged.

Father Zebulun stepped onto the road and squinted. He nodded in satisfaction.

"We're not far from my house. We can walk the rest of the way. With luck nothing will interrupt us this time."

"I'm not going anywhere with you until you explain where that gun came from!" Zephyr tried to stalk towards him but winced—her right shoe was still MIA and the asphalt was not pleasant on her feet. "And how it can take down demons! This is Massachusetts! Do you even have a license for that?"

"It's not safe out here," Father Zebulun said evenly. "We must get off the road. Now."

———

The first thing Zephyr noticed about Father Zebulun's home were the animals.

The dogs made quite the racket as they walked up a dirt road towards a forest-green farmhouse. Close by was a three-story barn painted sky blue and a few acres of pasture. The area was bucolic, pastoral...peaceful. Zephyr was glad of it. The fire demon had sent her into a panic she hadn't experienced since she was young. Fire was the one element Zephyr would have nothing to do with.

A German shepherd, a collie, and a chocolate lab immediately ran towards the group, barking their heads off. The chocolate lab went straight for Father Zebulun, its movements graceful considering its three legs. The collie set to work sniffing each and every one of them, and when it was Zephyr's turn, she saw the milky-white film over its eyes—the collie was blind.

Meanwhile, the German shepherd went straight for Samael, growling threateningly.

"Easy, Goliath," Father Zebulun called to the German shepherd as he scratched behind the lab's ears. "It's all right."

He pointed at the collie. "That's Lucy. And St. Francis is the lab. You'll also see Apollos and Titus wandering around too…Goliath, I said *easy*."

Goliath shot Samael a mistrustful look and padded over to his master. Father Zebulun led them his front door, unlocked it, and gestured them all inside.

The inside was warm and welcoming, with knotty pine paneling and hardwood floors. Father Zebulun brought them into his kitchen, a sunny little room with plenty of space to cook and an excellent collection of port. Samael immediately helped himself to a bottle and dropped the still-snoozing Orobas on a purple beanbag that was presumably used as a dog bed. Zephyr smelled pine cleaner and cat litter—she was not surprised to see a couple of cats milling about. The cats immediately darted over to her; cats could sniff out a witch better than any Catholic. She was, however, deeply surprised by a floppy-eared bunny who scampered away from them, and a potbelly pig that eyed them suspiciously from the living room.

Father Zebulun cleared his throat. "Easter and Christmas. Some parents enjoy delighting their children with chicks or kittens or rabbits or piglets or puppies…and then regret it and wish to dispose of them. I…intervene."

He shooed a black cat off the island counter. The cat glared at him in deep offence and promptly leapt into Zephyr's arms. She sighed wearily before intoning, "It smells like a zoo in here."

"So is there…is there a plan?" Emerie leaned forward, resting her elbows on the countertop. "What did your priest buddies say? Are they coming to Milton?"

Zephyr's lip curled. Great. More priests. That was just what this situation demanded. The black cat purred in her arms and she scratched its ears. The black cat turned its golden eyes towards her and she mentally asked him his name.

My high priest calls me Dragon.

She bit her lip to keep from giggling. Of course the cat assumed Father Zebulun was a priest to its divinity. All cats were like that. Goodness...it had been so long since she'd had a familiar...she had a sweet orange and white familiar in high school she called Marigold who passed away while she was in college. The thought of giving her heart and magic to a new cat was out of the question. But with Dragon in her arms, it struck a pang of longing within her.

Dragon's high priest bent under the sink and pulled out a first aid kit. He crooked a finger at Emerie and she obediently went to him, seating herself on one of the barstools. He dabbed a bit of ointment on her cheek.

"They will be coming. But the demons won't wait for them and neither should we."

"Agreed," Samael called from across the room, popping open a 1984 bottle of port. Father Zebulun scowled at him but returned to his nursing, placing a bandage with cartoon princesses on it over Emerie's cheek.

"What are we going to do?" Emerie crossed her legs.

"*We* are going to do nothing." The priest turned to Zephyr and gestured for her to come to him. Zephyr ignored the motion and set Dragon on her shoulders before she reached across the island counter to grab the first-aid kit. She would take care of her own cuts and bruises.

Father Zebulun turned to Emerie. "You're already in quite a bit of danger, young lady. You are going to wait right here while I clean up your mess."

"Now hang on!" Emerie raised her hands in protest. "What makes your house any safer than mine? Aside from there not being a portal to Hell in your attic...you know what I mean! Demons can find me any place in Milton!"

"My house is...somewhat fortified from such influences. And it will be doubly so once I leave." Father Zebulun went to the kitchen pantry and began removing boxes. Emerie quirked her head.

"Ugh," Samael muttered as he took a swig of port. "Is that why I feel so nauseated here? This whole place reeks of priestly rites and crucifixes."

Father Zebulun looked at him frankly. "Of course, that one will have to accompany me. Unfortunately, he was right. As he was the first one summoned, he will need to be the one to enact the rite."

Zephyr snorted as she gingerly dabbed her forehead with an alcohol swab. Dragon rubbed his nose against her cheek and licked one of her cuts. "I'm sure Samael would be more than happy to provide that particular service."

"He will do it." Father Zebulun's voice was quiet as he withdrew a large crossbow from the cardboard box. "Willingly or unwillingly."

Samael took another swallow of port. Zephyr eyed the crossbow dubiously.

"Okay, priest, you and I need to chat." Zephyr looked at Emerie. "Would you excuse us, please?"

Emerie sighed. She looked at Samael who grabbed a bottle of chardonnay before scooping Orobas up by the scruff of the neck. They exited the kitchen and entered the living room.

Father Zebulun set the crossbow on the counter. Zephyr picked up one of the arrows and twirled it between her fingers. "I'm guessing you're not going to explain about the gun."

The priest averted his gaze. "Miss Moon, I assure you, it's not important. It is a limited tool I acquired through…less than scrupulous means. I'd prefer not to use it again."

Zephyr gripped the arrow tightly. "Well, that might not be an option. If that thing can really take down a demon—in one shot—"

"It has limited viability." Father Zebulun checked the strings of his crossbow. "And it's only one gun. One gun versus a thousand demons is practically useless."

"Fine, whatever. But regardless of that—have you noticed anything strange about Samael?"

"No more so than usual." Father Zebulun's voice was curiously resolute. Zephyr quirked a brow as he withdrew several brightly colored water pistols from his pantry and set them on the countertop.

"Okay, I admit my demon experience isn't much compared to yours. But Samael? Why isn't he attacking Emerie? Why hasn't he possessed her by now? Why is he—just *allowing* us to go after his brethren like this? Especially considering when we send them all back to Hell…I mean, he's going to be first in line." Zephyr lifted a toy water pistol between two fingers.

"Good." Father Zebulun pulled out a duffel bag and began to pack it. Silver knives, multiple crucifixes, water guns, the large crossbow—it was like something out of a B-movie. Zephyr was surprised she didn't see silver bullets.

"But that isn't *normal* demon behavior, is it?" Zephyr crossed her arms. "Azazel possessed my mother—but he seemed more interested in the house. Beelzebub took over Emerie's house, but didn't go after Emerie. These major demons are occupying *houses* rather than people and Samael is just letting them. Don't you think—don't you think something might be going on?"

Father Zebulun stopped and looked at her coldly. "Like what?"

"I don't know." Zephyr made a face at a picture of Jesus hanging on the wall. "Like I said, demons aren't my area of expertise. But Samael has developed an odd sort of protectiveness over Emerie—did you see him pull her out of the minivan? And protect her from that fire demon? That *isn't* a demon's modus operandi. Surely, you can at least see that."

His expression flickered for a moment. But then he returned to packing his duffel.

"Zephyr." His voice was methodical. "Demons are little more than spiritual vermin. Demons lie. It's what they do. They lie, they cheat, they load the deck, they twist words and meanings. Every year they get better at it and every year they seduce more and more people into their web. I do not understand the machinations of the demon Samael—nor do I care to. All I know is there is an infestation in Milton that must be purged immediately. They *must* be kept from hurting any more people—Samael included."

Zephyr raised her hands. "I'm not arguing with that. I'm just saying…there's a weird amount of organization in all this that concerns me. Negative spirits like this wreak havoc, they are chaos incarnate. But why did the great and powerful demon Amy target us so quickly? Have you had interactions with that demon?"

Father Zebulun slowly shook his head. "Not with *that* demon. But—"

"If something is going on—if these demons are *planning* something— then we'll need to—"

"Miss Moon." Father Zebulun faced her squarely. "You admitted to me yourself that you do not have experience with demons. And while I would prefer not to go into detail—I do. I know their machinations. I know how they operate. Demons do not *plan*, not in the way you and I plan. They may pledge their allegiance to Lucifer, they may be united in the destruction of humanity, but they have no concept of personal loyalty. They bicker amongst themselves, they consume each other for power and strength, they fight like wild dogs over human hosts. They—"

"That's exactly my point!" Zephyr shouted. "They're *not* doing that! We've been dealing with them one-on-one; don't you think an entire flock of demons would be *interested* in taking control of a priest or a witch? Why are we dealing with them one on one? Why didn't Beelzebub come after us? Why was he more interested in taking over the *house* than corporeal bodies?!"

"It doesn't matter." Father Zebulun zipped the duffle shut. "The bigger problem is Miss Fox's connection with that demon. Demons can be…alluring. They are excellent…seducers."

Zephyr watched him with a raised brow. "You sound like you have experience with demon 'seducers.'"

"Emerie's the problem," Father Zebulun's voice was heavy. "She does not see Samael as a demon. She sees him as…as her friend."

The kitchen door flung open and Emerie strode inside. She crossed her arms and glared at them accusingly.

"Stop talking about me behind my back."

Zephyr rolled her eyes. "Emerie, leave please. The adults are talking."

"If you think I'm just going to stay here while Milton is under siege, you've got another 'think' coming," Emerie shot them both a nasty look, "I said from the beginning this was my mess and I would clean it up. I don't just wait around for other people to do my chores."

"Miss Fox, you have no idea how dangerous a situation we're in." Father Zebulun pinched the skin between his two brows. "And you have no idea what dangerous company you're in."

"Look, I get that you don't like Sam—hell, I don't blame you, I'm not real sure about him myself." Emerie glanced at the doorway. "But I wouldn't be worried about him. I wouldn't be worried about Orobas either. They're—"

"They are demons." Father Zebulun strapped the duffle across his back. "They are dangerous. They—"

There was a loud crash coming from the living room, quickly joined by a cacophony of barking dogs. The three humans sprinted into the living room. Samael and Orobas stared at them like a deer caught in the headlights—Orobas had his hand trapped inside a pickle jar and seemed to be in a hopeless struggle with the jar. Samael pulled at the little horse as hard as he could in a futile attempt to help, but the jar would not release. There was pickle juice all over the hardwood floors.

"Did you cast some kind of spell on this jar?" Samael gripped the pickle jar hard enough that it was a surprise the glass hadn't shattered.

"No." Emerie rolled her eyes. "Orobas, let go of the pickles."

He obeyed and easily slid his hand out. Father Zebulun watched the exchange in fascinated horror. Zephyr grimaced as she shook pickle juice off her bare foot.

"See?" Emerie glanced over her shoulder. "Something tells me we can handle *these* demons on our own."

Father Zebulun did not respond.

———

Samael dropped Orobas like a sack of potatoes. The humans retreated back into the kitchen, presumably to debate how best to annihilate his kin. There was a deep stone fireplace against the far wall, several squashy armchairs, and an old-fashioned television. There was also a piano—smaller than Emerie's grand, but the sort of instrument a church lady might use to practice with the choir.

Orobas eventually went off to explore the rest of the house. He meandered into the kitchen and Samael heard the clink of dishes and silverware. He hoped the little horse demon would stay away from the kitchen knives. Kitchen knives and demons were always a bad combination.

Emerie returned from the kitchen and flopped onto the leather couch. Lucy the collie snuffled up to her and she rubbed the collie's ears. Samael could hear Goliath the German shepherd's claws clack against the linoleum in the foyer—the dog was pacing, probably filled with anxiety at all the strangers in his house, human and inhuman.

Samael went to the piano. Instruments rather fascinated him, the way they could convey a universal language through sound and tones. He delicately pressed on the keys and experimentally tried a chord.

Emerie spoke. "So, you play."

Samael flinched. He cast a dark look towards her and Emerie shivered at how his eyes glowed burnt orange in the shadows. "Heresy."

"Hell has heresies?" Emerie tucked her feet underneath her.

"Yeah," Samael replied and scratched a wing absently. "Six."

She adjusted a blanket around her shoulders. "What are they?"

Samael was distinctly uncomfortable. This was dangerous territory— the less humans knew about the machinations of Hell, the better. He tilted his head, listening for the priest and witch. Father Zebulun and Zephyr's voices remained hushed while Orobas still moseyed about in the kitchen. Samael heard the blender go on and off every once in a while.

"That's one." Samael nodded finally towards the piano. "Music."

"Music?" Emerie looked alarmed. "Seriously?"

Samael nodded. "Yeah. Dangerous."

"The organ music you played to scare me?"

Samael cleared his throat. "I wasn't supposed to do that...sometimes Hell looks the other way if you're trying to scare someone."

"I mean, I guess I could see why demons wouldn't like—the Mormon Tabernacle Choir and Handel. But what about those crazy heavy rock bands? You know, the ones that dismember animals and worship Satan onstage?" Emerie asked. She looked like a little caterpillar, completely rolled up in blankets. It brought a strange feeling to the pit of Samael's stomach, something he couldn't quite identify.

He snorted at her question. "Please. They protest organized religion, right? That's one of our best successes and they're rejecting it for something more honest. That is...dangerous to our cause."

"Your...best success? You came up with organized religion?"

"Of course we did." Samael's claws twiddled between G and G#. "A giant bureaucratic institution that preys on the vulnerable? That cares more about rules than people? Obviously that came straight from Hell."

There was a long moment as Emerie processed this slowly. "What about all the good things church does?"

Samael mashed two keys together into a discordant chord. "We're pretty good about spoiling that kind of thing."

And so it was. It was one of the easiest tasks a demon received; encouraging a false prophet to keep charity funds, helping a church hide their predator clergymen, convincing a young girl it was her fault her youth leader came after her. A stray thought, an evil impulse, a good intention—it was easy enough to let it sprout like a weed and defecate any form of morality the church promoted.

Father Zebulun and Zephyr entered the living room. Emerie looked over her shoulder at them.

"Your house is freezing!" As though to emphasize her point, Lucy clambered on top of her and looked at Father Zebulun reproachfully.

"It's an old house." Father Zebulun adjusted his knapsack. "Come on, everyone. It's time to go."

SEVENTEEN

THE HARVEST FESTIVAL was in full swing.

Milton's Harvest Festival wasn't precisely a Halloween party, though it did harbor those elements. It was more of a preliminary Oktoberfest combined with a carnival. The local breweries and wineries showcased their best vintages, people snapped gorgeous pictures they shared online, candy got tossed around, and many people dressed up. It lasted a full weekend and was the highlight of their town.

Because of the elaborate costumes and pageantry, few people looked twice at the demons who walked the streets of Milton.

They emerged from the Hell House. Most walked out the front door, though a few climbed down the scaffolding and one enterprising creature that looked like a giant, bloated moth, flew out the attic window. Few Miltonians noticed this of course, and those who did assumed the new twenty-something owner had hosted a Halloween Party the previous evening. (And my, how creative the costumes were!)

One such character had a particularly fearsome outfit. He had the wings of a giant wasp, papery thin, like large flapping sheets of butcher paper decorated with throbbing red veins. His abdomen swelled and contorted to the point where some felt certain it might burst. But as the creature moved among the townspeople, his body contorted and twisted.

The insectile skin bubbled and boiled and before long, the demon had converted itself into the figure of a middle-aged man in a suit.

In human form, he was fairly nondescript. The adjective *beige* came to mind—beige features, brown hair, shiny teeth, an expression that seemed plastically fixed.

This was Mammon, demon of greed and avarice. He ran the accounts of Hell and was the great inventor of capitalism. He was a prince of Hell, one of the few dastardly demons mentioned in the same sentence as God —"you cannot serve both God and Mammon". The desire for earthly materials, the commercialism of Christmas, and televangelists were among his proudest accomplishments.

He would have preferred to be dropped off on Wall Street or a more affluent area—but everyone had to start somewhere. It was Mammon who whispered the idea of the American dream, that everyone was on equal plane, and if you just worked hard enough, you could become a millionaire. Mammon could do just as much damage in a small New England town as he could do to the stock market in Beijing.

It was a pity there were no megachurches nearby. But the local court-house was almost as good. Everyone knew that human law ran on money. He glided into the Corbin Courthouse with ease—there ought to be a few public defenders to terrorize. In his crisp dark suit, he was indistinguishable from the majority of people within.

Another demon who hailed from the Hell House attic headed towards the old Milton Library. He took to the skies, so not many saw him (and those who did assumed he was some sort of new-fangled drone)—a demon of sloth called Astaroth. He looked like a nude man with vulture-like wings and rode a dragonish beast while carrying a scarlet serpent.

The library was the perfect place for this particular prince of Hell. By the time he reached the library, his dragon became a Hummer and his wings turned into a tracksuit. He entered the library confidently and instantly, every student within minimized their homework and pulled up cat videos.

———

Emerie was grateful for the pageantry of the festival. It would be easy to blame Orobas and Samael's appearance on the Harvest Festival's celebrations. Samael would certainly not be the only demon meandering about—literally or figuratively.

They tried to remain as inconspicuous as possible. Father Zebulun loaned Zephyr a pair of his sneakers which Zephyr wore, but only begrudgingly. They hastily disguised Orobas, haphazardly stuffing him into a cranberry pea coat.

"Paper mache!" Emerie told a curious mother as they walked down the sidewalk. "Check 'horse mask tutorials' on Pinterest. Super easy craft for the kids."

At her insistence, they stopped briefly at a coffee cart, located conveniently in the center square where they could scope everything out. Emerie bought herself and Sam caramel lattes. After much deliberation, Orobas requested mocha cappuccino with extra whipped cream and rainbow sprinkles. Father Zebulun abstained from coffee, instead choosing to glare at Emerie in deep irritation for indulging demons with coffee drinks while Zephyr sipped a soy latte.

"Okay." Zephyr surveyed their surroundings. "I don't see anything yet—which is weird. They should love this kind of crowd."

Emerie wiped Orobas' snout with a napkin (he'd immediately dunked his face into the drink). "Sam said he had to be the one to enact the ritual, right? So how do we do that? Can we do it right now?"

"Not right this second." Zephyr scrolled through her phone's contact list. "It would be helpful if I could find more witches to help...a full coven could take care of this a little easier."

Father Zebulun whirled around. "Excuse me? There will be absolutely *no* black magic in this town."

"Wait, is it black magic or an exorcism?" Emerie wondered as Zephyr took a deep breath to argue. "Or is there a difference?"

"*Of course there's a difference.*" Father Zebulun boomed and Zephyr gritted her teeth.

"Look, you sanctimonious ass, you were the one who needed this done urgently! A coven of women is the quickest way to do that!"

"Like your mother?!"

"You leave her out of this, you know she's useless!"

Emerie noticed Samael had slipped away from the group. She scanned about her quickly and spotted him across the street. He was talking to a middle-aged woman in spotless New Balance tennis shoes. He looked deeply irritated.

As Father Zebulun and Zephyr continued to quarrel, Emerie took a few steps back. She crossed the street to see what on earth Samael was doing—he appeared to be speaking with the woman.

She withheld a groan at the sight of the woman. In college, Emerie had worked front desk at a hotel and on sight, she *could tell* this was just the type of guest who would come downstairs and complain about the sheets on her bed being wrinkled. A blonde middle-aged woman, wearing yoga pants and a bright pink polo. Her hair was that awkward razor cut which just screamed she ate kale on purpose. Emerie noted several buttons on her shirt: KEEP THE CHRIST IN CHRISTMAS! and JESUS IS THE REASON FOR THE SEASON. This was the sort of woman who would complain viciously about a menorah display and thought taking prayer out of school directly caused school shootings.

"Yo, Sam!" Emerie called out. "What are you doing?"

Samael turned. He looked so alien, standing there on the sidewalk, ignoring the pedestrians who complimented him on his "costume." Alien and yet so...Emerie shook herself. What on earth was wrong with her? Demons weren't supposed to be attractive, they were supposed to be terrifying. Right? Father Zebulun's warning flitted through Emerie's mind and she swallowed her nervousness. Sam made to cross the street and rejoin her, but the woman grabbed his upper arm.

"We're at *war* here. There are children present, young man. You'd better rethink your costume choice next year!"

He jerked away from her and started towards Emerie. She tilted her head in question.

"What'd she want?"

Samael exhaled sharply. "Just wanted to invite me to her church and warn me about leading young people astray for celebrating Halloween. Oh, and to remind me that Dungeons and Dragons is a path to the devil. Like I didn't already know the path to the devil. Honestly. Where would I even find a dragon in Milton?" His tone was fairly light, and yet he still seemed more on edge.

"Sounds about right..." Emerie decided not to explain what a role-playing game was. "Look, are you really going to do this? Are you going to do the ritual for us?"

Samael looked at her. She was suddenly overwhelmed by the feeling of how ancient he was, how outside her orbit. His ember eyes held secrets she couldn't possibly understand and while she knew logically that Father Zebulun was right, she shouldn't trust demons...she couldn't help but do so.

"What do you think?" He folded his arms against his broad chest. Emerie felt a stab of annoyance.

"I think," she said as she led him back to Father Zebulun and Zephyr, who appeared to have resolved their argument, "that you're not as evil as you want to be. And I think you will help us."

He frowned at her but neither confirmed nor denied this. Emerie looked at the witch and the priest. "Okay, mom and dad, are you done flaying each other in public? Can we stop fighting and start coexisting please?"

"I am trying." Father Zebulun's tone was overly patient—the voice one might use to explain to a toddler why they couldn't crawl inside a dryer. "But we do not have the luxury of time. Beelzebub, Azazel...these are princes of Hell. High-ranking demons. They must not be allowed to linger."

"What the hell is a Prince of Hell?" Emerie felt it necessary to ask. She stuck her bokuto into the dirt and leaned on it like a staff.

Orobas opened his mouth to respond but Samael answered first.

"It's just a dumb ranking, Emerie. Hell is a bureaucracy, like every-thing evil in this world. They're stupid powerful and enjoy a level of prestige that is very undeserved."

Emerie was about to respond when she noticed Zephyr was frowning at the bottom of her cup. She looked like she'd discovered a gnat in her drink so Emerie peeked over her shoulder. She only saw foam and coffee grounds. But Zephyr seemed to see something more.

She looked at all of them. "I don't think this is an accident."

Father Zebulun exhaled through his nose. "Please do not tell me you were scrying with your coffee."

"Shut up and listen to me," Zephyr commanded. "Look. I'm a witch.

That means—that means shit doesn't happen by accident for me. Everything is intention and everything is intentional."

To prove her point, she brought her coffee cup forward to the rest of the group. Emerie blinked and realized the foam and grounds made a distinct pentagram. The realization sent a shiver down her spine and a choked giggle out of her mouth.

"Look!" Emerie was slightly offended. "It was not *intentional* that I accidentally created a portal to Hell in my attic."

"Not that!" Zephyr snapped. "The spirits. They've set themselves up in a...in a sort of arrangement."

Father Zebulun frowned at her. "Miss Moon, I already told you. This is an infestation."

"I'm not saying these spirits aren't vermin!" Zephyr crumpled her cup. "There are things here that are clearly here to cause havoc. President Amy, Legion, Orobas—no offense."

Orobas picked up a bright orange mushroom from behind a garbage can and took a large bite. Emerie blinked at him, perhaps considering telling him that particular breed of mushroom was poisonous—but she apparently thought better of it and turned back to the rest of them.

"But the bigger ones, like Beelzebub—he's *squatting*. Squatting in Emerie's house."

"So what?" Emerie fidgeted with the lip of her coffee cup. "Wouldn't demons be attracted to places like that? Haunted houses, I mean."

"Not *those* spirits." Zephyr shook her head. "I don't even think they'd stay in Milton that long—they'd want to go to bigger cities. They could do a lot more from there. But they're staying here and—look, it's strange that Beelzebub kicked us out rather than killing us."

"Miss Moon, what are you implying?" Father Zebulun's eyes narrowed.

"This sign in my coffee cup—it's an omen. The demons are trying to do something. They're taking over spots in Milton with a lot of demonic energy, a lot of bad history. They're preparing for a bigger spell—a bigger ritual. I think they're trying to summon something."

"This is ridiculous."

Father Zebulun clearly had heard enough. Zephyr's eyes flashed and she tossed her cup in the garbage can. They faced each other angrily—

the priest towered over her but that didn't seem to impress Zephyr one bit. Emerie watched them nervously. Samael looked at them with an inscrutable expression.

"You do not understand demons." Father Zebulun's voice was a forced calm. "You do not understand their motivations, what they do, who they harm. You don't even believe they're evil."

"I think we've established that I don't see the world as black and white as you do," Zephyr hissed. "and you're right—I don't know demons. But I do know witchcraft, and I'm telling you, they are planning on doing a little conjuring themselves."

"This is a theory." Father Zebulun gestured to her greenery design. "A supposal when we have no time for supposals. Milton is in danger. We need to dispel Beelzebub and the rest of the demons *now*, not chase after your black magic."

"We *need* to find the demon that's setting the stage! The person who's directing the demons to set up camp here!"

"Guys!" Emerie forced herself between them. "Seriously, my arms are too short to box with you both. We have to work together here."

"I'm attempting to do so, Miss Fox." Father Zebulun crossed his arms over his chest "However, if Miss Moon refuses to follow my lead and declines to acknowledge my superior experience at handling demon infestations—"

"Oh, that is *it*!" Zephyr kicked his sneakers off and furiously stuck her remaining heel back on. "I'm out of here. I'll find the caster of this myself."

"Oh, feel free!" Father Zebulun said sarcastically. "I'll simply save the townspeople of Milton on my own."

"No, no!" Emerie attempted to grab Zephyr's sleeve, but she shook her off angrily. "We can't split up! Horror movie rules, people! Bad shit happens when the group splits up! Right, Sam?"

Samael was hardly paying attention—instead he was staring at the Corbin Courthouse with that strange look on his face. He sighed a little bit at Emerie's appeal. "It doesn't matter what I say. The priest and the witch don't trust me like you do."

His tone was neutral—it did not indicate whether or not Emerie was right in trusting him.

"Depending on the expertise in expulsion and eradication," Orobas intoned as he retrieved Zephyr's crumpled coffee cup from the garbage, "separate groups may eliminate more demons from the town. However, it may also be easier to entrap us in the end." He took a contemplative bite out of the Styrofoam cup.

"I'm telling you, Exorcist rules here!" Emerie crossed her arms. "Never be alone with a demon, that's when Regan breaks your neck!"

Samael looked at her. "Haven't you broken that rule about thirty times by now?"

Emerie didn't have a response to that. But it didn't matter. Father Zebulun had walked away from the conversation, apparently tired of the bickering. Zephyr was long gone, her purse swinging violently back and forth on her hip.

"Well, shit!" Emerie smacked her forehead. "What are we supposed to do now? Who do we follow, the Catholics or the pagans?"

Samael looked at her. "You're asking the wrong demon, Emerie."

———

What were the princes of Hell *doing*?

Somewhere along the line, Samael must have missed the memo. He *had* been stuck in Emerie's house for a while. But really, one-hundred and fifty years or so was barely a blip in the tormented eternity of Hell. And while Hell had many flaws in management, its reliable consistency was one of its virtues.

Demons—*especially* princes, like Azazel and Beelzebub—were not to show themselves to large groups of people. Targeting single individuals was fine, even encouraged, especially if the individual had a close, loving family. But this? Attacking cars, taking over houses, gathering crowds of people—that was *sure* to attract unwanted attention. They'd get the Vatican forces swarming in if they weren't careful, plus a thousand covens of angry witches.

Was that what they *wanted*?

Samael rather wished he could take one of the princes aside and ask for an update on current instructions, but that wasn't really feasible. It was a demon-eat-demon world in Hell—literally—and if you were left behind, that was too bad. But it was a little awkward, because Samael was a prince of Hell too.

He kept that quiet. He'd barely avoided utter annihilation by the priest and his damned cursed gun; he was not about to reveal this rank inconvenience to the rest of them. It was purely ceremonial, anyway. Well, sort of. It had its...perks.

Come to think of it, what on earth was *he* doing? Cavorting with a priest and a witch, hanging around the beguiling yet bewildering Emerie...he told himself it was purely for amusement and to regain control of the Hell House again.

But if more demons caught wind of it...he had no idea what he would do.

————

Father Zebulun watched the merry-go-round carefully and took note of every child that shrieked in delight. It wasn't uncommon for spirits to inhabit children—or demons to possess them. Children were rife with open possibility. They displayed a rare and beautiful vulnerability that engendered love and hope.

Evil *hated* children.

He sighed a little and pinched the skin between his brows for a moment. How on earth had he become mixed up in all this? He had sworn a long time ago that never again would he chase the darkness. And here he was, smack dab in the middle of it.

He supposed it was unfair to expect a quiet life after all he'd experienced—particularly since he'd chosen to retire in *Milton*, of all places. It was only a matter of time before something like this happened—but did it have to happen during his lifetime?

Something caught his eye and he sighed. He walked around the merry-go-round and took a seat next to someone who was hidden behind a copy of the *Wall Street Journal*. The pages of the newspaper riffled and the man next to him chuckle quietly.

"I heard you retired," the man remarked. He circled something with a red pen.

"You heard wrong." Father Zebulun crossed his arms. "And didn't I warn you what would happen if I ever saw your face again?"

"Undoubtedly." The man laughed and underlined the name of a columnist. "You'd send me back to Hell again."

"Well." Father Zebulun cleared his throat. "As long as we have an understanding. I can't let you linger, Mephistopheles."

The man lowered his newspaper. To the ordinary layman, he looked like an ordinary park-goer, someone who at first glance probably enjoyed cappuccinos and insisted on waiting for the tannins to develop in wine. Handsome, pretentious jawline, yet nondescript, like Joseph Quinn or Matthew Goode. But his eyes glinted disconcertingly. They were too dark for his complexion, for one thing. And far too clever.

"I mean, I can't say that Milton is where I wanted to rejoin the world," Mephistopheles said thoughtfully as he folded his newspaper. "I'd hoped for Manhattan. Or London. Tokyo, Beijing, Buenos Aires…I wouldn't even mind Kiev again. We had fun in Ukraine, didn't we?"

Father Zebulun did not answer. He stood up and heaved a large sigh. He then turned to face Mephistopheles.

"I will have to send you back to Hell," Father Zebulun said wearily. "Again."

"Hell?" Mephistopheles sniffed. "Hell hath no limits, nor is circum-scribed/In one self place, for where we are in hell, And where hell is must we ever be./And, to conclude, when all the world dissolves/And every creature shall be purified/All places shall be purified, All places shall be hell that is not heaven."

"I forgot how annoying it was when you quote your plays," Father Zebulun grumbled. "I cannot allow you to remain." His hand slipped into his pocket until it curled around his crucifix.

Mephistopheles didn't seem the least bit worried. "Shouldn't you be more concerned about my conjurer? After all, no one knows more than you how intoxicating the bond between conjurer and conjured."

"Stand, Mephistopheles," Father Zebulun said evenly. "Let's end this quickly."

Mephistopheles remained on the park bench. "Do you miss Lailah?"

The priest clenched his fist around the crucifix. His mouth went dry and he attempted to stave off the onslaught of emotion. The smell of lilacs, piercing violet eyes, an expression of sorrow and betrayal…

"Do you?" Father Zebulun asked quietly and *that* question finally seemed to irk Mephistopheles into standing. The newspaper was tossed carelessly to the side and Father Zebulun watched it ignite and flicker into ash.

"Careful, priest," Mephistopheles warned. "Even today, even now… still so insolent."

"Is this Love's chosen element?" Father Zebulun quoted quietly. "The fire o'er all my body stings me…But should I like, just once, to see you smile…"

"You're right," Mephistopheles tented his fingers. "Quoting my play *is* annoying."

Then he attacked.

It caught Father Zebulun off-guard. Mephistopheles was a dealmaker, a creature that existed between the fine lines of a contract, who rarely used his physical body for anything vulgar—and he considered physical fighting *particularly* vulgar. As Father Zebulun fell to the ground and struggled with the demon, it occurred to him that taunting Mephistopheles about Lailah right back must have *seriously* annoyed him.

Still, Father Zebulun wasn't entirely sure what the demon hoped to accomplish. It is never wise for something supernatural to attack a priest; like witches, they are nearly always prepared. Before long, Mephistopheles had retreated after being doused with holy water. Father Zebulun raised himself up on one knee, breathing heavily.

Mephistopheles' face broke into a smile. The holy water had pock-marked his face; he looked like a burn victim.

"Now, now, old friend. We lose our temper too easily! There's an easy way to settle this." He touched his face and the burns started to heal.

"I don't make deals with demons," Father Zebulun snapped. "Least of all with you."

"Fair enough, fair enough." Mephistopheles' face healed rapidly. "But this is a small deal, something even you could not turn down. I promise to return to Hell, quickly and quietly, on one condition."

"You cannot have my soul," Father Zebulun retorted. "Nor Emerie's, nor the witch girl's."

"Now, now now!" Mephistopheles raised his hands in defense. "Souls? Who said anything about souls? Nothing so dear as those. I know better than to try and barter souls with you, Boaz."

"You should know better than to try and barter *anything* with me," Father Zebulun growled. "I will not have it. You will return back to the shadows, fiend."

"All I ask," Mephistopheles plainly ignored him, "all I ask is the promise that Samael returns to Hell with me."

Father Zebulun paused in confusion. Mephistopheles grinned again, in a deeply unsettling manner. They watched the merry-go-round spin a bit. A little girl pushed a young boy off one of the brightly colored horses and he called her a swear word, realized Father Zebulun was watching, and both children guiltily apologized.

"What's going on?" Father Zebulun lifted his stern gaze from the children to Mephistopheles. "Are you...are the rest of you...*planning* something?"

"Oh, my!" Mephistopheles touched his heart in mock surprise. "Us? Work together? Plan something? Oh, you know how we all hate each other, how we enjoy devouring each other. And you know how deeply unpopular I am. If something *were* in the works, I'd hardly know."

"Do you know Samael?" Father Zebulun raised his crucifix. "Leave me out of your devilish politics."

"Only by hearsay. It's a small request, Boaz. If I must go, so must Samael."

There had to be some sort of trap in the words, but Father Zebulun could not detect it. Nor could he think of any way around the deal. It was imperative that Samael—along with all the bastions that had been unleashed—be banished back to Hell.

"I will say this..." Mephistopheles removed his hat and twirled it around his index finger. "Let's say there was something in the works, something I'm not allowed to be involved in because of my questionable loyalty—it would have to be *top brass* to force cooperation between all the princes of Hell."

"Listen well, fiend." Father Zebulun, batted the spinning hat away..

"*All* of the demons will be sent back to Hell. You, Beelzebub, Mammon, Orobas—and Samael. Princes or none. I can promise you that."

Mephistopheles' grin looked positively radiant. "Then we have an accord."

Before Father Zebulun could stop him, the demon seized his right hand and squeezed. White hot fire flooded Father Zebulun's veins and he screamed in pain and sank to the ground. When he regained his senses, Mephistopheles was gone.

EIGHTEEN

DEMONS MADE ZEPHYR NERVOUS.

She talked a big game about how they were all spirits to her, and she did truly believe that. However... ghosts were simple enough to eradicate—they were generally simple-minded, surviving on echoes of their former lives. What Emerie and the priest called "demons" were different. They were intelligent, sentient, and generally did not have good intent towards humans.

Zephyr had only come across a demon once, when she was a teenager. Her mother, the silly woman, had tried to contact her goddess but had completely botched the spell and channeled something far worse. It had taken nine castings and thirteen wards to clear the bad energy that had infected the house. Her mother hadn't even thanked her, too upset at her "interference." Sunflower often wavered between being deeply proud of her daughter's gifts and bitterly jealous.

Demons casting...demons summoning...what would they want to summon? More of themselves, surely...or something truly nasty. But why here? Why in Milton?

The Fall Festival was in full swing. Zephyr's hands fidgeted with her phone idly as she surveyed the area and opened all of her senses. If anything were amiss, she would know shortly.

For a long moment, she felt nothing, aside from the excited emotions of children and the patient exhaustion from parents. She inhaled deeply and the smell of crisp leaves and hot cider washed over her. Autumn festivals—*any* seasonal festival really—were excellent places to recharge.

Something brushed her cheek and she opened her eyes. There was nothing physically there—nothing except a path that led *off* the road and out of the town square. Zephyr's brow furrowed. That path led into the woods. It was one of the hiking trails, favored by tourists due to its zig zag through the forest and town which showcased Milton's best spots.

She felt a tug in her chest. Something wanted her to walk that path.

Her lips twisted slightly. That was the trouble with witchsense. You never knew if something positive or negative drew you, you only knew to follow.

Zephyr glanced behind her. She felt a brief pang of regret for storming away from the group, before she remembered her intense irritation with the priest. Never mind all that. If he didn't want to listen to her…if Emerie trusted a holy man over her…

She felt the tug again and turned back towards the path. A blonde woman bumped into her, power walking in the opposite direction and yelling at someone on her phone. Zephyr rolled her eyes and rubbed her arms. She threw one last look behind her before she took off down the path.

Zephyr regretted kicking Father Zebulun's sneakers off. Her heel sank into the soft earth, her other foot grew increasingly dirtier, and she tripped more than once.

Once she'd crossed the chapel yard, the path began to narrow and Zephyr could no longer hear the sounds of the Fall Festival behind her. There were fewer people too, though she strained her ears for the children's noise she heard earlier. All she heard was the territorial chatter of birds and the wind whistling through the autumn leaves.

She paused for a moment. Her heart hammered in her chest and her palms began to sweat. That wasn't a good sign. She was surrounded by forest. She *should* be in her element, she should be at peace. But the hair on her arms rose. The quiet around her was…unsettling.

Zephyr knew she ought to head back up the path and return to the festival. But the tug on her gut had not receded. There was something up ahead. She *knew* there was something up ahead.

It felt like she'd been walking for hours. Perhaps she had. Mysterious voices and eerie feelings tended to manipulate time and space for witches…she noticed the path had sharply inclined. Zephyr was half-tempted to give it up and go back to town—but her stubbornness won out, as it usually did. Raking her fingers through her hair, she continued up the path. Her ears pricked—the children's laughter. She heard it again.

Phantom calls in the forest…how obvious could you get? She shook her head in disgust. Nevertheless, she pushed forward, the forest shade closing in.

Zephyr reached a familiar clearing and exhaled slowly. She knew this place. They called this area the "witches' caves." She was barely in Milton anymore, she was almost in Framingham county. There was a cliff face around the Crenshaw creek, honeycombed with odd, manmade hutches. These were the real curiosity of Milton—perfectly rectangular, completely empty, and over two-thousand years old.

Sunflower used to take her here for picnics, breathlessly telling her these caves were a safe haven for witches, a sacred and ancient realm. Witches had run from the Salem witch trials and sought sanctuary in these stone hutches.

This was not precisely true, as Zephyr later found out. Historians agreed that some women did hide in these caves—but it was a stretch to claim they were witches. *Any* woman who was the least bit peculiar or independent could be denounced as a witch, and executed for her trouble. Witches, Zephyr believed, were far too clever to let a bunch of narrow-minded clerics exterminate them. Historians had no idea where the hutches came from, who created them, or what they were for.

Still, the clearing unsettled her. She paused and attempted to listen for whatever creature lay in wait. She heard no more phantom laughs, no bird chirps, no leaves' whispers.

Backing away, Zephyr turned to face the path that led her here. But before she could take a single step back to town, something struck her from behind.

———

"Here's a dumb question," Emerie remarked, a little dryly as they walked down the street. "If we find one of the demons, what do we do with it?"

Samael threw her an impatient glare. "First of all—I *am* a demon, Emerie. I don't know why you keep forgetting that. Secondly—it's probably best *you* do nothing. One hole to Hell in Milton is quite enough."

Emerie glanced at Orobas, who appeared to be eating a bicycle tire. She decided against asking where he'd found it.

"Do you know any handy exorcisms?" Emerie asked the little demon.

"I know all of the major and minor exorcisms," Orobas replied smugly, lifting his horsey head for chin scritches. "But they require more participants than an inexperienced human and a heretical demon."

Samael flinched. "I am *not* a heretic," he said crossly, "stop being so evangelical about those."

"Thus far, you have broken two of the heresies of Hell and are edging dangerously near a third," Orobas said matter-of-factly and Emerie rewarded him with more chin scritches. "Break three out of six, you are a heretic."

"What are the heresies of hell?"

Orobas cleared his throat but Samael quickly stepped in front of him. "You're not supposed to know them."

He yelped suddenly and glared downward. Orobas had taken a chomp at his leg.

"I *always* tell the truth to my conjurer," Orobas repeated righteously. "The six heresies of Hell are as follows: Love for humans, love for art, love for the Enemy, love of life over death, relationship over independence, and courage over fear. All are direct paths to anti-corruption, restoration, and redemption."

Emerie's brow furrowed. "I had no idea that Hell had—well—*rules*."

She considered some more. "Sam, you said music was a heresy of Hell...I guess that falls under the 'art' umbrella. And love for humans...I guess that means your failure to drag me to Hell or possess me or whatever."

"That's not *love!*" Samael assured her quickly. "That's just—me biding my time. It's all an elaborate plan to get you to trust me. Read Faust. Happens all the time."

"That's the German play with the guy who summoned the demon, right? Wait a second—*that really happened*?!"

"Faust summoned Mephistopheles properly," Orobas remarked, pacing as he lectured. "Had Faust accidentally opened a portal to Hell and unleashed legions of uncontrollable demons, Mephistopheles would not have protected him, he would have let them devour him. Therein lies the difference. Samael protected you, therefore—"

At this, Samael apparently lost patience with Orobas and promptly kicked him, the way one might punt a Yorkie over a garden fence. There was a great deal of force behind the action, so much so that Orobas went flying through the air. Emerie watched in brief horror as Orobas landed across the street. He didn't seem any the worse for wear, merely went on eating the bicycle tire, which had remained clenched in his little fist.

Emerie turned towards Samael, who looked sullen. "That wasn't very nice."

He opened his mouth to argue when something caught his eye. About a block away from them, a grubby-looking man had spread out a blanket. He pulled out a somewhat battered guitar and started to play. He sang along, harmonizing with the music his fingers expressed, something about autumn days and towns full of witches.

Samael looked enchanted. Or as enchanted as a horned demon with giant bat wings could look. Still, his wide eyes made Emerie smile.

"Milton has a lot of street performers." She tugged his sleeve. "Do you want to see?"

Samael's sweet expression vanished into his usual guarded manner. "Uh…"

"C'mon." Emerie grabbed his arm and dragged him towards the guitar player. She dug out a couple of dollars from her pocket and tossed it into the man's guitar case. He nodded towards her, breaking into a smile as he sang. Samael watched the man's fingers fly across the fretboard, utterly transfixed. Emerie couldn't help but find his wonder charming.

The man finished his song and looked up towards Samael. He grinned cheerfully.

"Want to try?" He held out his guitar.

Samael's eyes widened. He glanced at Emerie nervously, who nodded at him in encouragement. He also proceeded to look all around him, perhaps checking to make sure Orobas wasn't there to witness this indiscretion. He had little to fear. Orobas was currently dismantling a metal mailbox on the corner. He cheerfully ate the screws like popcorn and read the letters within with great interest.

So Samael picked up the guitar, a little awkwardly. He cleared his throat and strummed. He shivered at the vibrations.

"Put your two fingers here," the man directed, apparently unbothered by Samael's claws—or perhaps believing it was an elaborate costume. "Now try strumming."

Samael obeyed, wincing a little as the guitar buzzed unpleasantly.

"See that, that means your fingers are brushing up against strings they ain't supposed to," the man said. "Try again."

Samael tried again. This time, a chord rang out—Em.

"Good job!" Emerie clapped a little.

"Minor key is better than major." The man chuckled. "More honest, that's what I think."

Samael reverently handed the guitar back to the performer. Emerie put a couple more bucks in his case in gratitude. The street performer winked at her and began to play something new—it sounded like the intro to Ziggy Stardust.

"Get your boyfriend a guitar," the street performer advised Emerie with a wink. "He's got a lot of music in his soul."

Something between embarrassment and guilt washed over Emerie. "Oh, I mean, he's not my—"

"What does 'music in my soul' mean?" Samael wanted to know.

At that precise moment, Emerie's phone started to ring.

She looked apologetically at the guitarist and Samael and peered at her screen. Something panged in her chest uncomfortably. It was Dylan.

"Hi Dylan." She coughed. She noticed Samael scowl at the mention of her boyfriend's name. The street performer looked vaguely amused.

"Hi. Are you home right now?"

Emerie shook her head and then remembered she was on the phone; he couldn't see her face. "No, I'm out. There's a festival going on downtown."

"Oh. How are the renovations?"

Emerie glanced at Samael, who tapped his foot impatiently. "They've hit a, uh…snag."

"Snag?! What kind of snag?!"

"Well, we have kind of a…a pest problem," Emerie coughed again. "And I sort of made the problem worse."

"A *pest* problem?!" Dylan thundered. "Where? The kitchen?"

"More in the attic area…but now in the whole house…"

"Well, what are you going to do about it?"

Emerie bristled. "I've hired an exterminator."

"Yeah, like we have the money for that. We blew all our savings on that stupid house."

Emerie chomped the inside of her tongue to keep from reminding him that it was *her* savings at risk, not his.

"This guy is good." She scanned the area for Father Zebulun, but he didn't seem to be in her line of sight. "He's doing it pro bono."

"Why would he do that?"

"He's seriously…committed to Milton homes remaining pest free. Look, Dylan, I'm right in the middle of something. Can I call you back?"

"Hang on, Emerie, I didn't even tell you—"

She hung up. It was hard to have a domestic conversations in the company of demons. She needed to focus on closing the portal to Hell in her attic. She'd resolve things with her boyfriend after. She had to prioritize. What was the thing doctors had to do when deciding which parts of the body to operate on first after an accident? Ah, that was it—*triage*. Portal to Hell first, argument about the house with boyfriend second.

Emerie blinked. Samael had disappeared.

"Ah, crap!" She groaned. "Sam? Yo, Sam! Where did you go?"

———

Samael was in something of a pickle.

He had been glaring at Emerie as she talked to her lover on the phone, thinking sour and nasty thoughts—and then promptly wondered why it irritated him so. True, he had advised Emerie to dump the insipid mortal. Perhaps it aggravated him she wasn't listening. She *had* summoned him, after all. Why else would you summon a demon if not to gain its counsel? Or at the very least, his *services*. He was half-Incubus, after all.

Right at the moment Emerie started gabbing about "pest control," something had *yanked* Samael painfully. He had turned in outrage, thinking perhaps Orobas had sought revenge for the kick—when he realized he was no longer in the center of town. He was now standing in front of one of the oldest churches in Milton—the old Presbyterian church, where a minister had declared the town to be overrun with witches.

Samael blinked. Shadow travel...oh dear...

"Hi, Samael."

He flinched. Sure enough, it was *her*.

She was as beautiful as ever. The ancient perfume of Eden hung about her like a cloud. Hair the color of autumn, bright green eyes, creamy skin. She was tall and graceful, matching him height for height. Like him, her own wings were neatly tucked about her shoulders. Lilith hadn't changed at all.

Her expression held an odd sort of softness as she gazed at him. That was definitely not like her.

"What do you want?" Samael folded his arms and wings.

Lilith tried to look hurt, but her eyes glittered in mischief. "What do I want? I wanted to see you, of course. I was hoping you had broken out."

"I was the one who was summoned," he said shortly. "The rest of you lot are freeloaders."

———

Samael was in something of a pickle.

He had been glaring at Emerie as she talked to her lover on the phone, thinking sour and nasty thoughts—and then promptly wondered why it irritated him so. True, he had advised Emerie to dump the insipid mortal. Perhaps it aggravated him she wasn't listening. She *had* summoned him, after all. Why else would you summon a demon if not to gain its counsel?

Right at the moment Emerie started gabbing about "pest control", something had *yanked* Samael painfully. He had turned in outrage, thinking perhaps Orobas had sought revenge for the kick—when he realized he was no longer in the center of town. He was now standing in front of one of the oldest churches in Milton—the old Presbyterian church, where a minister had declared the town to be overrun with witches.

Samael blinked. Shadow travel…oh dear…

"Hi, Samael."

He flinched. Sure enough, it was *her*.

She was as beautiful as ever. The ancient perfume of Eden hung about her like a cloud. Hair the color of autumn, bright green eyes, creamy skin… She was tall and graceful, matching him height for height. Like him, her own wings were neatly tucked about her shoulders. Lilith hadn't changed at all.

Her expression had an odd sort of softness as she gazed at him. That was definitely not like her.

"What do you want?" Samael folded his arms and wings.

Lilith tried to look hurt, but her eyes glittered in mischief. "What do I want? I wanted to see you, of course. I was hoping you had broken out."

"I was the one who was summoned," he said shortly. "The rest of you lot are freeloaders."

Lilith laughed, high and clear. It almost sounded like church bells. "It's not our fault the mortal didn't know what she was doing. You know how strongly encouraged we are to seize every opportunity—or perhaps you don't. You haven't been below recently, have you?"

Samael shrugged. "I got stuck."

Lilith giggled again. "That is *so* like you, Samael."

He took a step away from her. Emerie was probably looking for him at this point…

"Samael." Lilith followed his footsteps, stroking his shoulders. "Now

Samael, I know you're frustrated with me. I don't blame you. But a thousand years gives one time to evolve. We ought to reconnect, you and I."

Samael snorted. "And break one of the Heresies? Relationship over independence?"

"The Heresies are ridiculous."

He looked at her, thunderstruck. "You came up with them! Right after you *dumped* me!"

Her lips quirked in amusement. "Are you still angry with me, Samael?"

He glared at her.

"Oh, my love!" Lilith attempted to take his hand but he wrenched it away, "We were all so young then. I came up with the Heresies for order. We were a *rebellion*, my love. Rebellions do not work without organization. The forces we fight against are quite unscrupulous, as you know."

"Has that changed?"

Lilith glanced at the church. "Not at all." Her voice became low with hate. "It has worsened, I think. The love for these *humans*. We must band together, now. You and I could do it again. We could challenge the status quo."

Samael started. "Challenge? What are you talking about?"

"Challenge Lucifer."

His mouth dropped open. He stared at Lilith, looking for any hint of amusement in her expression, but she revealed none. She was perfectly serious.

"Are you crazy?" Samael demanded finally.

"Lucifer is *losing*," Lilith impatiently flung her arms out, gesturing towards the town. "Surely you've noticed that by now. You've only been stuck two hundred years."

"Lucifer does not *lose*," Samael corrected, folding his wings about his shoulders like a cape. "Did you know he's here?! In Milton? He's aware of the portal to Hell and he *knows* you guys are spilling out everywhere! Do you think he's just going to allow us to rebel against him?!"

"He had his chance." Lilith's eyes glittered.. "Many of them, in fact. And all he has done is fail."

"Fail?" Samael said incredulously. "Look around, Lilith. This world is a mess. Lucifer is doing quite well, thank you. Wars, violence, humans hating each other because of their skin color, who they love, who they pray too…this is exactly what he wanted."

Lilith laughed bitterly and gazed up towards the church once more. "Oh, my Samael. You are so faithful. You always were, you know. It's one of the reasons I chose to be with you in those early days of the Garden."

"Until you dumped me," Samael reminded her flatly. "For Lucifer."

"You were wavering," Lilith said simply. "I did not have the luxury to entertain a weak-willed husband. At the time, we had to make a clear stand. You feared defying Michael, Raphael—you feared defying the Enemy."

Samael became quiet. He wanted to correct Lilith, snap at her that he'd hardly been *afraid*. But voicing the truth would be voicing a heresy.

He had not wanted to turn. He had not wanted to Fall, not really. He expressed doubt because he *loved* Michael and Raphael, not because he feared his brothers. And he loved…he loved…

But it would do no good to tell that to Lilith. Love was just a word to her.

"It hardly matters *now*." Once again, he backed away from her, and her expression tightened at the distance. "I *did* Fall. I chose Lucifer's rebellion. And after the great war, we were imprisoned in Hell while you scampered off with Lucifer to play with the humans. I don't forget abandonment, Lilith."

"Now who's breaking heresies?" Lilith demanded triumphantly. "You talk about 'independence over relationship,' yet you still hold a grudge over something that happened millennia ago? Besides. You got out yourself, you know, and were perfectly content wreaking havoc as well."

Samael had nothing to say. It was somewhat understood by demons the heresies were *impossible* to keep—but he was treading far too close to the line. No one wanted to be labeled a heretic.

Lilith smirked at his hesitance. "Oh, Samael. You've always hated to take sides. But there's a war coming, my love. This world does not belong to the humans and it does not belong to Lucifer—it belongs to *us*. And we have been kept away from it for far too long. Lucifer wouldn't have received any of his original support were it not for me. And I am tired of playing second fiddle. I didn't do it for Adam and I will not do it for Lucifer."

Samael jerked. "Wait—is Lucifer planning something in Milton? Has he set up the princes to enact—enact some kind of ritual?"

"Not while I'm here. The princes may be strong, but there are more of us than them. And if you, Samael—a prince of Hell yourself—turn from them…they wouldn't stand a chance." Her palm, soft as moonlight, caressed his cheek.

Samael swallowed. Lilith was conniving—she had always been extraordinarily ambitious, unafraid of anything or anyone. It was part of what made her so attractive. But she was vindictive. If something was in her way, she removed it, regardless of the cost. She was ruthless in her strategies.

The stories got her wrong. She wasn't Lucifer's right hand but she wasn't a hero to women either. She was somewhere in the middle.

Truth be told, most of them were somewhere in the middle.

"What about the humans?" His amber eyes flicked towards two women trying to distribute funnel cakes to their children. "What are your plans for them?"

To his satisfaction, Lilith looked confused. "What do you mean?"

"What are your plans for the humans?" Samael repeated. A little girl ran by them, gaped at Samael's wings, and shouted to her mother she wanted a pair.

Lilith's lip curled. She didn't need to answer. It was a stupid question to ask. Lilith was well known for her hatred of humans, and who could blame her? She was slighted by Adam and for all of her big words, Samael knew the heartbreak remained as fresh today as it did in the Garden.

"What a curiosity!" Lilith recovered herself quickly. "I do wonder *why* you're so terribly concerned about the matter—"

"THERE YOU ARE!"

Samael's heart sank. Sure enough, a furious Emerie Fox stormed towards him and snatched his wrist like a child.

"You can't just wander off!" She bellowed at him. "There are demons on the loose! We're supposed to get them *together*, not lone wolf it!"

Lilith's eyes widened. A wave of embarrassment swept over Samael, and he couldn't exactly pinpoint the reason why (though he couldn't help but be annoyed that once again Emerie had forgotten he was a demon.)

Emerie suddenly registered Lilith's presence. "Whoa, who are you?"

Lilith bristled. She *hated* impudence from humans. Samael took a tiny step in front of Emerie. Lilith caught the movement immediately.

"Well, well, Samael!" Lilith's expression was nothing short of murderous. "Your tastes seem to have changed."

"Oh, knock it off," Samael growled. "You've jumped to the entirely wrong conclusion."

Emerie sighed in exasperation. "Another demon?"

"You should be thanking her in any case." Samael tried to edge his wing forward in order to block Emerie, but she impatiently shoved it away, like an errant curtain. "This is my conjurer and therefore yours— she's the reason we're out at all!"

Lilith did not seem impressed. She glared at Emerie, who promptly glared back. Stupid human and her adorable fearlessness...

"I never would have thought." Lilith hissed, her eyes glowing red. "Samael the Accuser, Samael the Destroyer—all worked up over a little human girl."

"Who are you calling *little*?" Emerie's eyes flashed. "Sam, who *is* this?"

At the nickname "Sam," Lilith lost her temper. She screeched out a dreadful incantation. Samael watched in horror as dozens of venomous snakes emerged from the ground, heading straight towards Emerie.

"What the *hell*?!" Emerie cried out. She stamped a foot towards one and it snapped at her, its fangs digging into the heel of her boot. Another snake launched itself towards her, aiming straight towards her throat.

"*No!*" Without thinking, he rushed to her, lifting his arm to block the snake—

The snake was now in two pieces. The rest of the creatures hissed at him warily, but he backed off. Samael realized he was holding a sword.

"Where'd that come from?" Emerie asked dumbfounded.

The sword was golden. Flames licked its edges; it glittered in the sunlight and warmed his hand pleasantly. The sword positively *sang* as he raised it, as if rejoicing at its return. He hadn't seen this sword since Eden, since before the Fall. What—what did this mean?!

"It—it can't be…" Samael said shakily. "This was—this was taken away from me…"

Lilith stared at him in shock. He caught her gaze—he was bewildered beyond belief, but he lifted the sword towards her threateningly.

Lilith uttered just one word. *"Heretic."*

And then she vanished.

NINETEEN

ZEPHYR AWOKE TIED TO A STAKE.

Her first reaction was sheer rage at the cliché of someone or some-thing tying her to a stake. The second was registering how much her head *hurt*. God, she hoped she didn't have a concussion…

She was still at the witch caves. In fact, she was smack dab in the center of the witch caves; her stake was planted next to two of the largest hutches. The afternoon had turned golden and Zephyr could hear cicadas starting their chorus.

"This is a goddamn Monty Python skit. Are you spirits completely out of originality?" Zephyr struggled against the ropes. She couldn't see anyone. She swallowed hard when she realized there was a large stack of firewood at her feet. There were also markings in the dirt. She recognized some of them…it made her stomach churn.

"This is the lamest trap in the world…says the witch who fell into it…" She noticed her purse lying several yards away. Her keys…if she could reach her keys, maybe she could cut herself out. But she was tied too tightly.

"HELP!" Zephyr bellowed. "*SOMEONE HELP ME!*"

Only silence answered her and Zephyr wanted to cry in frustration. She squinted hard and mentally *threw* her cry for help towards anyone with an open mind. With any luck someone…*anyone* would hear her plea and be drawn to the witch caves. But how could no one be around? It was the Fall Festival for crying out loud, surely there was some family doing a little tourist trapping!

"Milton didn't even burn witches, you moron!" Zephyr screamed out. "They hanged them. And they weren't even real witches!"

Of course, the demon might not be going for historical accuracy. The demon might be aware of her greatest fear…her blood ran cold at the thought.

She tried to wriggle against her bonds, but the more she struggled, the more the ropes tightened.

"Look, you're not going to get away with this…" Zephyr said to her invisible assailant, with far more verve than she felt. "You've got about… I'd say five minutes to let me go before I *really* get annoyed."

The stake vibrated violently and Zephyr yelped in shock. She looked around her frantically, as far around her as she could. She took a deep breath and attempted to listen, both physically and mentally. Everything remained silent. But before she could cry for help once more, she felt the stake shift to the side, ever so slightly. Confused, she tilted her head upwards towards the sky.

Something was on top of the stake. A human face leered at her, its expression manic and gleeful. The thing had a strange chimeric body, somewhere between a lion and a goat. Cloven hoofs…with claws. Long, extended claws that wrapped around the top of the stake. Zephyr stopped counting the seven dragon heads, each with double split goat faces. His form *didn't make sense*. She averted her gaze. If a human stared directly at a demon like that too long, they would surely go mad.

"*We meet again.*"

"Azazel." Zephyr snarled. "Unbind me now. Or are you too scared to face me one on one?"

Her palms curled. So much of magic boiled down to hand gestures with intention…magic was fluid motion, as any dancer or artist could tell you. But while she was restrained, so was her magic.

"*Witch tricks bore me. Tis much more fun to keep you right here, where I can see you…*"

One goat face winked while the other opened his mouth—a long, slippery tongue slurped down to her jawline hungrily.

"Get your filthy tongue off of me!" Zephyr screamed. "What do you want with me?" She jerked. *A creek!* Her senses sang and she was so relieved, she almost didn't register the demon's answer.

"In ancient times, the practitioners of magic sacrificed themselves to me. They wrote their names in a book that signed away their souls."

"I am *no one's sacrifice.*"

She *pulled* at the creek and a swirling torrent of water crashed through the forest and slammed into Azazel, knocking him off the stake. Zephyr promptly threw up—the force and suddenness of the cast winded her.

But Azazel returned to his feet. He didn't even seem perturbed; more amused. "What can you accomplish, little witch?"

The seven dragon heads belched in unison. A ball of fire floated before them and a small, frightened sound came from between her lips. Fire.

She'd always hated fire. It was uncontrollable, angry, and wild— much like her own abilities. At eight years old, during a particularly fierce thunderstorm she witnessed a tree in their backyard get struck by lightning. It exploded into a blaze of flames that terrified her; she remembered feeling the heat through the glass of her window.

The worst of it was...she was never quite sure if she had summoned the lighting accidentally or if it was a natural occurrence.

The fire department had taken care of the inferno, but her fear remained. It was at that moment she tossed all her mother's candles and threw a fit if Sunflower tried to light a fire in the fireplace. Candle magic was out of the question, so Zephyr focused her abilities on the elements of water and air. But the fire issue remained a source of contention between them...a gap she'd never sought to bridge, especially after she moved out.

Azazel took a step nearer and then another—but before he lit her ablaze, he stiffened suddenly and crumpled at her feet. The ball of fire extinguished with a pop.

Sunflower stood over him, trembling violently. A silver athame, a witch blade, gleamed in the center of Azazel's back.

Cold fear flooded Zephyr. What the hell was Sunflower doing here? She struggled against her bonds. "Mom, get out of here!"

She was way out of her depth. For Sunflower, magic was essential oils, tarot reading, meditating, dancing with her friends underneath the full moon. It was not staring down demons or dealing with spirits. Least of all horrifying chimera-esque abominations.

Sunflower's hands shook as she knelt down and withdrew the silver athame from Azazel's flesh. She stumbled towards Zephyr and desperately started to cut away at the ropes.

"How—how did you—" Zephyr sputtered.

"I blessed it." Sunflower had cut away about a third of the rope. "I drew sigils and wards on it abhorrent to evil spirits."

She paused in her work a moment. "I—I heard your call."

Zephyr stared at her. "You did?"

Sunflower nodded. Her sweet, simple mother had never shown any sort of intuitive magic. But perhaps motherhood had its own magic. The Goddess had clearly led her here.

Azazel's dragon heads screeched like vultures. His chimeric bodies shifted and started to stand. Sunflower cast a frightened look over her shoulder and began to hack away at the ropes harder.

"Mom, please," Zephyr begged. "You need to run! I can take care of him myself, just get out of here!"

Sunflower opened her mouth to respond, perhaps a refusal to abandon her daughter—but was suddenly jerked away from the stake. Zephyr watched in terror as Azazel grasped her mother in its dragonish arms, flames licking the whiskers of each goat face.

"*All hail the great magician Sunflower,*" Azazel sneered. "*A knife in the back is all she's ever good for…*"

"LET HER GO!" Zephyr screamed.

"*Nay!*" The dragon heads began to drool in unison. "*Nay—you will watch us devour her, crunch each and every single bone, dance to every cry for mercy—then, and only then, will I set you ablaze, witchling.*"

The smallest dragon head went for Sunflower's throat. When its fangs sank into her throat, Zephyr Moon ignited.

The witch caves were suddenly engulfed in flame. Neither Zephyr nor Sunflower believed in Hell (Hell was a Christian concept, witches believed in a more complicated and layered spirit world which was morally gray) but it was impossible not to envision the flames of Hell all around them. Fire licked the trees and lava exploded from the caves. Azazel choked on the smoke and stared at the stake in confusion.

The remaining ropes snapped off Zephyr as she stepped towards Azazel. Her eyes had gone completely red and she walked through the fire untouched. Spaniel-sized lizards frolicked at her feet, each the color white and azure flames—salamanders, conjured from Zephyr's fiery rage.

"Release her."

Zephyr's voice was as harsh as wildfire, filled with smoke and power. It so startled Azazel the chimaera-esque beast *dropped* Sunflower like a sack of potatoes.

She lifted her arm and the flaming salamanders surged. The strange creatures fully covered every single misshapen head and opened their ember jaws. Zephyr watched expressionless as the salamanders fully devoured Azazel. The dragon monstrosity suddenly shrank into a pitiful black goat that bleated *"Mercy! MERCY!"* until the salamanders reached its head.

Then…only ash remained.

As soon as the demon was fully obliterated, the salamanders went out, like a blown-out birthday candle. The flames vanished into the ground and the lava cooled into black rock, certain to confuse local geologists for eons to come.

Zephyr ran to her mother. Sunflower's throat was punctured, but the bite was small. She marshalled the last vestiges of strength and placed her lips on her mother's neck. She sucked–although a myth humans can suck venom out, witches are able to extract dark energy from anything living. One, two, three, spit, one, two, three, spit, one, two, three, spit… her mother's eyes fluttered open.

"Hey mommy," Zephyr said softly. "Are you okay?"

Sunflower strained to sit up. "Did—did you do all this?!" Her eyes went wide at the blackened witch caves. Zephyr patted her mother's back, retrieving an embroidered handkerchief from her pocket. Sunflower coughed noisily into it.

Zephyr joined her in staring. "Yeah. I guess I did."

———

"Sam! Sam!"

Samael acted like he didn't hear her. He strode forward in a determined manner, but Emerie was fairly certain he hadn't the foggiest idea where he was going.

"Sam." She caught up with him. "Dude, you forgot your sword."

He glared at her. "Put that down, Emerie."

"I can't leave a giant-ass sword in the middle of the street," she argued. "That's dangerous. Someone could trip on it or a little kid could find it or something—"

"Humans can't pick it up," Samael said loftily.

Emerie glanced at her seemingly human hand, which held the sword easily.

"Well, they're not *supposed* to," Samael snapped. "This thing is just being contrary. I'm not taking it, Emerie."

"But didn't you say it was yours?"

"I said it was taken away from me, which means it isn't mine anymore."

"Well," Emerie said reasonably, turning the sword over in her hands. "Whoever took it away from you seems to have given it back."

Samael was quiet for a long moment. His expression hardened and he continued to walk forward.

"Hey!" Emerie fumbled with the sword's weight. "Don't get all broody and tortured on me. Despite what the YA books say, it's not a good look."

Samael sighed. "I just...I don't want it, okay?"

"Well, you saved my life with it." Emerie examined the sword, tracing an index finger over the designs on the pommel. "Speaking of which—who was the cranky chick that tried to Indiana Jones me to death?"

He blinked at her. "What?"

"The snakes." Emerie deadpanned. "Who the hell was that?"

To her surprise, Samael looked incredibly uncomfortable. "Um...that was Lilith. She, uh...she wanted to talk to me. She doesn't like being interrupted."

"Clearly. You know her? What did she want?"

Samael reached forward and took the sword from Emerie. In one fluid motion, he chucked it like a javelin. It sailed through the air and landed with a splash in the town square fountain.

"Make a wish," Emerie suggested.

"I wish to never see that stupid sword again," Samael grumbled. "Yes, I know Lilith. From a long time ago. We…were uh…."

Emerie stopped walking. "Involved? You dated?"

He wrinkled. "Demons don't *date*, Emerie. We…well…"

"I think I get the picture." Emerie radiated disapproval. "Well. She seems lovely. I see what you saw in her. Truly, she is the epitome of charm and grace."

"She's no worse than Dylan!" Samael growled in irritation. The sword had reappeared in his hand.

Emerie looked at him like he was crazy. "Are you seriously comparing my occasionally inconsiderate boyfriend with a demon chick that set a bunch of snakes on me?!"

"All I'm saying is they have similar personalities. Selfish. Inconsiderate. Unwilling to compromise." Samael flung the sword again. This time, it stuck itself neatly into the Baptist church steeple, much like a dart on a dartboard.

"Similar personalities?!" Emerie put her hands on her hips in outrage. "*She summoned snakes from the earth and launched them at my face.*"

"Undoubtedly—" Samael began to walk and roared in frustration as the sword, once again, appeared in his hand. "Undoubtedly, Dylan would be just as keen to exorcise me as Lilith was to destroy you. *I don't want the sword, take it back!*"

"Are you honestly comparing Dylan not liking haunted houses to Lilith sending her fanged minions after me?!" Emerie said incredulously. "That is the most ridiculous false equivalency—oh my God, Samael, stop throwing the sword, it's just going to come right back!"

This time, he had flung the sword high in the air. It pierced the clouds and disappeared from sight—maybe he aimed for the ocean. It became a speck in the distance and Emerie watched with a raised brow. Before she could say anything, Samael grabbed her arm and rushed away from the town square. Before Emerie quite knew what was happening, they had lifted off into the air.

She gasped and Samael's arms grasped under her legs, so he was carrying her. Emerie watched the town become miniature and choked as Samael flew through a cloud.

Under other circumstances, this could be rather enchanting. She could see the patchwork of autumn colors across Milton, the rolling green hills, and St. Julian's lit like a tiny dollhouse. But Emerie was too startled to really enjoy it and Samael flew like a drunk peregrine falcon. He nearly dropped her twice.

The Superman films have it wrong, she thought to herself grumpily, realizing she was completely soaked because Sam kept flying through clouds. She sank her fingernails into his arms for a better grip and he hissed in pain. *This is not romantic, this is TERRIFYING.*

He landed before her driveway with a thump and she scrambled out of his arms. Her heart was hammering against her chest and she glared at him. Samael didn't seem to notice, he was exhaling in relief.

"There," he said with satisfaction. "Now, we just—"

Emerie pointed. The sword had reappeared once more, this time in a nifty sheath attached to his belt.

"DAMN IT!"

Samael whirled towards her, as though it were her fault. But instead of raging about the sword, "Why are you even with him?"

Emerie was still reacquainting herself with gravity and trying not to throw up. "I'm sorry?"

"Dylan. Why are you with him? I've watched you guys for months. You don't enjoy each other's company, you don't have much in common, and you seem to have pretty different ideas of where your life is headed. What are you both doing?"

Samael, the relationship therapist. Geez. He sounded like her grandfather. Ji-Ji had met Dylan once, on a rare holiday excursion he'd taken while she was in college and had not been impressed. He pretended not to speak English the entire time and called him *saru*—a monkey who preened.

They had all the same classes together freshman year. Emerie and Dylan became so used to walking with each other and spending time together, it was only natural they became involved. They charmed each other as students—but when it came time to move on...Emerie realized she couldn't come up with a good answer.

"We just...we love each other." She shifted uncomfortably, trying not to think of the awkwardness of their most recent conversations.

Samael snorted. "When was the last time you had sex?"

Emerie gasped. "What does *that* have to do with anything? And also —none of your business!"

"You've been in that house for months, and I've never seen either of you—"

SMACK!

Emerie looked as shocked as Samael at the decisive slap. Her cheeks were stained pink and she looked simultaneously regretful and defiant.

"That," she took a deep breath, "is none of your business. Sex doesn't equal love. Furthermore, I can't believe you'd *watch*—"

Samael snatched her wrist and pulled her to him. His eyes blazed as he spoke in a husky whisper.

"What do you think I am, Emerie? Do you think I'm a little harmless lamb at your beck and call? I told you from the beginning exactly what I was, through the Ouija board. Of course I'd observe a beautiful woman and her lover. Though I'd hardly call him that. Not once did you do anything in that glorious bed but sleep."

Emerie stared at him, remembering the Ouija board conversation. Part Incubus...a demon of seduction. Of sex. She shivered at the intensity of his gaze.

"We've been busy." She hated how feeble her voice sounded. "It's been stressful since we moved..."

He smiled that terribly lazy smile, the one that made her feel like the ground was falling underneath her. "I can think of a lot of ways to relieve stress."

His clawed hand still clasped her wrist. Was he trying to keep her from slapping him again? Her whole body shuddered under his stare. Finally, after a beat, she wrenched herself away from him.

"Come on," she muttered. "We need to find Father Zebulun and Zephyr."

TWENTY

THE MILTON PUBLIC LIBRARY had an impressive statue out
front to greet patrons. A giant marble lion sank its dagger-length teeth
into an enormous serpent that coiled around its mane and torso. It was
one of the oldest sculptures in Milton and no one quite knew where it
came from. The librarians told curious visitors it depicted a scene from
an obscure medieval romance. Various religious groups believed it
depicted an epic struggle between good and evil. But most Miltonians
thought it represented two baseball teams that no longer existed.

Whatever the reason, no one expected the giant stone lion and
serpent to suddenly come alive.

Father Zebulun hadn't separated from the group long before he heard
a sudden screaming west of him. For a moment, he paid it no mind,
attributing it to the dunking tank that was usually set up outside the
library for the Harvest Festival. But when he heard the thunderous roar,
he knew immediately something was very, very wrong.

He withdrew a crossbow from his long jacket and took off toward the
library, sidestepping the panicked townspeople running in the opposite
direction.

There was good reason for this. The priest had never seen anything
quite like it (and he had seen a lot.) The lion was certainly *alive*; it

prowled in the front courtyard, tail twitching ominously. But it still seemed to be made of stone...every stride it made, Father Zebulun heard the scraping of cement. Its feet pounded along the courtyard steps like concrete and its stone muscles moved with pantherish grace. Its blood-red eyes narrowed as it stalked and something that appeared to be acid dripped from its mouth, sizzling as it hit concrete. The living stone creature suddenly crouched low—the monster was about to pounce.

The priest didn't ask questions. He raised his crossbow and shot.

The arrow landed with a satisfying thunk in the giant lion's thigh, but the creature looked at Father Zebulun as though he were a bothersome fly. Father Zebulun didn't waste another minute; he loosed another arrow and this time, it hit the monster directly in the eye.

The giant lion bellowed in pain. Its humongous paw lifted towards its eye in an attempt to rub the arrow out, but to no avail. Its paw slammed to the ground, causing a minor earthquake, and it roared towards the priest.

"Quiet, fiend," Father Zebulun murmured, loading another arrow. If he could *blind* the creature, then maybe—

But as he lifted his crossbow once more, a thought occurred to him. Where was the stone serpent?

The crossbow was abruptly knocked from his arms. The priest gasped for breath as something wound around his torso, squeezing the breath out of him. Spots floated in front of his eyes; he couldn't see what was happening.

"This is why people don't like priests."

The suffocation halted. He could still hardly breathe, but his vision slowly returned. A woman stood before him, leaning against the giant lion. As she came more into focus, Father Zebulun realized the formerly stone snake had wrapped its python body around him. He couldn't see the head of the beast, but he could hear its telltale hiss somewhere near his feet.

The woman gently tugged the arrow out of the lion's eye. She cast a reproachful look towards Father Zebulun and he took in her wavy auburn hair, the shape of her eyes, her creamy skin...

"L-lailah!" He gasped.

She clucked. "Wrong sister."

His stomach dropped. Her eyes were green, not lilac...this was Lilith.

The mother of demons, Adam's first wife, an anointed being...until she Fell. The stories varied on Lilith, but none of them were particularly pleasant. One such story stated she was the sister of the angel Lailah—the angel of night and darkness. They were supposed to be two sides of the same coin, polar opposites of each other...but with frightening amounts of power.

Lilith glared at him. "And what have you to do with my sister, Father? One of her little pets? Your sainted angels? You must have seen her before; few know how similar we look!"

The giant lion turned from them both and began to charge the library. The whole building shook and the priest could hear the terrified patrons within.

"Let them alone!" Father Zebulun choked out.

"They are hungry," Lilith snapped. "And I am not in the best of moods, priest, do not test my patience. Darling...you may have your snack."

For an instant, Father Zebulun wondered why Lilith had called him 'darling'. But then the snake's enormous head rose to his eye level and he realized who the endearment was directed towards.

The snake was coal black with the same flame-red eyes as the enormous lion. Father Zebulun's thoughts swam as he tried to think of a way out. But his arms were pinned to his sides—he had no way of reaching his crossbow, the Freischutz, even some holy water!

This was it. He would die and Milton would be cast into ruin because of his own blasted stubbornness.

The snake's jaws opened wide and Father Zebulun closed his eyes. But instead of being swallowed whole, there was a loud *BANG*. Father Zebulun fell to his knees and instinctively covered his face. An explosion of stones rained down around him and he staggered as he stood, trying to get his bearings. The snake was gone, but he was surrounded by rubble.

And Mephistopheles stood between him and Lilith.

The dapper demon tipped a feathered fedora to the fuming demoness. She seemed paralyzed in shock and rage. Father Zebulun had seen this sort of behavior once before—in Kiev. And it was directed *at* him, not in defense of him.

"You despicable little worm," Lilith hissed. "You would *dare* defend this human from my righteous vengeance?"

"Well, that's a rather obvious question." Mephistopheles flipped his hat off his head and twirled it around his index finger.

"You would side with this human against your own kin?!"

"Oh, in a heartbeat!" Mephistopheles assured her happily. "I rather like the priest, whereas you have always been a petulant harpy."

He took a threatening step towards her. "You may be older, dear sister…but you are none the wiser. The priest is *mine*."

Father Zebulun stared at the demon. He had heard these words before, but in a distinctly different context. Back when he had hunted Mephistopheles in Kiev.

He had been younger then, more foolhardy. Demons had overrun most of eastern Europe and the Vatican was losing exorcists left and right —mostly at the hands of Mephistopheles, one of the most vicious and clever demons in all creation.

In Kiev, Mephistopheles masqueraded as an exorcist priest himself— one of his most clever guises. He had as much access to humans as he wanted. At twenty-five, no one believed the green Boaz Zebulun that the priest he worked with in Ukraine was an ancient demon.

It was then he had the idea to fight fire with fire. He decided to use the medieval texts often used to summon demons for their own purposes. Zebulun's intent was not to summon a demon…but an angel.

The angel of night, guardian of conception, guide to the next world… Lailah. With auburn hair and lilac eyes, so similar to Lilith's human form…yet different. Lailah had none of Lilith's cruelty or malice, though her rage at being summoned by a human was fearsome indeed.

And…like young Emerie Fox…Father Zebulun's ritual malfunctioned. He ripped a hole to Heaven and Hell in the middle of Kiev and nearly jumpstarted the apocalypse.

All in an attempt to destroy the demon Mephistopheles—who now stood before him, protecting him.

"Shall we dance, Lilith?" Mephistopheles purred. "Shall we discover once and for all who has more power?"

A mighty scream ripped through the air. Father Zebulun clapped his hands to his ears and watched in horror as tawny wings burst forth from Lilith's shoulders. She arched her back like a raptor and talons erupted from her hands. Her head grew twice its size and her eyes almost appeared to melt into pits of darkness. Her button nose formed into a curved beak and her wings beat the air.

Father Zebulun watched the monstrous owl disappear into the clouds. He whipped around towards the giant lion and to his surprise, it had returned to stone—along with the serpent, somehow. Everything was as it should be, save the people still hiding in the library.

He turned towards Mephistopheles, who was dusting off his hands. "I did not need your help."

Mephistopheles arched a dark brow but did not answer. Father Zebulun considered taking him down now, while he still had a chance, while he was able to snatch the Freischutz...

He decided against it. "Why did you save me?"

Mephistopheles sniffed. "It is against my purposes to allow you to die at the hands of Lilith."

"Why should you care how I die?"

"I don't," Mephistopheles tossed him something. "I care how you live."

Father Zebulun caught it. In his hand were car keys—he blinked and realized his Cadillac (which was supposed to be parked outside his house) was right behind them.

"You better listen to the witch," Mephistopheles advised. "I'll grant you that us demons don't work together at the best of times...but she is correct. There *is* a plot going. Something I don't care to be a part of. I find it...distasteful. Earth is already overcrowded with evil, it doesn't need anymore, don't you agree?"

There was a great deal Father Zebulun wanted to say. The fact Mephistopheles had shown some sort of morality in saving his life—the fact the demon did not *want* the gate to Hell in Emerie's attic open— raised a great many questions he would have frankly preferred over a bottle of wine. Twenty years ago, they'd been enemies. Now they were... what? Allies?

He didn't have the luxury to turn the favor down.

———

"I don't like cheating."

Sunflower looked at Zephyr in surprise. She sneezed and Zephyr quickly removed her suitcoat and wrapped it around her mother's shoulders. Zephyr's teal pantsuit was probably ruined; the sleeves were singed (and still smoking), but it would keep her mother warm until they reached the shop. The temperature had dropped and the shaded forest path was enough to give anyone a chill.

"Cheating? What on earth do you mean?" Her mother snuggled into the suitcoat contentedly.

"You know," Zephyr sighed. "The magic tricks I could do. How everyone wanted to be my friend in elementary school. How I accidentally charmed my second-grade teacher into giving me the lead in the school play. It always felt like cheating."

"It's not cheating!" Sunflower's pale gray eyes widened in horror. She took her daughter's arm and squeezed it. "These are your gifts! Your talents! They're who you are!"

"Or who you wanted me to be."

There was another pause as they walked through the forest. Birds chirped above them and both women breathed in the sounds of the forest simultaneously—forests were grounding, no matter the amount of magical ability. Sunflower did not let go of her daughter's arm. Sunflower seemed to be mulling Zephyr's words over. They weren't far from the town—they could hear the sounds of the festival (and a few sirens, worryingly) from a few miles off.

"If you—" Sunflower's voice cracked and she tried again. "If you—if you never wanted to use your magic ever again…there's a way."

Zephyr tripped over a root and turned to stare at her mother in shock. "What?"

"There's a way. I know of a spell to…sort of stopper your magic. Freeze it, until your death, and it's released to another soul being born at the same time. If that is what you truly want…we can enact it."

"I already do that myself."

"Your masking." Sunflower's expression fell. "But it carries such a heavy toll, Zephyr. If you don't release it somewhere, it will...it will make you gravely ill."

Zephyr took a deep breath. "Mom—"

"It wouldn't have to be me!" Sunflower added hastily. "For the ritual, I mean. I know of—other witches. More—more experienced witches who could help. And you could have your life of...normalcy and—and *pantsuits.*"

She couldn't help but shudder and Zephyr laughed at the reaction. The trees began to space out as they grew closer and closer to the town. She considered her mother's offer and ruefully realized she'd burned her extensions off.

They reached the walking path which led to the town square. Zephyr knelt and picked up a stray soda can. She aimed and tossed the can into a nearby recycling can—across the street. It landed perfectly.

"If you'd asked me last week, I would've taken you up on it," she murmured. "Can't though. Even if we close the gate to the spirit world... even if we get rid of all these horrible energies and sprits...there's something about this town that doesn't sit right with me, Mom. It needs protection, and not just from Father Holier-Than-Thou. I have to keep my magic."

Zephyr took a shuddery breath. "I have to...stop hiding my magic. I have to be okay with it. Because you were right, Mom. It is who I am and for a long time I've been ashamed of it. But..."

She tilted her head upwards towards the October sky. "Maybe it was never me who had to hide my magic from the world. Maybe it's the world that needs to make room for me."

Sunflower's eyes shone and she grasped the sleeves of Zephyr's suit-coat tightly. "I...I oh my sharp mustard seed. My little fairy. My spring breeze."

"Ugh, no cutesy nicknames, Mom, you know I hate it!" Zephyr complained as they crossed the street. But she didn't really hate it. It reminded her of some of the better moments in her childhood with her mother...her mother's off-key lullabies, the sweets for equinox, her stories about the gods and goddesses...it was nice. Even if they fought like wildcats in an hour, at least her mother had offered her a way out, despite her pagan principles.

When they reached the curb, a Cadillac pulled up next to them. Father Zebulun blinked at them both and cleared his throat.

"Miss Moon." He nodded at her mother. "I believe…we should talk."

Zephyr crossed her arms over her chest. "Is it about how the demons are casting a spell and how you found out about it on your own instead of choosing to believe me and now you need my help?"

The priest winced. His pained expression satisfied Zephyr's pride and she nodded. She turned towards her mother.

"Mom, go home. It's time for us to finish this once and for all."

Sunflower's brow furrowed. "I want to help!"

"You'll help the most if I know you're safe at home." Zephyr took her mother's palms and squeezed them. "I love you, Mom. I'll be home soon. Get some of your cheap wine—we'll celebrate a successful cleansing."

Sunflower managed a weak smile. She hugged her daughter fiercely and Zephyr kissed her cheek. Then the witch brusquely got into the priest's car and they drove off to find Emerie and her demon.

———

"You guys are back!" Emerie exclaimed. "And not fighting! Awesome!"

Father Zebulun looked to have aged ten years as he slowly got out of the Cadillac. They had found Emerie and Samael near the town fountain. Samael sulked while Emerie ate a caramel apple and gave Orobas her core. Zephyr followed the priest out of the car calmly, with the air of someone who had been proven right and was about to let the whole world know about it.

"I was right," she announced to the company in a tone tinged with smugness. "They're casting. They're using ley lines to—"

"Wait, ley lines?"

Zephyr sighed noisily. "Remember the drawings you made in your botched attempt to get rid of Samael? Your house is on a ley line—a place of magical energy where you can draw from to cast. The demons are gathering on ley lines to—to cast something. Probably summoning."

Samael jumped up and yanked a sheathed sword off his belt. "Here, priest. Have a sword."

Father Zebulun examined it closely, but did not take it. "That is an angelic sword. I can't accept this. It will burn my arm off."

Emerie raised her hand. "I picked it up!"

Father Zebulun looked at her in disapproval. "Were you trying to give it back to him?"

She nodded.

"There you are," he said in satisfaction. "Though I'm not sure why a *demon* should possess an *angelic* sword." He glared at Samael suspiciously.

Zephyr stared at the priest. "How the hell do you know all this stuff?"

"And speaking of." Zephyr added, blocking him bodily. "Are you going to tell us about the gun? The gun that can apparently take down demons with ease, and yet you are somewhat reticent to use? Let me guess; it's witchcraft and you don't like being a hypocrite?"

"No," Father Zebulun snapped. He started to say something more but paused—a family with a large collection of pumpkin-shaped balloons walked by them. The dad yelled to Samael, "Great costume!" Samael tried to offer the four-year-old the angel sword but Father Zebulun quickly intervened.

Zephyr, however, was not about to let the conversation drop. "What is it? Can it help us disperse the spirits?"

Father Zebulun watched to ensure the family was out of earshot. He faced the group. "It is called Der Freischutz. An old weapon I received long ago. There are seven bullets. Six of them will always hit their mark. But the seventh…"

Samael finished the sentence. "The seventh belongs to Lucifer."

A cold breeze rattled the trees and Emerie shivered. Father Zebulun crossed his arms across his chest. Emerie could see one hand brush up against his shoulder holster.

"The seventh belongs to the Devil," Father Zebulun assented. "But it was never something I wanted to use regularly."

"You used one of them." Emerie pointed out. "On President Amy."

"Yes. Five bullets left."

The group digested this unpleasant information.

"Never mind," Father Zebulun flexed his fingers. "Miss Moon, I think it's time we assisted Miss Fox in getting her house back. Why don't we all return to her home and have a little chat with Beelzebub?"

TWENTY-ONE

HAD Emerie not abruptly hung up on Dylan, she would have learned Dylan had decided to cut his trip short and would be arriving at the Hell House that very afternoon.

He wasn't in a particularly pleasant mood. He couldn't stop thinking about the utterly magnificent apartment he'd discovered in Boston. It was just off Beacon Street and only four blocks away from his work. Sleek, modern, fully furnished—with a twenty-four hour maintenance crew on standby. He had begged the real estate agent to hold the apartment for them, just long enough to get Emerie on board—but they had refused. It had been now or never. Dylan had put down the deposit and first month's rent. Well, technically he didn't exactly...they didn't have a joint checking account, so technically *Emerie* put down the deposit and first month's rent. At least, he'd signed her name and used her bank details. He rationalized that once his name was on her bank account he'd be able to persuade her Boston was the right way to go. He'd been given one key—a key he vaguely planned on duplicating after a tough conversation with his girlfriend.

As he pulled into the driveway, he felt a twinge of guilt for overriding Emerie's wishes and using the last of her savings. He had tried to talk to her about the apartment, a few times now. He couldn't believe she'd actually hung up on him.

Dylan sighed. He let his car idle for a few minutes as he stared up at the looming house in front of him. They were at a crossroads, Emerie and he. She could either join him in Boston or not. And Dylan had a pretty good idea of what her choice would be…he'd better get a head start on packing now. Emerie would definitely want the flat screen, but he could sneak it into his car now if she wasn't home…

He stepped out of the car and walked up towards the front door. The neighborhood was quiet for a Saturday, something he attributed to whatever festival was going on in the main square blocking off half the routes to the house.

Dylan fumbled in his pocket for the key but realized with annoyance the door was unlocked. That Emerie…did she leave the back door unlocked too?

He entered the house and was immediately met by a miasma of stench. It smelled like death defrosted, a combination of rot, feces, and his middle school locker room. He retched a little and realized in horror trash practically *tiled* the floors—everything from old magazines, yellow-crusted shirts and towels, potato chip bags and half-full pizza boxes.

"What the *hell*?!"

He stumbled into the living room and rushed towards the window. He wrenched it open and took deep gulps of the fresh autumn air. What on earth had *happened*?! He'd known for years that Emerie was messy, but this was ridiculous…this couldn't all be Emerie. Did she have a party? For the Garbage Pail kids?

"Emerie?" Dylan shouted. "Are you home?"

No one answered and he scowled in frustration. He went for his phone in his pocket and fumbled a few seconds before he realized he left it in his car.

He started to wade back towards the front door and promptly tripped. He landed on all fours and squawked in pain—he'd cut his hand on something that felt like a knife. It turned out to be an old soup can with the jagged edge of the lid glinting in the sunlight. Dylan looked frantically for something to wrap his bloody hand in, but the questionable nature of the crusty, soiled clothes littering the ground made him hesitate. He also realized in surprise none of the clothes belonged to him *or* Emerie…in fact some of the trash seemed to be from things Emerie would never touch, like Bud Light cans (she hated light beers) and plastic gallons of two-percent milk (most dairy upset her stomach.)

His hand throbbed. He might require stitches—he needed to get to Urgent Care or an ER as soon as possible. He forced himself to stand and hobbled towards the front door. As he reached for the knob with his non-injured hand, he heard the unmistakable sound of the front door lock click.

Dylan stared in confusion. But before he could even try the door to verify he somehow had become locked in, despite the fact he held a key, a loud horrifying BUZZ ripped through the air. He turned around wildly and a thick cloud of black flies swallowed him completely.

———

"That's Dylan's car."

The group stopped short. Emerie looked at the priest and witch nervously. Samael ignored her comment and flung his sword again in a graceful arc, but as soon as it winked off in the distance, it reappeared in his hand. He sighed wearily.

Emerie wordlessly pulled out her phone and tried to call Dylan. There was no answer, but Emerie heard the faint sound of the Bee Gee's —Dylan's ringtone—from somewhere. She approached the car and saw his phone buzz against the driver's seat.

"He…must be inside…" Emerie swallowed. "What do we do?"

Father Zebulun quietly withdrew a crucifix. Zephyr flexed her fingers. Samael looked bored.

"I say, we pour a drink out for him and move on," Samael leaned against Dylan's car. "He was an annoying little prat."

"He might not be dead!" Emerie's voice cracked. "He might be—possessed! Or he might have run away!"

"There's only one way to find out." Zephyr swiveled on her heels toward the house. "Let's go."

Dread pooled at the bottom of Emerie's gut. She would never forgive herself if something horrible happened to him…she marched like a determined knight. She barely hesitated as she turned the doorknob—it was unlocked—and hurried inside.

To everyone's shock, the hoard had disappeared. The inside of the Hell House no longer looked like the underbelly of a dump. It appeared —*normal*—or as normal as it ever was. There was no rotting stench either, in fact, there was now a distinct lack of scent. No fresh paint, no sawdust, just…nothingness.

"Was it all an illusion?"

Zephyr asked the question they all were thinking as they cautiously stepped forward into the foyer. Emerie thought she would feel relief at the fact it was only an illusory trick of Beelzebub to wreck her house, but instead, she felt fear. What did this all mean?

"Do you smell that?"

Father Zebulun's voice broke through the quiet. Emerie inhaled through her nose and realized what she was smelling. The faintest, stalest scent of cigarette smoke was in the air and it came from upstairs.

"Sam?" Emerie whispered. "What's he doing?"

"He's…" Samael closed his eyes. "He's no longer feeding off the house. That's why it was a pestilent wreck, he was absorbing its energy. Now he's…absorbed something else."

Something else…something like Dylan.

With little warning, Emerie raised her bokuto and screamed like a vengeful samurai. She pounded up the steps, heedless of her friends' cries of warning. When she reached upstairs, she swung her bokuto wildly, furious at the fact she had no idea what to expect next. The smell of nicotine increased and she noticed the door to her office was ajar. She kicked it open and burst inside.

It was dark. The sun had started to set outside, but the lacy blue curtains Emerie had carefully chosen were drawn. The lace cast strange eye-like shadows on the wall. It was also *freezing* in the room, just as it had been in Zephyr's mother's room. Emerie nearly dropped her bokuto, she shivered so hard. And that was when she saw her boyfriend.

He was sitting in her chair, the lovely violet chair from the thrift store Dylan said belonged in a bordello, not in a professional office space. He was also smoking.

Emerie lowered her bokuto. He used to smoke in college, until Emerie told him she wouldn't kiss him again and he quit.

"Dylan?" she asked tentatively. "You okay there?"

"Emerie!"

The group had finally joined her. In that freezing cold room, it seemed like she'd been upstairs for hours, though it was only a few seconds. And at that moment, Samael *shifted*. His expression became less human-like and more otherworldly, his eyes became sunken black pits. His mouth widened across his face, revealing a row of needle-sharp fangs. His horns became rimmed with flames and he hissed at the silent, smoking figure of Dylan. A forked tongue emerged from Samael's lips, tasting the air. Emerie gasped—his wings expanded and reached across the room. She noticed strange symbols tattooed across their breadth. He seemed to grow more arms—or limbs, perhaps.

Dylan lifted his head. She couldn't see his eyes. "Is that supposed to intimidate me?"

"*Get out of him.*" Samael's eyes glowed. Father Zebulun looked between the two of them, as though unsure of which demon he needed to exorcise first.

"Brother, I'm doing you a favor." Dylan's voice was raspy. "Let me take the pawn. You're free to own her now."

"*I don't need your help on that. GET OUT OF HIM!*"

Samael attacked. It was a vulgar, brutal, animalistic display that briefly shocked the humans as he dove for Dylan's throat. It felt like slow motion. But Dylan—or rather Beelzebub—laughed throatily and took another drag of his cigarette. By the time Samael reached him, he exhaled —not smoke, but a thousand black flies which enveloped all of them.

Emerie choked. She couldn't see anything, couldn't *hear* anything, just the tickle of black flies crawling up her skin and the sharp stings of their bites. They were in her mouth, in her ears, and she wheezed and dry-heaved flies. She swung her bokuto wildly and ended up hitting Father Zebulun in the knees. He barely noticed, too intent on his own swam of black flies pulsating across his form.

But something had fallen from Father Zebulun's jacket. A flask of something—vodka? Water. Holy water. Holy water *that Father Zebulun believed in*. Inspiration struck and Emerie groped towards the bottle and unscrewed the cap. She doused her bokuto with water and to her triumph, the black flies halted their cloud. In that single pause, she saw Dylan stare at her in confusion and she flung her bokuto at him.

The holy water-drenched wooden sword hit Dylan solidly and he—or the demon inside him—shrieked. What looked like third-degree burns and steaming welts appeared on his skin and he screamed in agony. He fell to his knees and the black flies rained to the ground—they'd lived out their short life expectancy.

Emerie spat flies. "Samael!" She coughed and shuddered. "Sam, your sword!"

The demon groaned, but did not miss a beat. He lifted the golden sword and held it to Dylan's neck. A thin red line appeared on her boyfriend's throat and he glared at Samael hatefully.

"You'll kill the human?" Beelzebub's voice was dry as ash.

"What do I care for a human's life?" Samael growled. "Get out of him."

"You care more than you admit. *Heretic.*"

Samael pressed the sword harder into Dylan's neck. Blood trickled down his skin and Emerie felt paralyzed.

But just at the moment she thought her demon would surely decapitate her boyfriend, Dylan's mouth opened like some sort of twisted frog. Emerie couldn't help but scream as a tornado of black flies thundered out of her boyfriend's maw and soared past them, outside of the room. Zephyr ran after them, perhaps intending to banish them for good, but they easily eluded her—down the stairwell they flew, while the front door banged open, until they disappeared into the fading twilight.

Emerie ran towards Dylan and helped him stand. He hacked and wheezed, while Emerie helpfully pounded on his back until every demonic insect was out of his body. She noted wryly she would need to mop the dickens out of this room—little piles of dead flies littered the hardwood floors.

Father Zebulun joined her and pulled a Band-Aid out of his pocket. Dylan watched him dazedly as the priest carefully applied it to the cut on his neck. Emerie was pleased to see they were Star Wars Band-Aids.

"Mm." Father Zebulun examined Dylan's hand. "Don't worry, young man, I've seen worse. Emerie, would you bring me your sewing kit, please?"

"Do you really think I have a sewing kit?" Emerie snorted.

"Here." Zephyr sighed, pulling a small travel case out of her purse. "And rubbing alcohol to disinfect."

Dylan's sanity returned right as the priest started stitching his wounds. "What—the hell—happened?!"

Emerie flinched at how raspy his voice was. Demon possession must be hell on the throat.

She opened her mouth to come up with some sort of colorful explanation—drug trip? The fumes from her fumigating the house? But unfortunately, Father Zebulun had no intention of covering for her.

"You were possessed by a demon, young man. You are lucky to be alive."

The full setting of the room slowly dawned on Dylan. His bloodshot eyes drank in Father Zebulun, the dead flies on the floor, Emerie hovering next to him, Samael leaning against the far wall, wings half-cocked, and Zephyr stepping back into the room and sprinkling what appeared to be salt on the doorframe. His head swiveled towards Emerie.

"Why is there a priest, a demon, and a suit in my house?"

Emerie glanced at the company around her, who carefully avoided her gaze. She cleared her throat.

"Remember that pest problem I told you about? They're uh…helping me with it."

"Pest problem." Dylan's voice was faint. "The thing that possessed me…"

"Right," Emerie nodded. "But unfortunately, that's not the only one. There are more. Lots more. So we have to—"

"Get the hell out of Dodge!"

Dylan scrambled to his feet. Wild manic adrenaline coursed through his features and he grabbed Emerie's arm and tugged her towards the door.

"Boston—phone's in my car—we can have our stuff shipped there!" He yanked on her arm, but Emerie remained solidly planted. "We can sell this house online! Everything can be taken care of online! Let's—*go!*"

Emerie shook her head. "Dylan, I can't just leave. It's my fault the demons are here. I have to help get rid of them."

Dylan stared at her like she was insane. She supposed her tone was a little too offhand about the whole situation.

"EMERIE CASSIDY FOX WILL YOU LISTEN TO YOURSELF?!" Dylan bellowed. "THERE IS A DEMON IN OUR HOUSE. IT IS TIME TO GET THE HELL OUT OF MILTON AND NEVER COME BACK!"

There was a pregnant pause. For a moment, something like realization crossed Emerie's features, as though she just registered how strange her life had truly become. She glanced over at Father Zebulun, Zephyr, and Samael, who looked concerned, bored, and resentful, respectively. Orobas was nowhere to be seen; presumably he was downstairs snacking on coffee filters. She sighed and turned towards her boyfriend.

"I'm sorry, Dylan." Emerie's voice was small yet firm. "I have to stay."

Dylan spluttered something unintelligible that had the connotation of a curse. "Emerie—I am leaving this house and I will not be coming back. Do you understand that?"

She sighed again. "I understand. Text me your new address, I'll have your things shipped to you."

He looked at her in disbelief. Something like regret passed over his features, as though he considered changing his mind for a brief moment. But when he glanced over at Father Zebulun, Zephyr, and Samael, his expression hardened and he stood. He walked out the door, slamming it behind him.

Emerie exhaled. She hadn't realized she was holding her breath. She stared at the door thoughtfully, trying to sort out her emotions. It was unfair of her to expect Dylan to remain in all this craziness. It was unfair to expect *anyone* to acclimate themselves, really.

Truth be told, they were probably on the verge of a breakup anyway. Between the responsibilities of home ownership and exorcising demons, their commitment had an expiration date.

"Are you all right, Emerie?" Father Zebulun rumbled. "Why don't I go after him? I'm sure I could calm him down."

"Nah, it's okay." Emerie stretched a little. "It's better this way. Keeps Dylan out of danger, at any rate. Anyone hungry? I'll order a pizza."

TWENTY-TWO

FATHER ZEBULUN RETIRED into the room that would eventually become Emerie's office, and Zephyr invaded her bedroom. Emerie planned on taking the loveseat, but she wondered what arrangements she should make for Samael and Orobas. Did demons sleep? Did demons dream? She wasn't sure. However, there was a comfortable recliner and she dragged a few throw pillows into the center of the living room to create a sort of pillow nest for Orobas.

After she changed into her pajamas and lit some candles (Orobas had a particularly pungent aroma, something between a horse and a dirty fish tank), she noticed Samael seated on the couch. He stared broodingly at the sword. He had put it on the coffee table and it looked particularly splendid, sparkling in the candlelight.

Emerie walked over and sat down next to him. "You okay?"

Samael glanced at her in surprise. "I should be asking *you* that."

She shrugged. "I'm sure I'll be upset about the breakup later on—especially when I get the first round of bills for this house. But we've got bigger things to worry about, haven't we?"

He gave her that familiar incredulous look and returned to glowering at the sword.

"Do you want to talk about it?" Emerie ventured.

Samael sighed. "It's a long story, Emerie."

"What did you mean about the sword?" Emerie scooted closer. "That it was taken away from you?"

"I..." A shadow crossed over his face. "Do...do you really want to know?"

Emerie nodded.

"If you want to know, I can show you."

She blinked. "Show me?"

"Do you remember the night I possessed you for five minutes?"

Emerie glanced around, verifying that Father Zebulun wasn't in the vicinity. She had a feeling the priest would exorcise Samael right then and there if he heard that. She nodded in answer.

"Most humans don't know this." Samael leaned back on the couch. "But possession can work two ways. Demons can possess humans—and humans can possess demons."

Emerie could not disguise her immediate revulsion at the idea. Samael caught the look and nodded.

"It can have pretty horrifying results," he admitted, "just as a demon possessing a human can. But if you'd like to know about the sword, how I got it, how I lost it...I can show you. Through my memories."

Emerie considered this for a long, quiet moment. She didn't quite understand what he meant—it sounded as though she could access his memories through possession. But why did Samael want to show her this way? Why not just tell her? She then turned towards Orobas, who was finishing off Zephyr's discarded pizza crusts and the cardboard pizza box intermittently.

"Orobas," Emerie tossed the little demon a bread stick. "Is Father Zebulun asleep?"

Orobas looked up, his horsey-nose red with pizza sauce. The breadstick plonked against his lower lip and he slurped the breadstick up. His eyes glazed a bit but then he shook his head. "No. He is deeply engrossed in his readings, though."

"Is Zephyr asleep?"

"She is in deep meditation."

Emerie crossed her legs in order to get more comfortable on the couch. "All right. Orobas, do you think Samael intends to take over my body and use it for wretched purposes?"

"He *should*," Orobas remarked as he took another bite out of the pizza box. "But he won't. He's grown attached to you and is well on the way of becoming a true Heretic. A part of him longs for you to understand why he is the way he is, which is why he offers you this opportunity. A human possessing a demon is far more dangerous to the demon than to the human."

Emerie expected Samael to flinch or become embarrassed by this proclamation. But instead, he simply stared at her intently. His eyes glinted a little in the candlelight and Emerie found herself feeling a little flushed.

It was dangerous. But then again, everything Emerie had done up to this point had been dangerous. She had a fairly good track record for reckless shit. Aside from ripping a hole between dimensions and unleashing the forces of Hell from her home, she had made a lot of good friends. That made the whole nightmare worth it, in her opinion. She was already planning on getting Father Zebulun and Zephyr *temiyage* gifts—a Japanese thank you-gift for all their help. Probably castella cake, which was impossible to screw up…she'd like to prove she could do *something* correctly without ripping open a hole to Hell.

"Okay." Emerie said decisively. "Show me."

Samael hesitantly took her hand. It did not escape Emerie's notice how small her palm was in his—and how alien his large clawed hand was. She had a crazy urge to feel how sharp those talons were.

"Close your eyes," he directed. "Take a deep breath. Try and clear your mind. Focus on me and our connection. Remember the feelings you experienced when I possessed you. Don't be afraid of what happens next."

She nodded slowly, trying to keep her mind blank. It was easier said than done. She took a few deep breaths and concentrated on the rise and fall of her chest and Samael's hand. Why was his hand so soft? Shouldn't a demon's hand be scaly or slimy? He had claws, but she had yet to feel them…

Emerie gasped. She couldn't feel anything. The smell of the scented candles had vanished along with the crunches Orobas made. Her surroundings had completely disappeared; all she saw was blankness. It felt as though she was standing on a white sheet of paper.

"Samael?" She called and started at the sound of her voice. It sounded far away from her body.

"I'm right here."

Emerie turned and exhaled in relief. He stood right next to her and still held her hand. He squeezed it—a strangely comforting and human gesture that warmed her.

"Get ready," he warned her. "I'm going back to the memory...it will be overwhelming for you."

"As long as you're here."

A strange look crossed his face. He nodded and suddenly the nothingness collapsed.

She wanted to scream at the abruptness, at the feeling of being hurtled through the stratosphere, but it was over before it began. She felt herself enveloped in a world of dizzying colors—every shade of green, crimson, violet, turquoise, and gold exploded before her. It was so overpowering, it took Emerie a moment to focus.

They were standing in a forest, that much was certain. Maybe a rainforest—Emerie could see an emerald canopy above her and heard a discordant harmony of bird calls all around. Flowers twined up the trees and, to her shock, great lumbering beasts plodded past her. She could not identify them, but they looked familiar—as though she had read about them in a science textbook.

"Where are we?" Emerie whispered.

"The garden," Samael replied, his expression sad.

"What garden?"

He fixed his steely gaze upon her. "I'm sure you've heard of it. The garden. The garden where everything began. Where paradise fell."

Emerie blinked. "Wait—are you talking about—*the Garden of Eden*?!"

"What else?"

"I just—I just didn't realize it was a real place, that's all." Next thing you know, Samael was going to tell her that Avalon and El Dorado existed too. She wouldn't put it past him.

"Truth isn't always literal," Samael said. "Especially for humans and demons. Sometimes we walk in metaphors and poetry and all things in between. Come with me."

He took her arm and Emerie allowed herself to be guided along. She looked downwards, as if trying to find a path, but everything seemed to be wild, tangled up brambles. Garden indeed! She felt like she was breaking trail through a jungle. She'd be right at home with a safari hat and a machete. The air was overly warm too—Emerie could tell the deep green canopy protected them from the worst of the sun's rays.

Eventually, the trees cleared and revealed a wide, turquoise river. The river was nothing short of spectacular, with pink and yellow flowers that lazily floated between the currents and silver fish which leapt to and fro in a sparkling dance. But then Emerie saw something that made her clap her hands to her mouth to stifle a scream. She pointed a trembling finger across the river.

"Don't be afraid." He smiled a little. "That's me."

"That's *YOU*?!"

The thing across the river was the most terrifying creature Emerie had ever seen. She couldn't look at it for too long, as she felt sure her knees would buckle. The first word that came to mind was *dragon*. There was something like scales all around the creature that burned like coals on a barbecue. What was worse, it had a body like a writhing water serpent, which wriggled here and there in a restless, chaotic manner. She could clearly see six wings that were covered in bright, disturbing eyes, two of which were framed by the copper wings. But each time she tried to take it in, the creature's feathers and eyes moved and formed a new position, a new posture. It was like an alien dragon from another dimension.

"How is this thing scarier than your demon form?!" Emerie was thunderstruck.

Samael cast an annoyed glance towards her. "Okay, first of all, that is incredibly insulting. Secondly—every visitation with an angel begins with the phrase, 'Be not afraid.' Now you know why."

"Be not afraid," Emerie said aloud. "Does that work?"

"Rarely," Samael said dryly. "But we have to say it, it's in the manual."

The   serpent-monster-angel-thing-with-too-many-eyes-and-wings
paid them no heed. One of its wings twitched towards the water and
playfully splashed upwards. A cascade of water rained down and the
monstrosity began to glide across the water towards some unknown
source.

"Come on." Samael sighed and directed Emerie along the river,
across from Samael's angel form. They kept pace, walking a parallel path
along the river. But Emerie couldn't look at the angel monster for too
long, so instead she drank in the sights around her. She recognized some
birds as different kinds of parrots and songbirds, along with hawks and
falcons. There were mammals, some which looked like giant rats that
lumbered along, snuffling at fallen seeds and fruits. Emerie gasped when
she passed an ape-like creature with a distinctly human face. It stared at
her with an unsettling sort of knowledge.

"Look." Samael pointed.

The angel monster had stopped. Emerie's eyes widened. Across the
river was an entire *menagerie* of animals. Deer, elk, horses, wildcats,
wolves, lizards, tropical birds, hawks, every animal Emerie could think
of. It was an amazing sight, to see them all gathered in a haphazard
circle. They surrounded a tall, dark figure who stood at the center of the
menagerie. He was a handsome young man with midnight skin and
warm brown eyes.

"Adam."

"*The* Adam?"

"Yes. The very first man."

She stared, her mouth dry. He was incredibly beautiful. Finely toned
skin, handsome rugged features, and an overwhelming kindness in his
expression as he scratched a wild boar's ear. It occurred to her he was
also naked, but Emerie couldn't muster any sort of embarrassment or
lust. It was like looking at an old painting with vibrant colors—you did
not notice the nudity, it was simply part of the painted presence.

"Wow," Emerie whispered.

A golden sound erupted which shook the trees and stirred the river. It
was the most beautiful music Emerie had ever heard, the sound of a
thousand singing voices, an orchestra of crimson beauty. Her eyes filled
with tears when it finished.

"What—what was that?" Her voice shook.

"It is not good for man to be alone," Samael intoned.

"Huh?"

"That's what that meant. It is not good for man to be alone."

Emerie's jaw dropped.

Samael only nodded. There was an odd mixture of expressions on his face, longing tinged with anger, wistfulness framed with hatred. She couldn't begin to guess his mood as they explored his memories.

Two other angel monsters appeared next to Samael's angel form. They looked as horrifying as he did, with too many wings and eyes, but while Samael's form was a brilliant copper, theirs were silver and white, respectively. The silver angel monster squirmed briefly, as though it strained to do something. Emerie yelped when the creature exploded— but in its place was a humanoid figure. It walked towards Adam awkwardly in stiff, jerky movements.

Emerie recognized the figure. It was Lilith.

Lilith said something to Adam but Emerie couldn't begin to guess the language. She turned towards Samael for explanation.

He sighed. "Right. Hang on." He stood behind her and placed his fingers in her ears, being careful not to nick her with his claws. Suddenly, the language shifted to English.

"Choose me," Lilith was urging Adam. "The Garden was created for us. I shall take away your loneliness. It shall be our Garden, not simply my protectorate."

Adam smiled at her and touched her cheek gently. "Oh, Lilith. Why do you shift forms? What game are you playing?" Emerie couldn't help but sigh. His voice was deeply melodic, a rich bass timbre that made her knees weak.

"To stave your loneliness," Lilith was excited. Happy. Almost innocent. It made Emerie uneasy to see such light and enthusiasm from someone who'd recently tried to kill her.

"HE does not want you to be alone. This form is HIS favorite. Therefore—"

"HE creates you to be you, Lilith," Adam interrupted. "And you misunderstand. I want...I want a family. Not someone to rule over, not to have dominion over the garden. I want a family like me."

He gestured towards the animals around them. "You have Lucifer and Samael and Raphael and Michael and Lailah and all the seraphim and cherubim of Heaven. The animals have each other. I want a family such as this. Like me…"

"But I can *look* like you!"

"But you are not like me." Adam's voice was tender. "Lilith is Lilith, she is angel. She is kin of the cosmos. I want kin of the earth."

Lilith stepped away from him quickly. Adam did not seem to register the disappointment and hurt on her face, so he turned back to the animals, this time playfully throwing a stick for a tan and black dog. Emerie expected to see Lilith revert back to her angel monster guise, but she stayed in her human-ish form. She walked to the water and concentrated on her reflection. She frowned, and made tiny little shifting movements—corrections to the planes and angles to her face, growing her hair longer, changing the color. She was trying to perfect a human appearance.

The Samael from the past—the angel monster—moved towards her. "Why do you do this?"

"You should follow suit, Samael." Lilith did not look up. "HE loves the humans more than us. We must earn HIS love back."

Samael's past form shifted his wings uncomfortably and all of his scattered eyes widened in shock. The agitated rustle of his wings sounded like an assortment of glass bells, tinkling in the wind. He moved away from Lilith and glided upwards.

"She scared you with that," Emerie noted.

"She did," Samael admitted. "But I didn't believe her initially." He stared off into the distance. She noticed his wings were trembling slightly.

"Come on. I'll show you."

A kaleidoscope of colors flashed around Emerie, which briefly jerked her out of the garden. But within moments, she regained grounding and found herself looking at a group of humans. Her eyes widened in surprise. She had expected to see Eve next, not a crowd of people, some of whom appeared to be children. But near the center of it, Adam was seated. He roared in laughter at something someone else said.

"Who…who are these people?"

"Adam's family." Samael smiled as a little boy ran past her, yelling something at his older brother. He returned the endearment, and both giggled, sharing some private ancient joke.

"You're probably looking for Eve—she's over there."

He pointed. Emerie followed the gesture and swallowed hard. There was a beautiful woman nearby, who busily plucked a large assortment of mango-like fruits. She turned and gave a bright smile toward Adam, who blushed in response. Emerie shivered.

She exhaled. "She's so beautiful."

Eve shared the same warm brown eyes as Adam and her skin was a deep ebony. She had gorgeous wild black curls Emerie immediately envied. She selected each fruit with long tapering fingers. There was a hint of mischief in her expression that reminded Emerie of the look she'd give when she wanted to pull a prank in high school. But the unsettling part of Eve's figure was the recognition Emerie felt as she looked at her.

It was a ridiculous impossibility. Obviously, there was no way Emerie Fox could ever have met Eve, the mother of all women, the apparent blame for the fall of man. But she couldn't seem to shake the familiarity she saw in Eve's features. The sly smile, the joyful eyes, the strong limbs, the broad curves, the beauty, the charm, and the intelligence. Emerie had seen it on her mother. On her high school English teacher, Mrs. Staude. Her best friends in high school. Her college roommate. On *Zephyr*.

Emerie had seen the face of Eve on every woman.

"Okay." Emerie snapped herself out of it. "I get Eve. But who are all these other people?"

Samael looked at her like she was stupid. "Adam's family. Didn't you hear him earlier? He said he wanted a family."

"Well yeah, I just figured that when Eve came along, he'd have kids with her and…" She drifted off and blinked at Samael's slightly patronizing expression.

"Emerie." Samael folded his hands. "Adam and Eve *just met*. They're still getting to know each other. They are the first, yes—but family isn't just a mom, dad, and kids. Family is what you make of it. Adam, Eve, and the rest of them—they get to choose their families. Just like you do."

"But who are they?" Emerie pressed. "Why haven't I heard of them?"

Samael sighed. "Well, your Sunday school stories are notorious for leaving things out."

Emerie stared at the cluster of people. She noticed two young women holding hands while a little child snacked on something that looked like a leaf. Adam said something to them and the two women laughed and threw a berry at him playfully.

"Wait!" Emerie whirled towards Eve. "Is she doing it now? Is she picking the forbidden fruit and damning all of creation?"

"No," Samael said impatiently. "She's just making a fruit salad for lunch."

He appeared to be correct. Eve took a bite of something that looked tart and spiky. She smiled in pleasure and passed around her fruit to the children first. She sat next to Adam and whispered something in his ear.

Emerie glanced around. "Where are you in all this?"

"Over there." Samael pointed across the way. Sure enough, there was Samael the angel monster. Eve noticed him too and immediately stood. She ran over and offered him some fruit. She laughed when he turned her down—but began to ask question after question. What did the angels eat? If they did not need to eat, could they eat for enjoyment? Did they drink? Did they care to? If they were curious enough to try it, would HE be angry?

Samael the angel monster answered all her questions patiently and Emerie got the distinct impression he enjoyed himself, though it was hard to tell from his lack of human expressions.

Eve finally tired of her questions and returned to the group of people. A white angel
monster joined Samael as the humans enjoyed their lunch. It was then Emerie noticed the sword.

"Your sword!" She gasped. Sure enough, Samael the angel monster held it—though *how*, Emerie wasn't quite certain. But she could see it glint in the light as it caught the rays of the sun.

"Our job—" Samael cleared his throat. "Our job was to guard them. We didn't know from what—we didn't even really understand what guarding meant. We just knew that HE loved them, so we should love them."

His expression darkened. "But they were the real danger."

The white angel monster next to Samael's angel monster started to transform. But instead of Lilith's human form, he turned into a long, ivory colored snake. Samael again placed his taloned hands over Emerie's ears so she could hear the conversation.

Samael the angel monster sighed. "Now *you're* shifting?"

"Just a humble worm," the white snake replied. "Nothing more, nothing less. I don't see why Lilith wants to be like them, anyway."

"Yes," Samael agreed. "We ought to rejoice in what we are."

The white snake hissed in agreement. "Indeed. Why does Lilith wish to look like them?"

"She believes HE loves them more than us," Samael replied uncomfortably as he flicked a butterfly away with a wing.

"Nonsense," the white snake declared. "Look at them. They are weak. They have no wings. Their skin is so easily breakable, I'm almost curious what would happen if one of the plants stung them. No sense of smell, bad eyesight, they cannot see the garden without the sun…ridiculous, flabby creatures. Lilith worries too much."

Samael's angel monster went through an assortment of reddish shades, as though he were blushing in embarrassment. He mumbled something about "created in HIS image" that Emerie couldn't quite catch.

The white snake snorted and slithered up a tree. "Hardly. HIS image indeed! More nonsense."

"That's what HE said."

"HE must be testing us. That is not true."

Samael's copper wings shook angrily. "HE would not test us that way. That is cruel. HE is never cruel."

"HE is either testing us or is a fool. Which is better?"

Samael grew quiet. The white snake reached out from the tree and nudged him gently.

"I upset you," the snake apologized. "My passions fly away with me. Never mind me, little brother. Just like Lilith, in a way. Too much passion, not enough sense."

"You ought to talk to them," Samael suggested. His wings perked a little at the white snake's words. "They are interesting. They are not…

they are not like us, but they are interesting. Inquisitive. Creative. Funny."

"Perhaps you are right." The snake slithered down the tree. "I will talk to them. For all their silly appearances, they must be wise. I shall think of a question to ask them and hear their wisdom. Raphael is forever telling me to humble myself; he is absolutely right. I shall talk to them."

And with that, the white snake slithered off into the grasses.

"Let me guess." Emerie looked at Samael, who seemed unnerved to watch this as a third party. "The snake that tempted Eve?"

"Lucifer," Samael replied softly. She was surprised at how sad he looked.

"He really was Satan?"

"His name was *Lucifer*," Samael growled suddenly. "You humans gave him *that* name. Satan. Accuser."

His voice was so fierce Emerie actually took a step away from him. She noticed his horns began to smoke a little—she wondered if that was something that happened when he was angry.

Samael noticed her step back and sighed. He folded his wings and his arms. "He was...he was complicated. And he was my brother. Is my brother. He is my brother, Emerie."

"Look, I get shitty family." Emerie raised her arms in defense. "And I *really* get shitty brothers. But seriously. You thought it was a good idea to let him go off by himself and talk to humans? You didn't suspect *anything*?"

"Emerie," Samael's voice was weary. "This was before evil. This was before suspicion. We had no concept of wrong. There was only good. Us. The humans. It was all good. I thought Lucifer was trying to connect with the humans."

"Do you still think that now?" Emerie wanted to know.

Samael looked past her. He watched a streak of snow slither along the grasses before it disappeared from his eyeline. He closed his eyes.

"Some days I do. Some days I think he Fell before any of us and we weren't aware. Some days I think he Fell during his conversation with Eve. I don't know. I'll never know."

His voice cracked and Emerie couldn't help but take his hand. She squeezed it gently and he looked at her.

"Did you see it?" Her voice almost a whisper. "Did you see…Eve eat the fruit?"

Slowly, Samael shook his head. "I wasn't there for that. I just…I saw what happened next. Because that's what…that's when I…"

"Can you show me?"

Samael frowned at her. "You sure you're ready for that?"

Emerie took his hand in response. He stared at her hand in his. His intensity made her nervous. But then he closed his eyes in concentration.

The world shifted once more, and Emerie was dazzled by the dizzying array of colors around her as she swirled through his memories. When everything stopped spinning, she inhaled deeply and frowned. The smell of ozone was in the air. She couldn't see the sun anymore; the sky was overcast. Something rumbled like thunder.

"Sam?" Emerie said nervously. "What's…happened to the garden?"

The colors seemed muted—less real, as though she was looking at an unfocused photograph. Samael's expression was stony.

"Where are you in this?" she asked. Before Samael could answer, something emerged through the trees.

It was Samael's past form—the angel monster. He moved forward every few paces and paused. She couldn't be sure—there were too many snake-like limbs and wings to keep track of—but he appeared to be searching for something.

Emerie felt Samael place his hands over her ears once more. She concentrated on the Samael from the past.

"Eve?" His voice was vulnerable. Afraid.

"Adam? Where are you?"

"You're looking for them?" Emerie whispered. "Where did they go?"

"I didn't know." Samael's voice was quiet. "The sky went dark and everything changed. I became afraid for them."

Samael the angel monster continued to comb through the green. Then he stopped short and peered under a rock outcropping. Emerie squinted —there was someone there, cramped and shivering.

"Eve?" Samael the angel monster asked in confusion. "What are you doing? What is on you? Where is Adam?"

214 KAT D. COFFIN

"Shh!" Eve trembled. "Shush-hush! HE's coming! HE'll find me! *He'll see me. He'll see who I am and what I've done.*"

"Who?" Samael went nearer to her. "Who do you mean? Who are you scared of?"

"Get away from me!"

Samael faltered. His wings stopped shifting and became still. The dozens of eyes that decorated his form focused in on her.

"You're not like me," Eve whispered. "You're other. Different. You frighten me."

His wings started to tinkle and chime again—Emerie recognized this as a nervous habit—he was agitated. Samael—the Samael next to her—watched the exchange expressionlessly.

"I didn't know what else to do." her Samael said. "I didn't know how else to help."

Samael was justifying himself. But why? Emerie looked towards Eve and his past self and gasped. Samael the angel monster changed form—or at least tried to. He seemed to deeply struggle with it, but eventually a human shape emerged. He now looked much like the Samael holding Emerie's hand—dark curly hair, expressive brown eyes, an odd combination of mischief and compassion tangled up in his features. Emerie noted he had no horns or claws, but his wings remained.

"I don't mean to frighten you," the newly transformed Samael said to Eve anxiously. "I'm just trying to help you. What has happened? Why are you so scared? Where is Adam?"

"Hiding." Eve whimpered. "He is hiding. As I am. HE will kill us when HE finds us. We have disobeyed him. We ate from the Tree."

Samael's eyes widened. It was a relief for Emerie to finally understand his expressions.

"Why would you do such a thing?" Samael whispered.

"The serpent." Eve shivered. "The serpent told me to."

Samael's expression tightened. "The serpent?"

Eve buried her head in her knees. She flinched when he tried to touch her, so he stepped away, his head cocked towards the wind. He nodded and turned from her.

"Why did you walk away?"

"HE asked me to get Lucifer," Samael said heavily. "And HE... wanted to speak to Adam and Eve alone."

"You mean God."

"Yes."

Emerie crossed her arms. "I didn't see God."

"You don't want to see HIM," Samael replied. "So you don't."

This didn't make sense to Emerie. "But I'm in *your* memories. Aren't I seeing what you see?"

"I don't want to see HIM either," Samael answered, turning away from the scene. "Come on. We're losing my past."

They followed Samael's past form, who looked increasingly more troubled with every step forward. He also called for Lucifer, but the angel did not appear. Emerie sighed heavily.

"I've never understood this story," she confessed. "It always seemed unfair."

"What did?" Samael asked absently. Clearly his mind elsewhere.

"Eve's punishment. Why did God even put the stupid tree in the garden in the first place? Seems like a pretty nasty test to me. I mean, it was the Tree of Knowledge of Good and Evil, right? If God really didn't want us to have that knowledge, why present the temptation in the first place?"

"HE did want them to have the knowledge." Samael quickened his pace. "But in HIS time, not yours. HE never said they wouldn't ever be able to eat from the Tree, HE just didn't want them to right then."

"Why not?"

"Because they weren't ready yet."

Emerie was about to ask what he meant by that when Samael halted. He pointed towards his past self, who had also paused. He spoke to something entwined around a tree limb. It was the white snake.

Samael placed his hands on Emerie's ears yet again. She heard the snake's voice, desperate and small.

"Brother." Lucifer touched his nose to Samael's. "Brother, you must help me."

"Help you?" Samael was baffled. "What is the meaning of all of this? Why did you tell Eve to eat from the Tree? And why do you hide from HIM?"

"Did she tell you that?"

Emerie recognized Lucifer's tone. It was the tone politicians used in order to engender trust and cast doubt on their opponent. But it was a tone Samael didn't understand.

"She said you told her so," Samael replied warily.

"She *lies*."

Samael blinked in confusion. Emerie realized he didn't recognize the word.

"She speaks other than the truth," Lucifer elaborated. His tongue flicked back and forth.

Samael shifted uncomfortably. "Brother—she was so scared, brother."

"Liars are always scared," Lucifer hissed. "They are scared of getting *caught*."

"I don't—I don't understand," Samael stammered. The fear in his gaze was palpable. Emerie's heart broke. he wished she could squeeze her Samael's hand, but he was still gently touching her ears, allowing her to understand the language.

The past Samael took a deep breath. "Brother, HE wants you. HE is calling for you. HE sent me to fetch you."

"I cannot go to HIM."

Samael stared at the white snake. "What do you mean?"

"Don't you see?" Lucifer's voice became urgent. "Brother, the humans are *liars*. They tell *stories*. Do not deny it, you have seen them create stories. Stories are lies, brother. Even as we speak, they are *lying* to HIM about me."

"What do you mean?"

"They blame their sin on me. I went to them for wisdom and they turned against me. HE will choose the humans over me—over us—because Lilith was right. HE loves them more."

Samael stepped away from Lucifer as he shook his head. "No. That cannot be true. Brother, that *cannot* be true."

"You know it is true." Lucifer's voice became heavy with sadness. "The truth is, little brother, we were not enough for HIM. We were not good enough. For this reason HE created the humans to replace us. Therefore...you must not let HIM find me, little brother. You must protect me. We only have each other, Samael. We cannot trust anyone else."

"Brothers."

Samael and the snake started. Emerie gasped—two of the angel monsters had entered the clearing.

But these did not look like Samael's angel monster form. They were less serpentine and monstrous, though Emerie hesitated to call them human-ish. They still had at least six wings, two of which covered their faces. They glowed with an unearthly light and were about three feet taller than Emerie.

"Archangels," Samael explained quietly. "Michael and Raphael."

"Brothers!" The past Samael's expression melted into relief. "You must help us. Everyone is so afraid—Eve believes HE is going to harm her. I cannot find Adam anywhere. And Lucifer—Lucifer needs us most of all. He believes—"

"Step aside, Samael."

Raphael's voice was hard and terrible. It sent chills down Emerie's spine and made her mouth go dry. She took a step back from him, never mind she was only a witness, not a participant. Still, something about Raphael's beautiful and terrible demeanor frightened her.

The past Samael faltered. "Brother…did you not hear me?"

"We heard you," Michael said gently. His voice was soft as a child's and there was deep sorrow inflected in every word he spoke. His voice was almost musical. Emerie realized both archangels carried swords as well, similar to Samael's.

"Step aside, Samael," Raphael ordered again and drew his sword. Samael's eyes widened.

"What—what do you intend to do?" He took a step in front of Lucifer.

"Samael." Michael's voice was quiet. "You do not know what he has done. You must move. The garden, the world, the humans—all of it is in terrible danger because of Lucifer."

"If he escapes the garden," Raphael said as he raised his sword, "he will spread his iniquity throughout the earth. It will be completely poisoned."

"I don't—I don't understand!" Samael looked bewildered. "Iniquity? Poison? We are brothers, Raphael. Surely—"

"I told you." Lucifer's voice was dark and suspicious. "The humans have corrupted them."

"Corrupt?" The word clearly meant nothing to Samael. "Lucifer—"

"Face us, brother," Michael said sadly to Lucifer. "In your true form. Samael will not protect you from the consequences of your actions."

"Won't he?" The snake turned towards Samael. "Are we not brothers, Samael?"

"Of course we are," Samael became increasingly more upset. "Michael—"

"There's no time," Raphael said brusquely. "Trust us, Samael. This is what needs to be done."

Before Samael could respond, he raised his sword and in a flash, sliced through the air towards the snake. Emerie cried out, certain she would see two halves of a snake on the ground. But instead, Samael had drawn his own sword and blocked Raphael from destroying Lucifer.

"I will not forget this, brother," Lucifer hissed. In a flash of white, he disappeared into the grasses.

The three angels stared at each other. Righteous fury was etched on Raphael's expression. Michael looked at Samael stonily.

"It's come to this." Raphael's voice was hard. "You have made the same choice as Lucifer."

"Choice?!" Samael bit out. "You were trying to unmake him!"

"You don't know what he's done, Samael." Michael reached out towards Samael, who jerked away from his arms. "You don't know what he will do."

"He's confused about the humans," Samael argued. "And—how do we know he isn't right? Suppose HE truly does love them more than us. How can we worship someone who favors one over the other?"

Raphael's wings lifted from his eyes. Emerie could not see their color, but they blinded her temporarily, as though she tried to stare directly at the sun.

"Is this it, then?" Raphael said in a deadly voice. "You are choosing Lucifer over HIM?"

"He's our brother!" Samael shouted. "He's our *family*!"

"No, Samael." Michael shook his head. "He has Fallen."

"And so, it seems, have you," Raphael added.

The sword in Samael's hand disappeared. He stared down at it in confusion, then slowly lifted his head towards his brothers. Raphael's expression remained resolute, Michael's resigned.

"N-no, wait," Samael stammered. "You can't—"

"You have let Lucifer escape." Michael's voice was barely above a whisper. "You do not know what evil this will cause. We could have stopped him here and now...but now..."

"My sword." Samael's voice began to shake. "Give me back my sword!"

"You were given that sword to protect the Garden," Raphael's voice was cold. "To protect the humans. You have failed to do that."

Samael's features filled with rage. "How can you say that to me?! How can you turn your backs on Lucifer?! How can you trust so blindly?!"

"Goodbye, brother."

The world was suddenly engulfed in darkness. Emerie screamed in terror as everything around her rocked back and forth, as though she were in the eye of a storm. But as quickly as it started, everything stilled. She realized she no longer stood in the garden. She was in a barren place, perhaps a desert. And she saw Samael.

He was on his knees, hands clenched in the sand. Horns sprouted from his forehead and oozed blood down his face. His beautiful feathered wings became leathery skin, like a bat's. She could see his claws digging into the ground and her heart broke at the wretchedness on his face.

He was enraged. He was broken. Emerie swallowed and knelt next to him. She gently touched his shoulder.

His head rose and he met her gaze.

Suddenly, Emerie was back on the couch in her living room. Neither of them had moved and her gaze at Samael remained unbroken. He looked at her, his expression interminably weary.

She brought her hands to his cheeks. He looked at her, somewhat startled at the gesture.

Emerie could not stop looking at his sorrowful ember eyes. His hands slowly rose and clasped her wrists, gently stroking her pulse points. He looked into her eyes and she suddenly felt keenly aware of herself...her thin cotton pajamas, the tender heat in his expression, the fact she had just broken up with her boyfriend...

"Emerie."

Father Zebulun's voice broke the spell. Emerie jerked away and hopped off the couch, stretching her legs, which had fallen asleep.

"I would like to speak to the demon privately," he said pleasantly. "Would that be all right?"

"All right." She scratched her neck. "I'll make some tea. Don't exorcise him while I'm in the kitchen."

Father Zebulun did not answer.

TWENTY-THREE

THE DEMON WATCHED the priest warily. Father Zebulun was not happy, which to be fair, was his general attitude in regards to demons. But things were getting out of hand with this demon and if he couldn't exorcise him, he at least needed to communicate the gravity of the situation to Samael.

He took a seat on the couch and began without preamble. "You let Emerie possess you."

His tone was an odd mixture of accusation and bewilderment. He knew such a thing was possible; but the idea of a demon willingly allowing a mortal to access their infernal abilities and vulnerable memories...it was unheard of. Samael raised and lowered one shoulder in response.

"She had questions," he said, scratching one of his wings. "I tried to answer them."

"In all of my interactions with demons," Father Zebulun's voice was slow and methodical, "I can't think of a single time a demon allowed a human to possess it. To have that kind of access to its memories."

Samael narrowed his eyes. He jerked his head towards Orobas, who waved casually as he read last month's issue of *Cosmopolitan*.

"Your friend did not tell me, I heard you." the priest said. "As I was getting a cup of tea. I nearly put a stop to it, but…" His curiosity trumped his base instincts. He wanted to see what the demon would show her. Whatever it was, it engendered sympathy for Samael and that could be problematic.

"She wanted to know," Samael repeated, a little defensively. "This was the best way to show her. More to the point—how do you know that about demons? In fact, how do you know *so much* about us? In all *my* interactions with humans, I've never met a human who knows so much about angel swords and demon abilities."

"It's my business to know," Father Zebulun rumbled.

"Yeah?" Samael challenged. "You're saying the Catholic church has some kind of secret club that teaches officiants about the creatures of Heaven and Hell?"

"I'm not at liberty to divulge that," Father Zebulun said delicately. "And I am the one asking questions here."

"Whatever." Samael leaned back on the couch. "I guess you guys are the experts on inquisitions."

"Funny," Father Zebulun said dryly. "An inquisition joke. I've never heard one before."

There was a long pause as the two sat in silence. Father Zebulun cleared his throat.

"Do you know…the demon Mephistopheles?"

Samael started a little. "How do you know *that* name?"

"We've met," Father Zebulun's gaze was tense. "In Kiev. A long time ago. And he's back in Milton. He…saved my life."

Samael's eyes widened in confusion. That didn't bode well. Father Zebulun had hoped the demon might explain why Mephistopheles would do such an irregular, *ethical* thing. But Samael looked lost.

"Are you—friends?" Samael asked. Father Zebulun scowled.

"Certainly not. It was my intention to destroy him and I nearly succeeded—at least I sent him back to Hell."

Samael rubbed his eyes—an oddly human action. Perhaps he was picking up some human habits. The priest cleared his throat but did not speak, allowing the demon to gather his thoughts.

"Mephistopheles is a wildcard," Samael's expression was wary. "He's not one of the princes, he's not part of the bureaucracy. Most demons don't like him because he just does whatever he wants instead of following orders. If Zephyr's right, and the demons are casting…I don't see Mephistopheles involving himself. He does play favorites, though. Maybe he decided you were a favorite."

Father Zebulun looked displeased at that idea. Samael inhaled.

"Or maybe," he added. "The politics of Hell are more complicated than what your *church* has taught you."

Father Zebulun sniffed. "If you're implying some of the demons of Hell are actually *good*—"

"I'm implying," Samael interrupted. "That shit is complicated. And as much as you and your precious religion want to believe shit's black and white, human or demon, mortal or supernatural—*shit is complicated.*"

———

There was another long silence. Father Zebulun stood from the couch and began to pace around the room. Samael watched his agitation motionless—only his tail flicked back and forth, like an impassive cat.

Finally, Father Zebulun faced him. "It should be clear by now I don't trust you on this plane."

"Really?" Samael feigned shock and swung his legs on the coffee table. "And here I thought we'd been bonding."

"Quiet," Father Zebulun snapped. "I'm in no mood to humor you. I just want a straight answer from you. What do you want?"

Samael looked taken aback. His eyes narrowed suspiciously, as though sensing some sort of trap in the question. But he couldn't seem to figure out what it was.

"I don't know what you mean." Samael rose from the couch. He went to the piano and began to play a concerto. Father Zebulun tapped his fingers on the top of the piano.

"What do you *want*?" Father Zebulun repeated over the delicate sounds of Mozart. "Is it her? Do you want Emerie?"

Samael switched to a minor key. The priest waited. But Samael didn't know how to answer him. Demons often took special interest in human hosts. They were sources of energy, playthings, tools for mayhem and destruction.

But this...was different.

"You see," Father Zebulun tapped his fingers in response to Samael's tune, "that was my theory. You wished to possess her. I've known many a demon that's gone after a pretty young girl."

Samael picked up a picture frame of Emerie perched upon the grand piano. It looked like a family picture—a snowy day in front of a rather creepy looking house in Japan. She stood next to a wizened old Japanese man who looked barely tolerant of the picture-taking. Emerie was laughing, her cheeks cherry-red from the snow, pretty ornamental clips in her messy dark hair and wearing some type of Japanese traditional dress...a kimono. She seemed carefree and joyful...a perfect target for a demon. A perfect target for Samael. He could have her in an instant, if he wanted...

"But the sword...complicates the theory."

Samael flinched.

The priest's gaze fell towards Samael's sword, which still lay haphazardly on the coffee

table. Samael set down Emerie's picture.

"That is an angel sword," Father Zebulun informed Samael, as if he didn't know. "Demons cannot wield them. They can't even get *near* them. Which leads to another, far more unlikely theory."

The music halted and Samael visibly bristled. He did not like where this was going.

"Are you, in some form or fashion, seeking redemption for your sins?" Father Zebulun asked in perfect seriousness. "Do you wish to join the heavenly hosts once more?"

"*No!*" Samael burst out, utterly horrified at the idea. "How could you even *think* that?!"

"The sword—" Father Zebulun began.

"I didn't want it back!" Samael slammed his claws on the piano which resulted in an unpleasant noisome sound. "It just appeared and now I can't get rid of it! I just used it to keep Emerie from getting struck down by Lilith!"

Father Zebulun's brows rose. "You used it to protect a human?"

There was a supremely awkward pause. The ends of Samael's talons began to smoke and he seriously considered smiting the priest out of spite.

"Technically," Samael growled. "But it was happenstance. I don't *care* about humans!"

"You care about Emerie," Father Zebulun pointed out. "Enough to protect her from your malevolent brethren. What can that mean?"

There was another long silence as Samael struggled to form words. His right paw plinked up the scale of keys in a lilting, ascending melody.

"I don't know." The piano music danced right back down the scales again, "But I'm not—I'm not seeking *redemption*, let's make that perfectly clear. I have no interest in the angelic hosts. They spat me out, I won't crawl back to them again."

Father Zebulun frowned in disapproval. "Obviously, I do not know the details of your Fall. Nor do I want to know. But consider, Samael. Your relationship to humans is not singular to Emerie. We have been together, alone, in this room, for twenty minutes and you have not tried to destroy me—though I'm sure you've thought about it. You have spent significant amounts of time with Zephyr, who deals with the supernatural and is therefore more susceptible to its influences—and yet you have not tried to attack her. Why? What end are you seeking?"

"I don't know!" Samael's wings abruptly unfurled and nearly knocked the priest over. But it wasn't intentional. The demon stood and walked away from the piano, beginning his own sort of anxious pace.

"I don't know. I don't want to hurt you all but I *don't* want to follow your God either—how could I follow someone who so easily threw me away? And why should I? Your world is a mess! I see nothing but chaos and brokenness from all corners of the earth. Which is why I don't know. Why isn't that good enough for you?!"

Father Zebulun felt uncomfortable. He had heard this sort of talk before…but not from demons. From parishioners as they struggled with the daily hardships of life. He went to Samael and found himself lifting his arm to Samael's shoulder to stop his frantic pacing.

"Angels and demons deal with absolutes, Samael," Father Zebulun said gently. "The fact you're falling somewhere in the middle…well, that's rather a human trait."

Samael did not answer.

———

Emerie turned her stove on and leaned back against the cabinets. She stared at her reflection in the metal teapot idly. She looked tired—dark circles rimmed her eyes and her face seemed paler than usual. She ran her fingers through her dark hair and frowned at how easily it tangled. She hadn't had much sleep. Who could blame her?

Sighing, she turned towards the kitchen cabinets and selected three mugs—a Star Wars mug, a pretty blue mug with an E on it, and a mug decorated with Jane Austen quotes. It was nearly dawn. Maybe she could whip up some omelets. She had a feeling both Father Zebulun and Samael might be in the mood for tea.

She thought back to what she had seen in Samael's memories. The whole experience had both exhilarated and terrified her. There had been so much beauty and pain. She swallowed as she thought of the broken-ness in Samael's expression. He hadn't *wanted* to Fall.

Emerie made a face. She had experience with this—Lucifer had manipulated his brother. He had played Samael like a fiddle, like an abusive parent gaslighting their child. She rather wondered if Samael saw it that way.

The kettle whistled and Emerie went to it, intent on moving it off the burner. Her gaze focused on the reflective surface of the kettle and she gasped, whipping around.

Lilith stood before her, her gaze critical.

"Jesus!" Emerie exploded.

"He won't help you," Lilith picked a bit of lint off of Emerie's shirt. "Emerie Fox, is it? You and I should talk."

"Uh…" Emerie glanced out of the kitchen, towards the living room. Father Zebulun and Samael still seemed deep in conversation.

"Privately." Lilith showed her teeth. "Without any meddlesome influ-ences. Away from that dratted priest and my ex-husband. Don't worry. I think you and I have a lot in common, actually."

Before Emerie could let out an appalled *"Your ex-WHAT?!"*, Lilith snatched her wrist. They both vanished in the proverbial puff of smoke.

———

Zephyr was lost.

She sat on Emerie's sleigh bed, legs neatly crossed under her. She kept her back perfectly straight and her eyes closed. She gradually let awareness flood her senses until she could no longer hear her heartbeat.

Breathe in. Breathe out. Breathe in. Breathe out.

Breathing was hard. Her brain ran a mile a minute, reviewing her current caseload, the spirit hauntings in Milton, worrying for her mother. Her mind would not accept the present moment without a fight.

Breathe. Listen. Accept.

Acceptance. She did not have to mask her magic. She could live and exist as a witch. She would not hinder it anymore, and she would listen to the magic coursing through her heart. She would learn to love its quirks and tempers. She would allow it to shift her soul.

Zephyr mentally called her magic to her, asking for aid, for power, and for peace. Her magic greeted her like a happy puppy. It tingled through her fingers and warmed her chest. She had pushed it away for a long time. Unable to resist, she let her hands dance, magic sparking from her fingertips. Her hands flapped more and multicolored lights bounced across the walls.

Breathe. Listen. Accept.

Her palms flapped with each word and Zephyr's peace grew.

She could feel her spirit pull away from her. She suddenly noticed herself sitting on Emerie's bed. Her expression was so serene, oblivious to the chaos around them. Zephyr rather envied her body and critically noted her poor suit had seen better days. (She wondered if her dry cleaner handled ash and sulfur stains…)

Her spirit free, she allowed herself to float to the ceiling of the room. Her shoulders lightened considerably and she passed through the ceiling into the attic. It was better to examine Emerie's Circle this way, without her physical body present. Waltzing upstairs might attract…unpleasant curiosities.

Nothing looked to be emerging from the large crack in the ground. The room was dark, save for one lamp someone had left on.

She inhaled deeply. Darkness seeped into the corners of the room, like a bad leak. She could feel spirits on the other side—they pushed against the crack and painted Circle. It was too easy an opening. They thought it must be a trap. But they wouldn't believe that for long.

Zephyr raised her hand. With two fingers, she drew an intricate design in the air—a sigil, a ward of sorts—an attempt to purify the attic. It halted the flow of darkness, but it was a temporary measure.

Something prickled against her neck and she turned towards the curious little stove at the end of the attic. Something there? She allowed herself to glide towards it.

There was empty space around the stove, as though it held something important once. Her hand passed through the metal, she felt coolness and warmth. This stove used to warm this room. This attic used to be a meeting area—for a previous owner of the home.

Zephyr inhaled sharply. She could feel a spirit—something that hid in the corners of the house, too afraid to emerge. "It's all right. Come on out."

Something shifted in front of her. An orb of light shot out of the stove and hovered before her in hesitation. Zephyr took another deep breath and waited patiently for the spirit to materialize.

The orb began to shape into a figure. The figure seemed flat, two-dimensional, like a large photograph. But as the spirit found its footing, it slowly formed into a middle-aged woman.

She could not have appeared before Zephyr if Zephyr had ventured to the attic physically. But through this spiritual projection, a skill Zephyr mastered as a child, she could converse and communicate with whatever spirit was nearby. And though Samael occupied the house for a hundred years or so, Zephyr felt fairly certain there were one or two spirits about that hid from him in various objects within the house. She didn't blame them. If she were a lost spirit, she'd hide from an inhuman entity too.

"Is this your house?" Zephyr asked patiently. Her voice seemed to encourage the spirit to regain more form.

She slowly took the shape of thin, twig-like woman in a Victorian dress. She was neither handsome nor beautiful; she was somewhere in the middle. Her face drooped somewhat like a basset hound and her silver hair was caught in an untidy bun. As her features became more pronounced, Zephyr noticed she had a habit of twisting the rings on her finger.

"Tell me your name," Zephyr ordered.

"Fairy Lemp."

Her voice was high-pitched, like a little girl's. Her pitch grated against Zephyr's skin, but the witch ignored the discomfort.

"Were you the one to summon Samael?"

The spirit's eyes bulged out; Zephyr took a step back. Her nondescript features became quite bizarre when she was provoked.

"It was I!" Fairy Lemp said mournfully. "A demon of great charm and affluence, who, if properly summoned, could guarantee me eternal devotion and riches beyond my wildest dreams!"

Zephyr frowned. "Right…if *properly* summoned."

It was not precisely possible for a spirit to look abashed, but Fairy Lemp was darn close to it. She kicked a ghostly foot awkwardly.

"Conjuring requires great courage…alas, alack, mine failed me that fateful night…"

"Thereby trapping the demon in your house." Zephyr sighed. "And you couldn't even manage to release him?"

"I dared not!" Fairy Lemp's spirit hovered to the attic ceiling in her exuberance. "I dared not trifle with the spirits once more!"

"So rather than fix the problem, you just…left it a mess."

Fairy Lemp stared down at Zephyr before she suddenly broke into a brokenhearted wail. The wail reverberated against the walls and Zephyr plugged her ears.

"Knock it off!" she shouted. "That's quite enough! Now look…why did you summon Samael precisely? There are a thousand inhuman spirits that could grant you servitude and wealth. Why Samael?"

Fairy Lemp sniffed. "Another spiritualist recommended him. Someone far more powerful than I."

"And who would that be?"

"I cannot…I cannot recall…"

The figure of the spirit began to warp back and forth. Zephyr sighed again. Spirits' memories were paper thin and rarely substantial. At least now she knew Fairy Lemp was not a part of all this. Someone…or something…put her up to the whole mess. Zephyr wondered how long this plan had been in the works.

But before she could retreat through the floor back to her body, she felt a violent force *SHOVE* its way into the attic. Zephyr whirled around and found herself face to face with the spirit of a furious, elderly, Japanese man.

She gaped at him and he slammed a transparent cane against the wall.

"What do you think you are doing?!" He thundered. "My grand-daughter has been taken!"

"*What?*"

"Emerie has been taken! Right out from under your nose! *Aho*! Get going! Before it's too late!"

It was with a jolt and a rush that Zephyr smashed into her body.

———

Zephyr blasted into the living room without preamble. "Emerie's gone!"

Samael leapt to his feet, eyes flashing. "What do you mean she's gone?!"

"I sensed something enter," Zephyr informed him. "It broke through my wards like they were nothing! Something really powerful—I think it took Emerie. I don't feel her aura here."

Samael rushed past her into the kitchen. Zephyr heard him gallop across the tiles, open the basement door, and bellow Emerie's name. She met Father Zebulun's gaze.

"Samael." Father Zebulun slowly walked into the kitchen. "Samael—it is pointless. She has been taken."

"*By what*?!" Samael slammed his fist against the counter which cracked the granite. "What took her?! How can we find her?!"

"Lilith."

The three of them turned towards Orobas, who calmly entered the kitchen and inspected Zephyr's wards on the wall. Sure enough, they seemed to have peeled, like fading graffiti.

"How can you be sure?" Samael asked slowly.

"I never betray my conjurer," Orobas said simply. "And my conjurer is in danger."

"Why didn't you *do* anything?!" Zephyr ground her teeth. "Or yell for help?!"

"Anything *I* would have done," Orobas retorted coolly, "would only have made matters worse for my conjurer. Furthermore, do not forget what I am. Just because Samael breaks heresies willy-nilly does not mean I will as well."

Samael snatched up Orobas by the throat. Zephyr cried out in protest.

"Where did she take Emerie?!" Samael demanded. "Tell me!"

"You are *not* my conjurer." Orobas didn't even blink, although he was turning a nasty purplish color. "You cannot *threaten* me this way, even if you technically have more power."

"Do you have any idea what Lilith could do to her?!" Samael roared.

"Enough!" Father Zebulun thundered. "This isn't getting us anywhere. Samael, put Orobas down. He will either help us or not help us, but cajoling and threatening will do no good."

Reluctantly, Samael released Orobas, who fell to the floor like a sack of potatoes. It didn't take long for the horse-headed demon to recover, and he promptly wandered into the living room. Samael watched Orobas mosey off, his expression filled with hatred. Then he turned back to Zephyr and Father Zebulun.

"What do you propose we do, priest?" Samael spat.

"I propose we stay calm." Father Zebulun noticed the burner on the oven was still on. He walked over and switched it off. "We will get Emerie back."

"Why did she take her?" Zephyr wanted to know. "Just to be a dick? What's her beef with Emerie?"

"It may be my fault," Father Zebulun leaned his head against the pantry, closing his eyes in thought. "We had a...disagreement outside the library earlier today. She failed to kill me and this may be her form of vengeance."

"It's not," Samael interrupted.

They all turned and looked at Samael. Samael's gaze fell to the floor.

"It's not your fault." His tail drooped and his words were stilted with guilt. "Lilith's being spiteful. She's angry with me, angry our conversation got interrupted. That's why she took Emerie."

Father Zebulun's eyes narrowed. "What conversation? What did you talk about?"

Samael sighed. "She wanted to join forces with me to rise up against Lucifer."

Zephyr sucked in her breath. A glass with a festive toucan suddenly shattered behind her. The priest looked at the witch to ascertain if she was all right, but Zephyr didn't move.

"I don't understand." Father Zebulun returned his attentions to Samael. "They are both of Hell. Legends say they were lovers. Why would she want to fight against him?"

Samael eyed him. "Remember what I said. Shit's complicated. And she and Lucifer have been over for eons. Actually, she and I...we had... an affair of sorts, in ancient times. You might, uh...might call it 'marriage.' Ahem. I guess she thought that was enough to get me to join her."

"But you said no, right?" Zephyr's question sounded more like an order.

"Well, I should have, but I was extremely drunk at the time..."

"To joining up with Lucifer!" Zephyr elbowed his wing. "Not marrying her!"

"I said going against Lucifer was a bad idea," Samael said defensively. "Which it is—at some point you humans will realize that. My loyalty is to my brother. Then Emerie interrupted and Lilith got pissed."

"Where might she take Emerie?" Father Zebulun picked up the pieces of a broken Star Wars mug. "Has she been to Milton before?"

Samael flung up his hands. "I have no idea what she did after we split up! I was in Hell! She was gallivanting on earth, probably causing all kinds of trouble. This is pointless. It's probably too late—she's probably snacking on Emerie's intestines by now!"

"Samael, do not panic." Father Zebulun placed the pieces on the counter. "Lilith knows there is an exorcist and a witch in this house. She clearly knows your affection for Emerie. She will want to toy with you. She will not kill Emerie right away."

The priest was right. Lilith wanted to be *chased*. She wouldn't slit Emerie's throat until Samael was there to see it. But finding her would not be an easy matter.

"Give me a second to go to Emerie's room." Zephyr headed toward the door. "Let me see if I can do a tracking spell...I'm rusty with spellwork."

The priest nodded. "I will make some calls." He pulled his cell phone out of his jacket and Samael glowered at both of them.

No good. Lilith fancied herself the goddess of witches and the basic witchcraft Zephyr would throw her way would probably be unusable. And it didn't matter how many monks or priests Father Zebulun knew... there was only one certain way to find Lilith.

Samael strode towards the bookshelf and pulled Harriet the Ouija board off. He impatiently shoved his angel sword off the coffee table and set the board up. He knelt down and folded his wings, trying to calm the fast beat of his heart.

Brother...brother help me! Help me find her!

————

"Not that I'm against sightseeing...but why are we here?"

Lilith ignored her. She knelt down and placed a gentle palm on one of the stone memorials. Dionys Stevens, thirty years old, hung for the crime of witchcraft.

There were at least twenty stone memorials in the little park, along with a large unmarked monument at the center for every unnamed woman who lost her life. The Milton Witch Memorial County Park was a favored place for picnics and festivals, though it seemed deadly quiet at the moment. There were booths lining the park but Emerie noticed uncomfortably that they were empty. She wondered if Lilith had scared them off.

Lilith sighed wistfully as she traced the edge of the memorial.

"The hatred mankind has for women," she declared as she straightened, "is despicable."

"Agree with you there," Emerie replied dryly. "Did you see the last election?"

Lilith smiled. "What did I tell you? I told you we had much to discuss and even more in common. I'm sure you believed I was going to kill you right here, didn't you? But I am not like the demons you've met. I am your ally, Emerie. I serve women. *Real* women."

Something about the way Lilith said "ally" bothered Emerie. It reminded her of a white girl Emerie knew in college, who informed her she shouldn't have worn a yukata for their summer carnival, as it was 'cultural appropriation.' Or that fraternity that refused to let Falcon rush because he was trans.

"You did set a bunch of snakes on me." Emerie folded her arms against her.

"I apologize for that." Lilith laughed. "You walked in on a rather… emotional moment for me. We have a *long* and *passionate* history, Samael and I."

Emerie frowned. Now Lilith sounded like a girl on Emerie's high school basketball team who got upset when Emerie started dating her ex.

"Yeah, sure," Emerie humored her. "All's fair in love and war, right?"

"Love?" Lilith's expression became rather fixed. "Did I hear you right? Do you love Samael?"

Emerie blinked. "Um…That's kind of a loaded question."

"Not at all." Lilith took a menacing step towards her. "I admire you for it. Proclaiming to love someone with Samael's history…what a marvelous example of grace you are."

Her pause indicated she expected a response, so Emerie gave a half-shrug as she surveyed her surroundings and kept an eye out for an escape route. She wished she had her phone—all it would take was a sneaky text to Zephyr and her friends would be there in an instant…

"Samael the Seducer…" Lilith casually stroked the side of Emerie's jaw. "He strikes again. But what of Samael the Accuser? The Destroyer?"

"What are you talking about?" Emerie tried to take a step back. Her heels hit one of the stone memorials.

"Even before we Fell," Lilith whispered. "They called him the venom of God. The poison of God. Do you know why?"

Something lurched in Emerie's stomach. That name hadn't come up in the Garden of Eden. Had Samael kept part of the story out?

"I know more than you think," Emerie shot back. "I've seen—I've seen what happened. I've seen your Fall."

This was a lie. Emerie knew for certain she had seen *Samael's* Fall—but the lie didn't bother her too much. It was almost worth it to see the shock and rage on Lilith's face.

"Well, it seems Samael has shared a lot with you." She pulled Emerie towards her and wrapped her arms around her waist. "Why don't I share some secrets as well?"

Emerie attempted to twist away from her…fighting to break out of her embrace. But once she caught Lilith's striking emerald gaze, she became immobile. What was happening? Lilith's irises were spinning… what was this?

And suddenly, Emerie's world shifted around her, just as it had when Samael allowed her access into his memory. Lilith was attempting to possess her! Emerie tried to scream, tried to regain control of her faculties, but every movement felt paralyzed and stiff, as though there were iron weights attached to her limbs. She couldn't see anything at all. She tried to speak and heard her voice bounce all around her. It echoed, as though it came from far away.

If she focused, she could see. She could still see herself by the witch memorial. Her hand rose and it flexed of its own volition.

No, no…*Lilith* was flexing her hand!

"STOP IT!" Emerie screamed.

This was nothing like her shared moments with Samael. This was *violation*, an utter invasion of consciousness. To her relief, her screams seemed to have an effect on Lilith, who raised Emerie's hand and pinched the bridge of her nose, as though she had a headache. Emerie suddenly realized the corporeal Lilith—the form she had been talking to —was nowhere to be found.

"You absorbed me," Emerie felt herself say. "Don't be so angry. Most humans like possession, whether they admit it or not. I'm sure you have felt the intoxicating connection with Samael more than a few times."

But that was with *Samael*, Emerie tried to scream. Lilith did not acknowledge the thought.

"Shush hush," she said aloud. "I am going to show you something, just as Samael did. I think he left out a few memories for you to peruse."

That is none of my business, Emerie thought angrily.

"I'm making it your business," Lilith purred. "Pay attention."

They were no longer at the Milton memorial. In fact, Emerie wasn't entirely sure *where* they were—the world seemed to spin all around her, as though she flew past cities and worlds. Lilith was taking her somewhere. Lilith wanted to *show* her something. Why?

Water. They flew over water. The ocean? She glided over an endless expanse of sea that churned and twisted all around her. The waves folded every which way, as though unsure of what direction they wished to go.

Emerie cried out. There were *things* in the water—with every crashing wave she saw a limb, a wing, a head bobbing amid the sea foam.

"Look long and well." Emerie felt her mouth move and she realized Lilith was speaking to someone else. "Look at your murdered brothers."

Emerie's heart jolted in her chest when she realized Samael soared next to them. His face betrayed no emotion as he took in the countless dead in the sick-gray waters. Emerie tried to call out to him, tried to say his name. But Lilith tightened her expression.

They flew to what looked like a mountain peak that barely crested over the giant waves. Samael still said nothing, his gaze fixed on the endless ocean all around him.

Lilith tilted Emerie's head and forced her to smile. "Do you see now?"

Samael looked at her.

"Do you see how much you are hated?"

Something shattered in Samael's expression. He turned away from her and launched himself into the gray clouds. Lilith made Emerie smile in satisfaction.

Through great effort, Emerie was able to speak, her lips attempting to revolt at every word. "What...is this? Where...where...are we...? Who...?"

"The Flood," Lilith answered inside her head. "We had made progress, you know. Lucifer had nearly conquered the entire earth. But HE wrecked everything and allowed the humans to escape. We could no longer come out in the open. We had to go...underground, you might say."

She gazed at the waters. "We lost many of our cause."

Emerie tried to respond, to ask for clarification, even to express horror a flood in fact did overwhelm the earth. Or was any of it real? Samael had said something about walking through metaphors and dreams, that poetry was closer to truth than memory. But Lilith would not allow her to dwell on this new information. Like a bird took to the air, she followed Samael's path into the sky.

What is this? Emerie thought frantically. *I'm seeing Lilith's memories... how is it switching between my body and hers? I don't have wings...but I feel her moving my mouth, my limbs...what is happening?!*

"Possession is an intimate thing," Emerie heard Lilith call out. "It blurs the lines between body and mind. But surely Samael would have explained that to you!"

Emerie couldn't focus. Lilith was dragging her somewhere else, forcing her into a new memory, a new world. It felt as though the sky crumbled on top of her, as though she bore Atlas' burden for a moment, but then immediately her senses returned. They were no longer above the clouds. Instead, they were in what appeared to be a city. An ancient city—the walls were made of stone, and chariots and wagons lined the streets. But the city was silent and dark.

She shivered. There was something awful and unnatural about this darkness. She looked up and realized she could see no stars at all. It was as though the night sky had been blanketed in storm clouds. She thought she could smell ozone.

Someone approached. Emerie couldn't help but cry out—but this time, Lilith did not try to thwart her. Instead, she allowed Emerie her faculties, perhaps to make sense of her surroundings.

"Why?" Emerie whispered. "You want me to see this? You want me to...to know what this is?"

Lilith didn't answer. The footsteps grew louder and Emerie inhaled sharply as someone turned the corner.

It was Samael. Emerie exhaled in relief. He didn't seem to notice her as he paused outside of every door. He halted at one and she watched him raise an arm for a moment before he entered.

Confused, Emerie followed him inside. There was no lamp or any sort of light illuminating the home, but Emerie could still see more clearly inside. The dark outside of the house was oppressive, almost like a fog. She noticed a young woman curled on a mat next to the far side of the hut. She held a baby in her arms as she slept, and there was another young boy asleep next to her, perhaps four years old.

Samael walked towards them and knelt down. His expression never wavered and Emerie was shocked to see how cold his eyes were. He reached towards the young boy and touched his forehead.

Emerie heard something like an exhaled breath. Silver flowed through the boy and into the ground. Emerie watched it split into several rivulets that chased each other out of the house. She followed the things quickly and poked her head out of the house—and started a little. Why was Lilith allowing her this control over her senses? Emerie watched the rivulets snake through the streets and disappear into houses.

She turned towards Samael and stiffened. The woman had awoken. She rubbed her eyes blearily and kissed her sleeping baby. She kissed the young boy's forehead.

Something was wrong. The woman's brow furrowed. She gently touched the little boy's shoulder in an attempt to wake him. Emerie's throat constricted as the little boy's head flopped side to side.

He was dead.

The woman screamed. She shook her son harder and tried to breathe life into his mouth. She said one word over and over, her voice becoming more hysterical with every movement.

Samael exited the house. Emerie barely registered anything, paralyzed. The mother still sobbed over her dead child. Emerie couldn't move. She had just seen Samael kill a child.

"The death of the firstborn," Lilith whispered in her ear. "The last plague of Egypt."

Nothing made sense. Didn't God send the ten plagues of Egypt? Locusts, frogs, the river into blood…and death of the firstborn. Why was *Samael* the one to do this? Did the stories have it wrong? Her stomach churned and she tried to keep herself from throwing up.

"HE protected HIS people," Lilith whispered. "While Samael destroyed the rest. Do you understand now? Do you understand why he is called Samael the Destroyer? He *warred* against humans. If he had not been sent to Hell, perhaps you all would be wiped out."

"I want to go home." Emerie's voice broke. "Please take me home."

"Stop fighting me, then."

Emerie gave up. Her shoulders relaxed and Emerie retreated into the corner of her mind and allowed Lilith to take complete control.

TWENTY-FOUR

"WHY WOULD she be at my church?"

Samael avoided his gaze and mentally cursed himself for it. Why on earth was it suddenly so hard to lie to the priest? Demons were the *masters* of lies! It should come as easily to him as Enochian, his mother tongue. But he felt a curious weighty sensation at the pit of his stomach.

Humans thought the slightest touch of a Ouija board could summon Satan, but frankly, he was far too busy to terrorize preteens at a sleepover (which was when the majority of Ouija sessions occurred). But Lucifer answered Samael through the Ouija board almost immediately. Nine letters. STJULIANS. He immediately interrupted Zephyr mid-spell and Father Zebulun mid-mobile phone conversation and insisted they leave that very second.

"You're not the only one with contacts." Samael fists clenched as they strode down the street. "She's wrecking your church. I'd be a little concerned."

The priest was still suspicious, but he didn't argue. Their pace quickened as they made their way through town. The remains of the Harvest Festival were still in the town square. There were empty stalls, and littered bits of kettle corn danced across the street, soon to be cleaned up by yawning volunteers.

When they reached the church, an elderly woman in a khaki suit and heels dashed outside and blubbered to Father Zebulun *something* had invaded the sanctuary. Furthermore, it had an assortment of monsters and beasts—*demons*, the woman seemed hesitant to say—that ripped up the hymnals, razed the organ, and terrorized the morning prayer parishioners, most of whom had evacuated. Father Zebulun listened with a grim expression.

"Maggie," he directed. "Take the rest of the day off."

Maggie was so distraught, she didn't even notice Samael standing before her, wings half-stretched. She let out a tearful wail and ran for her car. Father Zebulun went to his Cadillac. He knelt underneath the car and pulled out two large, plastic, neon orange water guns.

Zephyr stared. "You have *got* to be kidding me."

Father Zebulun checked the tanks of his guns, which were filled to the brim with holy water. "Do I look like I'm joking?"

Without another word, they strode towards the large church doors. Father Zebulun flung open the doors of the sanctuary, pulled the Super Soakers from his jacket, and blasted whatever he saw.

The inside of the church was chaos. Demons, great and small, were everywhere—some drew lewd pictures on the stained-glass windows, others dismantled the church organ, and one rather fussy looking demon was busy turning every cross upside down.

The chaos was so manic, Samael almost didn't register he was able to walk into the church easily.

That was abnormal. It was one thing for Lilith to be able to stand the Holy Ground, as well as her minions—she had quite a bit more power than he. Perhaps she'd weakened the sacred barriers somehow…?

Samael gasped when he saw the altar.

Emerie lounged on the wooden platform carelessly. In her hand was a Communion chalice filled to the brim with wine. She had kicked her boots off, her expression raised towards the ceiling of the sanctuary. She didn't look the least bit bothered by the pandemonium around her.

"Emerie!" Samael yelled as he ran towards her.

"Samael, wait!" Father Zebulun shouted. "Don't go near her!"

Samael blanched at the warning in the priest's tone. The smell of sulfur filled his senses and a sinking feeling settled in his gut.

At the priest's shout, Emerie sat up. She took a large gulp of Communion wine and grimaced at the taste.

"One would suppose that one of the oldest cathedrals in the country would have better wine," she remarked. "Here I go again, expecting more out of humans than they deserve."

Samael stopped short. It was Emerie's voice he heard—but those were not Emerie's words. The mannerisms, the clipped tone, the expression that oozed cruelty and wickedness…

"Lilith." His voice was dry.

Emerie's lips pursed. "Why the long face, Samael? Now you get the best of both worlds—myself as your consort, once again, in the body of this human you like so much. This is what we might call a win/win situation."

"No." Samael shook his head. "I don't want that. I don't want—I don't want *you*. Leave her body!"

Emerie laughed and poured herself another glass of wine. "Oh, Samael. She doesn't want me to leave. Truth be told, she doesn't really want to see you right now."

Samael's blood ran cold. "You're…you're lying."

"I don't lie, Samael," Emerie said idly as she traced a finger around the edge of her chalice. "That's the big difference between Lucifer and me. What I tell you is true—Emerie doesn't want to see you. She knows the truth about you, my pet. I didn't even show her *half* of what you were up to on earth—but the barest taste was enough to turn you off you forever."

"That isn't true!" Samael shouted desperately. "Let me talk to her!"

She smiled again and paused for a moment, as though asking Emerie. The moment passed and she repeated, "She doesn't want to talk to you."

Something deep inside Samael shattered. He staggered and nearly lost his balance. But Father Zebulun stepped forward, took his arm, and hoisted him upwards. He glared at Emerie's unimpressed figure.

"I have heard enough," he boomed and lifted his crossbow. "This body is not your own. You are to leave Emerie's body this instant!"

Emerie looked at the priest fondly. "What are you going to do, little priest? Are you going to shoot Emerie full of holes with your silver arrows? I'm sure it would be quite painful—I won't feel anything, of course, I transfer all mortal pain to the mortal soul."

"This isn't for you," Father Zebulun said grimly. To prove his point, he shot at something slimy that was crawling up the belfry. It shrieked in pain and fell to the church floor with a sickening thud.

"And what do you propose?" Emerie casually hopped off the altar. "I'm assuming you won't call my sister for help?"

Zephyr blinked in confusion and then looked at Samael. He shrugged in response—the words were meaningless to him. Lilith must have meant an angel; after all, angels and demons were estranged brothers and sisters. But whatever she meant, it seemed to stir Father Zebulun to anger.

"I can handle filth like you on my own," he growled. "Zephyr! Get ready!"

The witch looked bewildered. "Me?! I'm not Catholic!"

"It doesn't matter!" Father Zebulun yelled. He tossed her a small black book. "Turn to 'the rite of exorcism'—I need you to speak the responses!"

Zephyr flipped the pages frantically. Father Zebulun started towards Emerie.

"Emerie." His voice became gentle. "If you're in there—I swear on my vows as a priest. I will get you out from under her control. Your friends are here. And no matter what you've seen, we're not giving up on you."

There was the smallest instant of a flicker in Emerie's expression—as though a far-off memory took her attention into daydream. But Emerie's body smiled in response, smiled so hard the lips became dry and cracked. Little rivulets of blood flecked her mouth.

"*Lord have mercy,*" Father Zebulun began in a thundering voice.

"Uh—Lord, have mercy!" Zephyr called out.

"*Christ have mercy.*"

"Christ, have mercy!"

"*Holy Lord, almighty Father, everlasting God and Father of our Lord Jesus Christ, who once and for all consigned that fallen and apostate tyrant to the flames of hell...Strike terror, Lord, into the beast now laying waste your vineyard!*"

Emerie began to laugh uproariously—though the laughter was *not* Emerie's laugh. Samael knew Emerie's laugh, it was low and cackling, like a drunk hag. *This* laugh was more like a harpy shriek, like an untuned violin. It hurt his ears to listen, but he stared desperately, and wished for the first time in his long life, an exorcism would be effective. As the words grew more pronounced, filled with spiritual power and the witch's own internal magic, Samael felt his skin begin to burn.

"Fill your servants with courage to fight manfully against that reprobate dragon, lest he despise those who put their trust in you—Let your mighty hand cast him out of your servant, Emerie Fox, so he may no longer hold captive this Emerie whom it pleased you to make in your image, and to redeem through your Son; who lives and reigns with you, in the unity of the Holy Spirit, God, forever and ever."

Father Zebulun's thundering voice roared through the church. The exorcism was not directed at Samael, but even he felt its power—it singed his horns and compressed the air, as though he were suffocating in a small coffin. Samael watched Father Zebulun in shock and some awe —this human showed no fear whatsoever towards Lilith. He knew exactly who she was and where she came from, yet he defiantly chanted out the exorcism as though he'd exorcised her a hundred times before.

But Lilith continued to puppet Emerie—she barely seemed to notice his words.

"Who do you think you are, priest?" she jeered. "You can present me before the pope himself and I would never release hold of this sow!"

This did not faze Father Zebulun. He stared hard into her dark eyes and roared out, *"I command you, unclean spirit, Lilith, along with all your minions now attacking this servant of God, by the ascension of our Lord Jesus Christ, by the descent of the Holy Spirit, by the coming of our Lord for judgment —depart, you devils!"*

There was a raucous screeching all around them. Samael watched in fascinated horror as all the demons scattered about the sanctuary cater-wauled in pain. Father Zebulun had ordered them to depart—and it seemed as though they were being forcibly removed. Even Emerie looked pained, lines creasing across her face and her eyes flashing in anger.

It was in this moment Samael realized the exorcism did not hurt him.

He was uncomfortable, certainly—he could feel the weight of the exorcism press in against his chest. It slightly scorched his horns and skin—but he did not feel the uncontrollable *tug*. The pull that would lead all exorcised demons back to Hell.

"*I adjure you, ancient serpent,*" Father Zebulun hissed toward Emerie. "*By the judge of the living and the dead, by your Creator, by the Creator of the whole universe—yield. Make no resistance nor delay in departing from this woman, for it has pleased Christ to dwell in man and woman. It is God Himself who commands you. Depart, transgressor, depart seducer, give way, you monster, give way to Christ!*"

"I AM NOT SOME WORM FOR YOU TO COMMAND, HUMAN!" Emerie screamed.

"Samael!" Father Zebulun bellowed. "Hold her—I must lay my hands on her!"

Samael didn't wait to be asked twice. He flung himself into the air and his wings caught the strange currents of air that emanated from the priest's voice. But Emerie saw him coming for her and dodged easily. She crab-crawled up the wall of the sanctuary and took refuge in the choir balcony.

"Is this who you take orders from, Samael?" Emerie's laughter was high and mocking, so different from her ordinary pig-snort chuckle. "You cavort with priests and apostles? I knew you when you commanded a legion of ten thousand demons. How far you have fallen!"

Fallen? The word settled oddly in Samael's mind. Was he falling from the graces of Hell? Or was he...rising?

He was disgusted to see Emerie's head swivel around her back.

"Stop it!" Samael complained. "That is such an old trick the humans are making films about it. Come down here this instant!"

Emerie continued to crab-crawl across the sanctuary ceiling and sidestepped him as he attempted to snatch her. She began to laugh that horrible harpy laugh, delighted in the futility of his movements.

"You're pathetic, Samael," she jeered. "Panting after this girl like a dog in heat. You can't even—oof!"

Her litany was abruptly interrupted by a hymnal smacking her in the face. Zephyr, who had grown tired of Father Zebulun's exorcism and Samael's frantic chase, had taken matters into her own hands. She had climbed up the pulpit and flung the heaviest hymnal she could find towards an unsuspecting Emerie.

It worked. Shocked by the action, she fell from the ceiling, but before she could break her neck, Samael swooped in and caught her.

"Nice one," Samael told Zephyr gratefully as he landed next to the altar. "I think you gave her a black eye, though."

"She was overdue for one." Zephyr winked. "Bring her to the priest."

But Samael didn't have to move. Father Zebulun was already approaching. His expression was stony; he shot Zephyr a disapproving glare for her methods. The latter shrugged this off.

"Emerie." Father Zebulun gently laid his hands on her forehead. "Emerie—come back to us."

Her eyelids flickered and Samael's chest filled with hope as she dazedly opened her eyes. There was a brief moment of innocence as she gazed at her friends—but it disappeared into shadow. Emerie wrenched herself from Father Zebulun's grasp. She laughed hysterically and made a mock cross motion across her chest.

Something violently flung Father Zebulun across the church. He landed with a sickening thud against the giant statue of Christ that overlooked the altar, in a pointed mockery of the crucifixion. Samael dove towards her to try to hold her down, but was thrown to the ground—several minor demons had snatched his wings and started to nail them to the pews.

"Father Z!" Zephyr ran towards the priest, who had been knocked unconscious. "Oh Goddess—are you all right?"

Father Zebulun did not answer. Furiously, Zephyr turned towards Emerie, who laughed maniacally as she floated above them. Her dark hair made a Medusa-esque halo and the church began to rumble.

"My fun is over," Emerie declared and her eyes turned violet. "It is time for all of you to die."

TWENTY-FIVE

POSSESSION WAS STRANGELY RELAXING.

Lilith puppeted her body like a marionette, but the more Emerie got used to it, the more she felt soothed. There was a distinct sense of relief. She no longer had to make decisions. She was no longer in control. Responsibility was completely out of her hands.

And so Emerie sat, curled up in the corner of her mind, and didn't even bother to watch Lilith's machinations. She considered sleep—she was *terribly tired*—when she realized someone was seated next to her.

"Whoa!" Emerie squeaked, scooting away. "Who the hell are you?"

"Who the hell?" The stranger's voice was unquestionably cross. "Such disrespect! Don't you recognize me?!"

He *did* look somewhat familiar. He looked about her age, with dark hair and eyes, and a crooked smile. His clothes were a little old-fashioned, but clean cut—neatly pressed slacks, a pale blue button-down shirt. He wore a gray fedora. Emerie tried to place him. He also looked quite a bit like Falcon.

"Seriously." Emerie narrowed her eyes. "Who are you? This is my head, what are you doing here?"

"Well, it seems as though you're letting just about anyone into your head these days," the stranger replied grouchily, "but I told you a long time ago I would always be with you. I live inside your heart."

The words rang through Emerie's head. Someone had said that to her a long time ago…her grandfather. Right before he died.

"You're…*Ji-Ji?!*"

"Who else would I be?"

Emerie continued to stare. The longer she looked at him, the more his appearance became familiar. Long, aristocratic fingers, sparkling eyes, and of course the fedora…she swallowed. It was because of Ji-Ji she was able to buy her home in Milton.

Emerie felt a lot of emotions as she stared at the young man seated next to her. Confusion was one of them—Ji-Ji looked like a stranger instead of her beloved grandfather. Furthermore, he held a bamboo cane in his arms, one that Emerie knew for a fact opened up into a blade. But didn't Falcon inherit the cane? And his hat?

Ji-Ji eyed her skeptically. "You're taking things a little too literally, Emerie. We are seated in the corner of your mind. I have a say in my appearance—as do you."

"But what are you *doing* inside my head?" Emerie scooched away from him.

"What am *I* doing in your head?!" Ji-Ji thundered. He banged his cane in emphasis. "What is *she* doing in your head?! The little red-headed hussy?! Have you no respect for yourself?!"

"Ji-Ji, she possessed me!" Emerie stood up in anger. He mirrored her movements and it occurred to her they were precisely the same height—she got her petite stature from her grandfather.

"What was I supposed to do? I've been *possessed!*"

"This is not The Exorcist!" Ji-Ji boomed and Emerie flinched at his volume. "You have a choice to let evil into your heart or to rebuke it, no matter how hard it gets for you! This is *your body,* Emerie Fox. Your soul. No one else's."

Ji-Ji had *never* yelled at Emerie before. In fact, Emerie was probably the only person in the entire world who he hadn't yelled at. He yelled at her mother for marrying an American. He yelled at Falcon for not getting good grades. He yelled at her father for not taking his grandchildren to visit him in Hokkaido often enough. He yelled at the mailman for not arriving precisely at eleven a.m.

Ji-Ji was a cantankerous, ornery, and thoroughly abrasive gentleman. But for whatever reason, during Ji-Ji's long life, Emerie was his special favorite. The rest of the family was subject to long lectures and criticisms, Emerie received presents—and most of his inheritance.

Emerie wasn't entirely sure how to handle Ji-Ji being pissed with her.

Ji-Ji began to pace. "Look at what's happened. I thought for sure you would do something sensible with the money I left you."

"I did!" Emerie protested. "I bought a house!"

"You bought a spirit-infested house!"

At the echoing of her mother's words, Emerie could not help but pout. "I thought you would think it had character."

Ji-Ji glared at her, but Emerie saw the corner of his lip quirk. She grinned at him in triumph. He knew perfectly well his daughter had told her children haunted house stories and that his own penchant for the obscure and strange had skipped a generation.

"Well, I never," Ji-Ji's dark eyes blazed, "would let an evil spirit into my body. I learned to live in peace with the spirits in my old home. Why couldn't you do the same?"

Emerie wasn't sure how to answer this. It hadn't really occurred to her to just let sleeping demons lie. She assumed if your house was possessed by a demon, the best thing to do would be to get rid of the demon. This was a rather western idea—no wonder Ji-Ji was annoyed.

"Okay, I get it," Emerie said sullenly. "I was scared. I got freaked out by who—or *what*—Samael is. And I'm still kind of freaked out by it! He's done a lot of bad stuff, Ji-Ji. Evil I can't even imagine."

"That is true." Ji-Ji reached up and fidgeted with his fedora. "Ancient spirits like Samael have a long and dark history. They live longer, so they have more time to fall into evil. However—he does have a certain trust in you. And he is helping you and your friends. That is unusual."

Emerie stared at her shoes. She fidgeted with the fabric of her jeans and picked at the frayed edge. Ji-Ji sniffed pointedly.

"But whatever he's done or not done," Ji-Ji said sternly, "that is no excuse. You have always been so sure of yourself. In everything you do, you know exactly who you are. It is one of the reasons I knew it was a good idea to leave you my inheritance. Where was this certainty of self when Lilith entered your body? You have listened to fears, child."

Emerie ripped a thread out of her jeans and rolled it between her fingers. Ji-Ji was right. With everything that had happened—a thoroughly haunted house, witchcraft, exorcisms, accidentally ripping a hole between dimensions and unleashing the forces of Hell into her small town…she thought, however falsely, that she had it all under control. But when Lilith took over…she wasn't in control anymore.

She raised her head and met her grandfather's gaze.

"I'm sorry, Ji-Ji."

Tears pricked Emerie's eyelids and she wiped them furiously. She buried her head in her knees. Her grandfather tapped her shoulder stiffly, just like he did when she was a little girl. He was always so awkward about physical contact; it was cheering to know this had carried over into the afterlife. She hiccuped a little and finally looked forward. She could hear the shouts and laughter more clearly—there was a fight going on outside her body. She sighed.

"Well, Ji-Ji…how exactly do I get my body back?"

Ji-Ji harrumphed and banged his cane. "How do you *get* your body back? It's *your* body!"

Emerie tilted her head curiously. "Yeah, but…aren't I possessed right now?"

"Possession is not like it is in the movies."

He did not say anything else. Instead, he muttered something under his breath and glared at her. He would do the same thing when Falcon got frustrated with his homework. Emerie stood and began to pace.

"It's not like in the movies…" Emerie muttered. "Okay…well, they all seem to involve young girls, don't they? Innocence corrupted, I guess. They're overpowered by the demonic influence, which is what makes them so scary…"

She considered. She'd briefly allowed Samael to possess her, before she summoned him. He'd made a dirty joke and she ordered him *out*… and he actually got out.

Ji-Ji watched her carefully. He tilted his head back and patiently waited for her to find the answer.

"You know," Emerie said thoughtfully, thinking of Samael. "Possession is a pretty horrifying process. It's a violation, after all. Maybe a lot of people lose the will to fight—or think they *can't* fight. I mean…this is *my* head. *My* body. I mean, isn't that why Lilith showed me all that stuff about Samael? To freak me out? Psychological manipulation? To make it easier for her to invade my head?"

Ji-Ji's expression did not alter but his dark eyes twinkled. Emerie's revelation proceeded to make her even more furious.

"This is bullshit!" she shouted. "She can't have my body! She just wants it to freak out Samael! It's all a head game! I'm over it! I'm taking my body back!"

Emerie froze suddenly. She slowly looked at Ji-Ji, an expression of pure deviousness etched across her features.

"Ji-Ji." Her voice was steady. "You know…Samael let *me* possess him for a little bit. He said that was a little known fact about possession… humans can possess demons."

Ji-Ji snorted. "He sounds like an especially foolish spirit to tell you such an obvious vulnerability."

She went to him and wrapped her arms around him. He froze—just like she remembered, so uncomfortable with hugs! She smelled vanilla and tobacco, familiar, warm scents. "Ji-Ji…I miss you so much. I miss you every single day."

"There's no need to miss me." He tapped his head with his cane and then pointed at her heart. "I'll always be right here."

Emerie smiled at him and Ji-Ji's features turned stony.

"And don't let me ever catch you *leaning* on your bokuto like it's a *cane*, again!" He snapped. "Be more respectful!"

———

The moment Lilith announced through Emerie's mouth they were going to die, Samael knew it was over.

Of course, *he* would be fine. Lilith still wanted him for her own purposes. But he was overcome with fear for Father Zebulun and Zephyr —which was an entirely unnerving experience. It was odd enough being worried for Emerie, but adding two other humans to the mix was another matter entirely.

Emerie raised her arm. The large statue of the crucifixion overlooking the altar groaned powerfully and lurched off the wall. It pelted the altar with debris and nails. Emerie cackled and flicked her wrist—the crucifix statue shot like a missile, headed straight for Father Zebulun's heart.

"No!" Zephyr screamed and threw up her hands. The crucifix statue slowed its course and Emerie narrowed her eyes. She jerked her head and there was a thunderous clang. Samael watched in horror as several of the organ pipes attacked Zephyr like snakes and wrapped around her, turning her into a metal mummy.

"Get off!" Zephyr shrieked as she resisted the pipes. *"Get off of me!"*

Emerie lifted her hand and smirked. Zephyr had probably formed some sort of barrier or sacred space—but it was ineffective with her immobile. The crucifix resumed its journey and cruised towards Father Zebulun's unconscious body. Samael roared as he flung himself in front of the two and slashed his sword towards the crucifix.

"Look at what you're doing, heretic." Emerie gloated. "Protecting humans! Protecting *two* humans—and one of them a priest! Do you have any idea how many brothers and sisters this mortal has banished? Do you know of his liaison with my sister?"

Samael blinked in confusion. He would have turned towards Father Zebulun for an explanation, but the priest was still out cold. Zephyr struggled against her bonds and frantically searched for some way to fight back.

"One last chance, Samael." Emerie flicked her hand. Water floated from the baptismal font and splashed across the statue. The giant statue of the crucifixion was now drenched in holy water. She edged the statue nearer to him, and the holy water sizzled as it dripped.

"Let's find out if heretics can still burn."

Samael lifted his sword. But before he could attempt to stave off the attack, Emerie stiffened.

Something contorted in her face, as though she had a nervous tic all of a sudden. She scowled and her hands went to her forehead, almost like she nursed a terrible migraine. The statue groaned and fell to the ground.

"What's happening?" Zephyr tried to run to her, but Father Zebulun caught her arm. "What's she doing?"

Samael could hardly dare to hope. It seemed as though there was an internal conflict in Emerie's body—yes! Emerie was fighting back!

"Emerie!" he shouted. "We're here! We can get you out!"

"Shut up!" Lilith within Emerie screamed. "What are you doing?! Your body is *mine*, vile sow! *How dare you!*"

Before Samael had a chance to wonder at her words, she let out a terrible howl. Her body convulsed, and strangely, seemed to phase in and out. One moment she was Emerie, another she was Lilith—and when she was Lilith, she choked out:

"This is my body, you bitch—get out, get out!"

Her voice was decidedly Emerie's. Samael gaped as Emerie continued to scream and jerk, her head wobbling like a bobble head. And then, she began to cough, and fell over the baptismal font as though it were a toilet. Her chest started to heave and without warning, something was *pushed* out of her, which screamed when it hit the baptismal font and fell to the floor. The thing was transparent briefly, but slowly regained form, like a Polaroid picture.

"Holy shit." Zephyr was awed. "She just fucking vomited Lilith out of her body!"

She was right. The light in Emerie's eyes had returned and she placed her hands on her knees. Her breaths were short and hard. She threw a dirty look towards Lilith's crumpled form, which lay on the floor of the church.

"I need a taco." Emerie groaned and hot relief flooded through Samael.

He ran to her and halted. He remembered that Lilith had shown Emerie some of the more traumatizing parts of his past—he had no idea how much Emerie had seen. He looked at her nervously but she gave him a small smile. He was confused until she rolled her eyes and hugged him tightly—*she was hugging him.*

"It's okay, Sam," she mumbled into his shoulder. "It's okay. We all have our demons."

Samael groaned. "You've been waiting all week to make that joke."

She smiled at him unrepentantly and he had the simultaneous urge to either kiss her or throttle her for the bad pun (bad puns generally produce this urge). Kiss her...he should kiss her...it had been a while since he kissed a woman...

He held back. Something told him if he kissed her...it wouldn't simply be a kiss of lustful passion. He wouldn't be able to stop. Not simply the physicality of it all, but the emotion. He fell once, in a garden long ago, and now...if he kissed her, right now, regardless of the priest or the witch...would he fall again?

Samael was abruptly interrupted by Father Zebulun's moan.

"Father Z!" Emerie broke away from Samael to run over to him. With Lilith temporarily immobile, Zephyr had managed to free herself from her organ-pipe cage. She had slipped something into Father Zebulun's mouth that woke him up.

"My mom doesn't have a lot of magical talents." Zephyr chuckled. "But she's really good at herbal infusions. Feeling better, Father?"

Father Zebulun made a face. "What on earth am I chewing on?"

"Woke you up, didn't it?" Zephyr slapped his back heartily. "Make sure to swallow it whole. It's good for the colon."

Father Zebulun grimaced and suddenly registered Emerie's presence. "Emerie! Are you all right?"

"I'm fine," she assured him. "I got her out of me—long story. But she is, y'know, still..."

Father Zebulun stood quickly, ignoring Zephyr and Emerie's protests. He strode towards Lilith, who remained on the ground. She mumbled a little and tried to sit up. She failed. Apparently being vomited out of a human tended to daze demons.

"Well, Emerie," he rumbled as he shook a bit of sick off his shoe. "Are you ready to send her back to Hell?"

"*Hell* yes." she grinned. They both glanced at Samael, perhaps to see if he would object. He scowled at Emerie's quip but shrugged.

———

"Hm." Father Zebulun turned towards the witch. "I would appreciate it if you'd draw a seal around her. Trapping Lilith will only take a moment."

Looking surprised and pleased, Zephyr hopped towards them. She dug a piece of chalk out of her bag. Emerie obediently sat in a pew and watched Zephyr draw a perfect circle around Lilith, adding little doodles and characters here and there.

"Damn. Zephyr makes it look so easy."

"That's why you should only perform exorcisms with a trained professional," Samael chastised. He took a seat in the next pew up. He tried to fold in his wings so he fit better but only ended up knocking a couple Bibles off the pew.

"Smooth," Emerie commented. Samael grumbled about the narrow pews and how they were ill-made for anyone of a proper size.

"You're sure you're all right?" His volume rose over Lilith's screams and Father Zebulun's powerful voice.

She nodded. "Yeah, I am. Sorry for freaking everyone out."

He shrugged. "I can't believe you were able to break out of her hold. Lilith is one of the most powerful demons in Hell—and you managed to *possess* her for a time. And break out of her control. That's…unheard of."

"You were the one who told me humans could possess demons. I bet if more people knew that the possession rate would go down. Besides, I had help." Emerie lifted her legs and rested them on the pew in front of her.

Samael's brow furrowed. "Had help?"

"Yeah." Emerie rolled her shoulders. "Ji-Ji."

"Who?"

"My grandfather. He died about two years ago. He left me some money—that's how I bought the Hell House in the first place. And boy, was he royally pissed I gave up my body to Lilith…"

Samael looked completely lost. It was almost endearing. She twirled a hymnal ribbon around her finger and watched Zephyr mark something on the squalling Lilith's forehead.

"Bodily autonomy," Samael said finally, "is particularly important."

"No argument here."

"So now that you have your body back." He tilted his head. "Do you have any plans on what you're going to do with it?"

There was something immensely inappropriate about how he said this, but Emerie couldn't help but grin.

"I'm open to suggestions," she replied airily and Samael's brow quirked with interest. He opened his mouth to respond but was suddenly interrupted.

"Emerie," Father Zebulun called. "Come up here, please."

She hopped off the pew and walked towards the priest. Lilith was fully awake now and she glared at all of them hatefully. She appeared to be trapped inside the curious chalk circle, right in front of the altar. She did not look at all comfortable.

Emerie squatted next to Lilith. "Ready to go home, buddy?"

"*Vile sow! I will feast on your entrails and wear your skin as my raiment!*"

Emerie tilted her head towards Father Zebulun. "She is just so sweet to me."

"I would like you to observe this exorcism." Father Zebulun handed Zephyr a prayer book. (Zephyr held it between pinched fingers, as though it was dirty.)

"Why?"

"I want you to prepare yourself. The rest of the exorcisms we will complete will be much bigger and probably more violent. You must steel yourself."

"I'm sure I'll be fine." Emerie leaned against the baptismal font. "I got Samael here without a fuss, right?"

Zephyr and Father Zebulun exchanged an exasperated look. Before Emerie could skirt the obvious issue of how her last ritual had unleashed the forces of Hell, Samael looked down the aisle and exclaimed, "Orobas!"

The little demon greeted them all with a nod of his horse-like head. He paused briefly to chew the stray organ pipes, which earned a disapproving frown from Father Zebulun. The priest was beginning to register how much damage the church had endured.

"Where have you been?" Zephyr snapped at Orobas.

He raised a brow. "Did you think I would help you fight Lilith? I am ill-equipped for battle and Lilith would quickly destroy me."

"Coward!"

Orobas shrugged this off, as though it were of little consequence.

"What does it matter? You will be banishing myself and Samael soon enough."

There was an awkward silence. Emerie's chest tightened. Samael said nothing, just looked towards the witch and the priest. Zephyr looked away and inspected the circle they'd trapped Lilith within to make sure it was secure. Oddly, Lilith was also quiet, with something close to a smirk etched on her face.

"We spoke about this earlier, Emerie," Father Zebulun said finally. "After we exorcise Lilith, the next ritual we will enact to rid the town of these demons will...banish them. All of them."

She felt nauseated. She turned towards Samael. He carved doodles into the church pew in front of him with an extended claw. He cast a curt glance at them, and then slowly rose from the pew.

"I won't go without a fight. Just so you all know."

Father Zebulun's hand lifted to his jacket. Emerie could tell he was feeling for his pistol.

"You agreed to enact the ritual." The priest said quietly.

"Yeah, well." Samael glanced toward Emerie. "Maybe I'm not so keen on going anymore."

Zephyr's fists clenched, and a cold chill seemed to emanate off her. Emerie stepped between them.

"Can't we..." Emerie crossed her arms in front of her chest. "Can't we find a different solution? Compromise? We're sending Lilith back on her own, can't we send the rest of them back one by one?"

"Jesus, Emerie, do you know how long that would take?" Zephyr stumbled slightly on the steps of the altar and grabbed Father Zebulun's elbow for balance. "The longer we wait, the more spirits will spill out of the portal in your attic. It would be one step forward, two steps back—"

"But it's not fair!" Emerie took a step in front of Samael. "Sam's been helping us do this from the beginning. From the moment he was summoned, he's been protecting all of us! Doesn't he deserve to be here?"

Something flickered in Samael's expression. She noticed him look down at his sword, still snugly (and annoyingly) secured. "Emerie—"

"I was afraid this might happen."

Father Zebulun stepped away from the altar and placed a firm hand on Emerie's shoulder. She shook him off brusquely. He gave a heavy sigh.

"I understand you have a connection with this demon. I understand more than you know. A long time ago...I was involved in a summoning gone wrong. I had my own doubts and reservations about correcting my mistake. In the end, it cost me everything."

He looked squarely at Samael. "In the end, no matter how helpful, no matter how connected, he is a *demon*. He has done terrible things. He has committed great evil on this world. The earth is no place for him."

"I thought Catholics were supposed to forgive!" Emerie stepped in front of Samael, as though shielding him from the priest's terrible stare. "Isn't that your whole deal? Confession and repenting? He's told me the evil he's done. He's helping us track down the demons. What kind of repentance do you want? Does grace only matter when it's convenient?!"

Father Zebulun didn't move. For the first time since she'd met him, he seemed at a loss for words. His expression fell on Samael, as though he expected the demon to explain himself. Samael opened his mouth to respond but was suddenly interrupted.

"The girl has a point. There is no grace among humans—not truly."

Emerie turned towards the interloper. Down the aisle of the church, a middle-aged woman watched them. She had entered through the main sanctuary doors.

Emerie gasped. She recognized this woman! This was the Karen with all the churchy pins on her pink polo. She had that distinctive soccer mom haircut. Now she observed them with great interest.

"*Oh!*"

Lilith had cried out. Emerie glanced at the trapped demon for a moment and then turned back towards the stranger, brows raised.

"Um...we're kind of in the middle of something." Emerie coughed. "Can we help you, ma'am?"

"I certainly hope so, Emerie," the middle-aged woman responded with a smile. "In fact, I'm counting on your help."

She grinned and looked directly at Samael.

"It's good to see you again, my brother." She started to walk down the aisle as she took a sip of a frozen latte. "I see you have made some friends. Acting quite the rebel, aren't you, befriending humans? That's all right, little brother. I see you've trapped Lilith. She's been most naughty lately—it was good of you to keep her for me."

Samael's expression was murderous and scared. Emerie felt him tremble next to her.

"Lucifer."

TWENTY-SIX

"YOU'RE LUCIFER?!"

Emerie hadn't meant to blurt it out. But how could this woman be the Lord of Hell? She had Prayer Club written all over her. Emerie had seen her Suburban. It was littered with Marriage = 1 Man + 1 Woman and Jesus fish bumper stickers. But the woman ignored her.

"Have you had fun?" Lucifer's voice was warm and maternal. "I know you've been stuck in that house for a while. I do hope you've enjoyed yourself."

Samael stared at the floor, unable to meet Lucifer's eyes. His wings shivered and Emerie felt a rush of affection for him. She reached out, took his hand, and squeezed it gently.

Lucifer noticed the movement immediately. "Well, how about that! You *have* been having fun, Samael. The other incubi will be very proud."

"Shove off," Samael muttered. "It's none of your business."

"Fair enough." Lucifer took another sip of latte. "I don't really care about that, anyway. I heard you managed to trap Lilith—and I will reward you handsomely for that, little brother."

Emerie had little sympathy for the she-demon that possessed her. But the look of absolute fear on Lilith's usually pert face moved her.

Lucifer paid Lilith no heed. She rested an elegant and perfectly manicured hand on one of the pews. Finally, she acknowledged the frightened she-demon.

"Well, Lilith?" she called out to her, in a slightly scolding tone. "What do you have to say for yourself? Do you think I was ignorant of your little plans? Did you really think my little brother would betray me for *you*?"

"Go to hell," Lilith hissed.

"Not me." Lucifer chuckled. "But I can promise you I will talk to Beelzebub before you're banished. I'm sure he'll have something special cooked up for you."

Lucifer straightened and turned towards Father Zebulun. "Well, Father, proceed with the exorcism."

Since Emerie had met Father Zebulun, she had known him to be a tempest beneath calm waters. He never lost control, never lost his temper, and remained resolute and sure in everything he did. She expected Father Zebulun to stride forward Exorcist style, tell the interloping Lucifer *the power of Christ compelled him*...

But Father Zebulun hadn't moved. He seemed rooted to the spot, his expression frozen. The moment Lucifer's stare fell upon Father Zebulun, he had become paralyzed. One hand dropped the crossbow and it clattered to the floor.

Zephyr was aghast at his immobility. She stomped in front of the priest and bit out, "Get lost."

Lucifer smiled at her gently. "How I miss the days when witches worshiped me properly. Nowadays, they sanitize their own history and profess not to believe in me. It *is* disappointing."

"Did I stutter?" Zephyr threatened as she drew chalk from her pocket. "If I can seal Lilith in a circle, I can seal you."

"Oh, child." Her voice was almost sympathetic. "Just like your mother. You deal with forces beyond your ken."

Without warning, Zephyr mugged Father Zebulun's water gun from his jacket. She looked vaguely disappointed, as though she intended to grab the proper pistol, but missed. Still, she pumped several times and pointed it directly at Lucifer, who looked on, unimpressed.

"One last chance!"

"Zephyr, don't!" Samael roared. "You don't know what you're doing!"

She ignored him and pulled the trigger of the water gun. But instead of water, *white hot flames* shot out from the gun, coursing straight towards Lucifer. Her jaw dropped as the streams of flames slowed and halted in front of Lucifer's face.

"Oh dear," she murmured as she fiddled with one of her Jesus buttons idly. "The priest's weapon seems to be malfunctioning. Better get that looked at."

The flames suddenly reversed and sped towards Zephyr. She screamed and dropped the water gun, but the flames kept their course. Milliseconds before she was engulfed, Samael leapt in front of her, shielding her with his wings. He gritted his teeth as the smell of singed flesh overwhelmed the church.

Lucifer's lip curled. "You've been on earth for too long, Samael. Your sympathy for these creatures is misplaced."

"Whatever." Samael averted his gaze. "Just—let them be."

Lucifer sighed in exasperation. "I swear, little brother, I do spoil you so. Very well. Humans—your services are no longer needed here. Leave the church. Go to your houses. Netflix and chill."

No one moved. Zephyr shakily wiped ash from her arms and Father Zebulun remained in his semi-catatonic state. Emerie decided to take action. She planted herself in front of the soccer mom and placed her hands on her hips.

"What are you going to do?"

Lucifer scrutinized her with interest and took another long draught of frozen latte. Emerie scowled at her bored expression.

"Well, well. The conjurer speaks." Lucifer chose to smile. "I do owe you a boon, human. You opened the door a crack and now I'm able to throw it all the way open."

Emerie wasn't sure what she meant but the entitled, pompous tone infuriated her. "Piss off!"

Lucifer tossed the empty plastic cup aside and it clattered on the floor, leaking mocha residue onto the ground. She passed right by Emerie and approached the circle. Lilith stared at her in fear, still trapped in the seal.

"Hey," Emerie shouted. "I was talking to you!"

Lucifer glanced at her and Emerie shuddered. She hated Lucifer's eyes. They looked like oil spills, dark and thick, poisonous to the soul.

"Samael," Lucifer said softly. "It's time."

Emerie slowly looked at Samael. He didn't move, but he stared at the floor of the church. What did Lucifer mean?

It didn't take her long to find out. Lucifer snapped her fingers and Samael reluctantly stepped forward to join her. He met Emerie's stare.

"They all warned you, Emerie."

"What are you doing?" Emerie tried to race towards him but Lucifer flicked her wrist and she slammed to the ground. "Sam, stop it!"

"All of the princes have gathered." Lucifer smiled at Samael and caressed his shoulder. "Mammon to the east. Abaddon to the west. Moloch to the north. Azazel below. Save one. Shall we return to the Hell House?"

"What are you talking about?" Emerie bellowed.

Lucifer pointed at Zephyr, who'd fallen to her knees. "The witch knows."

Zephyr shook violently. Her face was pale and clammy and she looked like she was about to be sick. Father Zebulun staggered to her side.

Lucifer raised her arms and then clapped her hands slowly and methodically. With each clap, the hanging lights went out with a pop, immersing the sanctuary in darkness. She pointed towards the unlit candles at the altar. They flamed and shot long columns of fire straight to the vaulted ceiling. Emerie's eyes widened—when she'd first tried to exorcise Samael, her candles had acted similarly...right before a gate to Hell ripped open.

Lilith screamed. The chalk circle around her glowed scarlet and she tried to move away from the symbols, as though each mark burned her. She could not leave the circle, but there were *things* that started to crawl out.

"One more piece," Lucifer told Samael, who looked away. "You called me, brother. Don't forget that."

"You *what*?!"

Zephyr found her voice. Emerie didn't understand. But the guilt in Samael's eyes was clear.

"I had to, Emerie. I had to call him. I used Harriet."

"The *fuck*?!" Zephyr bellowed.

"My Ouija board!" Emerie shouted back. "He used my Ouija board to summon Satan!"

"Don't call him that!" Samael begged. "He's my brother, Emerie! I had to get him, or Lilith would've—"

"*YOU IDIOT!*"

Emerie marched over to Samael. White hot rage coursed through her and she raised her arm and *SLAPPED* Samael across the face as hard as she could.

Samael lurched from the blow. Lucifer quirked her head curiously. Emerie took a deep breath.

"That was as stupid a thing to do," she inhaled deeply through her nostrils, "as it was for me to attempt an exorcism by myself."

"Have to agree." Lucifer's eyes were bright with malice. "Now, then. Since the little love affair is over...shall we?"

Samael swallowed hard. For a halting moment, Emerie wondered if he would defy Lucifer.

"Remember our deal. I told you where to find the girl. You agreed to take your throne...as Prince of Hell."

Emerie gasped. Samael bowed his head. He turned his back on the group and went towards Lucifer.

Without warning, they suddenly vanished.

Emerie backed away from the front of the church, where Lilith still screamed in pain, and grabbed Father Zebulun and Zephyr's arm as she retreated down the aisle. They might have to make a break for it—but before she could proceed, she heard the church doors slam shut. Unseen hands shot the bolts, locking the humans in.

She whirled around. Fat, pudgy little devils that looked like flying sausages leered at her as they flapped away from the church doors. More and more demons crawled out of the circle. Lilith continued to shriek, sprawled within the circle. It almost looked as though she was giving birth to the horrifying beasts.

"What the hell!" Emerie shook her priest, in an attempt to snap him awake. "What the hell just happened?"

"A ritual." Zephyr gritted her teeth in pain. *"I told you...Lucifer is casting—"*

Zephyr stifled a scream. Emerie, who'd been trying the main doors, jumped back. A centipede like monstrosity the size of a refrigerator crawled across the front doors. It raised a horrifying head covered in pincers and clicked at them menacingly. Emerie turned towards the side doors. Slimy, black eels the size of school buses creeped across the stained-glass windows and came to rest across the side doors of the sanctuary.

It was at that moment Emerie realized there was someone standing at the altar.

Beelzebub grinned at them warmly. "Hello again, my friends."

TWENTY-SEVEN

"HELL IS EMPTY," Lucifer mused. "And all the devils are here. Or will be."

"Please stop. I hate when you quote."

Lucifer and Samael stood before Hell House. Emerie's home was bathed in red, as though the sun were setting. Samael was pretty sure it wasn't sunset though—but wherever Lucifer was, linear time had a tendency to fracture.

"Didn't I tell you, Samael?" Lucifer gestured to the front door as it swung open in welcome. "Everything would shake out. It was extremely fortuitous the Lemp woman tried to summon you—that gave us an opening."

Samael cast a dark look at the house before they entered. "Right. Everything happens for a reason?"

Lucifer smiled tenderly. "That was my most successful propaganda for the humans, you know."

They came into the living room. Lucifer flopped onto the couch like a housecat and stretched comfortably. Samael didn't look at his brother, instead retreated to the bookshelves and examined the titles, like a disinterested house guest. Lucifer watched him curiously.

"Why so glum, chum?" Lucifer snapped her fingers and another frozen coffee appeared in her hand. "Everything worked out perfectly."

She set the plastic cup down on the coffee table. Samael winced involuntarily. Emerie would be *furious* that the Devil wasn't using a coaster.

"Where are the other princes?" Samael turned pointedly away from the wet ring on Emerie's coffee table.

"Moloch is at the Witch's Memorial, Abaddon at the witch caves—Azazel was *quite* a disappointment to me, unable to kill one little witch. Mammon is at the Corbin Mansion, Baphomet at the old library, and of course...you are here." Lucifer swirled her index finger in the air and another frozen coffee appeared. Samael watched in quiet judgment—Lucifer had apparently traded his love of wine and spirits for caffeinated frozen beverages.

"And the church?"

"Beelzebub is there." Lucifer yawned. "Oh, don't look so worried, little brother. Your little human girl will be fine. I can't say the same for the witch who destroyed Azazel—stupid of him, but my heart does break. And of course, that priest has been a thorn in my side for decades."

Samael turned and traced some dust on the shelf with his claw. That had been the second part of the Ouija conversation. After Lucifer had revealed Emerie's location...but Samael had made him swear he would not harm Emerie. That if he allied himself to Lucifer, Emerie would live.

He drew a pentacle star in the dust. He felt that same uncomfortable, dreadful feeling in the pit of his stomach as he thought of Father Zebulun, comforting him about his doubts and confusion. And Zephyr...the little witch was correct. Lucifer was casting—he intended to make the gate to Hell *bigger*.

Lucifer was going to turn the town of Milton into a portal to Hell.

———

"Okay, does anyone have any bright ideas?"

The interior of the church grew darker and darker. Zephyr couldn't tell if it was due to the giant bugs blocking the windows or if daylight was dying. Beelzebub stood at the end of the aisle, on the altar. He clicked at them genially and seemed in no rush to fly at them. Instead, he knelt down and they watched in horror as his proboscis extended. The proboscis sucked up two flittering moths the size of housecats and he slowly chewed them up. Saliva and insect entrails oozed down his face. Zephyr had the uneasy feeling he was making a point—this would soon be their fate.

But now that Lucifer had disappeared, Father Zebulun returned to himself. Breathing hard, he fumbled in his jacket and withdrew the Freischutz.

"I'll need a clear shot." He stared down the aisle directly at Beelzebub.

But before he could gun down the insectile demon, Beelzebub's mouth fell open. *Literally* open. His jaw dropped to the ground like a perverse scroll; his black fanged maw faced them directly, a sort of grotesque cavern. There was a horrible buzzing and then all at once, a thick cloud of black flies erupted from his mouth.

Father Zebulun bellowed in rage. Emerie shrieked and batted them away uselessly. Zephyr choked and gagged. The black flies quickly swarmed the church like a heavy smog—they completely obliterated Beelzebub from view.

"*Damn it!*"

Zephyr had never heard Father Zebulun swear. But there was no way to point this out to him without ingesting a thousand black flies. Instead, she grabbed Emerie's arm and Father Zebulun's elbow and pulled them towards one of the side staircases. The cloud of flies grew thicker and thicker as they rushed up the twisting stairs. Father Zebulun bypassed the balcony and swerved to the left. They stood before a set of rickety wooden stairs and what looked like an attic door. Father Zebulun clambered upwards and jerked it open.

"The bell tower!" he yelled at them. "Quickly!"

They scrambled up the splintery steps and found themselves in a dark, cramped room. Emerie nearly ran headlong into one of the great bronze bells. Father Zebulun yanked the door shut behind them and bolted it quickly. There was a strange tip-tap against the bell tower door —as though the swarm of flies were tentatively knocking.

Zephyr coughed deeply. "Now what?"

They started to cross the room carefully. Nothing seemed particularly secure—the floorboards creaked dangerously underneath and Zephyr took care not to touch one of the church bells. There was a large window across the room, latched shut. Emerie kicked the rusted latch and the window opened easily. She poked her head through and whistled.

"It's a long way down."

"Of course it is," Zephyr muttered. "I thought all this shit was computerized nowadays." She gestured toward the bells.

Father Zebulun looked offended. "This church and this bell tower are over a hundred years old."

There was an ominous thud against the bell tower door that caused the whole tower to vibrate. Zephyr took another look at the open window. Emerie was right. This was beginning to look hopeless.

"Well, Father, I don't suppose you have a grappling hook in your jacket?"

"Indeed not," Father Zebulun said grimly. "We'll have to risk climbing."

"Are you kidding me?" Zephyr gestured towards the tiny opening. "I am not a rock climber! We will flatten ourselves on the concrete!"

"Do you have a better idea?"

"Wait!"

Zephyr turned towards Emerie. Her eyes were bright and she cleared her throat for emphasis.

"Zephyr, do you have a broom?"

The witch's mouth fell open. Father Zebulun closed his eyes for patience. There was another ominous THUMP against the door.

"A broom?!" Zephyr shouted. "That's your idea?! You want me to fly us off this tower on my *broom*?! I don't have a broom! This is not Harry Potter!"

"WHAT'S THE POINT IN BEING A WITCH IF YOU DON'T GET A BROOM?!" Emerie shoved her bokuto at Zephyr in emphasis.

"That's not—we don't—the brooms are not used for that purpose!" Zephyr blustered, trying to bat the bokuto out of her face.

"What are they used for if not flying?!"

"They're—we—*it is a phallic metaphor, Emerie.*"

The fact there were literal demons at the door was forgotten. "Wait, so you *bang* the broom?!"

"Could we please focus on the issue at hand?" Father Zebulun's eyes flitted to the door.

Zephyr took the wooden sword roughly from Emerie. If only it were as simple as enchanting a broom to fly them out…but there was something she *could* try. She bit her lip. Casting…she was so out of practice! But if they didn't do something, they would die.

She placed two fingers on the bokuto. She closed her eyes in concentration. *Spirits of air…guide us. Help us! I know I've been lost, I know I've turned away from the powers of the universe…help me save my friends.*

The bokuto glowed, as though it had been heated in a stove—but it did not catch fire. Zephyr opened her eyes and gave a jerky nod. Now or never.

Another THUD rattled the room and ended with a sickening crack. The door was not going to hold. Zephyr pushed a lock of dark hair out of her eyes.

"I have no idea if this is going to work," she announced. "Grab hold."

Without protest, Father Zebulun and Emerie each grasped an end of the bokuto. Zephyr stood in the middle and supported it with both hands. With a yell worthy of Xena, Zephyr charged towards the open window, with Father Zebulun and Emerie in tow. They clutched the bokuto tightly and Zephyr squeezed her eyes shut as they leapt out the window.

The wooden sword did not precisely fly—though Zephyr suspected it could do the job if it only had one passenger. Instead, it sank slowly to the ground as they all held onto it like some sort of hovering monkey bar. She could feel the spirits of air all around her, little elementals sustaining and supporting her. Spirits and witches lived in a symbiotic relationship; they fed off each other. This kind of magic *drained* the practitioner.

About a foot before they reached the ground, Zephyr slipped into unconsciousness.

———

They landed safely. As soon as Zephyr let go of the bokuto, she collapsed to the ground. Emerie grabbed her before she hit her head on the pavement and Father Zebulun gazed up at the church tower regretfully.

Emerie examined her surroundings as she helped Zephyr up. The witch leaned on her heavily and Emerie wasn't sure if Zephyr was exhausted by the effort of her spell or if the town of Milton had led her to despair.

The whole town looked like the setting of a horror film. It was only three in the afternoon, but the streetlamps were alight and blackish clouds sank low over the houses and businesses. All of the houses were dark, the streets were completely silent—empty festival stalls littered the sidewalks and Emerie could just make out the center square, cloaked in shadow. The stillness in the air was eerie, like the greenish calm before a tornado. The deathly anticipation turned Emerie's stomach.

"Where is everyone?"

It was Zephyr who spoke. She still leaned against Emerie, her eyes were wide with fright.

"Why is it..." Emerie gulped and turned towards Father Zebulun, who stared at the road before them motionless. "Why is it so quiet?"

"They're preparing the rite," Zephyr whispered. She seemed to regain some of her strength and shakily released herself from Emerie's support. "That must be it. This town has been plunged into the in-between—the existence between worlds. Like Purgatory for demons. Every Prince of Hell on every ley line...they're about to nuke that gate to Hell until this whole town *is* Hell."

"Oh, no they won't." Emerie faced the priest and the witch. "We're not going to let that happen."

"Emerie, it's already happened..." Father Zebulun's voice shook. "We need to get out of Milton."

"We're not running away!" Emerie banged her bokuto on the ground in emphasis. "Listen. I have a plan."

Father Zebulun and Zephyr exchanged a doubtful look.

"Okay, I know I sort of caused this whole mess and my plans haven't exactly been stellar as of late—but just this once—please trust me on this. I have an idea, but for it to work...we need to get to the Hell House. Please, Father. Please, Zephyr. I know we can do this."

The idealism in Emerie's expression was potent and contagious. The fact was, the situation in Kiev had seemed hopeless too, but Father Zebulun had stuck it out anyway. He would die in Milton taking a stand, if he had to. And, of course, there was certainly no way Zephyr would leave her mother's fate in the hands of demons and spirits (no matter how much Sunflower might enjoy it).

"Okay, Emerie. Ball's in your court."

TWENTY-EIGHT

YOUR BROTHER'S A DICK, SAM. GTFO

Samael stared at the glistening pink paint on the wall of the house, his mouth slightly open. He'd heard something outside the living room window and had told Lucifer he would check it out. Lucifer was confident Beelzebub had taken care of them; that his demon insects now feasted on the bones of the priest and the witch.

Lucifer was usually right. Samael took that for granted. He assumed the disturbance outside the house was unruly devils knocking over the trash bins instead of keeping the fast until Lucifer's ritual was complete.

The graffiti on the wall was a shock.

Emerie was still alive. He wasn't sure if this made him joyful or fearful—perhaps a bit of both. How on earth had she escaped Beelzebub's pincers? And why in Hell's name did she come back *here*? Why send a message to *him*?! She knew he was a demon. She knew where his alliance stood.

He wondered if the priest was alive too and remembered suddenly the weapon he carried. But Beelzebub had been aware of the Freischutz —Lucifer had stated most condescendingly that Beelzebub was prepared for the weapon.

It must've been the witch then. Some natural power of hers Lucifer had not foreseen. Or perhaps all of them together…?

There was a loud kerfuffle from the back of the house. Concerned, Samael circled the building until he reached the backyard shed. Emerie hadn't done much with the shed since she moved in here—the grass that surrounded it was littered with paint chips and splintered wood. Nothing within the shed was Emerie's.

Unless…that's where she was hiding.

Samael hesitated. If he found Emerie there—or the priest or the witch —he would either have to smite them on the spot or bring them to Lucifer for judgment. Lucifer would know if he set them free—Lucifer *always* knew. Nothing got past his big brother; it was one of his most annoying faults.

But Samael didn't *want* to smite them. The idea of hurting them put knots in his stomach.

He glanced down at his sword. Lucifer had tactfully refused to mention the return of his angel sword and Samael kept hoping the thing would go away the longer he stood in Lucifer's presence. But the weapon stubbornly clung to him. It was a weapon forged to protect humans. If he tried to use it to destroy Emerie…would it leave him in peace?

His gut twisted horribly and Samael took a deep breath. Completely at a loss at what to do, he stormed towards the shed and flung the doors open.

Orobas sat peaceably on an old riding lawn mower as he chewed a radio antenna.

"Orobas!" Relief flooded Samael. "I was wondering where you disappeared off to!"

"Not a place for minor demons like me." Orobas plucked a bit of sulfur from his shoulder. "Lucifer and Lilith and Beelzebub…best to lie low." He tossed a few stray screws into his mouth.

"Is that what Emerie is doing? And everyone else? Lying low?"

Orobas shook his head. "My conjuror has a message for you."

"For *me*?!"

"Indeed. She said she is haunting you. Just like your conscience."

"Conscience!" Samael spluttered. "I don't have a conscience!"

Orobas eyed him critically. "You're not supposed to have an angel sword either. And yet—"

"Oh, shut up. You say she's *haunting* me? How is she doing that?"

"She has already begun."

At that precise moment, the lights of the Hell House went dark.

———

"This idea is crazy."

Emerie backed away from the power box. "Some of the *best* ideas are crazy!"

"I'm afraid I must agree with Zephyr," Father Zebulun said worriedly. "We cannot terrorize a *demon*."

They were in the basement of the Hell House. There were two official entrances into her basement—the outdoor cellar doors which faced the side street and the traditional door in her kitchen. But there was another entrance into the basement—something Emerie and Dylan had discovered for themselves shortly after moving in. There was a sort of jar room below their shed. A compartment door led them into a cramped little space lined with shelves. Dusty and broken mason jars filled every shelf, some with vegetables, others with unidentified liquids. Dylan *hated* the room; said it was creepy. But Emerie poked around a little more and found an odd little corridor—that led directly into her basement.

They weren't really sure what the passage was. It could've been built for storage; possibly it was an extension of the jar room. Or as a way to get firewood from the shed inside the house, to avoid the often dangerous New England blizzards.

Regardless...it was how they got into the house.

"We're not trying to terrorize them." Emerie waited for her eyes to adjust to the darkness. "We're sending a message."

"Tagging your own house with an insult to Satan is a message?" Zephyr asked dryly.

"Sam will get it." Emerie crossed her arms. "He left me annoying messages on the walls when I first moved in."

Zephyr sighed and looked away, like an older sister who was resigned to her younger sibling's foolishness. Father Zebulun crossed himself. They didn't believe her. She couldn't exactly blame them, but their negative attitudes were getting on her nerves. She remembered how frantic Sam was when she was possessed by Lilith. There was a part of him that cared for her—a part of him that cared for humans. He just didn't want Lucifer to know that.

"You still have the gun, right?" Zephyr asked Father Zebulun as Emerie dug around in one of the boxes.

"Yes," he replied doubtfully. "Though I...I'm not sure what the effect will be on the devil himself."

"Guess we'll find out." Zephyr stretched a little and bent to touch her toes. She straightened and punched her fist against the flat of her palm. It looked like she was preparing for a fist fight, but she closed her eyes and inhaled deeply—she was centering herself.

"Okay!" Emerie announced. "I'm ready."

She held a large bundle of green coils in her arms. As she started towards the basement steps, a metal tube dragged along the concrete—Zephyr stooped and picked up the head of the garden hose. She tucked it between the rubber coils helpfully.

Father Zebulun took one look at her and said, "Oh dear."

She ignored him and tramped up the basement steps, Father Zebulun and Zephyr at her heels. When they reached the door, Zephyr reached around and quietly turned the knob.

The door silently swung open. The kitchen was completely dark, but there was a distinct and unpleasant aroma—like sulfur or rotting meat. Emerie nodded at Zephyr who pulled an incense burner out of her bag, along with several sticks of incense.

A common symptom of a haunted house was a bad smell. Therefore, Emerie figured the best way to haunt a demon would be to fill the home with a *pleasant smell*. Luckily, a good witch always had incense sticks on hand.

"I'm nearly out of sage." Zephyr fretted as she lit her first incense stick in the kitchen. "The rest are passion fruit, China rain, clean cotton, sex on the beach, and cherry blossom."

"That should be enough," Emerie inhaled deeply. "We just want to hit the main areas of the house, anyway."

Father Zebulun stared at Zephyr. "Did you say 'sex on the beach' was a scent for incense?"

Emerie disappeared into the little hallway. She rummaged about in the laundry room before she returned, carefully unspooling the garden hose. She looked at Father Zebulun expectantly.

"Hand it over." Father Zebulun unwound a crucifix from his wrist with a sigh. "I think this is a foolish idea—but we're out of time and we may as well go down fighting."

———

Samael was pummeled by the scent of incense when he reentered the house.

He held Orobas by the scruff of his neck, like an errant kitten. Lucifer was still in the upper room, the attic, presumably preparing for the ritual. He had to be, for if he smelled the rank stench of sage and frankincense permeating the living room and entryway, he would be *furious*.

"What is this?" Samael shook Orobas a little for emphasis.

Orobas inhaled deeply and retched a little at the scent. "Cleansing incense."

"I know what it is, you infernal creature, what is it doing *here*?! At the center point of the ritual? We can't have this garbage here, it'll mess up the rite!" He flung Orobas on the ground and snatched the incense on one of the little tables. He stuffed it in his mouth to stifle it. It tasted like holiness and ash.

Orobas brushed himself off, unfazed by the rough treatment. "They are preparing to stop Lucifer."

"Idiots! Where are they?!" He found the second incense stick on the bookshelf in the living room and furiously shoved it in his mouth too.

"You are not my conjuror." Orobas sniffed. "However—my conjuror cordially invited you to join her to 'kick Satan's ass' upstairs."

"You have got to be kidding me."

Samael bolted out of the living room and galloped upstairs. He raced down the hallway and abruptly tripped. He landed flat on his face with a mighty thump, and furiously scrambled up. The culprit was a thin green garden hose that trailed down the hallway and stairwell, and disappeared into the kitchen. Utterly confused, he tugged it a little and then started to follow it.

The garden hose led to the end of the hallway, where the attic stairwell door was ajar. His sense of unease grew as he pushed the door open further followed the garden hose up the steps into the attic.

The attic was empty, save the throbbing, pulsing circle at the center— Emerie's original Circle. His stomach lurched; he had no idea where Lucifer was. Everything seemed ready—a lamb had been slaughtered; its corpse lay at the center of the markings as a profane mockery of the Enemy. Black candles bathed the room in a warm, ominous glow. Samael realized he still held the garden hose in his hands...he hadn't reached its snout.

Before he could find the end of the garden hose, it was suddenly tugged taut. In surprise, he dropped the hose.

"SUCK IT, SATAN!"

A burst of water erupted from nowhere, and Samael dodged the stream with a sharp yelp. Some of the spray hit him briefly and sizzled against his skin—holy water! But it was not aimed towards him, instead, the holy water blasted across the attic floor, and, somehow, scrubbed away the paint markings. He realized Emerie and Father Zebulun were standing across the room, right in front of the old-fashioned stove. Emerie held the garden hose and Father Zebulun had two fingers placed in front of the nozzle—he murmured something under his breath. He was *blessing the holy water.*

Samael didn't know whether to be furious or impressed.

"Emerie, stop!" Samael shouted. "You're going to get yourself killed!"

The stream of water halted as Emerie kinked the hose. She frowned at Samael like a displeased teacher.

"We are *trying* to stop the end of the world, Sam," she informed him haughtily. "And by the way, do you have any idea what this water will do to my hardwood floors?"

She flung her last remark at him like an accusation, like it was *his* fault she was drenching her attic with holy water in order to wipe away a Circle. He stared at her aghast.

"Out of our way, Samael," Father Zebulun rumbled. "My pistol's shot is not for you, but I will not hesitate to use it."

"You all are insane," Samael hissed. "Do you have any idea what Lucifer will do to you when he finds you? Get out of here while you still have a chance!" Perhaps he could set the ritual aright again...they could escape out the window, he could redraw the Circle, maybe Lucifer wouldn't notice the giant puddles of holy water.

"Why do you care, Sam?" Emerie asked him. "Why are you telling us to get out of here instead of yelling for your shitty brother?"

Samael had no answer for that. But he felt an uncomfortable warmth near his hip—the sword, the angel sword, glowed and sang to him, a song only he could understand.

"Quiet, you," he muttered to the sword.

Emerie unkinked the hose and more water sprayed the attic. Samael growled in anger and leapt up to the rafters to avoid the acid spray. He yelled something in a harsh, sibilant language which Emerie pointedly ignored as she continued to spray her attic down.

But suddenly, without warning, the stream of water halted. Emerie frowned and shook the hose a little.

"Zephyr! Turn the spigot back on!"

Nothing happened. Until Zephyr slowly walked through the attic doorway, her face drawn and tight. A silver dagger gleamed against her throat, the blade pressed tight against the taut skin.

Lucifer smiled at all of them, her brow delicately furrowed. She clucked as though they were naughty children.

"My, my, what a mess you've made," she murmured. She deliberately stepped into one of the holy water puddles. It steamed under her pink tennis shoes, but she didn't even flinch.

Father Zebulun's hand drifted towards his jacket. Lucifer noticed the motion and laughed.

"Go ahead, priest. Please. Waste another of your bullets, edge your fate closer to me."

His hand froze. Samael shook his head violently at the priest. Could the Freischutz work against Lucifer? His brother did not seem worried by the weapon, which could only mean its powers would be ineffective. The priest's hand dropped.

"Let her go."

Emerie released the garden hose and stalked towards Lucifer. Zephyr tried to speak, perhaps to warn her off, but the silver knife tightened at her throat. Emerie stopped short when she saw a red line dot the witch's throat.

"Little girl, do not test me." Lucifer's smile became fixed. "The witch here is going to fix your mischief and redo the Circle. I will keep you alive for Samael's pleasure, but do not try my patience."

"Gross!" Emerie was appalled and threw Samael a dirty look.

Samael looked simultaneously outraged at Emerie's disgust and embarrassed at this concession from Lucifer. His brother shoved Zephyr away from her, into the wet chalky remains of the Circle. The silver dagger floated in front of her as a hovering threat; it inched nearer to Zephyr if she made a move to get away.

"Redraw the circle, witch."

"Do it yourself!" Zephyr spat. The knife wafted in front of her face, its point dangerously near her eyeball.

"Test me." Lucifer's eyes glowed red and Emerie shuddered. There was something truly horrifying about a soccer mom with demonic red eyes.

The silver dagger drew nearer. Zephyr took a ragged breath, her body quaking as she reached for a piece of chalk, a few feet away next to a box of knick knacks. Slowly, she picked it up. She hesitated.

"Now."

Zephyr's chalk touched the hardwood floor. She began to drag it along and ever so slightly started a small curve.

"YAAAAAAAAAAAHHH!"

Like some sort of berserker warrior, Emerie ran towards Zephyr, her bokuto held aloft. She slammed the wooden sword against the silver dagger, as though she were playing T-ball, and the knife clattered to the floor.

But Emerie wasn't done. She then turned her attentions to Lucifer and promptly brought the wooden sword down squarely on the Devil's head.

She hit her target with a sickening THUD.

There was a brief silence as Father Zebulun, Zephyr, Samael, and Lucifer all adjusted to the fact Emerie had clobbered Satan on the head with a wooden sword. Lucifer didn't even look angry for a good twenty seconds, she just looked confused.

Lucifer came to her senses. Emerie attempted to hit her again with her bokuto. This time, unfortunately, Lucifer's hand shot upwards and snatched the wooden blade mid-strike.

Emerie met Lucifer's crimson gaze. "You know, I think maybe we got off on the wrong foot."

Lucifer jerked her wrist; the bokuto snapped in half and Emerie flew across the room. She would've slammed into the wall, but Samael, unable to resist protecting her from this onslaught, snatched her in midair.

"I have had enough."

Lucifer's voice reverberated across the room. The attic shook ominously and every black candle flared into a roaring orb of fire. But just before they would surely have been annihilated, a small voice cleared its throat.

Lucifer paused. Orobas stood in the middle of the room. He busily scrawled something on the ground with Zephyr's discarded piece of chalk. Once he finished, he tossed the nub of chalk into his mouth and chewed noisily.

"Oh, Orobas...what have you done?!"

The little horse demon shrugged at Samael's moan. A giant, gleaming white cross intertwined with a five-pointed star covered the room. It gleamed in the candlelight and Emerie looked at Samael in confusion.

"Holy ground...he made this holy ground...*Lucifer can't enact the ritual.*"

Lucifer did not move. She spoke, barely above a whisper. "What have you done?"

Orobas peered at Lucifer inscrutably. He bowed solemnly before Emerie. He then turned towards Lucifer and said clearly:

"I never betray my conjurer."

Lucifer gazed at him in shock. Then hot rage overtook her features. Fire haloed her face and Emerie suddenly realized Lucifer's face was *changing.* Her mild, harmless soccer mom features became enveloped in fur. Her eyes widened into golden, feline orbs, the flames shifted into a silver-white mane, her hands grew into paws the size of dinner plates with dagger-like claws.

The white lion pounced on Orobas and devoured him, scattering flesh, blood, and sinew everywhere.

————

"No!" Emerie screamed. The sheer violence of the action hobbled her; she fell to her knees and a sob escaped her lips. Samael made a noise like a wounded animal.

Father Zebulun, however, drew his gun.

His hand shook badly, but there was a sudden explosion as he shot the Freischutz. The air seemed to collapse and compress within the room and the lion opened its mouth. Emerie thought she would hear a terrible roar, but instead she heard high, cruel laughter. The lion caught the bullet in its mouth and crunched it noisily.

Father Zebulun's eyes widened and he dropped the gun. Zephyr stepped in front of him.

"Bastard!" she shrieked. Her eyes began to glow as she lifted her arms. A hundred Christmas ornaments rose from the cardboard boxes, along with several paperback copies of torrid romance novels Emerie hadn't figured out where to keep. They began to pelt the beast viciously. Lucifer growled in displeasure and batted the books and porcelain Christmas trees away like an annoyed cat.

Emerie's face hardened at Samael, who stood paralyzed. Furious at his inaction, she snatched at his belt and attempted to tear his sword out of his sheath.

She may as well have tried to yank Excalibur from its stone; the sword would not budge and Sam turned on her furiously.

"What do you think you're playing at?!" he shouted furiously. "This sword isn't a toy!"

"We have to do *something*!" Emerie screamed back. "He killed him! He murdered Orobas! Orobas was our friend!"

"Go on, then, Samael," the lion spoke, but they heard Lucifer's maternal voice. "Will you turn against your brother? Become a heretic of Hell? I've seen you, you know. Delighting in music, glorying in friendships…you've had numerous chances to take control of this girl and you haven't. But you are my brother, Samael. You saved me that day in the Garden and I have never forgotten. I will forgive you, Samael, for your crimes. But you must stop this heresy."

"Sam!" Emerie's voice was loud and hard. "You told me yourself, in our first conversation, he was a dick."

Samael's anguished expression softened at the memory.

"Will you betray me, Samael?" The lion carefully stepped over the cross-star design. "Holy ground is no matter to me. I can easily burn this house to the ground and finish the ritual in the ashes and flames. You are a prince of Hell, my brother. These pestilential humans are unworthy of you."

Samael's sword blazed suddenly with a glorious golden light. He drew it from its sheath. Rays of light danced across the room and Lucifer averted his gaze, as though the brightness hurt his eyes.

"Where were you, Lucifer?" Samael asked. He kept his sword low, but still raised. "When I was stuck in this damn house for two-hundred years? When I was trapped between planes? I know you knew I was here. Why didn't you free me?"

The lion stood on his back paws. His form thinned and shifted back into a yoga pants-wearing soccer mom.

"Am I my brother's keeper?" she sneered. "Do you require a babysitter, little brother?"

Samael lifted his sword. Lucifer's brows rose.

"You once used that very sword to save my life. Will you use it now to strike me down?"

"I abdicate."

Lucifer froze. "What did you say?"

"I abdicate. I renounce my title as a Prince of Hell."

Silence filled the room. Emerie leaned towards Father Zebulun. "Is he allowed to do that?" she whispered.

Lucifer chuckled as her hand came to a rest on one of her Jesus fish buttons. "You abdicate? And so what? You will return to the heavenly hosts to string harps and play as a gopher?"

"No." Samael shook his head. "I don't know what I'll do. But I won't serve you any longer."

Emerie smiled at Samael. He smiled back at her, and Lucifer looked at the two of them in utter rage. Father Zebulun looked bewildered. Zephyr was the only one to call out a warning right before Lucifer attacked.

It happened so fast Samael almost didn't even react. It was as though he were struck by lightning. But in one heartbeat, he found himself wrestling with a silver-white lion the size of an elephant. He couldn't move to defend himself—Lucifer's paw trapped his sword arm against the floor as the beast had began to tear his wing off. The pain staggered him; all he could do was scream.

"GET OFF OF HIM!"

Emerie's voice rang out as she heaved up an artificial Christmas tree and swung with all her might. It landed on Lucifer with a solid thump, but did not seem to have much effect. Lucifer was apparently irritated at the interruption and paused in the disembowelment—enough to turn towards Emerie and snarl.

"Lord of Hell!"

Father Zebulun stared across the room and aimed his plastic water gun. He pumped madly and a stream of holy water hit directly in Lucifer's eye. The silver-white lion roared in agony and Samael scrambled out from underneath him to find Zephyr close by. She drew runes and designs with a sharpie along the edges of Orobas' last design and in an instant, Samael realized what she was doing.

"Sam," Zephyr said without looking up. "Get her in the Circle."

Samael did not ask for clarification. He charged the silver-white lion and shoved the beast with all his might into the center of Orobas' inscription. Furious, the lion pounced at Zephyr—suddenly slamming hard against an invisible barrier. The collision stunned him for a moment. Lucifer was trapped.

And so, unfortunately, was Samael.

"Father Z!" Zephyr's voice was loud and terrible. "Start the exorcism."

"Wait!" Emerie shouted and tripped over herself. "Wait—Sam's stuck too. We have to get him out first."

"There's no time for that."

Samael stared at Emerie, who covered her mouth in horror. He nodded at the priest. "Give me the book."

Father Zebulun withdrew a small leather book from his jacket. He tossed it within the Circle and Samael caught it easily. Lucifer stared at him in astonishment and shock, too stunned to try and rip it from his hands. The priest then turned towards Zephyr.

"Miss Moon," he requested. "As we discussed."

Zephyr closed her eyes. She fell to her knees and was immersed in a pure white light. Emerie stared at her in wonder; suddenly, the sound of church bells filled the house.

Emerie had no idea how the witch had conjured the sound of church bells. But sure enough, there was a frightful cacophony of howls and screeches. Lucifer clawed at its ears and screeched in pain. Emerie ran to the attic window and realized the sound of church bells enveloped the entire town of Milton; along with a chorus of demon screams.

"Do it now!" Father Zebulun bellowed. Samael opened the prayer book.

Lucifer's eyes narrowed. He suddenly shifted back into a human woman, still in her yoga pants and polo. But her eyes looked positively serpentine.

"Your little ritual," she hissed. "Will do nothing, Samael. It won't send me back to Hell, it will only send *you* back to Hell. I will always be here on earth. I will always cause destruction and enmity, I will always enact violence, and *I will never die.*"

"Yeah, well…" Samael took a seat in the Circle and made himself comfortable. "It'll send everyone else back to Hell. And it'll at least get rid of you for the time being."

Lucifer's eyes flashed. *"How dare you defy me!"*

She snatched Samael by the throat. But before she could devour him, Samael began to chant.

The wind picked up and the church bells stopped. Zephyr crumpled to the floor, completely spent. The Circle shone in unearthly brightness once more, a vivid golden color that showered the attic with light. Emerie watched in petrified fascination as Lucifer and Samael were bathed in gold. Lucifer continued to hold Samael by the throat—but she closed her eyes, as though tired, and accepted the immersion. The Circle suddenly became concave, and Lucifer fell into blackness.

The wind became a tempest. The attic windows burst open and

demons of every shape and size poured through. They howled and screamed and tried to escape, but as Samael's voice grew louder and louder, they too were pulled into the golden circle. Emerie nearly got clocked in the head by one of the giant eel beasts, but it was sucked powerfully into the circle, like water into a drain.

The demon continued to chant. His languages shifted from English, to Latin, to Greek, to some language she couldn't recognize. The tempest raged around them ferociously, but Emerie, Zephyr, and Father Zebulun were unaffected, as though they stood in the eye of a hurricane. The chaos roared. Emerie suddenly realized that although Lucifer had fallen through the golden Circle, Samael still remained. He seemed as confused as she was and for a moment, Emerie wondered if the exorcism would spare him.

The roof of the attic exploded in a roar of splintering wood and cardboard boxes. Even more demons—hundreds of thousands of them—were ripped into the vortex, all to the tune of the most horrific caterwauls. The winds went faster and faster as they collected demon after demon and shoved them all into the circle. Each one disappeared into a black void.

In the final moments, Samael looked up. His lips moved, but she could not hear what he said.

"No, don't!" Emerie cried out.

"I BANISH YOU ALL IN THE NAME OF JESUS CHRIST!"

She wondered why the name did not seem to pain Samael any longer. She desperately tried to reach him.

"Wait!" Emerie cried out. "Wait—I don't want him to go to Hell! He doesn't *deserve* to go to Hell!"

Father Zebulun did not look at her, but she saw tears streamed down his face. Zephyr stared hard at the golden Circle.

"GO BACK INTO THE PIT OF HELL, FOUL DEMONS! YOU ARE BANISHED IN THE NAME OF THE LORD JESUS CHRIST!"

Samael cradled his injured wing. He said one final word, nodded at all of them, and allowed himself to be drawn into the portal.

Tears fell down Emerie's cheeks. Zephyr looked towards the sky, unable to face it. The three of them saw Samael disappear into the darkness. The circle's golden glow turned into a white-hot flash, blinding all of them briefly.

And then there was silence.

Emerie wrenched herself away from the old-fashioned stove. She ran towards the Circle. But there wasn't a portal there any longer. Just a chalk sketch, like any creative child might make. She touched one of the sigils, letting chalk dust kiss her fingers.

She looked at Father Zebulun as her eyes overflowed with tears. "Can't we...?"

He shook his head. Zephyr went to her, helping her situate herself.

"Come on," she said, in a gentler tone than Emerie recognized. "Come on. We all need a drink."

TWENTY-NINE

SAMAEL AWOKE to the smell of sawdust.

He frowned as he attempted to gather himself. He lay on the ground, for one thing. He was blanketed in morning light. Somewhere in the distance, he thought he heard the song of a sparrow. He inhaled deeply —he failed to detect the familiar, hellish scents of sulfur and rot.

Well, he hadn't been to Hell in a while. Perhaps they upgraded?

Samael rose slowly. He couldn't hear the rage screams of his demon brethren, nor could he hear the sounds of wrath and despair that echoed in the halls of Hell. He had expected to wake up before Lilith or Beelzebub, who would quite happily feed him to a giant centipede or some other nasty torture. Hell was creative in its punishments.

Instead, all he could hear was a faint chopping sound. Curious, he stood shakily and noticed his half torn-off wing had somehow healed. It was a little sore, but there were no markings or scars that indicated his battle with Lucifer.

Weird. Where am I?

He could see windows, for one thing, and beautiful wooden walls. Perhaps he was in a log cabin? He was surrounded by large tables covered in sawdust and wood pieces, with various odds and ends scattered about. Lumber was neatly stacked against the wall and Samael saw at least three different saws hanging on the wall from pegs.

Maybe they wanted to heal him and then take him apart again?

The whittling noise suddenly turned into a rhythmic sawing. It came from the next room over. Warily, Samael followed the sound. He couldn't help but stare at the various half-finished projects on the work tables—everything from birdhouses to benches to wine racks. (There seemed to be a *lot* of wine racks.)

The steady axe on wood led him down a short hallway into another workroom. *This* room was even stranger than the first—mainly because everything within seemed to be broken. A grandfather clock had been shattered beyond repair and sagged sadly against the wall. There were dusty old record players from the 1920s that couldn't possibly work any longer. Cracked benches, broken chairs, even little figurines that seemed malformed. What's more, Samael kept tripping on various odds and ends scattered beneath his feet. It was as though he'd walked into a workroom's rubbish area.

It was darker in this room—fewer windows. When Samael's eyes adjusted to the shadows, he noticed a youngish man off to the side, busily at work at a wooden workbench. He cautiously approached him clearing his throat awkwardly.

The man looked up. He was in his early thirties and looked as though he might be Syrian, or Palestinian, with dark skin and warm, kind eyes. His hair was a mess of black curls and his flannel shirt was covered in dirt and sawdust. He smiled at Samael, revealing deep dimples. He looked as though he'd been expecting him. He set his saw down and wiped dusty hands on his jeans.

"Hi, Sam," the man greeted him cheerfully.

Samael started. Only Emerie called him 'Sam.'

"Who...who are you?" Samael asked in bewilderment. "Where am I?"

"You don't know?" the man questioned. His hands twitched—he seemed uncomfortable standing still. Samael watched the restless hands pick up some long metal wires and inspect them carefully.

"You seem kind of familiar," Samael acknowledged.

"I'm glad to hear that, at least," the man laughed. "I'm the Carpenter. This is my workshop."

This meant nothing to Samael. He looked about him and tried to gather context clues. All he could see were broken pieces.

"Your workshop?" Samael asked. The Carpenter nodded absently. He started to thread the metal wires onto something.

"Some workshop," Samael said critically. "Everything in here is damaged."

The Carpenter nodded in agreement, his brow furrowed. "Yes. I'm afraid that is so."

"Why don't you just pitch it all?" Samael asked. "Start from scratch?"

The Carpenter gazed all around him, at all the bits and pieces, the shattered fragments. He smiled at each of them fondly as his finger traced the edge of his work table.

"I like to fix things," he said simply. "Kinda like your friend Emerie."

As if that settled the matter, the Carpenter returned to his work. He continued to twist little metal wires onto a long piece of jagged wood. Samael winced—he seemed to get a lot of splinters for his trouble.

"Why am I here?" Samael asked finally.

"Good question," the Carpenter agreed. "Why are you here?"

Samael stared at him.

"You wouldn't be here unless you really wanted to be," the Carpenter explained. He ducked under the table and heaved up a few thin pieces of wood. Each was battered and scratched. As he spread them across the table, Samael noticed the Carpenter's wrists. Both had a pale, ugly scar.

Samael's eyes widened. He recognized those scars. They came from a particularly gruesome form of torture Hell had given the Romans.

He took a few steps backwards and nearly crashed into another bench.

The Carpenter tilted his head. "Everything all right?"

"It's you." Samael's voice shook. "I know who you are…"

The Carpenter watched him quietly.

"What—what do you want with me?" Samael tried to muster his courage, but all he felt was fear.

"What do *you* want with *me*?" the Carpenter asked.

"Stop answering my questions with questions!" Samael shouted. "Why—why am I here?! Why am I not in Hell?!"

The Carpenter sighed. He came around the worktable and hopped up onto it. He swung his legs like a child and grabbed a small piece of wood. He started to whittle.

"Sam," the Carpenter said, biting his lip in concentration, "what was the last thing you did on Earth?"

Samael stared at him suspiciously. The Carpenter did not look up from whittling.

"I—I enacted the ritual." He cleared his throat. "To seal the gates shut. To send all of the demons back to Hell."

"Yourself included," the Carpenter noted.

"Well, yeah," Samael snapped. "The priest said the ritual had to be performed by a demon. So—so I did."

"And why would you do something like that?" The Carpenter kept his eyes on the wood. It began taking on shape. A fish? A chalice? Samael couldn't tell.

"What do you mean?" Samael asked warily. "I had to. Emerie was in danger—so was Father Zebulun. And Zephyr. They would've been killed—or worse."

"You did it to protect them," the Carpenter mused. "You gave your life for theirs...despite it being a 'heresy of Hell'. Why?"

Samael did not know how to answer.

The Carpenter stopped shaping the piece of wood and raised his head towards Samael. His expression conveyed nothing but tenderness.

"You and I have something in common, Sam," the Carpenter said gently.

"Oh yeah?" Samael challenged.

"Oh yes," the Carpenter nodded. "You committed the most dangerous heresy of Hell, dearheart. You dared to love—even to the point of damnation. You loved them—Emerie, Boaz, and Zephyr—enough to give your life for them."

The affection in the Carpenter's tone bewildered Samael. He wanted to argue, wanted to say he was a demon, *he did not love*...but what other explanation was there for his actions?

"But…" Samael started to tremble. "But…I am a demon."

The Carpenter's eyes filled with tears. "You are my child."

Something broke in Samael. He felt something hot run down his cheeks and he touched his face. Tears? Was he crying too? Why was his hand shaking?

"Oh, Sam," the Carpenter said sadly. "If only you knew. If only *all of you* knew. I have nothing to do with the torments of Hell—that was your own creation. I would do anything to have you all back in my arms once more. I would give my life for all of you back…indeed, I have and will do so, a hundred thousand times again and again. For as long as it takes for you all to come back to me."

He gazed off into the distance, out the window. Samael heard thunder rumble and suddenly registered the Carpenter had carved a small horse-like figure. He wondered what the significance was.

"You don't—you can't know what I've done," Samael whispered. "Otherwise you'd—you'd never want me back."

"I know everything you've done." The Carpenter closed his eyes, wiping his own tears away.

"After two thousand years," he murmured with a soft chuckle. "No one quite understands the radical scandal of grace."

Samael was not sure how to answer this.

"I love all of my creation," the Carpenter said levelly as he turned the small wooden horse over in his hands. "But you, Samael…and so many of your siblings…you made the mistake of thinking I loved humans *more* than your kind. That was never the case."

The Carpenter exhaled slowly. "And now…I think perhaps you understand a little more *why* I love humans the way I do. Emerie has shown you this, hasn't she?"

Samael wrinkled. "Was that why she was created? So that by falling in love with her, I'd come back to you?"

The Carpenter chuckled. "Hardly. Emerie is her own person, with her own goals, with her own purpose—all separate from yours. But every relationship, every connection, every interaction shapes people. A million varying choices in one person, a hundred million stories out of every gesture, every expression…she is breathtaking in her stubbornness. As is Boaz in his ferocity. As is Zephyr in her authenticity. I love them dearly and I will admit...I hoped you would, too."

Samael's knees gave way and he fell to the floor. The Carpenter joined him and placed an affectionate hand on his shoulder.

"Sam," he said softly, "I never abandoned you. I never abandoned Lucifer. I have loved you from before the worlds were shaped into being, before the stars began their courses, before everything. You were always welcome here. You were always wanted here. I love you and I always will."

Hot tears dripped onto the dusty floor. The Carpenter pulled him into his arms fiercely, and Samael cried like a child.

When the tears were finished, Samael pulled away, and sniffed. The Carpenter dug a bandana out of his pocket and handed it to him.

"I'm angry." Samael's voice was hoarse. "I'm still angry."

"You're allowed to be angry."

Samael frowned, lifting his head. "But what now?"

"That, dear heart," the Carpenter helped him stand, "is entirely up to you."

Samael blinked in confusion.

"If you so choose, you are welcome to join the heavenly hosts once more," the Carpenter told him. "Gabriel especially would be delighted at your return."

Samael rolled his eyes.

"But there is another option." The Carpenter looked thoughtful. "It has been a long time since Nephilim roamed the earth...with good reason. When they first walked on mortal ground, I had hoped they would be protectors of man, to defend against your...misguided brethren."

Samael listened.

"Obviously that went awry," the Carpenter sighed. "But...if you wish it, Sam, you may return to earth. I will make you a Nephil—one of the Nephilim."

Samael's heart leapt in his throat. He gazed around the junkyard of a workshop, and weighed both options. He thought of Emerie's stricken face as he had fallen into the gate to Hell, thought of Zephyr's anguish, and Father Zebulun's regret.

He thought of Lucifer—his brother, his enemy, his shame. Could he simply abandon him like this?

He looked at the Carpenter.

"I've made my decision."

THIRTY

THE HELL HOUSE (or Hell Haven, depending on which neighborhood you lived in) was no longer haunted.

It didn't escape its bad reputation, however. The townspeople of Milton muttered and gossiped, and continued to warn Emerie about the evil that plagued the house. Besides, what was a single girl going to do with such a big house, anyway? Better cash it in now and get a studio apartment.

Emerie ignored them all, as was her habit. She spent the next month and a half pouring all her energy and motivation into refurbishing the house. She took Dylan to small claims court and managed to wrest her savings out of the apartment he'd leased. (Dylan's father bailed him out, of course.) She then used the remainder of her savings from her grandfather and her property insurance to fix her roof. (The town of Milton could not quite remember the tornado that swept through the town, but no one could deny the curious damage it wreaked on the historic landmarks.) She gave every room a new coat of paint. She bought bright colored quilts for the beds. And she hung all the grotesque garage sale art she found to her heart's content, including a beautifully mounted Tyrannosaurus head, a painting of a demure skeleton in a pink 19th century gown, and a fine collection of mini-statues which turned out to be saints—or vodou deities, depending on who you asked.

Most importantly—since her attic was now holy ground—she set up her shrine to Ji-Ji. His disapproving gaze would watch over her house from now on and she never forgot to place sake and rice cakes at the front of the shrine every morning, asking for his blessing.

Zephyr was one of the concerned citizens who suggested multiple times she abandon the project. But Emerie wasn't a quitter. She preferred fixing things.

"On your own head be it." Zephyr took a long sip of wine. "I wanted to talk to you about something else, anyway."

Emerie had decided to host a housewarming party, to celebrate her finished work. Unfortunately, none of the superstitious townspeople had shown up, which meant the party consisted of herself, Zephyr, and Father Zebulun.

"And what would that be?" Father Zebulun examined one of the figurines, a pretty woman with a candle wreath on her head.

"Well, you're not gonna like this," Zephyr said bluntly. "But I've been contacting the spirit world, and, well, Samael ain't there."

Father Zebulun choked on his Guinness. "What do you mean, *you've been contacting the spirit world*?!" he thundered. "Didn't I expressly forbid any sort of action?! Do you want to open *another* gate to Hell?!"

"I don't believe in Hell," Zephyr replied saucily. "And I know how to open and close out a circle—unlike *some* people." She jerked her head towards Emerie, who shrugged.

"Geez," she commented. "You open a portal to Hell *one time* and no one ever lets you forget it."

"*Anyway*," Zephyr continued as she poured herself another glass of wine. "Samael isn't in the spirit world."

Emerie stilled. Father Zebulun tapped his hand on coffee table in irritation.

"Not in the spirit world?" she asked. "Not in Hell? Where else would he be?"

"Don't know." Zephyr took another drink. "I wasn't planning on *summoning* him again." She shot an irritated glance towards Father Zebulun. "Just checking in. But my usual sources swore up and down he wasn't there."

"Usual sources." Father Zebulun snorted. "They are undoubtedly lying."

"Maybe," Zephyr said doubtfully. "Still—it's something to consider."

There was a knock at the door. Emerie heaved herself off the couch and downed her glass of Guinness.

"Finally," she remarked. "Let's hope we actually have some normal guests."

Father Zebulun looked offended. "*I'm* normal!"

"Yeah, what gives?" Zephyr chimed in. "What's more normal than a witch attorney having a conversation about the afterlife with a Catholic exorcist? Speaking of which, it's Halloween—we should watch *The Exorcist*."

"Please no," Father Zebulun requested. "I detest that movie."

"You detest it?!" Emerie heard Zephyr demand in great offense. "How could you detest it? It's about priests exorcising demons!"

"All the priests die," Father Zebulun deadpanned and Emerie couldn't help but laugh as she walked into the foyer and opened the front door, ready to let new guests in.

She dropped her empty glass. It fell to the floor and shattered.

"Hey, Emerie," Samael said in a perfectly normal tone. "I seem to be homeless. Would you mind if I crashed on your couch?"

———

Thank you for reading! Did you enjoy? Please add your review because nothing helps an author more and encourages readers to take a chance on a book than a review.

Don't miss more from Kat Coffin at www.katcoffin.com

And find your next read, UPTON ARMS, by Scott Craven. Turn the page for a sneak peek!

You can also sign up for the City Owl Press newsletter to receive notice of all book releases!

SNEAK PEEK OF UPTON ARMS

BY SCOTT CRAVEN

FIVE YEARS AGO

After more than six centuries of predatory dominance, it had come to this.

Cargo pants.

The vampire hadn't been this depressed since the Great Famine, which mortals called the Black Plague.

Yet here Vlad was, outside a Chili's, wearing pants with far too many pockets, the majority of which were empty. His hunting skills had deteriorated to a point where camouflage, rather than a fangs-out assault, was his best option.

There had been a time when this particular all-you-can-slay buffet would fly well below Vlad's radar. Inside was the bland and tepid blood of those who spent weekends watching sports, washing cars, and screaming at kids. In a different era, he'd hunted only gourmet meals provided by the smart and the strong. Their fighting spirits enhanced their flavor, like sipping wine of an exquisite vintage.

That was long ago and far away. For reasons hinging on both his abilities and morals (more the former than the latter, if Vlad was honest with himself), his diet consisted of small mammals, from squirrels and chipmunks to the occasional feral cat. He avoided raccoons due to their feisty nature and the cuts they left behind, now that even flesh wounds took days instead of seconds to heal.

Still, Vlad needed a cheat day every few months, if for nothing more than to give him a reason to keep living. The centuries had taken their toll, and he had to make a few lifestyle adjustments to his aging body and powers when it came to enjoying a human dish.

But a Chili's? Now he knew how seniors felt joining those tours adapted to people with walkers. This was the vampire version.

If he had to be here, Vlad was going to make the most of it.

An hour before, he had donned his Ordinary Guy costume of blue oxford shirt, khaki pants, and loafers. It was one of the few times Vlad was thankful vampires didn't cast reflections, though he remained curious as to what he looked like (not to mention how handy it would be to see himself when shaving).

Though the sun had set an hour before, the heat and humidity slapped Vlad's face as soon as he exited his apartment in a rundown duplex. At least it was biologically impossible to break a sweat, since his skin was either cool or flaming, based on the presence of UV light beamed directly from the sun.

He walked the half mile without once looking skyward, bored more than a century ago with the planets and stars locked to the only world he knew. Soon he was outside Chili's, where he was a lion visiting a watering hole filled with lumbering, dull-witted, and often intoxicated wildebeests. Vlad headed straight to the bar, the vampire deli counter. Casting about for the weakest in the herd, his eyes settled on the out-of-shape, forlorn gentleman sitting at the end. From the Crocs to the plaid shirt tucked into cargo shorts, the outfit screamed, "Prey here, get your prey here!"

No need to open the menu, Vlad knew what he wanted. He nudged into a narrow gap and put his elbows on a wood surface that had likely absorbed a thousand spilled Bud Lights. He ordered just that, not wanting to upset the flock. Vlad pretended to take a sip every few minutes, figuring the patrons were oblivious to their surroundings and wouldn't notice the always-full beer in front of him. He glanced down the bar every now and then, realizing he was definitely in the mood for Mexican (assuming, wrongly, his catch of the day was from Mexico).

The vampire settled into what he called "Brad mode," that genial guy who blends into the background to the point he fades away, sip by faux sip. Vlad liked to think it was related to his (dwindling) power to hypnotize, but in honest moments realized it was because he was just another poorly dressed white guy at America's most generic bar.

Vlad glanced over just in time to see his mark lay a twenty on the bar and push away. Vlad followed, maintaining a hunting distance of forty feet. He pushed through the front door just in time to see his dinner round the corner. The vampire hustled, hoping his target had parked his car away from the halo of lights in the parking lot. If this spot didn't work out, there were other hunting grounds, starting with the Applebee's just down to the street, then the Olive Garden, and ultimately the Red Lobster, in descending order of decent meals. As he rounded the corner, Vlad's thoughts drifted to the last, hoping he wouldn't be stuck there because he was not in the mood for fish—

WHAP! Two bodies collided, and Vlad reluctantly pushed away his dinner because nothing was more awkward than bumping into prey.

"Excuse me," Vlad muttered, eyes down. He wanted to add a quick apology, but the hand squeezing his throat made it impossible to talk.

"I can smell the vampire on you," his (not) supper growled, tightening his grip..

Vlad caught a whiff of something too, an earthy scent behind the cheap cologne. *Werewolf,* Vlad thought. He'd dealt with them before. He was no match physically, not anymore, but he had other ways to deal with this unexpected encounter. Vlad gripped his foe's wrist, met the wolf's stare, boring down deep—

"Seriously?" the man said, digging his nails (bordering on claws) into Vlad's throat. "You think you can pull that hypno-vampire bullshit on me? I should go full-on wolf and tear you apart, except this is my favorite Chili's, and I don't want to burn bridges." The truth, as Vlad would learn in the coming days, was that this particular predator hadn't achieved full-on wolf in years, lucky to achieve Goldendoodle and rarely getting past a member of the rodent family.

At this point, however, Vlad felt at the wolf's mercy. He tapped his assailant's arm, motioning that he'd like to speak. Fingers loosened just enough for Vlad to stutter a clumsy apology to a meal starting to give him heartburn.

The werewolf released Vlad with a look the vampire had never been the recipient of—one of pity.

"Dude, I get it," the man sighed. "It doesn't get much lower than hunting at Chili's. Unless it's at Applebee's." He paused, seeing the defeated expression on Vlad's face. "Oh man, you were going there next, weren't you? Please don't tell me Red Lobster is on that list."

All Vlad could do was nod.

The man stepped back, analyzing Vlad in the dim light. "I'd say, five hundred and sixty-one years old? Give or take a decade."

"That's oddly specific," Vlad ventured, because he wasn't quite sure himself.

"The wrinkles, the liver spots, the creaky joints. Well, I'm guessing about the joints, though there was a time I could have heard them."

Vlad shook his head. "You're not far off. It's just that I stopped counting a long time ago. When I hit two hundred, I had a few friends over for an epic party that eventually led to a pretty horrific mural in Bucharest. There might even be a museum about it now. Since then, birthdays are just more math."

"I get it. My talents aren't what they used to be. I had no idea what I was going to do if you'd gone for my carotid."

Vlad shook his head, lips curling into something resembling a smile. "You were bluffing."

"I was indeed. Good thing because that saved us the spectacle of two ancient dudes slapping each other before collapsing in exhaustion."

"In a Chili's parking lot, adding insult to injury."

The man laughed and stuck out a hand with its stunted claws. "Luis. Sorry about starting to turn. Awkward, right?"

"Vlad," the vampire said, gripping the meaty half-paw. "Nice to meet a fellow supernatural. Don't run across too many these days."

"Dying breed. Literally."

"The night is young even if we're not. Care to join me for some fun? There's a place not far from here that offers a younger, much fresher clientele with an ABV high enough to give you a nice buzz."

With that, two creatures of the night hopped into a rideshare to a prey-bearing watering hole teeming with pretty. The TGI Friday's was bulging at the waistline with potential, a land of milk, honey, and cargo shorts. Settling in at the bar, the two ordered pastel drinks as camouflage and surveyed the menu that packed the seats. Vlad couldn't quite settle on what to have until Luis offered to do the bulk of the hunting.

"You mean give it to me on a silver platter," the vampire grinned.

"Yes. But don't say 'silver.' It's like mentioning 'cross' to a vampire."

"'Kryptonite' to Superman."

"'Subpoena' to any politician."

The two were still laughing when they chose a boisterous and inebriated twenty-something hipster off the late-night menu, a happy meal indeed. Once the sky had changed from black to deep purple and brightening every minute, they stood in front of Vlad's apartment.

"I'd invite you in but…" Vlad paused, unsure where to go.

"No worries. I'm not your type and frankly, you're not mine. No offense."

"None whatsoever."

Luis gave the duplex a once-over and shook his head. "You live in this dump?"

"Now I'm going to take offense," Vlad said. "Yeah, this is where I live. Not nearly as nice as a castle, but that was centuries ago."

"I have a suggestion if you have a little time."

"Sure." Vlad gestured to the eastern glow. "As long as it won't take more than a few minutes. I burst into a fireball at sunrise."

Luis scribbled something on the back of a Chili's napkin and shoved it into the vampire's hand. "Come by Upton Arms some evening. Head to Building C and ask for Worley. She'll take care of the rest."

Vlad had about a thousand questions, but held onto them when Luis pointed out how unhealthy it was to smoke. "Which is what your forehead is doing right now."

———

A week and seven rodent meals later, Vlad had nothing to lose. Little did he know it would be the start of a beautiful friendship.

Until he met a particularly cranky rainbowchaser bent on taking the gold right out of the golden years.

———

Don't stop now. Keep reading with your copy of UPTON ARMS, by Scott Craven.

And sign up for Kat Coffin's newsletter to get all the news, giveaways, excerpts, and more!

Discover more from Kat Coffin now at www.katcoffin.com

And then, find your next read, UPTON ARMS, by City Owl author, Scott Craven

————

What if eternal life wasn't all it's cracked up to be? Achy joints, cranky moods, and failing powers prove immortality is just late-onset death.

Such is the life of a six-hundred-something whose best years are in the rearview mirror—and Vlad can't even see himself in a mirror. Now living in Upton Arms, a retirement community for once-powerful supernatural beings, Vlad and his eccentric neighbors are learning a painful truth: life, even for immortals, is terminal.

Rising at dusk is a struggle, and turning into a bat? Forget it! Vlad's stiff wings are more likely to cause a crash landing than a graceful flight. And when it comes to his hypnotic powers, he can't even convince someone to grab him the remote control in the community room than control their will.

Just when Vlad thinks it can't get worse, Upton Arms faces something more dangerous than his existential crisis—foreclosure. Vlad sees it as the final nail in his coffin, even as the other tenants rally behind Luis, a werewolf and unofficial pack leader. Together, they'll fight for survival, and Vlad will discover a shocking truth: it's not too late to start living again.

Full of dark humor, supernatural drama, and unforgettable characters, Upton Arms is a must-read for fans of quirky paranormal fiction.

All reviews are **welcome** and **appreciated**. Please consider leaving one on your favorite social media and book buying sites.

Escape Your World. Get Lost in Ours! City Owl Press at www.cityowlpress.com.

ACKNOWLEDGMENTS

There is a misconception that writing a book is a solitary project. This is simply not true. It takes a village to create a book, and I am so grateful for my little village.

First and foremost, I must thank my mother, Linda Coffin. Through all of the trials and tribulations of my life, the only person I've ever wanted to be was you. I yearn to have your patience, compassion, and grace in all things. At the very least, I got your magical way of story-telling! Thank you for listening to my late night weepy phone calls, for bragging to K.A. Applegate about the book deal (I can't believe you did that, *mom!)* for stubbornly refusing to accept the possibility that this thing wouldn't be published.

Secondly, a thank you to my best friend Janice, the Ashburn to my Mullins. We have known each other since we were nervous fourteen-year-olds our freshman year of high school, giggling over Orlando Bloom pictures. So much has changed—and yet, not all that much! We've butted heads like sisters, but come back even stronger. Our friendship is a story of resurrection and I can't wait to see where we go next. Our politics and spirituality shifted, but our love didn't. I am so, so grateful for that and for your encouragement in all things.

Thirdly, thank you to my best friend Alex, the Tolkien to my Lewis. You are the sister of my heart and this goofy book would never have been finished if you hadn't expressed interest and allowed me to collapse dramatically on your bed every so often, wailing "HELL'S HERESIES WILL NEVER GET PUBLISHED!" You were right, as you generally are.

Thank you to *the group chat*—Brittany, Jenny, and Heather. You guys were incredible advocates for me and I can't wait for you to read it.

Thank you to Jess for always believing in me and being fiercely protective of me. I miss you desperately and treasure every FaceTime call. Jossi girl, you're too young to read this book, but I promise I'll write a fairytale for you.

Thank you, Angela, my beautiful and hilarious roommate, who had to hear my publishing woes every single day. You are braver than a marine (or at least have more patience.)

Thank you to my family, my brothers+ Chip, Tris, and Seth—you guys were the earliest audience to my stories, and I hope you know how much collaborating on stories and playing incredibly intricate games of pretend shaped my writing.

Thank you to my cousin Katie, who saw the ghosts and laughed at them.

Thank you to my big sisters, in blood and in spirit—Elnora, Abby, Stephanie, and my cousin Emily. I still want to be you when I grow up.

A thank you to my father, Lieutenant Colonel Charles F. Coffin.

Thank you to Mark, for being there for me when I needed it. Love you.

Thank you to Mads, who read an early draft and offered valuable insight and suggestions.

Thank you to the Washington University School of Medicine Kidney and Liver Transplant office. You do incredible work and I'm so proud I got to work there. Dr. Wellen, I assure you, your cameo is out of a deep love and admiration.

Thank you to Heath, specifically your album "Salem Songs", which provided a great deal of the inspiration and soundtrack for this book.

Thank you to my writer's group—Darling, Alison, Zahra, Seth, Del, and Adèle! I walk away from every writer's group extra inspired.

Thank you to the Hellcheer Discord Server! You guys have become invaluable friends, have been phenomenally supportive, and I feel so blessed and lucky that you all found me.

Thank you to Danielle DeVor, my phenomenal editor who took a chance on this silly book and shaped it into perfection. The moment I saw you on our first Zoom call together, I was instantly relieved—"Oh, she gets my book perfectly."

Thank you to Christi Cardenas, my magnificent agent. Thank you for understanding my weird sense of humor, for fighting for me, and making sure I had the best deal ever. I would be lost without you and I'm so grateful for you taking not one, but TWO chances on this strange book.

And finally, a special thank you to Jonathan the Ghost, who haunted my grandfather's house. You provided a wonderful inspiration for this story on how frankly funny you were—you taught me not to be scared of ghosts, but to enjoy them. I have been longing for another ghost to haunt my apartment ever since. Your references are all out of love. Miss you, buddy!

ABOUT THE AUTHOR

KAT D. COFFIN is a part-time serious academic and full-time writer and musician, currently residing in Brooklyn, NY. Her debut fantasy novel, *Hell's Heresies*, releases in 2025 from City Owl Press. She is one of the few writers granted permission from the C.S. Lewis Company to stage her play *Lost and Found: The Meditations of Susan Pevensie*, which imagines the grief and emotions Susan Pevensie endures after the events of *The Chronicles of Narnia.*
She enjoys singing opera, playing guitar, a good stout, and pestering her cat Dorothy L. Sayers.

www.katcoffin.com

instagram.com/KatinOxford
x.com/KatinOxford
tiktok.com/KatinOxford

ABOUT THE PUBLISHER

City Owl Press is a cutting edge indie publishing company, bringing the
world of romance and speculative fiction to discerning readers.

Escape Your World. Get Lost in Ours!

www.cityowlpress.com

facebook.com/CityOwlPress
x.com/cityowlpress
instagram.com/cityowlbooks
pinterest.com/cityowlpress
tiktok.com/@cityowlpress

www.ingramcontent.com/pod-product-compliance
Lightning Source LLC
Chambersburg PA
CBHW072344020726
47506CB00004B/999